Yesteryear's Echo

A Historical Psychological Thriller

Jane M. Bell

Copyright © 2024 by Jane M. Bell

All rights reserved.

No part of this publication may be reproduced, distributed, or transmitted in any form or by any means, including photocopying, recording, or other electronic or mechanical methods, without the prior written permission of the publisher, except as permitted by U.S. copyright law. For permission requests, contact Jane M. Bell at jane@janembell.com

The story, all names, characters, and incidents portrayed in this production are fictitious. No identification with actual persons (living or deceased), places, buildings, and products is intended or should be inferred.

Book Cover by Jane M. Bell

First edition 2024

For Colton, Trevor and Annika. I love you with all my heart.

Contents

1. Prologue — 1
2. Chapter 1 — 6
3. Chapter 2 — 15
4. Chapter 3 — 22
5. Chapter 4 — 29
6. Chapter 5 — 34
7. Chapter 6 — 42
8. Chapter 7 — 49
9. Chapter 8 — 58
10. Chapter 9 — 67
11. Chapter 10 — 76
12. Chapter 11 — 85
13. Chapter 12 — 93
14. Chapter 13 — 102
15. Chapter 14 — 111
16. Chapter 15 — 119
17. Chapter 16 — 128

18.	Chapter 17	138
19.	Chapter 18	147
20.	Chapter 19	156
21.	Chapter 20	162
22.	Chapter 21	170
23.	Chapter 22	178
24.	Chapter 23	188
25.	Chapter 24	198
26.	Chapter 25	207
27.	Chapter 26	217
28.	Chapter 27	225
29.	Chapter 28	233
30.	Chapter 29	241
31.	Chapter 30	250
32.	Chapter 31	259
33.	Chapter 32	268
34.	Chapter 33	281
35.	Chapter 34	292
36.	Chapter 35	303
37.	Chapter 36	312
38.	Chapter 37	321
39.	Chapter 38	329
40.	Chapter 39	332
41.	Chapter 40	336
42.	Epilogue	345

Also by	347
About the author	348

Prologue

Deep beneath her breast, her heart raced. Each beat a desperate plea for mercy she knew would never come. A forceful shove caused her to stumble forward through the jeering horde. Their cries were for blood. Her blood.

She lifted her eyes to the sea of faces as she passed. Their features twisted with loathing and an insatiable hunger for retribution. The swarm surged closer, their enraged shouts increased to a deafening crescendo. "Death to the Austrian whore!" shouted a man, his fist raised high in the air. The crowd echoed his chant until every stone in Paris trembled with their fury.

A guard she once commanded seized firmly upon her dainty arms. Her pristine gown was now a faded cruel mockery of her former existence. Its stained and tattered lace accents forced into a fretful dance as she moved.

She'd been a fool, that she now understood. Her frivolous vanity prevented her from acknowledging the suffering of the people she ruled over. However, even in her previous moments of darkness, she never could have imagined an end such as this.

The heavy metal shackles around wrists and ankles clattered as he pushed her closer to the scaffold. Her legs shook as she ascended each step of the platform. Splinters dug into the flesh of her delicate bare feet, but pain failed to register in her brain. The wood was slick, yet sticky with the blood of those who'd been there before her. Its metallic scent filled her nostrils, causing her stomach to churn and revolt. Bitter bile lingered in her mouth as she fought the urge to retch with extreme force.

Atop the platform, a priest awaited her arrival. His face displayed a solemn, pious mask. "My child," he intoned, "do you repent your sins?"

The woman's lips parted, but no words came. What sins could she confess that would satisfy him or this shrinking mob? Her birth? Her marriage? Her very existence?

The priest's eyes narrowed as he leaned in closer. "Your silence is your condemnation," he hissed. "May God have mercy on your soul."

She had always believed in God's mercy. But in this moment, her heart beat distant and hollow. Deep within her chest. What god would permit such cruel hatred?

The woman flinched without cause, as if struck by some blunt force. But something was wrong. These weren't her memories, her feelings. She — ?

The man's consciousness reeled as he found himself suddenly inhabiting the mind and body of Marie Antoinette.

The sensations were vivid and disorienting—these weren't his memories or feelings, but those of the ill-fated queen.

As he struggled to comprehend this bizarre experience, Marie's senses continued to bombard him with unfamiliar 18th-century stimuli, blurring the lines between his identity and hers.

"*Qu'est-ce qui se passe?*" he muttered, his words coming out in a mix of French and English. "Where am I?"

The executioner stepped forward, his face hidden by a black hood drenched with sweat. "*Madame,*" he said, his voice was deep and mocking, "it is time."

The roar of the crowd intensified as the guard forced him — her to her knees. The wood was hard and unyielding beneath her. With a heavy hand, he forced her head into position. The crescent-shaped recess of the blood-soaked bascule felt cold against her neck.

Panic surged through her — him. His breath became short, with ragged gasps. As he closed his eyes, hot tears flowed, uncontrolled, down his face. In his mind, he saw the face of the woman he loved, then their handsome baby boy.

When he opened his eyes, the sunlight glinted off the sharp heavy steel above him. His breaths became shallow, while his body trembled with a fear he failed to contain. The roar of the crowd grew louder in his ears.

Then, the sickening sound of metal sliding upon metal signaled the falling of the blade. A terrifying combination of his own voice and the woman's formed screams that caught in his throat.

Then everything went dark and silent.

Dr. Matthias Levi studied his test-subject with fascination and an underlying hint of concern. The man, strapped to the reclined chair, convulsed as if gripped by some incredible, invisible force. The subject's eyes rolled back in their sockets, then twitched and fluttered beneath their lids.

Levi's tone remained steady. Maintaining a certain professional detachment as he dictated his observations into a recording device. "Case 47, Subject Alpha. Psycho-Temporal Displacement successful. Subject experienced the vivid reality of Marie Antoinette's execution. Duration: approximately fifteen minutes."

He paused the recording. The ink soon flowed from his pen, as furious scribbles scratched against the pages of his journal. The room was quiet save for the soft hum of the machines and Alpha's ragged breathing.

The doctor's mind raced as he looked over his notes. The experiment was a resounding success, far exceeding his expectations. Alpha's experiences were far from mere hallucinations of an event. He had lived this experience as if he were Marie Antoinette herself. Alpha had just become more than just a silent witness to one of history's infamous moments. He became an actual part of that history.

The man's body jerked again. His muscles strain against the restraints that bound him. The light on the green screen began to spike and dip with erratic movement.

Curious, Levi leaned in closer. He recognized the signs of another displacement beginning, but this one was different. Alpha's face contorted in a grimace of pure terror. His lips moved, but his words remained silent.

Without warning, the man let out a piercing scream. His back arched from the reclined chair. Levi jumped back, his heart pounded in his throat. He stared with horrified fascination as Alpha thrashed and writhed. His mind was now lost to another vivid historic reality. This one beyond his cause or control.

The researcher's hand moved with a slight tremor as he wrote his observations. For a moment, his eyes remained fixed on Subject Alpha's contorted face. The man's anguished screams soon subsided, replaced by haunted, continuous whimpers.

Levi's thoughts raced, filled with implications of all he just witnessed. He leaned back in his chair. His gaze now moved to the various monitors and instruments surrounding him and his subject. The data provided here was invaluable. A window into the subject's thoughts as he navigated the unknown. Secrets of the human mind through this developmental theory he called psycho-temporal displacement.

He considered the other displacements Alpha had endured. The sinking of the Titanic had been a harrowing experience. Alpha had recounted the icy chill of the Atlantic waters. The desperate cries of doomed passengers stayed with him. The sickening tilt of the deck beneath his feet. Alpha had been there, a helpless witness to this incredible historic tragedy.

Alpha's account of the signing of the Declaration of Independence was a far less disturbing event. The sweat poured out of him as he sat in Independence Hall. The stifling heat made it difficult to breathe. Levi marveled at the details Alpha reported. Quills scratched against the parchment. The tension of heated arguments. The debates of the Founding Fathers as they formed a new nation. Such nuances were unattainable from any history book.

Julius Caesar's assassination haunted Alpha more than other experiences. Frenzied shouting mingled with the distinct smell of death. The look of betrayal in the Roman ruler's eyes. Their treachery registered in his brain. It all became a fixed part of Alpha's psyche. For days, visions plagued him. A dagger plunging again and again into Caesar's body. His warm, red blood spattered all over him.

Levi's voice took on a tone of excitement as he dictated his thoughts into the recorder. "The potential applications of psycho-temporal displacement were staggering," his words tumbled out in a rush. "The ability to experience distinct moments from history. He wanted to see these events through the eyes of the people who were there. The potential knowledge gained is immeasurable."

He paused, his brow furrowing as a darker thought entered his mind. "Of course, there are other possibilities as well," he continued, his voice lower. "The intelligence gathered, the secrets he'd uncovered. He now understood why the American CIA had plucked him out of WWII, Germany. The past holds incredible untapped information, and with psycho-temporal displacement, incredible knowledge was within reach."

Levi glanced back at the man's haunted eyes and ashen complexion. For the first time, a pang of guilt weighed heavily on his conscience. Was it right to cause these types of repeated traumatic experiences in another human being? "In the name of science." Was that enough to justify this research, his actions, this psychological torture of Subject Alpha?

The sensation faded as quickly as it had come, replaced by a growing sense of purpose. The potential benefits of his research already far outweighed any imposed discomfort this man might experience.

Levi continued to work late into the night. He knew he was on the cusp of something incredible and groundbreaking. Psycho-temporal displacement would alter the future. It would change the world as anyone understood it.

The researcher turned back to his leather-bound notebook. His pen flew across the pages as he recorded more details from his subject's latest experiments. The data he gathered revealed fascinating hidden secrets. Information about the collective human psyche. Levi aimed to become the master of the human mind and time itself someday.

Chapter 1

Dr. Thomas Bauer's eyes fluttered open. He often stared at the water-stains on his ceiling. They weren't all that different from the Rorschach inkblots he'd sometimes used at work. He thought one of them resembled the self-portrait of Leonardo da Vinci done in red chalk.

As he stretched, his hand bumped the edge of the nightstand. An empty whiskey glass crashed to the floor, shattering into pieces. A long sigh failed to dispel the weight of the day pressing down on his tired soul. Out of habit, he reached for his wristwatch on the nightstand to wind it.

Bauer rubbed his face with semi-calloused hands and sat up in bed. He looked around at the piles of clothes strewn about the place and the overflowing wastebasket in the corner. The space bore the telltale signs of a man consumed by his work and haunted by his past. Someone unaccustomed to bachelorhood.

His legs swung over the edge of the bed. He placed several psychiatric journals on the floor. A quick glance at one cover reminded him of a different stage in his life. Earlier in his career, he would devour the information contained within those pages. He was eager to stay abreast of new research. At the moment, they served as makeshift stepping stones to protect his bare feet from injury.

Navigating his way through the clutter and broken glass, he noticed himself in the bathroom mirror. He almost didn't recognize the man staring back at him. His deep green eyes had dark circles forming under them. His salt and pepper hair was disheveled. He splashed cold water on his face, hoping to wash away the remnants of another restless night.

As he went through the motions of his morning routine, his thoughts were consumed by the day ahead. The prospect of facing another round of mundane cases and bureaucratic red tape failed to excite him. He longed for the days when his career was still fulfilling and had meaning.

Bauer went to the kitchen and plugged in the coffee pot. As the rich aroma filled the air, his eyes landed upon a photograph stuck to his refrigerator. It was an image of a younger, happier version of himself with his family. He'd made some mistakes. He wanted to correct them, but he did not know how to mend the rift. His work had consumed him and his free time. He had drifted away from the people who used to bring him love and joy.

His gaze wandered to the photo of his parents. His mother sported a radiant smile. He realized he hadn't spoken to her in weeks. His eyes moved on to the stern countenance of his father. Bauer turned his eyes away from his father's image before his emotions caught up with him.

As he plunged two pieces of bread into the toaster. His eyes drifted to the only other picture in the kitchen. Propped up against the backsplash near the blender was a picture. It was a group of men and women in period costumes from the 1800s.

Bauer picked up the photo. A faint tug pulled at the corners of his mouth. He remembered the fun and laughter from that day's events and others just like it. Everyone's faces shined with camaraderie and excitement. Their activities were an escape from the pressures of career and his failed marriage.

The toaster popped, and his moment of nostalgia faded as fast as it had come. He returned the photograph to its place. Bauer poured himself a mug of coffee and took a sip. His face winced from the bitterness. It needed some half and half. He'd forgotten to pick some up on his way home the night before. Once again, he checked his watch. He was already running late for work.

Out the kitchen window he could see Mrs. Clendin, his elderly neighbor, across the street fetching her morning paper. He looked back at his bitter brew, turned to reach for a second cup from the dish drainer. He poured a second cup and headed out his front door.

Bauer apologized for the lack of milk as he handed her the warm coffee. She was gracious, appreciative of her neighbor's kind gesture. She excused herself and rushed back into her home for a minute. When she returned, she added a splash of cream to both their mugs. He glanced at his watch again, thanked her, and excused himself.

Dr. Thomas Bauer hurried back inside to grab his briefcase and jacket from the peg near the door. He gulped the last of his coffee. Some of it spilled down the front of his slacks. Glancing at his watch once more, he exhaled in frustration, then exited and locked his door. He inhaled deep, savoring the crisp morning air. His footsteps resonated along the quiet walkway. The world around him started to stir. Yet the demands of his day were already pressing down upon him.

Bauer's commute to work was a tired, worn route. He navigated through the bustling streets of Washington, D.C. His mind wandered through the rich history of this town. His car knew the way to his destination.

Saint Elizabeths Hospital was the first government run psychiatric facility in the country. Its historic Kirkbride design was state-of-the art at the time of its construction in 1855.

He pulled his car into his usual parking spot. He cut the engine and sat in silence for a moment. His eyes drifted over the classic facade that towered before him. The central administrative building stood shrouded in sprawling ivy.

As he entered, Bauer issued a polite nod to a security guard, who returned a silent, familiar smile. The lobby was empty. The east and west wings that flanked the administration wing were already bustling with activity. Nurses and doctors went about their respective duties with professionalism and efficiency.

The din of his footsteps echoed off the glossy floors. He walked through the corridors of the administrative building without a conscious thought.

He arrived at a modest wooden door tucked away in this quiet part of the hospital. He didn't notice the plaque on the door displaying the name Dr. Thomas J. Bauer, M.D., Ph.D.

Fumbling with keys, he unlocked the door and stepped inside. The familiar scent of musty old books, polished wood, and stale coffee filled his nostrils. He threw his coat on the rack by the door and sat in his well-worn leather chair. He let out a long sigh as he perused his day's schedule.

Bauer rubbed his temples, hoping to ease the dull ache that had settled behind his eyes. He needed to push aside the distractions of his personal life. The patients in his care required his focus. But he could not stop his own troubles from seeping into his conscious thoughts. This albatross was relentless as it drug him down deeper into his own despair.

Dr. Thomas Bauer was anxious and annoyed. He sat in a room designated for his clinical therapy sessions, waiting. He could never understand how a patient could run late for an in-house appointment. Especially when it was the first of the day. As he waited, his own thoughts wandered through weekend plans.

His first session was with a man named Rhyse Scott. He was a middle-aged veteran. His mind was forever scarred by traumas sustained in a combat zone years ago. The man had suffered for many years since he returned from deployment. Post Traumatic Stress Disorder, anxiety and depression now consumed his mind.

Rhyse had worked with several other clinicians at Saint Elizabeths with minimal improvement in his condition. He connected well with Bauer. Combining therapy and medication had been promising in recent weeks.

A nurse knocked on the door before escorting the patient into the room. The corners of Bauer's mouth moved upward. His eyes settled on the man taking a seat across from him. "Good morning, Rhyse. How are you feeling today?"

Rhyse's gaze darted to a flitting bird in a tree outside the window for a moment. The man's eyes then brightened as he watched the doctor settle into his own seat. "Mornin' Doc! Today's been alright, I guess. I got some good sleep last night. It's the first time in a while."

The doctor's smile widened as he grabbed his pen and yellow notepad. "That's wonderful news. It sounds like the new medication works well for you."

Rhyse nodded as he sat up straighter in his chair. "Yeah, I think so. I mean, I still have episodes now and again. But overall, I'm feeling the best I have in months," He then shook his head. "No, years."

The doctor made a few notes regarding his patient's improvement. "We'll stay with your current treatment plan for a couple more weeks. If you continue making progress like this, we can discuss some home visits."

Rhyse's face lit up at the mention of his family. "Visiting home? That would be amazing, Doc. I miss my wife and kids so much."

Bauer reached over to pat him on the hand to reassure him. "I know you do, Rhyse. And we're going to do everything we can to get you back to them as soon as we can. But we need to take things one day at a time. Make sure your current progress will continue to work, okay?"

The patient nodded, then leaned back in his chair. "Yeah, that sounds reasonable. "

A hint of warmth seeped into Bauer's chest as the man continued to talk. It was moments like this that reconfirmed his choice to pursue his career in psychiatry. Deep down, all he wanted to do was to help heal people like Rhyse. Individuals haunted by the most horrific experiences that continued to replay in their heads.

Just as the doctor was about to respond, Rhyse's posture shifted and became tense. His warm smile changed to a sinister, sarcastic smirk. It was as if a different person now sat with him. Rhyse's brow furrowed, and his eyes grew dark. "You know, Doc?" His words were gritty and barbed. Fear haunted his eyes and rage consumed him. "You sit there with your notepad and all those goddamn letters after your name. What the hell would you know about it?" The veteran held his body taut, like it was ready to snap at any second.

Bauer's own posture adjusted in response to the potential threat before him. "Rhyse, you've made fantastic improvements these last several weeks. Let me help you work through what's happening right now." His voice was calm, with an unmistakable hint of dread.

Rhyse's laugh was sharp. His eyes challenged Bauer. "Help? All your talk does nothing, and your drugs only make me numb. It doesn't keep me from the constant hell that I live through all day and night." His tone spiked with accusation. "Tell me, Doc, when was the last time your past haunted you?"

For a second, Bauer's professional façade faltered, as an internal thought escaped. "Every day—" The words fell from his lips before he could stop it.

"What was that, Doc?"

The doctor's attention snapped back to the present. "I — uh. Oh, nothing. I'm sorry to interrupt. Please continue."

"Has your heart ever just started pounding for no reason? The only thing my brain remembers is the shit I've been through. It plays in a constant loop."

Bauer tried to keep his patient from escalating. He kept his response calm and measured. " Yes, I have, — "

Rhyse failed to hear a word that came from the other man in the room. "After work, you go home to your Mayberry life. Say, do you remember things from your childhood? Dates with your wife. Playing with your kid?" The man's words dripped with sarcasm.

"Yes," Bauer responded as their roles shifted.

"The other day I spoke with him on the phone. He asked me about a time we played catch together in the park. I told him I remembered."

The conversation moved on to something more positive.

"You know what Doc?"

The patient fists crashed down hard on the table, catching Bauer off guard.

Rhyse stood and kicked, sending his chair crashing to the floor behind him. His stature was imposing, his tone threatening. "I had to lie to my kid, Doc." His words were thick with frustration and anger. "Ya know why? Because my mind can't remember. All I can remember is the goddamn shit I should never have survived."

The psychiatrist sat in silence, unsure how to respond. Rhyse's eyes flashed with a primitive wildness that made Bauer's voice quiver. "Rhyse, calm down. I want you to help me understand what you are experiencing right now."

"Calm?" The man broke out in a maniacal laugh. "My head is stuck in a damn war zone?"

Bauer pleaded, but he felt helpless. "Rhyse, please, let me help you."

"You just sit there in your safe little doctor world. You can't help me! Nobody can!" Rhyse's face twisted in a snarl. Then, in one fluid, terrifying motion, he upended the table and lunged toward Bauer.

Recoiling in fear, Bauer's fingers scrambled to press the red emergency call button on the wall. "I need staff here! Stat!" His shouts were almost inaudible over the man's rage.

After what seemed like an eternity, two orderlies burst through the door, followed by a nurse.

A burly man grabbed Rhyse, who lashed out like a trapped wild animal. His fury was raging out of control. The patient's fist caught the other man square in the jaw, dropping him instantly to the floor. Bauer stepped in to assist the other orderly. The nurse moved forward, plunging the needle into the man's deltoid, and injected the sedative. Rhyse fought and struggled for another minute.

As the medication took effect, Rhyse's combative behavior transformed into mournful cries and gut-wrenching sobs. They all observed as the medication took effect. In another minute, the hospital staff removed the patient from the room.

The doctor stood in the stillness of the now empty room. His heart was still pounding in his chest. Rhyse's anguished screams lingered in his head. The doctor took a deep breath, to compose himself. Seeing Rhyse in all his anguish remained fixed in his mind.

All he ever wanted was to help the man work through his trauma. The incident reminded him of watching his wife just before giving birth to their son. It was the only other time in his life when he felt so worthless.

Bauer reached to right the overturned table and chair, and began documenting what had happened. Static came over the hospital speaker system. The familiar dissonant tones caused him to freeze in place. Waiting for the calm voice full of information that always followed. "Code Blue, room 324. Code Blue, room 324."

"Room 324?! Oh my God!" Without hesitation, he sprinted from the room and down the hallway. His footsteps echoed off the walls as he ran. He popped into a stairwell and ascended two steps at a time until he reached the third floor. As he burst into the room, chaos greeted him. Nurses and a very green intern swarmed around the patient's bed. Their voices raised with bits of urgent information. The patient, a young woman in her mid thirties, lay motionless. Her skin was a sickly gray color.

Bauer's eyes scanned the monitors. As he pushed his way to the bedside, his mind raced through a practiced routine. The patient's condition was deteriorating fast, and what they were doing was not working.

"Report?"

A nurse looked at him. Her professionalism failed to hide her concern. "She's crashed, doctor. No BP, no pulse."

"I got an airway!"

"Someone get the paddles ready. Nurse push 1 gram calcium chloride, IV!" he ordered, his voice steady despite the adrenaline surging through him.

"1 gram? Calcium chloride?" The woman hesitated. "But doctor, the protocol — "

"I know," Bauer snapped. "But those protocols aren't working. We need to try something different."

He reached for the syringe himself, measuring the dose with shaking hands. He injected it into his patient's IV. He analyzed the screen for a moment. Then without hesitation, he grabbed the paddles and rubbed them together. "Clear!"

For the longest moment, the room fell silent, then the heart monitor beeped a familiar rhythm. Everyone in the room exhaled.

"We got her back!" Bauer shouted, with great relief in his voice.

The patient's vitals improved. Her heart rate grew stronger, breathing more even. The color returned to her cheeks. Bauer let out a breath he never knew he'd been holding.

As the patient continued to stabilize. The crisis passed. Bauer stepped back from the bedside, allowing the nurses to continue their work. His body shook from the adrenaline that coursed through his veins.

His decisions deviated from standard protocols. It was a risk. But it was necessary to save her life.

He would face condemnation from hospital administrators over his handling of this medical emergency. He didn't care. Deep down, he knew that if he had stuck to their protocol, she would be dead right now.

He glanced at his watch, then at the clock on the wall. How could it only be 9 am? It had already been a long, emotional, draining day, and lunch was still a few hours away. With a sigh Bauer turned toward the door. His mind was still reeling from all that had happened the last hour. Just before he stepped out of the room, he looked back to address the nurse in charge. "Please let me know of any changes in her condition."

"I will, Dr. Bauer."

His feet were heavy as they carried him from the room. He walked toward the elevator, too tired to take the stairs. As he descended floors, he noticed the dichotomy of his morning. He'd failed Rhyse during his breakdown. But was empowered after saving the life of the woman dying in room 324. All of it left him exhausted.

An old man strolled toward him in the hall, pushing his housekeeper's cart. Sam Harris' steps were no longer brisk, but they were never without purpose. This man was the longest tenured employee at Saint Elizabeths. He had worked in the same housekeeper position for decades.

Dr. Bauer passed by Harris on his way to his office. The housekeeper issued a silent smile. The doctor walked past the man and entered his office without even noticing him.

Chapter 2

Dr. Thomas Bauer closed the office door behind him. The click of the latch echoed through the stillness that surrounded him. With eyes shut, he pressed his back against the solid wood. His breath shuddered as he drew it deep into his lungs. He was exhausted.

He stood for several minutes. The familiar scent of old books and a faint hint of leather grounded him. This space was his sanctuary. A place where he could think, catch his breath, and escape responsibility for a little while.

Bauer pushed away from the door and shrugged off his white overcoat. He threw it over a hook on the coat rack without a thought. The worn carpet below his feet muted his footsteps as he walked to his desk. His chair creaked in protest as he sunk into its supple leather embrace.

He leaned forward, resting his elbows on the solid, unforgiving oak. He rubbed his face. The cactus-like stubble reminded him he had forgotten to shave that morning. Bauer dropped his hands and stared at the surface of his desk.

Papers lay everywhere. Layers of medical journals, patient files, and hastily scribbled notes. A half-empty coffee cup teetered on a pile of books. The cold dark contents threatened to spill at any minute. Pens, some without caps, lay about like fallen soldiers across some war-torn battlefield.

Bauer's workspace reflected his personal mental state. Overwhelmed, scattered, and pulled in too many directions. He was desperate to bring some order to the chaos, but at the moment, it was an impossible task.

A framed photograph near the edge caught his eye. It stood half-buried on his desk. This picture was of a younger, more carefree version of himself. In his arms was a beautiful woman who was also smiling. In front of him and his wife, Eleanor, sat their eight-year-old son, Simon. The family portrait was only three years old, however, it felt like a lifetime ago.

Bauer traced a finger over the glass, as if he were caressing her face. It had been six months since the separation, but the pain was deep, and the wounds were still fresh.

He set the picture back down. The frame made a soft click against the bare wood. This job demanded so much of him. His patients, the hospital, all needed him. Once again, he pushed aside his personal troubles to focus on his work. He had no time to dwell on his own wants and needs.

Bauer drew in another breath, held it, then let it out slowly. Then reached for Rhyse's file and flipped it open, forcing himself to concentrate on his entry.

As he worked, his mind drifted. The heated conversation with Eleanor the previous night still haunted his head. It was a harsh reminder of the distance that had grown between him and a family he still loved.

"Thomas, you're so consumed by work. Your thoughts are stuck in the past and future," she said. Her voice was tight with a mix of pain and frustration. "What about your commitment to me? To Simon? To us in the here and now?"

Bauer tried to explain. He wanted her to understand, but his words sounded hollow. Lame excuses, even to his own ears.

"I'm trying, Ele," he had said. "I'm doing this for us, all of us, for our future."

But Eleanor only issued a sigh, heavy with disappointment. She'd heard it all before. "No, Thomas. You do all of it for yourself. You always have."

She'd struck a nerve he longed to ignore. His work helped people. Why couldn't she grasp its importance? His devotion to unraveling patients' pasts and minds was a noble cause. Helping those trapped in their own personal hells seemed easier than facing his crumbling family life.

Gnawing guilt grew deep within his gut. His schedule had caused him to miss birthdays, anniversaries, baseball games, school music performances. On the rare occasions when he attended, his mind was elsewhere.

Yet a defiant part of him bristled at Eleanor's barbed accusations. His career was important. Vital. He knew in his heart he was on the cusp of something big, something groundbreaking. Something that would improve the level of care for his patients. He believed that whatever it was could alter the future of psychiatry.

Bauer rubbed his temples, then took a sip of his cold coffee. He hoped it would ease the ache that had settled behind his eyes. Eleanor was right, something had to change. His work was brilliant, yet somehow unfulfilling, without his family by his side. He needed to find some sort of balance. How could he mend the rift buried somewhere under the weight of his personal ambitions?

His glance fell once again on the photo on his desk. They all looked so happy, so unaware of the future that would tear them apart. Bauer picked up the frame. His fingers traced over the image behind the glass. Guilt weighed heavy in his chest. A lot would need to change if he was ever going to repair the damage he'd caused.

His attention returned to Rhyse's file. With eyes closed, he took a deep breath. He needed to focus, to push through this and get back on track. Patients and deadlines would not wait. He couldn't afford to get lost in personal struggles. Not now.

A clamoring noise, pulling the psychiatrist from his work and melancholic introspection with a start. He blinked, dizzy and disoriented. The insistent phone rang again, demanding his immediate attention.

He let out a sigh and moved his hand toward the handset. His hand stopped in midair, hovering, then he picked it up. "Dr. Bauer speaking," he said in a tone that sounded rough, even to his own ears.

"Hey Thomas, it's Andrew," the man said on the other end. "I hope I haven't caught you at a bad time."

Bauer was glad to hear the voice of Andrew Wilkins, his closest friend, on the other end of the line. Bauer's chair groaned beneath him as he shifted his body back in his seat. "Oh, no, it's fine. I needed to talk to you anyway. What can I do for you?" A slight tug pulled at the corners of his mouth.

"I wanted to check in with you. Do you need anything for your presentation about Saint Elizabeths Hospital and the Civil War this weekend?" Andrew asked. The caller's voice failed to conceal his enthusiasm. "We've got some excellent props for you. Oh, and I think the new uniforms will add a fantastic touch."

A spark ignited in Bauer's chest, pushing aside the weight of everything personal and professional. His historical reenactment group provided him with an immersive escape, at least for a day or two.

"That's great Andrew! This is going to be a blast!" Thomas said, adjusting his posture in his chair. "I've been looking forward to this weekend for months. Tell me more about the uniforms?"

As Andrew launched into a detailed description, his friend's spirits lifted. He listened, asked questions, and offered occasional suggestions. For a few stolen moments, he wasn't Dr. Thomas J. Bauer, MD, PhD. the exhausted psychiatrist with his crumbling marriage and estranged family.

Their words flowed as two passionate minds discussed shared interests. They talked about the upcoming presentation, the research they'd done, the historical details they checked and verified for authenticity.

The conversation shifted. "Oh, Thomas, I almost forgot," Andrew continued with the same level of enthusiasm. "Your hospital's administrators called me. They want our group to do a reenactment for their upcoming annual staff picnic in a few weeks."

"That will be a wonderful change from their usual entertainment. Let me know if you need any help with it."

"I will be in contact after I discuss it with the others in the group."

When he ended the call, he experienced a sense of renewed energy. His earlier depression was replaced by anticipation. He glanced at the clock, surprised by how much time had passed. Now *he* was late for his next appointment.

He just shook his head. He stood up. His long arms stretched skyward with an audible, satisfying pop. The tension he'd been holding in his spine since he woke up this morning, finally released.

He straightened up his tie, gathered up some files, then headed for the door. He paused with his hand on the knob and looked at the back of the frame almost buried on his desk. His deep personal problems were still unresolved. But for now, he had a renewed sense of purpose. It was something that had been missing from his life for a long time.

Bauer felt better about himself as he emerged from his most recent clinical session. It was nothing like the trauma and drama of earlier that morning. He turned on his heels to head to his office as his stomach issued an audible growl. Suddenly he paused as he remembered he needed a document for his weekend presentation. It was the perfect addition to his talk on a Civil War-era doctor who worked at Saint Elizabeths. He'd fetch it before heading to lunch.

He rounded a corner, his footsteps echoed off the polished floor. The archives were in the most historic part of the hospital. The space overflowed with row upon row of shelves. Books, boxes of old documents, photographs, and other research material filled each shelf. Bauer had spent countless hours inside. He enjoyed losing himself for hours in stories from the past.

His steps quickened as he passed by the nurses' station. He didn't acknowledge anyone. They were all busy with their own work. He focused his attention on what he needed from the archives.

"Dr. Bauer!" came an urgent voice from behind him.

The doctor turned to see Olivia Kendrick, a nurse he had worked with for many years. Her face displayed a look of concern. "The hospital administrators called while you were in your last session. They would like to see you immediately."

A knot formed in Bauer's empty stomach. "Did they say what this was about?"

The woman shook her head. "No, not a clue. Do you want me to call and tell them you're on your way?"

"Thank you, but that won't be necessary. I will head over right now."

"Okay. Hurry. They didn't sound happy."

Bauer sighed. His planned visit to the archives, followed by lunch, would have to wait. As his steps carried him to the administrative wing, his mind churned with potential scenarios. What could it be? Had there been a complaint? An incident? His thoughts scanned through weeks of work. He tried to pinpoint anything that might have caused such a sudden summons.

He reached the conference room. When he arrived, he was shocked to find the space filled with men and women. He recognized each of their stern faces. Dr. Marcus Sinclair, the hospital's director, sat with several other administrative officials around a large oak table. There were stacks of papers and patient files spread out in front of them.

Sinclair looked up as the psychiatrist entered. He failed to rise from his seat. He just gestured toward an empty spot. "Dr. Bauer. Please, have a seat." His tone was cold and blunt while he remained professional.

Bauer lowered himself with measured control. The high-backed leather chair creaked beneath him. He clasped his hands in his lap to keep from fidgeting. He tried to remain calm, but his heart pounded deep within his chest.

"Dr. Bauer, we need to address this morning's incidents involving Mr. Rhyse Scott and your patient in room 324." Sinclair stated, his stern gaze fixed on him.

Bauer's stomach sank. He had expected this conversation. However, the events were still so fresh. The timing of the confrontation caught him off guard. His mind raced; Rhyse's escalation had happened so fast. What more could he have done?

"We've reviewed the reports, and we must be frank, your handling of these situations concerns us," the director continued.

"With all due respect, sir, there was no way I could have prevented what happened with Mr. Scott. The man snapped, right before my eyes. And as for the woman upstairs, she is alive now because of the decisions I made. In both cases, my actions were based on the immediate needs of my patients. I won't deny what I've done. I take full responsibility for my actions. I'm unsure what more you expect from me," the psychiatrist said in his defense.

Sinclair leaned forward, his brow furrowed. "That's just it, Dr. Bauer. Your 'decisions' jeopardize the safety of this hospital. We have protocols in place for a reason. Ignoring them exposes us to liability and questions our practices."

"But Doctor, your standard protocols were failing her. Had I not intervened, she would have died," Bauer argued.

"Then you should have let her die," Sinclair retorted. His words were cold and distant. The searing gazes of the other administrators' eyes bore through Bauer.

Bauer stood stunned by Sinclair's callousness. To him, letting the woman die when there were still credible interventions was not an acceptable option.

"Our expectations for our staff are high, Dr. Bauer. Your recent actions, however, have become unpredictable. You must adhere to our protocols; they protect not just the hospital but also you and your license to practice medicine."

The discussion moved on to other incidents, policies, and criticisms. Bauer listened, only half-engaged, realizing that these administrators cared little for individual patient's outcomes. His jaw clenched as he responded, "I understand. It won't happen again."

Sinclair's expression remained unyielding. "See that it doesn't."

Dismissed from the meeting, Bauer's earlier enthusiasm had vanished. He trudged back to his office. The words " — you should have let her die," still echoed in his mind. He had taken the Hippocratic Oath, as had everyone in that room.

He mulled over the type of facility that prioritized liability over life-saving interventions. He despised being dictated to by those who never faced such critical decisions of the moment themselves. No protocol would stop him from doing what was right, what was best for any patients.

Back at his desk, Bauer surveyed the chaos of papers and his open briefcase. Now there were only two places in the hospital where he could sit in peace.

He glanced at his watch. There was just enough time to retrieve what he needed from the archives. He headed out, determined to find some solace in the familiar surroundings.

Chapter 3

Dr. Thomas Bauer's footsteps carried him through the long, less-frequented areas of Saint Elizabeths Hospital. A quietness haunted the air. The silence was broken only by an occasional, distant slam of a door or muffled voice.

These spaces held stories of countless souls who had passed through rooms and halls over the decades. It was the history that called Bauer to work at this facility following his graduate studies. When he began his career, he too became a part of that narrative. Here he felt like he was contributing to something greater than himself. Something that was as comforting as it was unsettling.

He moved further from the patient care areas, closer to the archives. The walls exhibited faded portraits of long-dead physicians, administrators, and a few auxiliary staff members. Their eyes seemed to follow him as he passed, critical of his every move. Bauer shook off the feeling and continued on to his destination. His mind was still reeling from the events earlier that day.

He paused for a moment in front of two pictures that hung on one wall next to each other. The first painting was of Dr. Matthias Levi. The well-renowned psychiatrist was a pioneer in the development of psycho-temporal displacement theory. Bauer stared at the portrait, taking in the details of his face. Levi's eyes seemed to bore through him, as if challenging him from beyond the grave.

The second mural was a great likeness of his father, Dr. Harold Bauer. Like his colleague, he too was once a well-respected figure at Saint Elizabeths Hospital. Pictures of his father always made him feel uncomfortable. His father's expression was dark and disapproving. A slight smile played at the corners of his old man's mouth. Harold looked like he knew something his son didn't.

The psychiatrist stood in the hallway. He stopped breathing, without conscious thought. He acted as if breathing would disturb ghosts in the stillness that surrounded him. He allowed himself to exhale, letting it out slowly. Then the silence broke as he took in another breath.

Secrecy always shrouded the tenure of Levi and his father. Mysteries that fueled a burning curiosity for years. His work had always fascinated Bauer. Rumors and the doctor's sudden disappearance added to the man's mystique. Over the years, he had gleaned snippets of information, heard hushed whispers, and found cryptic references of remarkable research.

Bauer reached out to touch the frame of Dr. Levi's portrait. His fingers traced the ornate gold leaf of the frame. He wanted to know secrets that man had taken to his grave. What discoveries had he made that never saw the light of day. The thought thrilled him more than it terrified him. Lack of time and resources kept him from learning more about the mysterious man.

A shift of awareness caused Bauer to turn his attention to the cold and familiar. The disapproving gaze of his father bore through him from the portrait next to Levi's. The senior Bauer's features were hard and always judgmental. Growing up, the two had sparse moments of closeness. Though his dad never discussed his professional life at home, Bauer knew his father's work was important. Harold Bauer had helped countless people tormented by the traumas trapped in their minds.

The psychiatrist winced as he turned away from his dad's image. It felt like someone had just struck him across the face. It was his sophomore year of high school when everything changed, without explanation. The pain was still fresh from that incident all these years later.

Bauer forced himself to look at his father once more. He studied the man's features more closely now. Many who knew his father often commented on the resemblance between them. Thomas never saw the likeness, until now. Their strong jawlines and intense gaze were similar. It was like looking into a mirror of his own life, both his past and his future.

A noise from down the long hallway brought him back to the present. When he turned to look, he could see the hospital's garden courtyard through a window. Branches of the trees reached high towards the dark clouds gathering in the sky. Bauer stepped back from the portraits. He knew this place held many mysteries, not just those involving Levi and his father. Following a deep breath, he pivoted and resumed his journey. The younger doctor felt the eyes of his predecessors follow him as he walked away.

Footsteps echoed off the polished floors. The long, dim lit corridor stretched out before him. In the distance, lightning flashed through the windows. The lights flickered overhead in response. Their eerie, dancing shadows were his only company as he continued.

Rounding a blind corner, the physician almost collided with Sam Harris. The old custodian that had worked at Saint Elizabeths for over thirty years. The man jumped. His hand grasped at his heart. A look of surprise displayed across his weathered face. "Dr. Bauer," he said, his gravelly and breathy voice seemed to match his age and demeanor. "I didn't expect to see you in this part of the hospital."

The doctor clutched his chest, then tried to regain his composure. He offered a tight smile. "I need to fetch something from the archives for this weekend."

Sam nodded, then looked straight into the doctor's eyes. "Something for your reenactment group?"

Bauer shifted his weight, yet his body remained taut. "Yes, — but how did you know?" he stuttered, with curious alarm.

"You and I talked about it last week. Don't you remember?"

The physician's stance relaxed. "Of course, I'm sorry. How could that have slipped my mind? I'm looking for a document about the early days of the hospital. It will add more authenticity to my presentation."

Without another word, Harris issued his coworker a slight yellow-toothed grin. Then, with a gentle nod, the old man turned to his housekeeper's cart and disappeared around the corner.

Bauer glanced at his watch, hurried on toward his intended destination. His footsteps echoed through the emptiness. His pace was now quick. He would have to hurry if he was going to make it to his next appointment on time.

The air in the corridor grew cooler and quieter as he drew closer to the archives. The intensifying thunder outside and his breathing were the only sounds. His hand reached for the ornate metal mechanism that secured the doors closed. Bauer pushed, putting some weight into his exertion. The heavy, hand-carved wooden archive door moved very little.

The hinges creaked in protest against Bauer's attempts to open the door. He put a little more body weight into his effort. The sound reverberated through the empty corridor and through the cavernous space beyond. The doctor stepped inside, letting the door slam behind him, under its own power.

As he moved further into the archives, the man relaxed. He drew in a deep breath. His senses registered the familiar scent of old paper, leather and dust. It was the comforting smell of knowledge combined with history. He inhaled again. The aroma filled his lungs and calmed his restless spirit.

The flicker of overhead lights followed another flash of lightning outside. Ghosts of the past seemed to dance with the shadows. The space was a sanctuary for Bauer. A place where he could lose all sense of time in stories and mysteries from long ago. He had spent many hours pouring himself into old research and notes. He enjoyed the hunt for clues and revelation of secrets long hidden.

The archives were a vast maze of shelving and filing cabinets that stretched deep into the room. The lights faintly illuminate the furthest recesses as he traveled deeper into the room.

Navigating his way through the stacks, the doctor's hands trailed along the dusty tomes. He scanned labels on boxes, searching for the one he needed. The silence was oppressive. The sound of his breathing accompanied the occasional creak of the shelves and distant thunder.

He moved efficiently, like he had done so many times before. His fingers touched on the spines of old books. His eyes searched the tomes and folders that lined each shelf. There was an incredible amount of information around him. However, what fascinated him most were the files and research that weren't here. Tales of data that had gone missing were as old as the hospital itself.

As he continued, Bauer's thoughts drifted back to the two portraits of Dr. Levi and his father. What secrets had they uncovered during their time at Saint Elizabeths? The things they had seen. He was certain there were discoveries they had found that never saw the light of day.

The rumors that pulled Bauer hardest had very little to do with his father. But it had everything to do with Dr. Matthias Levi. Over the years, the younger researcher had developed a curious obsession with the man and the myth. The strange legends, and pioneering research in psychiatry were pervasive.

What he'd heard about Levi's Case 47 both thrilled and terrified him. The man's sudden disappearance in the early 1960s, made the intrigue even more compelling. Many had dedicated years to their exhaustive, unsuccessful searches. Frustrated, they conceded their failure. Most discounted some of Levi's work to urban fables.

Bauer shook his head, trying to clear his mind of wandering thoughts. There was no time to indulge himself in such fantastic mysteries. He needed to get what he came in here for and scurry off to his next appointment.

He arrived at the section he was looking for. There in a dim lit corner sat dusty boxes brimming with files and yellowed papers. This area housed some of the oldest records, some of which dated back to the 1850s.

He pulled a box from the shelf and blew the dust off its top. Bauer coughed a few times then opened the lid. Inside he found a thick file filled with old information. The writing on some of them had faded from age. With great care, he lifted a file from its container to get a closer look.

His heart skipped a beat as he skimmed through a series of letters. One was written by one of the hospital's Civil-War Era patients. Through shaky handwriting, the person's thoughts were conveyed through the thin, pale ink. The lines appeared jumbled and confused. They also displayed raw honesty. It was a glimpse into the mind of someone struggling with the demons that haunted them.

In the silent, dim recesses of the archives, the outside world disappeared. Bauer immersed himself in the first-hand experiences without resistance. Their tears and joys came to life before his eyes.

The rattle of a nearby window pane accompanied the angry wind beyond. It pulled him from the patient's musings. He shook his head. This was not the time to get lost in the past. He made a mental note to revisit this box when he had more time. With great care, he returned what he had and continued with his quest.

His pulse quickened as his eyes found what he was looking for. He lifted the lid and sifted through the files. He had gone through over three quarters of the box's contents in vain. Just as he was about to give up, a slim folder tucked away in the back caught his eye.

Its label was faint and difficult to read. Bauer knew what it was as soon as he saw it. Written faded words taunted him with the stories inside. Trembling hands pulled the papers from their place. The history felt heavy, as ghosts from the past whispered in his ears. Bauer moved, seeking better lighting for a closer look.

Confident with his selection, he set the folder aside. He then returned the box to where it belonged. As he leaned over, the hair on the back of his neck stood on end. He glanced over his shoulder, but saw nothing lurking in the shadows behind him. A shiver ran through him. He froze in place, but all he could hear was the sound of his own breathing and distant thunder.

It was only him in the archives. He had passed by many rows of shelves as he made his way to the oldest sections, he reasoned. If anyone had entered after him, he would have seen or heard them. Bauer shook his head to dismiss his paranoia. The feeling persisted, a nagging sense that he was being watched.

He secured the file underneath his arm. His heart now pounded deep within his chest. Eyes darted from one row to the next, scanning one shadowy corner after another. The sensation of eyes upon him intensified. His breath hitched in his throat. He moved with caution through the aisles. His footsteps echoed soft in the silence.

He paused, straining his ears for any sound that might betray another's presence. But the only thing he heard was the distant thunder and the wind outside. Bauer tried to remain calm. He reasoned with himself. His imagination paired with the storm, messing with his logic. Tricks fueled by the eerie atmosphere around him.

He glanced at his watch. He only had a few minutes to get to his appointment on time. Without a second thought, the doctor tucked the folder under his arm and moved with purpose through the stacks. His eyes scanned the dim lit spaces for any sign of movement. The shadows seemed to shift and dance with each flash of lightning. They played on his already frayed nerves.

Just as he turned down the main central aisle to head back to the entrance, Bauer froze. A loud metallic crash shattered the silence. His heart jumped into his throat. The unmistakable slam of the archives door soon followed.

He ran toward the exit. When he emerged from the book shelves, he could see a metal trash can, still teetering in place. Kicked over, its contents lay strewn across the floor.

Chapter 4

Bauer raced for the door, in pursuit of whomever had been watching him. The shelves, filled with old texts and documents, loomed like guardians of the archives. An incredible amount of knowledge, both known and forgotten, surrounded him. Some of it, even forbidden. Bauer stood alone in the empty corridor. His heart thundered in his chest like the storm outside. The folder tucked under his arm slipped. He grabbed it before it fell, determined to protect its priceless contents. He scanned the empty corridor for any sign of human activity.

A faint light filled the corridor. The pale green walls were bathed by the intermittent flicker from overhead lights and the occasional lightning flash. In the air, there was a strong smell of wood polish and a hint of antiseptic. Smells reminiscent of Saint Elizabeths bygone heydays.

Thunder rumbled in the distance outside. Flashes of lightning created eerie shadows through the rippled antique panes. The Shadows seemed to dance with restless spirits. Bauer's heightened senses could feel himself being watched once again. The portrait lined walls had eyes that saw far more than what mere mortals could perceive.

Bauer swallowed hard as he scanned all directions of the long hallway. He was desperate for any clue of who might have been in the archives with him, watching him. The silence was deafening, broken only by distant thunder and the sound of his own ragged breath. His footsteps echoed as he hurried from one side to the other. The hospital was a maze of sorts. Where each doorway held long forgotten memories and hidden truths. Every passage was a portal to another layer of a long history.

He sprinted through the corridor, toward the primary patient care wing of the hospital. His own footsteps echoed loud off the polished floor. Bauer's eyes darted around, searching for any movement or hint of anyone. There, in the distance, something caught the doctor's eye. His heart leaped into his throat as he whirled around for a better look. It was only a poster on the wall, fluttering from the breeze of a nearby open window. Bauer cursed under his breath.

Bauer continued his search, checking every alcove he passed. The empty corridor before him seemed to stretch on for miles. Bauer's mind raced with possibilities. Who had been watching him? What did they want? Was it someone from the hospital, or an outsider who had somehow gained access to the archives?

His exhaustive search was futile. There was no one in that corridor with him. Bauer repositioned the file as it began to slip from under his arm. He turned on his heels to head back to his office. Just as he passed, a doorway near him opened. Bauer froze.

Sam Harris jumped, almost dropping the broom in his hand. "Oh! Dr. Bauer, you startled me," he said. His voice was thick with age and surprise.

Bauer exhaled. "Sorry Sam. Thought you were someone else," he mumbled, as he rubbed his chest.

Sam tilted his head. Curiosity was evident in his hazel eyes. "You okay, Doc? Look like you've seen a ghost or somethin'."

Bauer issued a weak smile. "I'm alright. Just another day — another dollar, Sam," he said, echoing the custodian's familiar catchphrase. The doctor's thoughts had already moved back to the mysterious figure from the archives. Sam gave a nod, then turned away to fetch his housekeeper's cart and continue his work in another room.

Bauer took a step, then turned back toward the old man. "Say, Sam. I don't suppose you've seen anyone else in this part of the hospital in the last few minutes?"

Sam turned back toward Bauer with an odd look on his face. The old man shook his head. "No. Just you."

"Okay, thanks." Bauer stepped away from Sam. The old man's presence provided a fleeting comfort that soon gave way to the doctor's anxiety once again. Questions swirled through his head as his paranoia shifted to reality. He could once again feel eyes upon him. Someone was still watching him, hidden, just out of sight. But who? Why did they run? Clearly, they didn't want Bauer to know they were there.

Bauer's frustration grew. His chase led him to the foyer without success. The area was teaming with hospital personnel and patients on their way to other parts of the facility. Bauer searched every inch of that corridor. But found no one.

The murmurer of private conversations mocked his desperation. It amplified his own racing heart in his ears. The storm outside had intensified. The wind now howled through cracks in the empty corridor behind him. Bauer failed to notice. He needed to get to his next appointment. He was already late.

As he took one last glance down the empty hallway, Bauer froze. There, in the distance, at the far end of the hallway, was a figure. It was too far away to make out any details. Bauer could feel the weight of their eyes on him. His heart raced as he took a step toward their direction, ready to confront whoever it was.

His pursuit was halted by the squelching noise coming from overhead speakers. "Dr. Bauer, please call the operator, stat!" The woman's voice was calm yet authoritative. She repeated the message, its tinny quality echoed off the walls throughout the hospital.

Bauer's gaze drifted for a moment from the figure as he muttered to himself under his breath, "Now what?" His tone was tinged with exasperation and weary resignation. When he glanced back down the long corridor, the figure had vanished, leaving behind an unsettling emptiness.

With a heavy sigh, Bauer turned and strode towards the nearest phone. The folder he'd picked up from the archives, still secured under his arm. He picked up the receiver and pressed zero.

"Operator," the same calm voice responded.

"This is Dr. Bauer."

"Dr. Bauer, you have a call from a Mrs. Clendin. She says it's an emergency and insists on speaking with you right away."

"Mrs. Clendin?" Bauer repeated. His body shifted with a mix of concern and confusion. It was rare for Mrs. Clendin to contact him, even at home. At least not with anything urgent. The seriousness in her voice was uncharacteristic and alarming.

"Yes, doctor. Please hold while I connect the call."

"Of course, thank you," Bauer replied, his mind spinning with curious possibilities.

The line clicked, and then a voice, frantic and frail, came through. "Thomas, thank goodness! You need to come home right away. There's been an incident at your home. You must come right away. I don't know too much, but please, please hurry!"

Bauer's heart skipped a beat. His knuckles were white as his grip tightened on the handset. "An incident? What's happened? Is anyone hurt?"

"I — I don't know the details. But there are fire trucks, police, and others all around your home. Please, come. As quick as you can!"

The line went dead. Bauer held the silent phone to his ear. His mind reeling with images of fire, police, and other unknown disasters. What on earth could have happened to prompt such a response?

With a grim expression, he then dialed his immediate supervisor. As he spoke, his eyes darted through the hallway, half-expecting the mysterious figure to reappear. Every shadow seemed to move. Each distant noise hinted at something ominous. Outside, the storm intensified, the wind blowing the trees with great force.

"I need to go. There's been an emergency at home," he explained.

"Of course, Dr. Bauer. I'll let the staff know you had to leave for a family emergency," came the response.

Bauer's attention drifted from the voice on the line as he hung up. Clutching the folder tight under his arm, he raced towards the main exit. The sensation of being watched persisted. Some unseen phantom presence that seemed to cling to the fringes of his perception.

Heavy rain lashed against the hospital's aged windows as he pushed open the door. The doctor stepped out into the storm. He paused under the awning. Cold wind whipped at his white coat. Blowing raindrops splattered onto his polished shoes. Thunder roared overhead. A bolt of lightning split the sky, illuminating the grand, classical facade of Saint Elizabeths Hospital.

Bauer stared out into the storm. His reflection distorted in the puddles on the cracked pavement. "What the hell am I doing?" he whispered, his voice lost to the howling wind.

Shaking off his hesitation, Bauer turned and rushed back inside the building. He made his way to his office, the folder still gripped tight. His fingers fumbled with the keys, betraying his anxiety. Upon entering, he took a quick, apprehensive look around. He half-expected the mysterious figure to materialize from one of the shadows. He placed the folder on top of his cluttered desk with care. The doctor grabbed his coat, hat, and briefcase, then rushed back out into the storm. He was driven by the urgent need to find out what awaited him at home.

Chapter 5

Dr. Thomas Bauer pressed against the doors of Saint Elizabeths Hospital's main entrance. Against the forceful winds and driving rain, he pushed to open the door. He hurried with futile efforts, trying to avoid puddles that soaked his leather loafers. He braced himself against the biting cold as he pressed forward. In the distance, his car sat waiting for him where he had left it only a few hours earlier.

Its once-pristine paint now dulled by the rigors of his life and the lack of attention. Bauer yanked the handle as he lifted it. Hinges on the door of the sedan groaned in protest. His car's interior mirrored both his home and office at work.

A pile of unread journals lay scattered across the passenger seat and the back. A thin layer of take out food wrappers decorated by a few coffee stains half buried the scientific publications. Papers from groundbreaking experiments lay strewn across the dashboard. Half of them slipped from their disorganized folders. Overdue bills and unsorted piles of mail peeked out from under the passenger's seat. Forgotten remnants of an ordinary life.

He threw his briefcase onto the passenger seat pile and climbed in. The door slammed shut by the blustery wind. He placed his hands at two and ten. His forehead came to rest at twelve on the steering wheel. Bauer's grip on the wheel tightened, turning his knuckles white. He sat alone. For a moment, sheltered from the world outside.

As the rain pounded without mercy against the windshield. Bauer sat motionless in his car. He took a deep breath and held it. A flash of lightning, followed by crashing thunder, jolted him out of his trance. Here, in the solitude of his vehicle, the weight of his day-to-day existence seemed to crash down upon him.

His reflection in the rearview mirror caught his eye. He didn't recognize himself. His once vibrant green eyes looked back at him, now dull and lifeless. Bauer now sported dark circles that spoke of the countless sleepless nights. His hair, once a rich chestnut brown, had become streaked with gray.

He ran a hand through his hair, feeling the coarse strands between his fingers. When had he gotten so old? The weight of the world had become heavier on his frame. He couldn't recall how or when it happened. However, this had been building for a while. The slow and steady erosion of his passion and his spirit.

He sat there. Staring at his haggard reflection. His thoughts played through his routine. Wake up, shower, and shave, when he remembers. Dress, eat a tasteless breakfast, and then off to the hospital .

At work he would spend countless hours listening to the troubles of others. He paid no mind to his own life crumbling around him. It was a grind as predictable as the rising and setting sun. However, his existence had become devoid of all warmth and light.

Bauer's hand sat lifeless in his lap. The storm continued to rage outside his car. He couldn't see much beyond the front of his vehicle. Fond memories had become distant dreams of the life he once enjoyed. He remembered the laughter that once filled days.

Bauer longed for the comforting touch of Eleanor. His wife's embrace had grown cold as they drifted apart. In recent months, he missed the bubbling energy of their son, Simon. Family dinners were a favorite way to end busy days. Eleanor's eyes would sparkle as she recounted the latest happenings at the downtown art museum. Simon was always entertaining with his tales of misadventures with friends.

Bauer's heart ached as he recalled playful moments with Simon. The two of them engaged in spirited games of chess. Each of their pieces moved across the board in a strategic battle of wits. Simon's face would light up with pride whenever he'd outmaneuver his father. An occurrence that Bauer cherished in his graceful defeat.

And then there were the quiet evenings with Eleanor. The two of them curled up on the couch. Each lost in the pages of a book. They would discuss the intricacies of plots, the depth of characters they loved or hated, and the beauty of stirring prose. It was those connections with his family that made him feel alive and loved.

But now, those beautiful memories had become painful recollections of what once was. The love and laughter were now gone. In its wake was a cold, defeating emptiness that consumed him. His silent, empty house had never felt like a home. Eleanor had become cold and indifferent. The distance that continued to grow between him and his son had suppressed Simon's zest for life.

Happier moments faded into the harsh realities of the present. And the rain continued to fall. Thomas Bauer wondered if he would ever find his way back to the light.

A tear welled up in his eye. Bauer shifted his thoughts to the events of earlier that day. His complete failure with Rhyse and the near-death of his other patient. The stern reprimand from the hospital administrators echoed through his mind. Their accusations of negligence cut deep into his already fragile psyche. They questioned his ability to treat his patients in an effective and meaningful way. In question were his methods, procedures, and judgments. Did administration have anything to do with the watcher from the archives? Was it the same person who stood at the end of the long corridor?

The hair on his arm stood on end. Once again, he felt eyes upon him. Bauer looked over his shoulder. All he saw were empty soda cups and takeout food containers mingling with old newspapers and other trash. His shoulders lowered as he exhaled and set his paranoia aside.

Bauer's mind once again returned to his workday. He had always taken great pride in his unorthodox approaches to his patient's treatment plans. He believed his innovative methods were key to unlocking the mysteries that made the human mind so fascinating. However, as he sat alone in his car, he wondered if maybe he'd been wrong. It seemed he'd been wrong about a lot of things, both personal and professional.

The potential threat of suspension by administrators loomed over him like the dark clouds that swirled outside the hospital. He reconsidered his ideas, his actions. Maybe his methods were nothing more than risky delusions. Some desperate attempts to find some sort of meaning in a world that had lost its luster long ago.

Bauer's hands gripped the steering wheel once again. His knuckles turned white as his grip twisted tighter. He could feel the burdens of responsibility. The expectations of patients, colleagues, administrators and family. He had carried it all, in silence for far too long. Deep inside, he knew he was nearing his breaking point. The doctor closed his eyes, and drew in a deep breath. All he wanted was to find some shred of order in the chaos that surrounded him.

But peace eluded him, as some new, unknown crisis awaited him at home. All he had left was bitterness, regret, and the knowledge that he had somehow lost his way. Not that long ago, the man who is now sulking in his car brimmed with purpose and promise. That same man who was obsessed with the human mind's ability to heal from extraordinary traumas. In a matter of months, he'd become nothing more than a shell of his former self.

Bauer stared out into the bleakness beyond his windshield. A world that seemed to have lost all color. Its once rich vibrancy, replaced by the dull gray that reflected the emptiness deep within his soul. Would he ever find his way back to the passion and purpose that had once driven him?

For now, he sat paralyzed by the darkness that threatened to consume him. He listened to the storm and the sound of his own breath. Something had to change, but for now, he had to keep going. There was now a more recent crisis waiting for him at home. Even though he lacked all strength and motivation, he couldn't escape responsibility and expectations.

With a heavy sigh, Bauer released his grip on the wheel and reached for the key in the ignition. The engine sputtered to life, a weary sound that echoed his own exhaustion. He pulled out of the hospital parking lot; the wipers engaged in a futile battle against the relentless deluge as he began the familiar drive home.

Bauer navigated his car through the rain-soaked streets of Washington, D.C.. His mind continued to ruminate on his life and the events of earlier that day. The historic architecture mocked him with their durable elegance on display in the pouring rain.

He turned onto a side street lined with classic-designed, modest middle-class homes. The car slowed for a stop sign. Bauer glimpsed a happy family enjoying life and each other's company. They were oblivious to the storm outside their home. As he passed, he winced. The love and warmth was now gone from his existence.

He paused at a stoplight. Bauer's gaze fell upon a weathered, old homeless person. The man pushed a cart filled with the last of his earthly possessions. Soaked, tattered clothes clung to the man's frail frame. The word "Vietnam" embroidered in bright yellow thread on his hat soaked with rain.

The man's eyes showed a haunting emptiness. A look Bauer knew all too well. He had seen it many times in some of his patients over the years. He'd also recognized sparks of it in his own eyes as they stared back at him in the mirror. A reflection, no, a premonition of his potential fate if things continued as they had the last several months.

The light turned green, and without thought, the vehicle sped forward. The soaked homeless man faded in his rearview mirror. However, he lingered in Bauer's mind. Choices always came with consequences, both good and bad. He had always worked hard and took pride in his work ethic and dedication. As he drove the city streets, he couldn't help but wonder if his dedication had become his undoing.

He turned down another neighborhood street. Bauer's attention came to rest on a withered tree in a neighborhood park. The park was empty because of the storm. The once vibrant leaves had turned yellow and brown. Whipping winds scattered the dead leaves about the playground. A few still clung to dying branches. The rain-soaked, lifeless branches drooped toward the ground. It was a sight that felt familiar to Bauer.

Bauer's heart raced as he turned the corner onto his street. His eyes widened at the sight of the flashing lights from emergency vehicles illuminating the rain-soaked gloom. The red, blue and orange strobes reflected off the wet surfaces, creating an eerie, surreal atmosphere.

As he approached the blockade, Bauer's hands gripped the steering wheel tighter. His eyes scanned the scene before him as his mind swam through possibilities of what might have happened.

A police officer held up an open hand, signaling him to stop. He then slammed his hand on the car's hood as he leaped out of the way. Distracted, Bauer slammed on the brakes. His tires screeched to a halt against the wet road. He threw it into park and jumped out of the vehicle. The rain soaked through his clothes without notice.

"Officer, what's going on? I need to get to my house," Bauer shouted. His voice strained to be heard over the pouring rain and the idling engines from emergency vehicles.

With a stern expression, the cop shook his head. "I'm sorry, sir, but I can't let you through. We have a situation, and we need to keep this area clear."

Bauer's frustration grew. His hands clenched into fists at his sides. "Please, you don't understand. I got a call from my neighbor, Mrs. Clendin. She said it was an emergency. I need to know what's happening!"

The officer's expression softened a little. However, his stance remained firm. "Sir, I understand. There is very little information thus far. Everyone is to keep out of this neighborhood until further notice."

Bauer ran a hand through his rain-soaked hair. His mind raced with worst-case scenarios. Was it a fire? A break-in? The lack of knowledge was driving him to the brink of panic.

He scanned the area, trying to look at his house through the sea of emergency personnel and vehicles. His eyes landed on a familiar figure standing out in front of her home, illuminated by the flashing lights. Mrs. Clendin, his elderly neighbor, stood in her drenched rain bonnet, her face etched with concern.

Bauer's heart hitched. If Mrs. Clendin was out here, he knew whatever was happening at his house had to be bad. He turned back to the officer, his voice rising with each word. "Officer, please. That's my neighbor over there. She's the one who called me. I need to talk to her. I need to know what's going on!"

The officer glanced over to where Bauer was pointing. He could see the old woman in the distance. He then turned back to Bauer. The officer looked conflicted as he seemed to weigh options. After a moment, he sighed. "Alright, sir. Pull your car to the side of the road. I'll walk you over. But I need you to stay with me."

Bauer nodded. A slight sense of relief washed over him. "Thank you. I'm sorry for causing any trouble. I just need to know what's happening at my home."

As the officer led him through the maze of vehicles, Bauer's mind continued to take it all in. His heart pounded in his ears. It drowned out the noise of the storm and the scene before him. Each step seemed tiny. The distance between him and his home seemed to stretch on for miles.

When he got closer, the look of fear and concern was clear in her eyes. "Mrs. Clendin, what's going on? What happened?"

The elderly woman's hands shook as she reached out for Bauer's arm. "Oh, Thomas, thank God you're here. One moment I was reading in my living room. The next I heard a commotion coming from your front yard. Lights and trucks filled the street. There was shouting and people everywhere. It all happened so fast. They won't tell me anything."

Bauer's eyes followed her gaze to his front door. A big, burly firefighter stood near the entrance. In his hands was a large ax, as another firefighter gestured toward the door. Bauer sprinted towards them, as the young officer chased after him shouting, "Sir, come back here! You can't go over there!"

Bauer ignored the policeman behind him. The firefighters's expressions were ones of confusion as he approached them, waving his arms and shouting. "Stop, stop." The officer caught up to him and tried to hold him back. "This is my house. Please stop."

The firefighter, with "captain" on his helmet, moved toward him. "This is your house?"

"Yes sir. I have my key right here."

One man turned and began shouting to others, "The homeowner is here! He just arrived."

The captain continued, "We need to get into your home right away. It's an emergency."

Bauer didn't argue with the man. Without hesitation, he just moved towards the door. He reached into his pocket for his keys. As he got closer to the door, the sound of rushing water grew louder and louder in his ears. He couldn't imagine what was making that kind of noise. His cold, wet hands fumbled with the lock.

The lock clicked open. Bauer pushed against the closed door, but it refused to open. The firefighter dropped his ax and came over to help. Together, the two men grunted as they struggled to push the door open a few inches. Water escaped with a rush as the door opened wider.

The deafening sounds of rushing water filled his ears. Bauer stood back from the doorway in shock as firefighters and city utility workers rushed into his home. All he could see, everywhere he looked, was water. Water flooded his entire home.

"The main break is over here!" yelled one man, as another rushed by with a large wrench in hand.

The sound of rushing water soon stopped. A man approached Bauer and informed him it was now safe for him to enter his home. All Bauer could do was nod as he stood in silence, staring through the doorway into his flooded home.

Chapter 6

Without a word, Thomas Bauer descended the two steps into his home. The water was chilly and came up to the middle of his calf. It soaked through his shoes and socks in seconds. A shiver went through him as it began to wick up the legs of his slacks.

With great conscious effort, he forced his feet to move. The sound of his legs sloshed through the flood that surrounded him. In the distance, he heard eerie drips and the lapping of small waves against walls and furniture. A musty smell filled his nostrils. The dampness permeated every corner of his abode.

Bauer waded further into the living room. Ripples swirled in his wake. The surface reflected the muted gray light from outside in a frantic, haunted dance. Fragments of his life bobbed about in the murkiness.

His eyes came to rest on a treasured family photo. He held Eleanor close, his arm around her waist, and her expression overflowed with joy. Simon was still a small boy, sitting with a huge smile on her lap. His own younger, smiling face stared back at him, submerged and distorted by the water. Bauer reached down, lifting the frame from the flood. Drops began to fall like tears from its edges.

A stack of sodden papers caught his attention. The ink had bled; the words blurred together in an indecipherable mess. Bauer's heart sank as he realized they were some of his handwritten notes. Important information that served as the foundations of his work for years. He picked up a page. Then watched in horror as the paper disintegrated in his fingers.

As he turned to another part of the living room, his foot knocked against something solid. He reached down to retrieve a wooden knight. It was from the chess set he and Simon once played with on quiet evenings. The memory of their conversations and laughter. Their fun as they moved their pieces across the board seemed so distant now. All of it drowned in the overwhelming reality before him.

Everywhere he looked, he saw fragments of his life suspended in the cold, murky water. His favorite books that had provided him with an escape, now sat swollen. He noticed that the covers had become warped. Their pages fused together and unreadable. The couch sagged under the weight of the water, its fabric discolored and stretched.

Bauer's mind swam as he tried to process the extent of the damage. With each step, he found another treasure, another piece of his world forever altered, submerged or floating. A heavy weight settled in his chest, making it difficult to breathe.

His eyes closed as he attempted to shut out everything around him. The sound of moving water and the unmistakable smell of dampness still assaulted his other senses. It was at that moment, surrounded by incredible destruction, Bauer felt lost and alone.

What would he do now? Where would he live? The uncertainty of his future loomed before him. The thought of salvaging what he could was daunting, as deep despair washed over him.

With a heavy heart, Thomas splashed his way into another room of his house. His movements were slow and labored. He picked up a soaked book and placed it on a nearby shelf. It was a futile effort. All he could do was try to piece together the fragments of what was salvageable. However, he knew in his heart that nothing would ever be the same. Everything he had worked for, everyone he held dear slipped through his fingers like the water flooding his world.

Bauer stood in the middle of his kitchen. The torrent lapped at his calves as he continued to survey the extent of the damage. Desperate to salvage anything he could, the broken man grabbed a mop bucket from the washroom. It hadn't been touched in weeks. He began scooping pail after pail of water into the basin. His movements were frantic, his heart pounded in his chest as he tried to remove an endless flood. The water sloshed around him. It had soaked through his pants, chilling him to the bone.

Buckets were emptied into the sink filled with dirty dishes. He shook his head as more water seeped back in from every crack and crevice. The futility of his efforts pressed down on him, threatening to crush anything that was left of his spirit. Still, he persisted, refusing to give up even as the water level remained unchanged.

His arms ached from the repetitive exertion. His breath came in short, ragged gasps. Sweat mingled with the moisture on his skin, and drenched strands of his hair clung to his forehead. He couldn't get the musty smell of wet paper, wood, and fabric out of his nose. The splashing of his own feet continued to reach in his ears.

As he reached down to fill the bucket once more, a gentle, caring voice carried over the ripples from his efforts. Startled, Bauer turned to see his neighbor standing there in her oversized galoshes. She had an arm full of dry towels in her hand. In the other was a steaming mug of coffee.

"Thomas," she whispered, her eyes resting on his, filled with concern. "Looks like you could use some help."

Thomas straightened up. His grip tightened on the handle. "I appreciate the offer, Mrs. Clendin, but I can manage."

With sadness in her eyes, she shook her head. "No one should have to face something this devastating alone. Please, let me help."

Bauer hesitated. His mental and physical exhaustion overtook his pride. He looked around the flooded room, then back at his neighbor's kind face. With a sigh, he nodded, accepting the mug of coffee she held in her hand.

The woman set aside the towels on the counter. She plucked pictures and papers from the water with a certain determined efficiency. Her moves were methodical, as she wiped the items she'd plucked from the water. Bauer watched her for a moment, then resumed his own efforts with the bucket.

Despite the chaos that surrounded him, Bauer found it comforting to have his neighbor there with him. Her quiet, caring support and practical help grounded him. For now, he had something to focus on beyond his own growing despair.

As they labored together, She shot a concerned glanced over at Bauer. "Do you want to talk about it?" she asked in a soft tone.

Bauer's jaw clenched as he shook his head. "There's nothing to talk about," he said, his voice rough. "Everything's a mess, and I need to get it cleaned up."

Mrs. Clendin nodded with understanding in her eyes. "Sometimes, talking can make the difficult stuff a little easier," she said. "But I'm here either way, for as long as you'll have me."

Bauer paused. The pail felt heavy in his hands. He saw the sincerity in her expression. A lump formed in his throat, and he swallowed hard, pushing down the emotions that threatened to overwhelm him.

"I — I'm sorry, Mrs. Clendin." he managed, his voice just above a whisper. "Thank you. I appreciate you being here."

The woman smiled as she reached out to pat his arm. "That's what neighbors are for." she said, then moved to pull another of Bauer's pictures from the flooded floor.

Thomas watched her for a moment. A flicker of warmth penetrated through the cold that had settled into his muscles. Then, with a deep breath, he turned back to the sink to empty his bucket.

The noise coming from the phone on the kitchen wall seemed out of place in the chaos. The shrill ringing disoriented Bauer as it assaulted his ears. He was surprised it still worked with all the water everywhere. He waded toward the sound. His hand trembled as he reached for the handset.

"Hello?" His exhausted voice came out as a whisper, filled with emotion.

"Thomas." Eleanor's tone was snippy, businesslike. "What time are you picking up Simon in the morning?"

Bauer's mind raced, his eyes darting around the room, desperate to find his calendar in the mess. He'd completely forgotten this was his weekend to have Simon over. "Tomorrow? I — " He stammered, struggling for words to explain his present situation. "Eleanor, I uh — he won't be able to stay with me this weekend."

There was silence on the other end of the line. It was a stillness that seemed to stretch on for hours. When his wife spoke again, her voice was tight. She didn't even try to hold back her frustration. "What do you mean? We had an agreement. This is your weekend, Thomas. You can't just back out on him, on us at the last minute like this."

Bauer closed his eyes, his free hand clenched into a fist at his side. "I know, I know. But he just can't come over here tomorrow. I've got too much to do around here."

Eleanor roared with anger through the phone line. "You and your damn work. There's always something with you, isn't there, Thomas? Some excuse, some reason you can't come through on your commitments."

Bauer's chest tightened. He took a deep breath to steady himself. "Eleanor, please. I'm not making excuses. This is a crisis." A lump formed in his throat. His entire body shook. "I'm sorry Ele. I just can't. There are things I need to figure out.

"And what about Simon? What about your responsibilities as a father? He was looking forward to spending time with his father. You're letting him down. Again."

His eyes stung with unshed tears. He gripped the phone tighter. "I'm not — I don't want to let him down. But I can't —"

Eleanor's voice rose as she cut him off. Her words were sharp and jagged. "Can't or won't? Because to me, it appears that you're choosing your own stupid problems over your son. Just like you always do."

Bauer opened his mouth to respond, but nothing came out. He looked around at the drowning fragments of his life, bobbing in the murky water. How could he make her understand? "I'm sorry," he managed. His tone softened. "I — I'll make it up to him. To both of you. I promise."

There was another pause, heavy with unspoken, pent-up emotions. When Eleanor spoke again, her tone was flat, resigned. "Don't make promises you can't keep, Thomas. Your son and I — we're used to disappointment at this point. We'll manage without you. We always do."

His wife was justified in her frustration with him. However, her words pushed him over the edge. He stood there for a long moment, the phone still pressed hard against his ear. The flood swirled around his legs and the weight of his responsibilities sat ready to pull him in further. "Ele, how can I have Simon over this weekend when I'm homeless?" The other end of the line went silent. She wasn't expecting the countering outburst that came from him.

"Homeless?" She gave a half sarcastic laugh. "Thomas, stop being so over dramatic."

"I'm standing in the middle of my kitchen in water up to my calves as I talk with you. This place is an absolute mess and I still do not know where I'm going to be sleeping tonight. Believe me, I'm far too exhausted for any more drama right now."

There was a forceful pounding on Bauer's door. "Hang on, Ele. There's someone at my door." Without waiting for her response, he left the phone teetering on the counter and went to answer it.

When Thomas opened the door to see several city employees in hard hats and yellow-colored rain gear. Behind them was a big truck maneuvering a trailer into place in front of his house. Attached to the trailer was a large piece of equipment. Several men stood in the downpour just outside his door with broad barreled hoses in hand.

"Dr. Bauer, we're setting up a pump out there. We'll connect a few lines so we can get some of this water out of here."

Grateful for the helpful offer, he stepped aside to allow the workers to enter. "Yes, of course. Thank you. Do what you need to do. Mrs. Clendin and I will stay out of your way."

Eleanor could hear the commotion in the background. People splashed around as they conversed with her husband and others.

When he returned to the phone, the line was dead silent. "Ele? Are you still there?"

She remained quiet for a second as the seriousness of her husband's situation registered in her brain. "Thomas, what's going on?" Her question was filled with concern.

"The city workers said a water main broke under the house. They turned it off, but there's still flooding throughout my entire house."

"My God, you weren't kidding when you said you were homeless. Were you?"

"No."

"Would you like to stay here for a night or two?" Her words tumbled out before she realized she said them. "Until you figure things out? I can fix up the spare bedroom for you."

Bauer couldn't believe his ears. Was his exhaustion causing him to hallucinate? His shoulders relaxed in response. Eleanor's offer was the nicest thing he'd heard that day. The only exception was his brief conversations with Andrew and Mrs. Clendin. "Oh, I couldn't impose on you and Simon like that. I'll just stay at a motel tonight."

"For God's sake, Thomas, why must you be so damn stubborn? I insist. Besides, it isn't an imposition. I offered."

He remained silent as he reconsidered. "Thank you Ele, I'm not sure how long I'll be here. There is still water everywhere. Once I get things somewhat under control, I will call you before heading your way."

"Sounds good." Then she hung up.

They'd been separated for many months, but they didn't hate each other. They still cared for one another, but had moved past trying to make their relationship work. They agreed long ago that they would remain amicable in their interactions for the sake of Simon.

After a few hours, the flood in his home was gone, but the mess remained. Bauer thanked the city workers, and his neighbor, for their help. Mrs. Clendin offered him a place to sleep for the evening. Thomas was polite as he declined her kind offer.

"But where will you stay? You can't say here, Thomas."

"Ele has agreed to put me up for a night or two."

"Eleanor?" The elderly lady's face lit up a little. Her eyes tugged a little at the corners of her mouth. She had always been fond of his wife. Their separation was something she never understood. Yet she knew it was not her business to meddle in their private affairs. She adored Simon. "She's right. After the day you've just had, being around your family tonight might be just what you need, Thomas."

Chapter 7

Bauer stood on the doorstep of Eleanor's home. The house he used to call home before the separation. His clothes clung to his skin, still soaked with water. In one hand he held a suitcase with some toiletries and the few dry pieces of clothing he managed to salvage. The weight of the day's events had settled onto his shoulders and back. The thought of stepping inside filled him with gratitude and a mix of emotions. His free hand hovered near the doorbell. He took a deep breath, preparing himself for the emotional flood that awaited him on the other side.

Eleanor opened the door. Her expression was of concern and something else he couldn't quite read. In front of her was the pathetic sight of her husband clutching a large suitcase. His whole body violently shivered. She took the bag from his hand.

He stood there in drenched clothes. "Where are your shoes?" She asked. Her eyes came to rest on his wrinkled, pale, bare feet.

"In the car. They're soaked through." Bauer was numb from wading through frigid water for hours. "I couldn't find any dry ones."

Her eyes moved past him. She could see that his vehicle was packed with a few things he salvaged before leaving his house.

"I think there's a pair of boots upstairs somewhere." She turned to yell over her shoulder. "Simon, can you please bring down a towel and a blanket from the hall closet?" She stepped aside and welcomed him into her home.

Thomas forced a smile. The muscles in his face felt awkward and unnatural. "Thanks, Ele. I appreciate you letting me stay here tonight" He walked over the threshold. The familiarity of this place hit him like a physical blow. The photographs on the walls, the shoes lined up by the door — it was all the same. Yet for him, everything was different.

Within seconds, Simon burst into the foyer. "Dad! I thought I would not see you until tomorrow," the boy said, his voice filled with excitement. Bauer's body convulsed as his boy wrapped the heavy flannel blanket around him and hugged him tight.

His wife closed the door behind Bauer and welcomed him into her home. She gave the suitcase to her son. "Take your father upstairs so he can take a hot shower and change into something warm and dry."

Thomas was too cold and exhausted to protest. She handed him the towel. Her fingers brushed against his as he took it. He could feel the warmth from the brief contact. It reminded him of the intimacy once shared between them. "Thank you," came silently through his quivering lips. His eyes turned away from hers. His feet ached as he climbed the stairs. Needle-like sensations filled his hands as the feeling returned.

Simon led him to the guest bedroom. It was the space that used to be his office. His familiar desk and bookshelves were gone. In their place was a bed and a dresser. It was then that he realized just how much had changed.

When Bauer reappeared in the kitchen following his shower. His wife sat at the dining room table. Her eyes moved from the magazine she was reading. "I heated some food." She said, "I thought you might be hungry."

"Oh Ele, you don't need to fuss over me."

She glanced at him. "From the looks of you, I'd say someone does." She jested. "Besides, it wasn't a big deal. Just some leftovers from our dinner earlier this evening."

Bauer's stomach growled in response. He couldn't remember the last time he'd eaten. "I appreciate it."

He sat down at the dining room table. The chair felt both familiar and foreign beneath him. Eleanor moved about the kitchen with efficiency. The sounds of clinking dishes and utensils scraping a pot filled the silence.

The scent of the warm food transported Bauer back to countless family dinners in this room. Moments when laughter and conversation flowed between them. He swallowed hard, pushing down the lump that was forming in his throat.

She set a bowl in front of him. Steam rose from the stew. She handed him a fork, her fingers once again brushing against his. This time, he met her gaze. This time, he didn't look away from the woman he'd fallen in love with all those years ago.

"Thank you," he said, his voice rough with emotion.

Her sad, knowing smile made his heart ache. "You're welcome, Thomas. Now eat, before it gets cold."

Bauer took a bite. Familiar flavors exploded in his mouth. It tasted like home with his family. Like everything he'd lost. He closed his eyes, savoring the moment. He knew it wouldn't last.

As he consumed his meal, the silence between them became laden with things left unsaid. He wanted to apologize, to explain, to beg her to take him back. But the words stuck in his throat like shards of glass.

Eleanor sat across from him, watching him with an unreadable expression. Her husband wondered what she was thinking. Did she regret inviting him to stay? He wouldn't blame her if she did.

The stew was soon gone. Bauer set down his fork, feeling a warm fullness in his belly. However, his soul was as empty as the bowl in front of him. He gazed up at his wife, trying to find something he could say. "Ele, I —" he started.

She held up her hand. "Not tonight, Thomas," she whispered. "Let's just — let's just get through today and tomorrow."

Her husband nodded as he swallowed hard. Deep down, he knew she was right. There would be time for them to talk in the coming days. For now, he was just grateful for her offer of a warm meal and a dry place to sleep.

He helped Eleanor clean up the kitchen. The two of them moved around each other in a dance that was both familiar and awkward. As he rinsed his bowl, he thought about all the times they'd done this before, as husband and wife, talking and laughing as they cleaned up after dinner.

Now, the only sound was the running water and the clink of dishes. This man was now a stranger in what had once been his home. He was an intruder in a life he was no longer a part of.

Their son came downstairs and joined his parents in the kitchen.

"Say dad, what are we going to do this weekend?"

Thomas sat silent for a moment. stalling with his response. "I'm sorry. There's been a change of plans—." A look of disappointment came over the boy, filling him with guilt. "I need to find a place to live and clear my things out of my house."

"You're moving?" Simon seemed conflicted.

"Only for a while, Son."

"Oh, good." The boy's entire demeanor shifted. "cuz that Mrs. Clendin makes the best chocolate chip cookies I've ever had."

"Better than your mother's?" Bauer said with a slight smile and a wink.

"Yeah," He then looked at his mother. "Sorry mom. She puts walnuts in hers."

"I didn't know you liked them with nuts, Simon."

"Neither did I until I had some from her —"

Eleanor's mood turned playful as she swatted at him with the towel in her hand, then pivoted toward her husband. "You know, Thomas, I still have a few boxes of your things. From before —" She stopped herself for a moment, then continued. "They're upstairs in the bedroom closet."

Bauer looked confused. He had forgotten about them. With the separation and the downward spiral of his life, they had slipped his mind. "What's in them?"

His wife shrugged. "Old papers, notebooks, maybe some photos, I guess. To be honest, I don't know. I've never gone through them. I just figured you might want them someday."

Bauer's thoughts filled with curiosity. What could be in there besides memories from better days. When his life wasn't such a mess. "I — yes, I will take those with me once I get settled somewhere."

Bauer checked the clock on the dining room wall. Was it eleven o'clock already? He yawned without conscious thought. It had been a long day. A day that had left him more exhausted than he'd been in a while.

The three of them went up the stairs. Thomas hugged and kissed Simon good night, then tucked him into bed. He returned to the guest bedroom.

Eleanor hovered in the doorway. "There are extra blankets in the closet if you get cold."

Her husband nodded, his throat tight. "Thank you again, Ele."

She gave him a slight smile. Her eyes softened a little. "Get some rest. You've got a lot to sort through tomorrow."

With that, she turned, closing the door behind her. He sat down on the edge of the mattress, his head in his hands. His exhaustion was physical and emotional. It left him drained. As he laid on the bed, he stared up at the shadows on the wall. Hot tears streamed steady from his eyes as he dropped off to sleep.

The unmistakable smell of bacon and brewed coffee roused Thomas from his slumber. He blinked at the ceiling above him. From outside the room, he could hear his son preparing for his school day. Eleanor called from the kitchen downstairs, "Breakfast is almost ready, Simon."

A yawn escaped him as he continued to lie there for another minute. He stretched and massaged his temples, taking in the former familiar surroundings.

His back ached from sleeping in the unfamiliar bed and the stresses of the prior day. The residue of events haunted his dreams. Bauer winced as he sat up. He rubbed his face, trying to shake off the lingering disorientation.

From the window, he could see that the storm that woke him several times during the night had cleared. Outside, the sun shone bright in a crystal clear blue sky. He thought about the previous day. Mrs. Clendin was the steadfast, kind lady she'd always been. However, Eleanor's offer of shelter and food was unexpected and complicated his mental state.

He followed the scent of coffee and the muffled voices of his wife and child as he made his way downstairs. As he entered the kitchen, Eleanor looked up from the stove. Her tone and expression became guarded. "Good morning, Thomas. Coffee's ready."

Bauer nodded, murmuring a quiet "Thanks" as he poured himself a cup. He added in a splash of half and half to mute the bitterness of the hot liquid. His first sip grounded him in the moment. Simon had already taken a seat at the dining room table. Simon issued a loving smile before turning his attention back to his breakfast.

The three of them sat in an uncomfortable silence. The clinking of utensils on plates disrupted the stillness of the room. Eleanor attempted small talk, asking her son about his upcoming school project, but her efforts fell flat. Bauer couldn't help but notice the tension she held in her shoulders. The way she avoided his gaze.

His eyes turned to his own food. He was hungry, yet eating felt awkward. Their strained relationship and the uncertainty of his future ruined his appetite. He wanted to push away the untouched plate, but knew doing so would be rude.

He watched as his wife glanced over at him. Concern flickering in her eyes before she caught herself and looked away. "Simon, go upstairs and brush your teeth. Grab your backpack. We've got to leave for school in a few minutes."

The boy left the kitchen. Eleanor turned to her husband. "I'll drop him off. You should probably start making a list of what all you need to do today."

"I will." Thomas nodded, his throat tight. "Thank you again, Ele. For everything."

She shot him a restrained smile, then went to meet their son at the foot of the stairs. Bauer sat at the table. His head in his hands. He listened as his family went about their business without him. Just before going out the door, Simon went back to the dining room to give his dad a hug. His father returned the embrace and gave him a kiss on the forehead. "Have fun at school." The boy smiled as his father released him. He soon headed out to the car, followed by his mother.

After they left, he found himself alone in the house. He wandered from room to room. His mind contemplated his grim reality. There were calls to make. It was time for him to put his life back together. He just couldn't find the energy. There he sat in the living room for the longest time, staring at the phone.

The first call was easy. Calling off work used to fill him with tremendous guilt. He hated letting his patients down. Today, that wasn't the case. He was glad it was Friday. He would have until Monday to make sense of his mess. The tightness in his shoulders released a little. There was now one less thing to worry about for a few days.

Next he called his friend. He didn't want to cancel the presentation. They had been working on it for months. Canceling made him feel like a defeated man. With a sigh, he picked up the phone and dialed.

"Hello?" Andrew's voice was bright and full of energy.

"Hey, Andrew. It's Thomas." Bauer's tone was heavy with resignation. "I apologize for calling you so early."

"That's all right! Actually, I was just thinking about you. Are you ready for tomorrow?"

He gripped the handset tighter. "Well, that's why I called. I — I can't make it this weekend."

"What? Why not?" There was a pause on the other end of the line.

"I just—I can't do the presentation. I'm sorry." Bauer took a deep breath, then closed his eyes and slowly exhaled.

"Is everything okay?"

"No, not really. My house flooded yesterday. I ended up staying with Eleanor and Simon last night. I need to pack up what's salvageable and find a place to live."

"Oh, man, that sucks." Andrew's tone softened. "But hey, don't worry about it. It can be rescheduled for another time. You just focus on getting your life back in order."

Despite his friend's genuine understanding, Bauer felt bad. He knew how much work they had put into that project. "I feel terrible. I let you guys down."

"You're not letting us down. Stop beating yourself up, life happens." Andrew reassured him. "Is there anything you need?"

"First I need a place to live. Other than that, I just don't know yet."

"Finding something that's suitable and affordable in this city is going to be a challenge. Rents have gotten ridiculous in recent months."

Bauer went quiet for a moment. Those considerations hadn't even crossed his mind.

"Please don't hesitate to reach out. We're all here for you. We'll help you get through this."

A lump formed in his throat. "Thanks. I appreciate it."

"That's what friends do. You aren't alone, ya know."

"I'm more alone than you think, Andrew." Thomas muttered to himself as he hung up the phone.

Bauer next phoned his landlord. The conversation was quick and to the point. Brief moments of concern and empathy were followed by a sigh of annoyance on the other end of the line. The man agreed to meet him at the house at ten o'clock.

He made a mental note about insurance as he finished his call. He placed his hands on his head as he sank further onto the couch. The three conversations had only reinforced the mess that was now his life. He just shook his head. All his dreams and ideas resulted in nothing but disappointment for his patients, friends, family, and himself.

He rose from the sofa and shuffled back to the dining room. His cold breakfast still sat waiting to be consumed. Lost in thought, he choked down his eggs without tasting them. He cleaned up the morning dishes, then went upstairs to change his clothes.

When Eleanor returned, she thanked him for cleaning up the kitchen. Then she left to get dressed for her day. When she came back down, she walked into the room. "Shall we ride to your house together, or take separate cars?"

His wife's offer surprised him. "Ele, you don't have—"

"You don't deserve this, Tom," she breathed. Her hand came to rest on his shoulder. "Let me help you at least assess the damage."

They made a quick stop at a local hardware store on the way to his house. When they entered the home, all the water was gone. However, the destruction was everywhere. Waterlogged furniture, ruined carpets, and the musty smell of dampness permeated the space. The tears fell unimpeded as waves of pent-up emotions caught up with him.

Together they moved from room to room, surveying each room. Bauer's landlord arrived later, and the process repeated. The landlord's visit came and went with impressive efficiency. He promised to be in touch once he spoke to the city's utilities department and his insurance company.

A soft knock on the frame of his open front door was followed by a familiar voice. "Thomas, are you in there?"

"Come on in Mrs. Clendin," Bauer returned. "We're in the living room."

The neighbor lady appeared in the room carrying two cups and a container in her hands. She acknowledged Eleanor with a smile as she handed her the hot brewed coffee. The kind woman then offered her a chocolate chip cookie. It was delicious, fragrant and still warm from the oven.

Eleanor turned to her husband. "You know, Simon was right about these cookies. I think they are better than mine."

Mrs. Clendin's pride from the compliment was brief. Her attention became overwhelmed by all the damage caused the previous day. She only stayed to help for about an hour then ran off to an appointment.

Thomas and his wife went back to the living room together. They tried to salvage whatever they could. She noticed a photograph of Bauer's parents on a bookshelf. Next to it was a water damaged picture of her, with her husband and Simon, that was rescued the night before.

"Hey Tom, why don't you call your mom?"

"My mom? What for?" her odd request confused him. It seemed to come from nowhere.

"She's lived here in D.C. since forever."

"And—."

"And maybe she'll put you up until your house is habitable again."

Bauer paused. The last thing he wanted to do was burden his mother with his personal troubles. However, the prospect of a familiar, comforting home tugged hard at his tired soul. "Do you think she'd be okay with me staying there?"

"Are you kidding? She adores you, Tom. And I'm sure she'd love to see Simon during his visits too. It could be nice for all three of you." Eleanor reasoned with a brief smile. "Besides, it's not like it's anything permanent. It would be perfect until you got back on your feet."

Chapter 8

Bauer scoffed at Eleanor's suggestion, his face flushed with indignation. "I'm not running home to mommy like a child." He snapped, dismissing the idea outright. "I'm a doctor, with a career."

Eleanor sighed. Her patience with him was once again wearing thin. "This isn't about running home to mother. It's about having a place to live while you get back on your feet."

Her husband wasn't listening. He tried to deflect the conversation. Instead, he wished to stay focused on practicalities. "My mother is finally enjoying her retirement. I don't need to disrupt that," he insisted, crossing arms in front of him.

"She's your mother, Tom. She'd be delighted to help you." Eleanor reasoned, as her tone softened. "Being a mother is a lifelong thing. Even after her children have grown and moved away."

Bauer shook his head. His jaw displayed his stubbornness. "I won't do that to her. She's done enough for me already."

His wife threw up her hands in exasperation. "Fine, Thomas. But you can't stay with Simon and I forever. You need to figure something out, and soon."

He nodded. His eyes once again came to rest on the picture of his parents. He knew his wife was right, even if he didn't want to admit it. The idea of asking his mother for help was for him admitting he had failed. After a lifetime of proving his worth against harsh criticisms, he was proud of his independence, maturity, and his ability to make his own way in this world.

"I'll come up with something," he mumbled, more to himself than to his wife.

She studied him for a moment, her expression unreadable. Then she just sighed and shook her head. Then his wife turned back to what she was doing before the idea popped into her head.

Bauer nodded, grateful to move on from the conversation. He knew he couldn't avoid the issue forever. But for now, he could focus on the tangible task of sorting through the wreckage of his life.

As they worked, Eleanor glanced at her husband from time to time. She worried about him. She knew him well enough to know that his stubborn pride was a formidable obstacle. It would keep him from accepting the help he needed.

But she also knew that pushing him would only make him dig in his heels. So she held her tongue and returned to the water-logged mess around them.

Thomas pushed the conversation from his mind. He didn't want to think about the baggage that came with Eleanor's suggestion. He didn't want to admit that he failed.

Instead, he threw himself into the work in front of him. Bauer sorted through sodden remnants with a grim determination. If he would just focus on the task at hand. He wouldn't have to think about moving in with his mother.

As he worked, the weight of his crumbling reality pressed down upon him. He was homeless. His career was not what he dreamed it would be. Now his wife was suggesting he run home to mother. It was all almost too much to bear.

He glanced at Eleanor. She didn't meet his gaze. He'd seen that look of concern in her eyes when Simon was sick or injured. Guilt replaced his stubborn pride. She was only trying to help. He knew that. But that had never come easy for him.

He sighed as he threw a ruined favorite book into the growing pile of debris in the middle of the room. "Look Ele, I appreciate what all you've done, and your suggestions. I really do. But It's just—I can't run to mommy every time something goes wrong."

Eleanor paused with a damp photograph in her hand. "It's not about running home to your mom, Tom. It's about humbling yourself and accepting assistance where and when you need it. There is a difference. And there's no shame in that."

Bauer was quiet for a moment while he considered her words. Part of him knew she was right. Something deeper was preventing him from picking up the phone and calling his mother. It nagged at the back of his brain. He couldn't quite place his finger on it.

"Let me think about it," he said. His voice was tight. It was the most he could offer. The closest he could come to a concession.

Eleanor nodded, understanding the weight of even that small admission. "That's all I'm asking, Tom. Just think about it."

Bauer's jaw clenched as he stared at the waterlogged photographs in his hands. In them, Bauer was a scrawny teen. It felt like a lifetime ago. In one, he stood beside his father, both of them smiling at the camera. But the smile on his father's face didn't reach his eyes. It never did.

His wife's words echoed in his mind. *"Your mother adores you and Simon… she'd love to see Simon during his visits too."*

She was right. His mother had always been there for him, even when his father hadn't. But the thought of admitting that he needed help stirred up old painful wounds he thought he'd long since moved past.

"It's complicated," he muttered under his breath. He couldn't bring himself to turn away from the photo in his hands. He was afraid that she might see the pain displayed in his eyes.

Eleanor paused. For a moment, she studied him. There was a tightness in his neck and jaw. She knew him well. There was more to his resistance than just personal embarrassment.

"Tom —" she began, her voice soft.

Bauer shook his head. Cut her off. "Not now, Ele."

In silence, she hesitated, then nodded. She would not push him. Instead, she turned back to sorting through pictures, books, and papers.

He felt bad for barking at her. He never asked her to help him today. Eleanor didn't have to be here. She volunteered. His wife didn't deserve that reaction.

"I'm sorry. I shouldn't have snapped at you." His eyes never moved from the photo in his hands. "It's just that I'm under a tremendous amount of pressure right now." Then poured himself back into the ruin that was his current life.

More photos took him back to his teenage years. His face cringed as he remembered one day in particular. It was the day he declared his future intentions. He wanted to become a psychiatrist and help people, just like his father.

Thomas would never forget the look on his father's face. The immediate disappointment in Harold Bauer's eyes. The way his mouth had tightened. "A shrink? You want to waste your life listening to other people whine about their problems?"

The son who always worked hard on his studies never expected this reaction. After all, his dad was a formidable pioneer in his field of research. He should have been proud he was following in his footsteps. Instead, from that day forward, there was a rift in their relationship. A coldness that came without reasons or explanations.

Now that his life was in shambles, a part of him longed for the comfort his mother provided. However, he could not bring himself to admit that his father was right. His stubbornness mingled with guilt. The frigid feelings between him and his father had nothing to do with his mother. He still loved her with all his heart. His pain had kept him from his mother for years. Worse yet, his own son had not been as close to his grandmother as he'd like in recent months.

Eleanor didn't bother her husband any further. This was his mess he needed to process, both external and internal. A little after 1:30 PM, she left to pick up Simon from school. He was by himself again in the space that was his house, but he didn't feel like he was alone. He glanced around, knowing full well no one else was there.

That evening, Bauer stood in the dimly lit guest room of his wife and son's house. This was a place of comfort and security. This had been his home. A space filled with memories, laughter, and moments shared with his family. Now he was in the room that used to be his office. He was a foreigner in a strange land.

He moved to the window, peering out into the darkness. The street was quiet, the only movement coming from the gentle swaying of the trees in the night breeze. Despite the tranquility of the scene, Bauer couldn't shake the knot forming deep within his gut.

As he turned, a shadow darted across the periphery of his vision. His heart pounded as he whipped around. There was nothing there. No one was in the room with him. Logic told him that. It was just the familiar bathed in the dim light from the outside.

He shook his head once again to dismiss the paranoia. "You're losing it, Bauer." He whispered to himself. His mind was playing with his vulnerabilities. The compounded stress of the last few days had caught up with him.

Thomas plopped down onto the bed. The mattress creaked under the sudden weight. The sound was unnatural, loud in the night's stillness. A noise from outside made him jump. His nerves were shot.

He laid back down and closed his eyes, trying to relax. Sleep remained elusive. His thoughts raced, unable to settle on any one thing for any significant length of time.

The exhaustion had settled into his bones. He drifted off into a fitful slumber. But Bauer's head would give him no peace.

Thomas was back in his parents' home. His father sat before him in his study. A place that was forbidden to him as a child. His father's cold eyes looked right through him. Disappointment showed in every line on his face.

"Follow in my footsteps," his father scoffed, his voice dripping with disdain. "You think you have what it takes to work in this profession? To delve into the murky depths of the human mind?"

A younger Thomas Bauer wanted to make his case. Prove his father wrong, but his words caught in his throat.

"You're not cut out for it, son," his father explained, as he looked away, shaking his head. "You won't be the first to crack under the pressure. This field will consume every bit of your soul. It will chew you up and spit you out without mercy, leaving you soulless and questioning your own sanity."

A crushing pain shot through Thomas' core. His mouth opened to protest, but his father's image faded back into the shadows of his subconscious.

The scene shifted. This time, he was now standing in the aisles of the hospital archives. The musty smell of old paper was neither familiar nor comforting. He moved through the stacks, looking for something. The sound of his footsteps echoed louder than usual through the space.

He turned down a row he'd visited a thousand times before, then froze. At the far end, he saw it. The ghostly silhouette of a man. This time, the shadowy person didn't run, but his face remained obscure in the darkness. He felt eyes on him. Watching, waiting. Then the figure started moving closer. The man's feet were silent.

Bauer ran back toward the exit. He cleared the aisle and crashed into Sam Harris, nearly knocking the housekeeper to the ground. Thomas grabbed the old man to prevent him from falling. Sam's eyes glinted with a hint of gratitude. His gaze was focused with an unsettling intensity.

"Be careful, Doc," The Janitor whispered. His tone was urgent and cryptic. "The past hides in the shadows of this place. Some things that are best left hidden."

Thomas bolted upright in the bed, gasping for air. He was disoriented. Lost in the unfamiliar. His heart pounded against his ribs. The dream clung to him like a second skin, making it hard to breathe.

Bauer's hand trembled as they ran through his sweat-drenched hair. He struggled to calm himself. The walls inched closer with each ragged breath he took.

He swung his legs over the side. His bare feet hit the cool hardwood floor. He needed air. He wanted to escape the confines of his head.

He stumbled towards the window. He glimpsed his reflection. His face was ghostly. Dark circles intensified his haunted eyes. He looked like a man on the edge. Teetering on the brink of madness.

Bauer slid the window open with significant force. He then pressed his forehead against the cold glass. He closed his eyes as he faced the breeze and the onslaught of mixed emotions. The dream was so real, so visceral. Bauer stood there for a long time, watching as the first tentative rays of dawn forced their way through the gathering clouds.

Bauer sat alone at the dining room table. He was beyond exhausted. He had no desire for company or more nightmares, like the ones that had plagued him the previous night. The images of his father's disapproving face and the ghostly figure in the archives continued to cast shadows over his thoughts. He stared into his coffee. Wispy tendrils rose and escaped his mug. The house was quiet. Eleanor and Simon enjoyed the extra sleep that came with slower Saturday mornings.

Bauer rose to pour himself another cup. As he replaced the half and half in the refrigerator, his stomach growled. He pulled out bacon, eggs, cheese, and an assortment of vegetables. He hadn't made breakfast for his family in ages. It was the least he could do in exchange for their hospitality the last two nights. He walked to the pantry to fetch some potatoes.

Eleanor woke to mingling aromas coming from the downstairs. In silence, she stood in the kitchen doorway. She watched as her husband went about preparing the meal. His wife noted his unusual lack of engagement and the dark circles that had formed under his eyes. She then issued a simple "Good morning" and strolled over to pour herself a cup of coffee.

Bauer failed to register her presence. He was consumed by mounting pressures ready to crush. He took a sip. The hot liquid scalded his tongue. The pain pulled him for a moment from his thoughts. As he set the mug back down, his eyes drifted to the framed photograph of his parents on the mantel in the living room. His mother's warm expression contrasted with his father's stoic expression. Bauer's chest tightened. His dream was still fresh in his mind.

Eleanor startled him when she walked over to the toaster with a plate of bread. "Tom, are you alright?" she asked, her eyes were soft and filled with concern.

"I'm fine, Ele." He forced a slight smile, but failed to make eye contact. "Just didn't sleep well."

She studied him for a minute, unconvinced, then changed the subject. "Well, eat something. You'll feel better."

Bauer nodded, picking up a piece of toast. He choked down a bite. He glanced over at his wife, heaping food onto a plate for Simon. The distance between him and his family, both physical and emotional, continued to grow.

His mind drifted back to Eleanor's suggestion the previous day. Maybe it was time for him to swallow his pride and accept the help he needed. The thought of calling his mother, of telling her he wanted to come home, filled him with more anxiety than comfort.

"Watch the potatoes. I'll be right back," he mumbled. He avoided his wife's gaze.

He went upstairs to the guest bedroom, closing the door behind him. He moved to the open window and stared out at the dreary morning. Rain pattered against the glass. Bauer sighed, then picked up the phone. His fingers hovered over the keypad, hesitating. This call was his admission of failure. It was what he needed to do if he was going to salvage anything he had left of his life.

Thomas pressed the last button and brought the handset to his ear. He expected her disappointment.

"Hello?" His mother's voice was sweet, comforting and familiar.

He swallowed hard. His throat was dry. "Mom, it's me."

"Tom! What a lovely surprise! How are you, dear?"

Thomas closed his eyes, leaning his forehead against the cool glass of the window. "I — I need to ask you something. I know it's sudden, but — can I come home for a while? Just a few weeks, maybe a month or two at most. I — I'm in a bit of a situation."

The words tumbled out, each one lifting a little weight from his shoulders. There was a brief pause on the line. Bauer's stomach sank. But then his mother's voice returned, filled with warmth and love.

"Of course, Tom. You know you're always welcome here. Stay as long as you need."

Thomas let out a breath he felt he'd been holding for days. "Thanks, Mom. I — I appreciate it. More than you know."

As he ended the call, Bauer was overcome by a mix of new emotions that swirled with the old. Relief, gratitude, but his nightmares continued to nag at the back of his mind. There were still so many uncertainties ahead. But for now, at least, he had a place to live. It was his first promising step in the right direction.

Bauer reasoned with a brief smile. "Besides, it's not like it's anything permanent. It would be perfect until you got back on your feet."

Chapter 9

Thomas Bauer pulled his car into the driveway of his childhood home. The gravel crunched beneath the tires. Staring at the familiar façade, his hands gripped tight on the steering wheel. He had avoided this place since he left for college. The house was the same as he remembered. Like no time had passed.

Edyth Bauer was a regular guest before her son's family relationship became strained. She loved reading to Simon or beating him at a spirited game of marbles. She enjoyed spending the holidays with them. Those visits made for some of the best memories.

Cherished family moments soon were collateral damage of their separation. At first, Thomas called her several times a week. As his life got more hectic, the calls were less frequent. As he sat in her drive, he couldn't remember the last time they had really talked, aside from their brief conversation earlier that day.

Bauer stepped out of the car. The midday sun dappled the ground as it shone through the canopy overhead. He popped the trunk to retrieve his beat-up old suitcase. It felt heavy in his hand, like it contained the burdens he kept with him.

He walked toward the front door. Memories flooded into his head. How many times had he'd raced up this very path as a child, eager to share something from his day? He remembered the late nights he'd snuck in as a teenager, hoping to avoid being caught. On the day he'd left this place for college, he was determined to never return.

Yet, here he stood, returning like some variant of the Prodigal Son. His steps slowed as he neared the door. Was he really ready for this? He knew that none of this trepidation had anything to do with his mother.

For a selfish, callous moment, he was glad he wouldn't have to face his father. To admit that he needed help. Thomas' pride bristled at the thought of confronting him.

He took a deep breath, then knocked on the door. The sound seemed to echo through the quiet neighborhood. Bauer shifted his weight from one foot to the other. He suddenly felt like a child again, waiting to be let in.

The door swung open to reveal his smiling mother. The years had been good to her. Her eyes were warm, and her demeanor was as sweet as ever. She had a few more wrinkles and a bit more gray, but otherwise, she was the same as she's always been.

"Thomas," she breathed, her face lit up. "Welcome home, my dear."

Before he could respond, his mother wrapped her arms around him in a tight embrace. His body stiffened for a second. He wasn't used to physical forms of affection other than hugs from Simon. The scent of her perfume filled his nostrils. He closed his eyes. For a minute or two, he was a child again, safe in his mother's arms.

"It's good to see you, Mom," Thomas managed. His voice was thick with emotion.

Edyth pulled away from him. She placed her hands on his shoulders and studied his face. "You look tired, Thomas. Come in, come in. Let's get you settled."

She offered to take the old briefcase from his hand. He pushed her hand away. He followed her into the house. His eyes roamed the familiar abode. The living room was exactly as he had remembered it, right down to the furniture arrangement. Family photos lined the walls, chronicling the passage of time. They were the only things that had changed. Bauer's gaze lingered on a picture of his father. His stern, unsmiling face stared back at him. He turned his eyes away.

"Your room is just as you left it," she explained as she led him up the stairs. "I always hoped you'd come visit once in a while."

A pang of guilt shot through him. He'd been so consumed with his work that he'd neglected more family than he realized. "I'm sorry, Mom. I should have visited more."

Edyth waved a dismissive hand. "Nonsense. You're here now. That's all that matters."

She pushed open the door to Bauer's childhood bedroom, and he stepped inside. It was a surreal experience. It was like stepping back in time. His old posters still adorned the walls. His books still lined the shelves. Even the bedspread was the same, a faded blue quilt his grandmother had made for him.

Bauer set his briefcase down, overwhelmed by the rush of nostalgia. His mother watched him from the doorway, her expression soft. "I'll let you bring in the rest of your things," she said. "Come down to the dining room when you're ready."

"Thanks mom." There was a distinct emptiness in his tone.

"Are you hungry? I can fix you something."

His stomach was in knots. The last thing he wanted was food. "I'm alright. I—uh, I had a big breakfast." The guilt that came with the graceless lie was instantaneous.

She patted him on the arm. "I'll make us some tea."

Thomas nodded, not trusting himself to speak another word. His mother smiled at him once more, then closed the door behind her, leaving him alone with his thoughts.

He walked over and sat down on the bed. The frame creaked under his weight. He ran a hand over his face. The stubble on his cheeks and chin reminded him he hadn't shaved for three days.

Being back in this room, surrounded by all these fragments of his youth, stirred up a flood of memories. Late nights studying and dreaming of his future. Arguments with his father that always ended with slammed doors, followed by long, bitter silences. The day he'd received his acceptance letter to medical school was the best and worst day of his life. His heart swelled with pride that day, only to be met by the crushing disapproval of his father.

And now, here he sat. A grown man, a respected psychiatrist, seeking shelter in his childhood home with his mother. It was an embarrassing situation he never saw coming. He still had a lot more to remove from his house before returning to work on Monday morning.

Bauer sighed. He rose from the bed. His back protested with familiar pains and stiffness. He couldn't stay here forever. *It's only for a few weeks.* He told himself.

He made his way downstairs, following the sound of clinking china and the aroma of brewed Darjeeling leaves. Edyth was in the kitchen, arranging several Franzbrötchen on a plate. He had the fondest memories of his mother's buttery, German cinnamon-roll like pastries growing up. She looked up as he entered. Her face was warm and welcoming.

"Ah, there you are. Come, sit. The tea is ready."

Thomas slid onto a chair at the table, like he had a million times during his youth. He watched as his mother poured the steaming liquid into beautiful china cups. She placed one in front of him, along with some cream and sugar and the plate of Franzbrötchen. Then she sat down opposite him.

For a moment, they just looked at each other. A wealth of unspoken words hung in the air between them. Then his mother reached out and placed her delicate hand on his.

"I'm glad you're here, Thomas," she whispered. "I've missed you."

He swallowed hard. Emotions caught in his throat. It had been a long time since anyone had said anything like that to him. "I've missed you too, Mom. I'm sorry, for not visiting more. For not being a better son."

Edyth shook her head. "You've always been a wonderful son. Your father — he was a tough man to please. But he loved you, in his own way. And he would be proud of you, of the man you've become."

He looked down at his tea, watching the steam curl up from his cup. "There's nothing to be proud of," he murmured. "I've made a mess of everything. My life, my marriage, my family, my career—"

She squeezed his hand. "You're a smart man. It will all work out. You just need some time and space to figure things out."

He looked up at her, his vision blurred by tears waiting to fall. "Thank you, Mom. For letting me stay here."

She smiled. Her own eyes glistened. "That's what mothers do, my dear. You'll get through this. You're stronger than you think." She said with quiet conviction. "Now, drink your tea before it gets cold."

Bauer finished his cup and second Franzbrötchen. He then left to rescue more of his belongings from his house. The sun shone bright, high overhead, casting a warm glow through the neighborhood trees. He drove back to his flood-damaged home. His journey felt familiar, yet strange.

At his house, he only concerned himself with the things he would need over the next few months. He would place the rest in the garage until his house was habitable again.

He took a load out to his car. In the distance, he heard a vehicle coming down the street. An old unfamiliar truck stopped in front, then began backing into the driveway behind his sedan.

Eleanor stepped out of the vehicle. Her auburn hair caught the sunlight just right. She was as beautiful and put together as ever.

Simon's lanky, graceless pre-teen frame emerged from the passenger side door.

She glanced at the boxes in Thomas' trunk. "Need some help?"

"Where'd you get the truck?" Asked Bauer, curious.

"I borrowed it from a gal at work. I figured it'd haul more than either of our cars."

He didn't expect to see them here. But he was in no position to refuse. "Thanks."

His wife issued a slight smile. "You're welcome."

The three of them worked to load up the rest of his car, then the truck.

"Is that it?" Eleanor inquired.

"That's it for this trip." He said. "I'll meet you at my mom's."

She nodded. "Alright. We'll see you there." She turned to Simon and placed a hand on his shoulder. "Come on, let's go see Grandma Edyth."

When he arrived, he noticed the truck already parked in the driveway. Standing in front of the truck were his wife and son. Together, they went up the walkway. Thomas knocked as he entered the foyer. "Mom, I'm back," he called.

His mom emerged from the living room. Her face lit up with joy as soon as she saw her grandson. She took the boy in her arms and hugged him tight. His mother stood nearby with a huge grin as she watched them embrace.

Eleanor stepped forward, her expression a little guarded. "Edyth, it's so good to see you again. It's been too long."

Edyth's smile was stiff, with a hint of coolness in her eyes as she greeted her daughter-in-law. "Yes, it has. But I'm glad you're here now."

For a moment, the tension was palpable. They never explained the reasons for their separation to her. All she knew was the deep pain it had caused her son. She soon focused all her attention on the boy.

"Simon, look at you! My goodness, you've grown since I last saw you. Why, you must be six feet tall already," she exaggerated.

A shy smile came over Simon's face as his cheeks turned beet red. "Not quite, Grandma. But I am almost the same height as my mom."

Grandma chuckled. The sound was lukewarm and genuine. "Well, that's too tall. She's such a petite little thing."

Eleanor's expression was strained, but she held her tongue.

Bauer became uncomfortable as he watched the interaction between his mother, wife, and son.

Edyth clapped her hands, her eyes sparkling with mischief. "You know what we should do? Play some marbles, just like we used to. I bet I can still beat you, Simon."

The boy grinned, and the tension in the room eased a little. "You're on, Grandma! But I've been practicing. I might actually get some of your marbles this time."

Grandma and grandson soon left for the game closet to get what they needed. Their joy and chatter echoed throughout the house.

Thomas and Eleanor stood alone in the awkward silence. His eyes met hers for a second, then darted to a window. Outside, their vehicles waited, still burdened with fragments of broken life. He turned back to see his mother and son, their heads bent together over a circle, their laughter mingled in the air.

He and his wife unloaded the vehicle. Bauer returned to the living room to inform his mother they were leaving for another load. As he approached, he could see they were still enjoying each other's company. They left Simon behind to make some fun new memories.

It took two more trips between his home and his mother's. It was all that he would need for the next few weeks. The rest would have to be moved into the garage before clean up and repairs could begin. He figured it would take a month, maybe three at the most, for the repairs to be complete.

Ready to depart, Thomas jogged across the street and knocked on Mrs. Clendin's door. She welcomed him in to sit for a while. Over a cup of coffee and her now famous chocolate chip cookies, He explained the details of his temporary living arrangement. He asked her to keep an eye on the place during his absence. As he stood to leave, she walked over to give him a hug.

"Everything is going to be alright, Thomas." She said, her head coming to rest on the middle of his chest. "It will turn out just like it's supposed to."

He held her for a second more. "Thank you Mrs. Clendin, for all your help," He replied. "Call me if you need anything, and I do mean anything. I'm still your neighbor, even if I'm not in the neighborhood for a while."

Hours later, he had returned to his childhood bedroom. Not much had changed. His mother came into dust on occasion, but otherwise, his things just as they were when he went off to college so many years ago. His mind became inundated by memories he'd forgotten when his life got busy.

In silence, he unpacked his belongings. The profound displacement had finally caught up with him. He was a failed grown man. His precarious existence, his absolute vulnerability, was now visible for all to see. It hit him like a gut punch that left him staggering and disoriented.

He sat on the side of his bed, his head in his hands. The water that flooded his apartment had washed away more than just physical possessions; it had exposed the parts of himself he tried so hard to keep from the world. The successful research, his stoic demeanor—they were just walls that hid insecurities and deep repressed emotional wounds.

His failed marriage. The growing distance between him and his son. He'd become disillusioned by his research. His once promising career had destroyed everything he ever cared about. His façade had shattered. He wanted to put the pieces back together, but the damage was done. His mask didn't fit right any more. It no longer concealed the loneliness and pain that consumed him.

His hand moved across one of the velveteen squares of fabric in the quilt his grandmother made. A faded photograph of her sat on the dresser with other pictures. He walked over to the well-worn desk, where he had spent countless hours studying. It was all familiar, yet unsettling. Once again, he felt eyes upon him. He turned around, but again, no one was there.

In the hallway, his mother stood. She had done all she could to welcome him home. However, she could see the hesitation and underlying discomfort that still consumed her son.

The guarded way he moved, his body racked with tension. She knew he forced his smiles when they didn't reach his eyes. His troubles were heavy. This was more than the loss of physical possessions. She knew he was at war with himself.

The knock on the frame startled him. He would have to get used to not living alone. He sat in silence for a few seconds, then took a deep breath. "Come in." His eyes didn't greet her as she entered.

"I made some dinner. I can fix you a plate when you're ready." Her voice was soft and filled with maternal concern.

"I appreciate that, but you don't need to fuss over me."

Edyth placed a hand on his shoulder. "Is everything alright, dear?"

Bauer held a half folded shirt in his hand. He gazed at her. Emotions clouded his green eyes. He cleared his throat. "I'm fine, mom. Just tired, that's all."

She knew better than to believe his hollow words. His weariness and stress were evident in the lines that had formed around his eyes and mouth. She took a seat next to him. The bed frame creaked under the additional weight.

She took his hand in hers. Her skin was soft and warm against his. "Thomas, I know things are a mess right now. Your house, your job, your family — it's a lot for anyone to handle."

Bauer nodded. He swallowed hard. He struggled to speak.

"I want you to know," she continued, squeezing his hand, "that you are always welcome here, regardless of the circumstances. This is your home, as much as it is mine. It always has been and always will be."

Some of his tension dissipated through his hand and she held it.

"Listen, you can't keep living in the past. Doing so only allows the old wounds to fester," she said. Her voice was gentle but firm. "Your father, he — he was a lot like you, even if neither one of you ever wanted to admit it. He had his own battles. But that doesn't mean you have to carry his demons and yours."

Her words sounded like something he would have said to Rhyse or one of his other patients at the hospital. His logical brain knew she was right. Thomas turned toward his mother. For the first time in years, he peered into eyes. He saw love in her eyes, strength in her face, and her simple wisdom of her presence.

Deep down, he knew something had to give. Pretending everything was alright, had been a complete disaster. This was not how his life was supposed to be. This was not how he wanted to spend the rest of his days.

This crisis was a wake-up call, a chance to reassess priorities and make corrections. Change meant confronting suppressed pain. Bauer took a breath to ground himself.

He reached over to give her a hug. "Thanks mom. Let me wash up, and I will be down in a minute."

Chapter 10

Following dinner, Thomas Bauer returned to his childhood bedroom. The space now crowded and cluttered with the remnants of his adult life. Despite the exhaustion that had settled into his bones, he unpacked more of his clothes and personal items. The out-of-date decor didn't belong to the current version of himself. He moved a few things around to make the temporary digs feel like his own. He found his quarters cramped, unlike the roominess that came with living alone.

As he sorted through boxes, his eyes fell upon the water-damaged photograph of him and his family. The same one he had rescued from the murky waters that flooded his home two nights ago. He lifted it from the box. His eyes fixed on the faces of himself, Eleanor, and Simon. It was a picture, from a vacation several years past. A moment frozen in time from their collective "former happier lives."

The smiles in the image, his own included, made him uncomfortable. His failures as a husband and father stared back at him from the image. Things needed to change, but he wasn't sure what that meant yet. He had a few weeks to contemplate those changes. Implementation would begin as soon as he moved back into his house. Bauer placed the damaged photograph on his old desk. He propped it up against a stack of books. It became half buried by piles of papers and journals.

Satisfied with what he'd done with his room, Thomas carried several boxes and several small pieces of furniture down to the garage. He stacked his belongings such that they would be easy to access if he needed them.

He surveyed the chaos. Bauer couldn't help but think this was the most organized he'd been in two years. However, despite his best efforts, the sheer volume of his possessions scattered about seemed to mock him. This was only a temporary displacement. He wanted everything to be different when he left. A bump in the road, a minor detour in his personal journey. Once the repairs were complete, he could start working on his relationships with his family. With any luck, he might salvage his career while he was at it. For now, it was all just a waiting game.

The familiar scent of his mother's laundry detergent wafted from the blanket that half covered him. Despite the tumultuous events of the past few days, a sense of comfort set in as he sat in the living room, surrounded by memories. Bauer's eyelids grew heavy as he watched the flames dance in the fireplace. His mind wandered as his body became more relaxed.

Transported back to the hospital archives, he found himself dwarfed by towering shelves filled with dusty tomes and fragile documents. It was difficult to breathe. The air was thick. Weighted down by knowledge and many secrets contained within these walls. He moved through the stacks, his footsteps echoed through the eerie silence.

Before him emerged a figure from the shadows. The same mysterious presence he had seen in the distance several days ago. Bauer watched him. He tried to make out the person's features, but they remained obscured. The man turned and looked at him. Then he motioned to Bauer, urging him to go deeper into the aisles of the archives.

Bauer's heart raced. His feet seemed to move against his will. He followed the phantom man through the maze of shelves. They came to a stop before a huge ancient-looking wooden door. Its wood was old, warped, and cracked. Its metal doorknob had become tarnished and discolored with age. The shadow gestured toward the door, then vanished at the end of the row.

With trembling hands, Bauer reached to open the door. When he pushed, the door refused to budge. He put more weight into his second attempt. The hinges creaked as it gave way to the man's efforts.

With caution, the doctor entered. Everything in the room had a thick layer of dust. Nobody had been in there for years. The room seemed eery, yet familiar.

In the center of the room was an oversized, old oak desk. The surface had yellowed papers scattered about. He walked behind the desk. When he sat, the chair cried out loud in protest under his weight. He noticed an old fountain pen sitting on top of a half written note. The script was delicate, but rushed. Its message interrupted.

He picked up the faded parchment. His eyes squinted as they danced over the page. He looked it over, puzzled. The writing was in German, and made little sense to him.

He set the document aside. He reached for the pen and inkwell with one hand, and a blank piece of paper with the other. When he applied the tip to the sheet, his hand moved on its own, without his effort. The penmanship was exactly the same as what was on the half-written letter. What he just wrote wasn't in English. How could that be? Unlike his parents, he wasn't fluent in German. "*Achtung!*" was the only recognizable word he scribbled.

Danger? What did it mean? Was someone in danger? Was he in danger? Bauer picked up the page. In the dim light, he couldn't make out any of the writing. He brought the parchment closer for a better look.

"You're not supposed to be in here, Thomas."

Bauer froze. His breath caught in his throat. He'd recognize his father's voice anywhere. A piercing scream shattered the silence between them as a hand clamped down hard on his shoulder.

Thomas jolted awake. His heart pounded under skin slick with sweat. He straightened up in the chair, trying to calm himself. Some details from the dream were already beginning to fade, but the unsettling feeling remained. He glanced around the living room, in an effort to ground himself in something familiar.

His mother entered the room. "Thomas, is everything okay?" She asked, noticing the panic in his eyes.

"What? Uh — yeah. I'm fine."

"It's late. You really should get some rest. I'm sure you're exhausted from all that's happened the last few days."

Bauer checked the clock on the mantel. It chimed, announcing the 11:00 hour. He didn't argue. She wasn't wrong. He nodded and yawned as he rose from the chair. "Good night, mom. I will see you in the morning."

"Welcome home, son." She said, "Good night."

Thomas made his way upstairs. He changed into his pajamas, brushed his teeth, and climbed into bed. He laid there for a minute, staring at the ceiling. Despite the strange nightmare, he had to admit that being back in this house provided an unexpected sense of comfort. Memories danced through his head. Glimpses of a life before the weight of responsibilities crushed him.

He pulled the covers up to his chin as he closed his eyes. With conscious effort, he pushed away the lingering remnants of his dream. As he drifted off again, he felt safe, surrounded by the familiarity of his old room.

Bauer opened his eyes. *Morning already?* His sleep was so deep. He found his head disoriented to time and place. A quick glance at the clock radio on his nightstand, allowed him to close his eyes for another minute. *Was it really 8:30 AM?* He stretched and rubbed his eyes. With a sigh, he swung his legs over the side of the bed. His muscles were stiff but rested. It was the first good night's rest he'd had in ages.

After a shower, he opted to go one more day without shaving. It would all come off before his return to work the next morning. He sat down to eat a hearty breakfast with his mother. The food was delicious and satisfying.

Following a second cup of coffee, Bauer set out to face the daunting task ahead of him. The drive to his house was short, but each passing minute seemed to weigh heavier on his shoulders. Pulling into the driveway of his once-cozy home sent a pang of loss and grief through him.

Not now, he thought to himself. There's too much work to get done today for him to wallow in self pity. He entered the house. The musty stench of damp wood, paper, and fabric assaulted his nostrils without delay. The squishing sensation beneath his feet made him queasy as he walked to the kitchen.

The place wasn't as warm and welcoming as Eleanor's or his mother's homes, but it was his space to live in as he pleased. The dishes still sat, piled in the sink, just as he had left them. He clasped his hands and placed them on top of his head. He now regretted leaving his simple domestic chores undone.

Following a deep breath, he walked into the living room. There were boxes, packing tape, and several unread newspapers with their rubber bands still attached, scattered about. Returning to the kitchen, he put everything on the table. He opened all the cabinets and emptied them.

He wrapped a favorite souvenir mug. He then packed it in a box, memories of family trips and lazy Sunday mornings inundated his mind. Conversations with his wife. Their hands intertwined as they talked about dreams and their future together.

Those ambitions were now replaced by the harsh realities of long hours and the growing distance between them. He pushed through the emotions stirring within him. With renewed focus, he completed his work in the kitchen; including the dishes from the sink.

Bauer moved on to the living room, where the damage was far more extensive. The once-plush carpet squashed beneath his feet, still saturated from the flood. He sorted through waterlogged books and papers. In the middle of the room, he created a pile of items to be discarded.

Water dripped from a stack of wet psychiatric journals as he lifted them from a shelf, then threw them on the refuse heap. He bumped against a side table next to his ruined favorite chair. A framed photograph tumbled to the floor. Bauer picked it up. His breath hitched as he recognized the image from his medical school graduation day.

The soggy photo held together only by its broken frame. He traced his finger over the cracked glass. His vision blurred as he stood there. He looked sharp in his black cap and gown. The golden cords around his neck accentuated the green in his eyes. The corners of his mouth reached his eyes as he gripped his diploma in his hands.

It was one of the happiest days of his life. But the memory wasn't all happiness and joy. His father, Dr. Harold Bauer, MD, PhD, flanked him. The photograph forever captured his dad's usual stern, disapproving glare.

Harold was a successful, world renowned research psychiatrist. He and his partner, Dr. Matthias Levi, were legends in the field. His dad seemed to be blindsided when his only child announced his college major. He never expected his son to follow in his footsteps. He never once encouraged it.

Thomas' mind flashed back to the day he got accepted to medical school. He ran into the house from the mailbox, shouting, screaming, waving the letter in his hands. Medicine would have been fine. However, psychiatry drove a wedge between the two of them.

Thomas peered closer at Harold's expression. Knowing his father as well as he did, the look of disappointment was unmistakable. His dad's eyes displayed hints of concern and fear. He never explained why.

Thomas worked hard his entire college career. He was on the Dean's List. He took advantage of some of the most promising internships. He did his best to prove himself. He wanted to earn Harold Bauer's acceptance and approval. Those accolades never came.

Now his father was gone, and his own life was in shambles. His dad tried to warn him. Psychiatry would chew him up and spit him out without a hint of remorse. Thomas' stubbornness had cost him a lot. Had it been worth it?

A tear ran down his cheek. With a heavy sigh, he wiped it away. Thomas then tossed the photograph onto the pile of unsalvageable mementos. It was a painful chapter in his life he wished to forget. He wasn't ready to admit his father was right.

This was just a temporary setback. Bauer kept telling himself as he went back to his work. He packed away the rest of his salvageable life's possessions and discarded items damaged beyond repair. He confronted the surfacing ghosts from his past, and the memories and regrets that had haunted him for years.

Thomas checked his watch, then placed the final book into a box. Waiting for his landlord to arrive, he moved from one room to the next. He wanted to make sure he left nothing worth keeping behind. The faces from the graduation photo in the discard pile caught his eye. Without thinking, he picked it up and threw it in with some other stuff and sealed it shut with tape.

He then added it to the stack of boxes that needed to be taken out to the garage. The musty, damp smell lingered in his nostrils. A constant reminder of the disaster that had disrupted his life. The sound of a car pulling into the drive diverted Bauer's attention. He watched through the kitchen window as a balding man in his late fifties stepped from a newer-model BMW. Bauer greeted him on the front stoop with a forced smile. He found it difficult to push down the emotions that gnawed at his stomach.

"Dr. Bauer," said the landlord, reaching out his hand. "Sorry to hear about what happened. My apologies for not getting here sooner. I've been out of town for two weeks and just got back last night."

His tenant remained silent as he led the man to his front door.

"Let's take a look, shall we?"

Thomas nodded, leading the way through the house. The man followed him into every room. The landlord shook his head as he discovered the extent of the damage. The man made notes on a clipboard of necessary repairs.

The doctor stood at his kitchen window, giving his landlord free reign to move about the house. Across the street, he could see Mrs. Clendin in her front yard, pulling weeds from her flower bed. He looked forward to returning to his normal life in the coming weeks.

"Dr. Bauer?" called his landlord.

"Yes." He answered as he turned and began moving toward the living room.

"I'm afraid I have some bad news," the man said, turning to face his tenant as he entered. "The dampness has seeped into the sheetrock and flooring. This is going to require extensive work. Because the city's faulty water main caused the damage, they'll be responsible for the clean-up and repairs."

Bauer's heart sank as he tried to contain the emotions stirring within him. His stomach twisted. The implications of his landlord's words hit like a wrecking ball. Working at a government-run hospital for many years had taught him everything he needed to know about bureaucratic red tape. The city's involvement would only prolong the process, turning weeks into months, or more.

"How long do you think it will take?" Thomas asked, not really wanting an answer.

"Hard to say. These things can drag on for a while." The man shrugged. "It could take a year or more." The landlord promised to keep him up to date, then turned and left.

Bauer placed the last box in the garage and returned to the living room. He sank into his favorite armchair. It was still damp and smelled of mold. He buried his face in his hands. He hoped that the damage would be minimal. But now this was no longer a temporary setback.

He sat in the ruins of his disrupted life. He knew he should be grateful for his mother's hospitality, but the thought of being stuck there, surrounded by constant reminders of his past, only added to his mounting frustration and embarrassment.

What would his colleagues think? His patients? His family? He had always taken pride in his independence, his ability to handle whatever life threw at him. How would he maintain his sense of self and purpose in this altered reality?

Bauer couldn't bear the thought of imposing on his mother for a year or more. He reached for one of the recent newspapers from the pile of trash in the middle of the room. He flipped through, looking for the classifieds. His eyes scanned the apartment and home listings, searching for anything that might suit his needs.

He grabbed the phone and began dialing. His fingers trembled as he punched in the numbers. He called friends, acquaintances, anyone who might have a lead on a decent rental. He even reached out to a few real estate agents, hoping they might have something off-market that could work.

Hours passed as Bauer made one call after another. Each one was more desperate than the last. The prices were astronomical, the options laughable. A tiny studio apartment for the price of a mortgage. A run-down basement suite that smelled of mold and despair. Every dead-end chipped away at his already fragile sense of self-worth.

It was getting late. His feet squishing in the damp carpet beneath only added to his growing frustration. He ran his hands through his hair, tugging at the salt and pepper strands, hoping the pain might somehow clear his mind.

He picked up the phone again, dialing the number of an old college buddy. Frank had always been there for him, through thick and thin. He would understand, would have some encouragement or a lead on a place to stay.

"Hey, Frank," He said when his friend answered. "It's me, Thomas."

"Thomas! Long time no talk. What's up, my man?"

Bauer hesitated, his words stuck in his throat. "I — I'm in a bit of a situation. My house flooded. I'm staying with my mom until I can find something. I was wondering if you might know of any rentals, anything at all."

There was a pause on the other end of the line. Then his friend chuckled. "Living with mommy, huh? Never thought I'd see the day. The great Dr. Thomas Bauer, reduced to crashing in his childhood home."

Frank's comments were a gut punch, forcing the wind out of him. He knew Frank didn't mean any harm, that it was just a joke between old friends. But he struck a nerve, raw with shame and vulnerability.

"Yeah, well, desperate times," He said, his tone was tight. "So, do you know of anything?"

"Sorry, man. I don't. But I will let you know if something comes up. In the meantime, enjoy that home cookin'."

Bauer forced a hollow chuckle. "Thanks Frank." His voice faded as he placed the handset in its cradle. Now he felt more lost than ever. Frank's words echoed in his mind, taunting him. *Living with mommy.* Was that his life now? A grown man, a successful psychiatrist, running back to his mother's skirts at the first sign of trouble?

He knew he would get through this. However, other than his mother, wife and son, no one would hear a word about his living arrangements or his struggles again. This was a journey he had to navigate alone.

Chapter 11

Bauer drove through the quiet suburban streets. The weight of displacement was heavy on his mind. The sun sunk lower in the fall sky. It cast long shadows across yards with manicured lawns and picket fences. Every pristine property was a picture perfect example of domestic tranquility. Each one similar to the ones he'd often seen in *Sunset* magazines. The peaceful drive clashed with his inner turmoil and bleak reality.

His car pulled into his parent's driveway. He called this place home for the first eighteen years of his life. The house looked the same as it always had. Its maintained landscape had an old oak tree in the front yard. But for Bauer, everything looked different. It felt like a trap. A cage that would restrict him to a history he wished to forget. A past he wanted no part of now.

He sat in his car for a moment. His hands gripped tight on the steering wheel. He closed his eyes and inhaled deep. *It isn't ideal, but it's better than being homeless,* he reminded himself. It was a mantra on repeat in his head for the past several hours. He tried to convince his brain that this was a temporary setback.

He grabbed the last of his belongings brought from his home from the trunk. Each step dragged as he walked toward the front door. He struggled to balance the remnants of his life. He shifted things in his hands, fumbling for the doorknob. After all these years, it felt intrusive to walk in without knocking.

Bauer entered, then kicked the door closed behind him harder than he intended.

"Thomas, is that you?" came a sweet voice from the kitchen.

"Yes mom," He returned.

The petite woman in her mid seventies peeked into the foyer. She had kind warm eyes and streaks of silver running through her hair. "Did you get everything done?" Edyth asked.

He paused at the foot of the stairs. He swallowed hard. "Yeah, I got it all packed and moved into the garage." He said without looking at her.

"I've made your favorite for dinner — pot roast with mashed potatoes."

"That sounds great." He forced a smile. He was hungry, but didn't feel like eating.

"Get washed up and come down when you're ready and I will fix you a plate."

"Mom, but you don't have to fuss over me."

She responded to the annoyance in his tone. "You're right, son. I just figured a good hearty home cooked meal would hit the spot after all you've been through the last few days."

"Home cooked meal" echoed through his mind like fingernails on a chalkboard after his conversation with Frank earlier.

He opened his bedroom door. The queen-sized bed remained unmade. Two dresser drawers hung half-open. The space felt different, yet it was just as he left it that morning. Then he was a visitor. Now he was a permanent resident, nothing was the same.

He set the boxes down on a chair and surveyed the room. There were pictures on the walls, family photos from years ago. He saw a picture of himself as a child, grinning gap-toothed at the camera. Next to it was a photo of his father, looking stern and serious in his white lab coat.

Thomas' guilt mixed with his frustration. His mother wasn't to blame for his current situation. His relationship with his father had been strained for as long as he could remember. It was forever fraught with unspoken expectations and disappointments. Years after his father's death, Harold Bauer's shadow still hovered over him.

He turned away from the photos and unpacked the boxes. He hung up clothes in the closet, trying to make the space feel more like his own. But no matter how he arranged his room, he still felt like a foreigner. Like he was a guest in someone else's home.

He put the last of his things away and went to the bathroom to clean up. Thomas scrubbed his hands several times, but he couldn't wash the smell of murky water and mildew from his hands. Bauer walked back downstairs to the kitchen. His mother was in the dining room setting the table for dinner. The aroma of meat and vegetables filled the air, reminding him of countless family dinners from his childhood.

"Smells delicious, mom," he said. "Do you need any help?"

"No, everything's ready. Please sit, and I will bring you your plate."

She smiled, then left the room. She soon returned with a generous portion of pot roast and mashed potatoes for him. "I'm so glad you're here, Thomas," she said, sitting down across from him. "I know this isn't an ideal situation, but we'll make the best of it."

Thomas nodded, picking at his food. He knew his mother meant well, but her words only continued to remind him of his conversation with Frank. He was a grown man, a successful psychiatrist, and yet here he was, living with his mother like a child.

They ate in silence. The only sound was the clinking of silverware on plates. His mother spoke a few minutes later. "So, how was your meeting with your landlord?" she asked.

Her son winced. "Not well."

"Oh?"

He took a deep breath as he pushed some peas around on his plate. "It looks like I won't be back in my house for a year, maybe more."

"I'm sorry to hear that, son." Edyth changed the subject. "Do you have everything you need for work tomorrow?"

"I suppose." He said, conflicted. The thought of returning to Saint Elizabeths had its inherent stresses. However, after the last few days, he welcomed the return to his familiar routine. "It will be good to get back to some sense of normalcy."

"It's amazing how much can change so fast."

Bauer sat silent, agreeing with her.

"Say, how is your work going?"

Her son shrugged. "Same as always, busy, stressful. Never a dull moment in psychiatry."

She nodded. "Your father always said that. He loved what he did, but it took a toll on him."

Thomas felt a wave of irritation as she mentioned his father. Every conversation circled back to "The great Dr. Harold Bauer" and his "brilliant" legacy.

"Yeah, well, I'm not dad," he said, a bit sharper than he intended.

His mother looked at him, her eyes soft with understanding. "I know that, Thomas. You're your own man, with your own challenges, your own path to forge. Your father would be proud of you, you know."

He scoffed. "Would he? Somehow, I doubt that."

"Of course he would," Edyth insisted. "He may not have always shown it, but he loved you very much. He just wanted what was best for you."

Her son hung his head. "Best for me, or the best for him? He hated me for going into psychiatry and research."

"Hated you?" She shook her head, then reached across the table to place her hand on his. "No, your father was a complicated man. He had his flaws, like we all do. But he did love you, and he was proud of you. Don't you ever doubt that."

He looked down at his food, feeling emotions swirling inside him. Anger, sadness, frustration, all tinged with a deep sense of loss. He had spent so much of his life trying to live up to his father's standards as a psychiatric professional. Thomas wanted to prove he could make it in this field. To show him he was worthy of the Bauer name. And yet, here he was, a miserable, failed man.

He pushed his half-eaten plate away. He wasn't hungry anymore. "I think I'm going to turn in early," he said, clearing his place setting as he stood up from the table. "It's been a long, exhausting weekend."

Edyth nodded with a look of concern in her eyes. "Of course, dear. Get some rest. Things will look better in the morning."

Thomas walked back upstairs to his bedroom and closed the door. The bed creaked as he sat down. He buried his face in his hands. He had nothing left, physical or emotional. The events of the several days had caught up with him.

He laid back and stared up at the ceiling. He thought about his life, about his choices. Bauer craved his independence. He prided himself on his ability to stand or land on his own two feet. But now, he relied on his mother and, to a lesser extent, his estranged wife to prop him up.

It was a humbling realization, one that made him feel small and vulnerable. He was used to being in charge, the one with all the answers. But now he had none of that.

His eyes closed as his thoughts raced. Focus was what he needed.

Concentrate on what you can control. He thought to himself.

He got up and started getting his stuff ready for the next day. Bauer thought about work, about Rhyse and the patients who relied on him. His life might be in shambles, but he wouldn't let that affect his professional life. He would help those in his care to the best of his ability.

A soft knock on the door broke his concentration.

"Thomas?" Edyth's voice called from the other side.

His jaw clenched. He'd hoped to avoid any more interactions with her that evening. "Yes, mom?" he responded, maintaining the edge in his tone.

"When you're ready, could you come downstairs? There's something I'd like to show you."

He closed his eyes and sighed, annoyed by the intrusion. "I'm getting my stuff together for work tomorrow. Can it wait?"

"It won't take long, dear. I promise."

His shoulders slumped further. "Alright, I'll be down in a minute."

He heard his mother's footsteps retreat down the hall. His eyes turned back to a spot on his ceiling, then he rolled himself to the edge of the bed. He exited his bedroom door. He was ready for this day to be over. He had a busy day ahead of him the next day. The last thing he needed was her doting over him. He wasn't a child.

Edyth waited for him at the base of the stairs with a warm, gentle smile on her face. "I'm sorry for the intrusion. I promise it won't take long."

"It's fine, mom," he replied in a curt tone. "What is it you wanted to show me?"

His mother seemed to ignore the bluntness in his response. She just turned on her heels and started walking towards the hall. "Follow me," she said, leading him to the back of the house.

Bauer followed. His irritation grew with each step. They passed the kitchen, where the scent of homemade apple pie and coffee lingered. She continued down the narrow hallway. As they approached the door at the end, Thomas felt a building sense of curiosity replace his annoyance and frustration. She stopped at the door to his father's old study. This was a forbidden room his entire life.

Edyth paused at the door. One hand rested on the knob, the other held in suspended animation. "I know you're going through some challenges. I just thought this might be helpful." Just as she was about to insert the key, Bauer moved his hand to stop her.

He balked at the thought of stepping through that door. His mind flooded with memories. Moments pieced together from glimpses he'd stolen as a child. Dark wood shelves lined the walls, teeming with many bound volumes. A large mahogany desk sat in the center of the room.

Unlike his own office at Saint Elizabeths, Harold Bauer's workspace was always neat and organized. Air seeped into the hall from beyond the closed door. The scent of old books, leather, and the faintest trace of his dad's aftershave yanked him back to his tumultuous teen years.

"I thought you might like to use the space as a home office," Edyth said, her voice soft. "For your work away from the hospital."

Thomas turned to his mother, mixed emotions swirling within him. Touched by her consideration, part of him bristled at the thought of using anything connected with his father. This study had always been a symbol of his father's authority. A room where the slightest intrusion came with a scolding.

"Mom, I —" he began, struggling to find his words. "I appreciate the gesture, but I'm not sure if this is a good idea."

Edyth's smile faltered a little. "Why not, dear? It's a quiet spacious area where you can work undisturbed. Your father always said it was the perfect place for deep thoughts."

Her son ran a hand through his hair. He struggled with the crash of emotions that mixed with exhaustion. "That's just it. This was dad's space. It wouldn't be proper, me being in there." Bauer half expected to hear his father's voice yelling at him from the other side of the door.

"Your father would have wanted you to use it." She insisted. "He always had high hopes for you."

Her words hit him hard. He turned away, trying to hide his anger and pain. "High hopes. for me?" he muttered, then shook his head in disbelief. "Right."

Edyth stepped toward her son. Her hand came to rest on his arm. "Look, I know things weren't always easy between you and your father. But believe me, he was so proud of you, even if he never showed it."

Bauer shrugged off her touch. He retreated down the hall. He glanced at the picture of his father hanging in the hall. His fingers ran along the bottom part of the frame. His stern, disapproving eyes bore through him. "Mom, I appreciate what you're trying to do, but I must be honest. I don't need this. I have my own methods, my own ways of working."

"I understand," she said, her voice tinged with disappointment. "I just thought — well, it doesn't matter. The offer still stands if you change your mind." She offered him the key in her hand, but he waved her off.

Bauer shook his head as he turned to face his mother. The hurt was evident in her eyes. He felt bad. She didn't deserve this cold, hostile treatment he'd given her since he returned from his house earlier. She was only trying to help. Just being near that study filled him with anxiety and constant reminders of the man he could never please. It was all too much.

"I should get to bed," he said, as the clock on the mantel chimed. "I have a long day ahead of me tomorrow."

Edyth nodded with a forced smile. "Of course, dear. I won't bother you anymore this evening."

Bauer scurried from the hall and went back upstairs. He stood before his dresser mirror, looking at his reflection. The dark circles that had formed beneath his eyes, and salt and pepper stubble on his face made him look old. After the last few days, he felt older than his years.

As he brushed his teeth, he thought about all the things that had happened since his father's passing. Has it really been eight years already? He wondered what his father would think of Simon. Would he be proud of the young man he was becoming?

He yawned, then glanced at his clock radio. It was only 7:30 PM, but his entire body ached with fatigue that had settled into his bones. He turned down the bedcovers and sat on the edge of the bed. He set the alarm for 6:30 AM, then laid his head down on his pillow.

As he waited for sleep to claim him, his mind returned downstairs. Knowing his mother as he did, she left his office untouched except for the occasional feather duster. If that were the case, the room was a virtual time capsule. It was the one place that represented all he had ever aspired to be in his younger years. It was also everything he rebelled against since his late high school days.

As his eyes grew heavy and his body relaxed, part of him was drawn to the dedicated workspace. He thought about how neat and organized his father's study was. However, the thought of sitting at that desk, surrounded by Harold's things, felt forbidden, intrusive, and suffocating.

Chapter 12

Thomas Bauer's eyes opened. He yawned and stretched. The amount of light coming in his bedroom window concerned him. His heart raced as he realized his alarm hadn't gone off. He took a quick glance at the clock radio, then fumbled for his watch.

7:45 AM. "Damn it," he muttered as he threw off the covers and stumbled to the bathroom.

Bauer cursed under his breath. Sharpened steel was drug across his wet face. He had five days' worth of whiskers to remove from his face. Clumsier than usual, he rushed through his morning routine in these new surroundings. He'd set out his shirt and slacks the previous night. However, he struggled to find a tie and his work shoes.

The smell of coffee and bacon drifted from downstairs. The breakfast he didn't have time for made his mouth water.

As he raced down the stairs, his mother's voice called from the kitchen. "Thomas? I have toast for you and —"

"No time, Mom," he cut her off. He grabbed his briefcase and coat from the rack. "I'm already late."

"But —"

The door slammed behind him before she could say another word. Thomas ran to his car. He tossed everything onto the passenger seat. As he pulled out of the driveway, he glimpsed Edyth's disappointed face disappear in the rearview mirror. Guilt washed over his sleepy brain, but he pushed it aside. He had bigger problems to deal with right now.

Bauer was grateful that traffic was not congested that morning. Every red light lasted an eternity. He drummed his fingers on the steering wheel, waiting for each one to turn green. On most drives, his mind prepared for his work as he drove. In his hasty departure four days ago, he never thought to check the upcoming week. That was part of his Friday routine. His appointments always started at 9:00 AM. He would have to zip through his notes and prepare for his day as best he could.

He pulled into the hospital parking lot at 8:40. This was the latest he'd been in ages. He hated being late for anything, especially his patients. His walk was brisk through the corridors. A curt nod to colleagues was all he had time for, as he avoided conversations that might slow him down. As he passed the nurses' station, he asked the head nurse the name of his first patient.

The woman noticed he'd just arrived, then looked at the clock. "It's Mrs. Parker, Dr. Bauer."

"Thank you." He said, reaching for the patient's chart, then continued on.

The doctor fished for his keys as he walked away. As he neared his office, his feet slowed. His door was slightly open. Had he forgotten to lock up in his rush to leave the other day? He was never careless about locking up when he left.It But then again, nothing that day had been normal.

He pushed the door, then stepped inside. His eyes scanned the room. Something wasn't right. His desk had its usual mix of papers and files. Organized in a way only he understood. However, this was not his mess. The half buried picture of his family, now laid flat.

Bauer's brow wrinkled as he moved past the coat rack. The bookshelf caught his attention. Several books were out of place. Others had haphazard spines protruding. Nothing was as he left it.

His eyes narrowed as he scanned the desktop once more. He'd placed the file from the archives on top of the pile before he rushed out a few days prior.

He searched every inch of his space for the documents. His heart sank. It was gone. Now he was sure someone had been in his office. Whoever it was, rummaged through his things and took it. But who? And why? No one had touched those papers for decades before last Thursday. The information it contained held no inherent value to anyone.

He ran a hand through his hair as his mind raced. He inspected the hardware on the door and windows. There were no obvious signs of forced entry. Bauer knew he didn't leave his door unlocked when he left. His own ingrained habit and obsessive-compulsive actions would have ensured he locked it, regardless of how rushed he was.

Whoever intruded into his personal space had a key. Bauer's jaw tightened as he logically considered everything and everyone he knew up to that point. The only thing that appeared to be missing was that file. The doctor shook his head, trying to make sense of it all.

This couldn't have been some random break-in. It was clear the person had access to keys. Maybe they were part of the staff. Someone who knew the hospital well.

He looked around the room again. Insignificant details jumped out at him. There was a faint scuff mark on the floor near his bookshelf. Bauer sniffed at the air. A scent lingered. Something he knew but couldn't place. The familiar scent mingled with the odor of cleaning solvents. Neither one he'd smelled in his office before.

He checked his watch, then shook his head. Now he was late for his appointment with Mrs. Parker. He scanned the room one more time. His eyes stopped on his filing cabinet. There, caught in the pull handle, was a single thread.

Bauer's breath hitched in his throat. He recognized that shade of blue. It matched the colored rags used by the hospital housekeeping staff.

Sam Harris?!

The realization stole the wind from his lungs. The old unassuming janitor had been a constant fixture at Saint Elizabeths since the early 1960s. The man always seemed to fade into the background. Bauer had passed him in the hallways countless times without a second thought.

Nah, it couldn't be him. Thomas thought to himself. *Could it?*

But why would he come in here and take that file? What could he possibly want with Civil War information from the archives?

The psychiatrist sank into his chair and ran a hand through his hair. His mind whirled with odd possibilities, each one more curious than the last.

He wanted answers. He would have to confront the custodian at some point, away from prying eyes and ears.

A knock at the door startled him from his thoughts. He sat up straight. "Come in."

The door creaked open to reveal Nurse Kendrick, from the northern wing of the hospital. "Dr. Bauer?"

"Olivia? Come in, come in—"

"I just thought you should know that Mrs. Parker has been waiting for you in the psychotherapy room for five minutes now."

"Oh, my gosh! It's been one of those mornings —" The doctor apologized. Looking at his watch, he bolted from his seat. Then he reached for a brand new yellow note pad and several pens from his drawer. He tucked the Parker chart under his arm. He grabbed his white coat from the rack and followed her out of the door. He checked the lock three times, then walked away.

He arrived at the psychotherapy room, disheveled and out of breath. He forced an uneasy smile. For the next hour, he had one job to do. His patient deserved his full attention. The mystery involving his office would have to wait. He did his best to push his suspicious thoughts aside.

Bauer's mind drifted as he tried to focus during his first session. The older woman droned on about recurring nightmares, but he found himself only half-listening.

"Dr. Bauer? Are you alright?" His patient's concerned voice snapped him back to reality.

He blinked, realizing he'd been staring blankly at his notepad. "I'm sorry, Mrs. Parker. Please continue."

As she resumed her story, the psychiatrist attempted to stay present. He jotted down notes with mechanical movements, but the churning in his gut persisted. The session concluded without further lapses in attention. However, he felt drained.

Following the appointment, he caught sight of Olivia Kendrick as he went to fetch the chart of his next patient. "Nurse," he called out, quickening his pace to catch up with her.

She turned, a stack of files clutched close to her chest. "Yes, Dr. Bauer?"

"I was wondering," he began, trying to maintain his casual voice, "have you seen anyone unusual around my office lately?"

Olivia's brow furrowed. "Unusual? No, I don't think so. Why do you ask?"

The doctor hesitated, unsure how much to reveal. "It's probably nothing. Just have a feeling someone might have been in there while I was out."

She scanned her memory briefly. "I can't say that I have," Olivia replied. "But I'll keep an eye out if you'd like."

"Thank you, I'd appreciate that," he nodded through a forced smile.

As the nurse walked away, Bauer's anxiety deepened. He made his way to the staff lounge, hoping to catch some of his colleagues between sessions.

When he entered, he saw two doctors huddled near the coffee machine. Their hushed conversation ended with an awkward silence.

"Morning, Thomas," Dr. Simmons greeted. "You're looking frazzled today. Everything okay?"

Bauer poured himself his first cup of coffee of the day, thinking about how to respond. "Actually, I wanted to ask both of you something. Have either of you noticed anyone around my office over the last week or so?"

Dr. Chen shook his head. "Can't say that I have. Why?"

"Just — curious," he replied in an evasive tone. "Nothing to worry about, I'm sure."

Simmons studied him for a moment. "Is there something going on? You seem edgy."

He took a sip of his beverage, avoiding eye contact. "I'm fine. Just a rough few days, that's all."

His colleagues exchanged concerned glances, but didn't press any further. Bauer excused himself, retreating to the relative safety of the corridor.

As he walked, he spotted Sam Harris in the distance, mopping the floor. The sight of the janitor's blue rags on his cart made Bauer's heart race. He debated confronting the old man, but then thought better of it. He needed more information first.

Throughout the day, the doctor questioned everyone he encountered. The receptionist, the cafeteria staff, even the security guards. Anyone who wandered the corridors. Each denial only heightened his anxiety.

By late afternoon, he felt like he was losing his mind. He sat at his desk, staring at the spot where the missing file was the last time he saw it. The break in gnawed at him, compounding the stress of his own personal recent displacement.

A knock at the door startled him. "Come in," he called, trying to steady his voice.

Nurse Kendrick poked her head in. "Thomas? I just wanted to check in. You seemed — on edge earlier."

The psychiatrist sighed, gesturing for her to enter. "I appreciate your concern, Olivia. It just seems to be one thing after another lately." He motioned for her to take a seat as he apologized for the mess.

She sat across from him, her expression sympathetic. "I heard about your house flooding. That must have been a stressful experience."

"It is," he admitted. "And now, with this —" His voice trailed off.

"What are you talking about?" She asked, curious.

Bauer hesitated, then continued. "Someone's been in my office. Things are out of place, and an important file is missing."

Olivia's eyes widened. "That's terrible! Have you reported it?"

"Not yet," He replied. "I wanted to gather more information first. But no one has seen anything unusual."

"That must be so unnerving, and frustrating," Olivia sympathized. "Do you need any help?"

Thomas shook his head. "I appreciate the offer, but I'm not sure what to do at this point. I just feel so — so violated, you know? Like I can't trust anyone anymore."

Olivia nodded. "I can imagine. Just remember, you're not alone here. We're all here to keep an eye out. To support each other."

She meant her words to be comforting. Instead, they heightened the doctor's paranoia. No one admitted to seeing anything. It was clear someone was lying. Or worse, were they all in on it.

As Olivia left, Bauer suddenly felt his chest tighten. He'd always viewed Saint Elizabeths as a hospital where he could prove himself. A place where he could make a difference in the lives of others. Now, everything was different.

He glanced at the clock. There was one more patient session before lunch. He needed a break from the suffocating atmosphere around him. He gathered his thoughts and headed toward the psychotherapy room. As he walked, he could feel eyes watching his every move.

The doctor continued to be distracted by paranoia and suspicion. Between sessions, he held his gaze with coworkers longer than was comfortable. He peeked around corners and scanned hallways, searching for any sign of who might have broken into his office.

His walk was brisk to his next appointment. A familiar sound stopped him dead in his tracks. The doctor's head swiveled to the right. His eyes fixed onto the source. Sam Harris was there, whistling as he pushed his housekeeping cart through the hallway behind him. The psychiatrist's head and heart raced as he watched the housekeeper go about his work.

The janitor's movements were methodical and unhurried. His demeanor was as unassuming as ever. For a moment, Bauer questioned his own suspicions. Could this really be the person who broke into his office?

Just then, the old man looked up. Their eyes locked across the bustling hospital corridor. The psychiatrist searched Sam's face for any hint of concession or guilt. The old man's expression remained impassive. His eyes gave away nothing. Sam nodded politely, as he always did. He then continued on about his business without a care in the world.

Thomas stood rooted in his spot, his mind whirling. Their brief, distant encounter left him with more questions than answers. He seemed to find himself face to face with this man more than usual. Or was he just more aware of the custodian's presence now? Each run in was a fleeting moment of eye contact or a polite nod. Then the housekeeper would continue on with his work.

In between patients, he spotted Harris again, this time mopping the floor near the nurses' station. He thought about approaching the janitor, but then hesitated. What if he was wrong? Such an accusation could damage the trust in their relationship. And if the janitor was indeed responsible, confronting him publicly like this might make things worse.

The doctor retreated to his office and closed the door behind him. He sank into his chair, rubbing his temples. The stress of his day caught up with him. He needed to focus on his patients, but the missing file and Sam's potential involvement consumed him.

He watched the clock. Dreading the moment, he'd have to leave for his next appointment, and potentially another encounter with Sam. Bauer took a deep breath, then stepped away from his door.

Sure enough, as he rounded the corner, there was the dutiful custodian. This time he was diligently cleaning an old frame that held a faded photo of his father and Dr. Levi. Bauer's steps faltered before he forced himself to continue on his path. As he passed, the man turned toward him. Their eyes met.

The psychiatrist searched desperately for any flicker of guilt or hint of nervousness. Anything that might confirm his suspicions. But the housekeeper remained stoic. His expression was neutral. If the janitor was hiding something, he hid it well.

The doctor's final session seemed to drag. He struggled to maintain his professional demeanor, his mind obsessed with the idea of the old man snooping around his personal space. The repeated encounters with this man throughout the day left him frustrated. He'd always prided himself on his ability to read people, to pick up on subtle cues that betrayed their inner thoughts and emotions. But Sam Harris was a mystery.

By 5:00 PM, Bauer was exhausted. He balanced pens and paper clips in random spots in his office. If anyone came in later, he'd know it. He gathered his things to leave. The doctor closed the door. He checked it three times then stepped away.

He watched the janitor push his cart towards a housekeeping storage closet down the hall.

Their eyes met. For a moment, He thought he saw something — a flicker of — something in Sam's eyes. But before he could process it any further, the man averted his eyes and continued his end-of-day routine.

In the parking lot, he fumbled for his keys, desperate to reach the relative privacy of his car. He slid into the driver's seat. In the rearview mirror, the old janitor was wheeling trash out to a dumpster near the building.

Bauer froze. Should he confront Sam now? Demand answers about being in his office? But what if he was wrong? What if this was all just paranoia born from stress and displacement?

He started the engine, deciding to let it go for now. As he pulled onto the street, the psychiatrist abandoned unanswered questions and mounting suspicions that threatened to crush what little sanity he had left.

When he arrived home, his mother greeted him with a warm greeting. "How was your day, son?"

Bauer forced a smile. "Fine, mom. Just — fine."

He retreated to his room and collapsed onto the bed. As he stared at the ceiling he thought about Saint Elizabeths Hospital and his coworkers. All of the dedicated professionals trained to help people with mental issues. Yet, here he was, feeling like he was losing his grip on reality?

Chapter 13

Bauer pulled into his mother's driveway, his knuckles white from gripping the steering wheel. The events of the day replayed in his mind like some warped vinyl record from ages ago: the break-in of his office, the missing file, and the repeated run-ins with Sam Harris. He sat in his car for a moment, trying to compose himself to face another person.

As he trudged up the walkway, Bauer's shoulders sagged under the weight of suspicions and everything that had happened over the last several days. He fumbled with his keys, dropping them twice before he unlocked the door. The familiar scent of his mother's cooking wafted through the open door, but it did little to lift his spirits.

"Thomas? Is that you?" Edyth's voice called from the kitchen.

Bauer grunted a response, hanging his coat on the rack with automated motions. He ran a hand through his salt-and-pepper hair. His brow showed lines from a day filled with deep thought.

Edyth emerged, wiping her hands on her apron. Her face lit up, but then her smile faded as she noticed his troubled expression. "I'm glad you're home, dear. How was your day?"

He pondered her words for a moment. For the first time in ages, he felt a hint of gratitude for being back in his parents' house. Bauer's gaze darted around the living room, not quite meeting his mother's eyes. "Fine," he muttered, his voice distant. "It was fine."

Edyth maintained her cheerful demeanor. "Well, I've made your favorite - sauerbraten with those little potatoes you always loved as a boy. Why don't you freshen up, and we'll eat in about fifteen minutes?"

Bauer nodded without thinking. His feet were already moving him towards the stairs. "Sure, Mom. Sounds good. I'll be down in a minute."

As he climbed the steps, she watched him. Her eyes filled with concern. She had seen him stressed many times before, but this wasn't the same. There was something different in his eyes that she couldn't quite place.

In the bathroom, he splashed cold water on his face, trying to shake off the cloud that had settled over him at work. He stared at his reflection in the mirror, noting the dark circles still under his eyes and the tightness of his jaw. "Pull yourself together, Thomas," he muttered to himself.

By the time he came back downstairs, She already had the table set. The aroma of sauerbraten filled the air. It was a comforting scent that had lightened his mood many times. Tonight, however, it failed to lift his spirits

"Sit down, dear," Edyth said, gesturing to his usual spot. "Tell me about your day. How are your patients doing?"

Bauer settled into his chair, his movements stiff and mechanical. He picked up his fork, pushing the food around his plate without seeing it. "Patients are fine," he replied, his voice flat. "Everything's fine."

His mother frowned. She attempted a different approach. "Oh, I almost forgot to tell you. Mrs. Hendricks from next door stopped by earlier. She was asking about you, wondering how you were settling in."

"Mrs. Hendricks?" Bauer's head snapped up, his eyes became alert. "What did she want to know?"

She blinked, surprised by his sudden outburst. "Nothing in particular. Just being neighborly, I suppose." Her words were slow and deliberate, as though she was trying to defuse a bomb. "Thomas, is everything alright?"

Realizing how his reaction must have been received, He tried to relax a little. "Sorry, Mom. I'm just — it's been a long day."

His mother reached across the table, patting his hand as she remained silent.

Bauer's expression softened when she touched him. "It's just—" He trailed off, unsure how to explain what he was feeling.

Her kind eyes encouraged him to continue. Her son stumbled over a few words. He wanted to tell her his suspicions about Sam Harris and the break in. That he felt like he was being watched everywhere he went in that hospital. How could he talk about the paranoia that consumed him without sounding unhinged?

He forced a smile that never reached his eyes. "It's nothing, mom. Just a lot going on at work. This sauerbraten and potatoes are delicious, by the way. Just like I remember."

Edyth's face brightened at the compliment, but her concern didn't wane from her eyes. "Well, I'm glad you're enjoying it. You know, I was thinking maybe we could go through some of those old photo albums this weekend. I found an entire box of them in the attic the other day."

Bauer nodded, grateful for the change in the subject. "Sure, mom. That sounds nice."

As they continued their meal, Edyth maintained a steady stream of light conversation. She filled him in on the latest neighborhood gossip and updates on many childhood friends he'd lost contact with. She hoped the familiar comforts and conversations might ease whatever burdens he carried.

Thomas tried to engage with her. He offered an occasional nod or curt response. But his head remained at the hospital. To the file, to his chats with Olivia, and his various encounters with Sam Harris and the man's unreadable expressions. He couldn't shake the feeling that he was missing something, something crucial, just beyond his awareness.

After dinner, Thomas helped his mother clear the table. He was still distracted. As he dried and put away the last plate, Edyth touched his arm. "Thomas, if you ever need me, you know I'm always here for you, right? You can talk to me anytime, about anything at all."

Bauer looked down at his mother. It was as if he was looking at a stranger. His mind was so far gone, he didn't hear a word she just said.

"What mom?"

She repeated herself now with more concern in her eyes.

For a moment, he considered spilling his guts and coming clean. But no words came. How could he explain something he still didn't understand himself?

"Thank you," he breathed. "I think I'm just going to turn in early tonight. It's been a long day."

His mother nodded, then lifted herself on her tiptoes to plant a kiss on his cheek. "Alright, dear. Sleep well. Things will look different in the morning."

As Bauer climbed the stairs to his bedroom, he doubted anything would change in the next several hours. The new light of day would only add to the shadows of doubt and suspicion that swirled within him.

He closed his door. As he leaned against it, a heavy sigh escaped him. The familiar surroundings of his old room failed to comfort him. Instead, they seemed to mock him, reminding him of simpler times when his life still made sense, when he felt in control of his life and his thoughts.

He sat on the edge of his bed, his head in his hands. In the last several days, Bauer's entire world was upended. He knew he should try to get some sleep, but instead he laid back, just staring at the ceiling.Thomas emerged in the kitchen about forty-five minutes later. Despite his exhaustion, his mind still refused to let him rest. He watched in silence as his mother bustled around, preparing a pot of tea and arranged cookies on a plate. Her constant movement and cheerful humming bristled against his frayed nerves.

With her back still toward him, her quiet melody stopped. "Would you like a nice cup of chamomile, Thomas? It always used to help you relax when you were a boy," she asked, without turning away from what she was doing.

"Mom, I'm not a child anymore." He snapped. "I don't need —"

She placed two steaming cups on the counter. The familiar scent filled his senses. Despite his objections, some of the tension released from his shoulders.

"Thanks," he muttered, as he took a seat and wrapped his hands around the warm mug.

His mother beamed at him, settling into the chair across from him. "Now, why don't you tell me what's bothering you?"

He opened his mouth to deflect, to once again insist everything was fine, but he couldn't lie to her again.

"I can see it in your eyes, Thomas. Something's not right."

He spoke. "It's complicated, mom. Work stuff. I don't want to burden you with my personal troubles."

"Nonsense," she replied, reaching across the table to pat his hand. "You're my son. Your burdens will always be my burdens, especially while you are here in my home."

The gentleness in her touch, the earnestness in her voice, stirred something in him. He wanted to pour out everything, but the part of him that had spent years building walls and maintaining professional distances balked at the idea.

He took a sip of tea, buying time to collect his thoughts, his words. "I appreciate it, mom. I do, but I think it's best for me to handle this on my own."

Edyth's eyes fell, but she nodded. "I understand. Just remember, I'm here if you need me."

As she stood to clear away the dishes, Thomas still felt guilty. He knew his mother meant well, that she was only trying to help. Deep down, a small part of him craved the comfort and security she offered.

His eyes wandered around the kitchen, taking in familiar sights. The old clock on the wall, its steady ticking an auditory constant since his childhood. Faded curtains his mother had sewn herself decades ago. The —

Bauer's gaze stopped and zeroed in on something on the refrigerator. A yellowed photograph held in place by a magnet shaped like the state of Maryland. He stood, moving closer to examine it.

It was a family photo, many years old. Thomas recognized himself as a teenager, awkward, standing between his parents. His father's arm rested on his shoulder, a rare gesture of affection. And there was his mother, beaming like always, with pride.

A lump formed in his throat as he stared at the image. When was the last time he'd taken a photo with his mother? He was absent after the separation.

"That's one of my favorites," Edyth said, noticing what had caught his attention. "Do you remember that day? It was right after you won that science fair at school."

Thomas nodded, unable to speak. The weight of missed moments, and years of distance, settled heavy in his core.

"Mom," he said, his voice was rough. "I'm sorry. I know I haven't visited you as much these past years."

Edyth's eyes softened. "Oh, Thomas. You've been busy with your work, your family, your own life. I understand."

"No," he insisted, turning toward her. "That's no excuse. I should have made more of an effort."

Edyth stepped closer, pulling him in for a hug. For a moment, her son stiffened, then relaxed. He then wrapped his own arms around her. Other than a few nights ago, he couldn't remember the last time he had hugged his mother.

As they separated, Thomas cleared his throat. It was difficult for him to regain his composure. He let his mind drift once again back through his workday. He knew that his work office was no longer exclusive to him. "Hey mom," he began. "If the offer still stands, I think I'd like to use dad's study, after all."

Edyth's face lit up. "Of course, it remains open! I think it would do you good to have a space of your own here to think through all those things in your head, Thomas."

He nodded as a mix of emotions swirled within him. The idea of using his father's den still felt strange and forbidden, almost sacrilegious. But he couldn't deny his practical need for a workspace. Somewhere he could spread out his notes and think without interruption, or feeling like he's being watched.

"Come," she said, as she moved towards the hall. "I've kept everything in there just as it's always been, but we can change stuff around to better suit your needs if necessary."

He followed her. His steps were slow and measured. As they approached the door, his stomach fluttered with anxiety.

Edyth unlocked the door and pushed it open. She flicked on the light. The room looked as Thomas remembered it. Dark wood bookshelves lined the walls, the massive oak desk dominated the center of the room, places on the chair behind it worn smooth from years of use.

He stepped inside, his eyes roving over the familiar yet alien space. The scent of old books and leather hung in the air, stirring memories he'd long suppressed.

Bauer's throat tightened. His relationship with his father left him conflicted. It was fraught with unmet expectations and unspoken resentments. This room held his father's legacy, and elements of his life's work. And now, it would be the place where he would try to sort through his consuming thoughts and maybe solve some of his problems.

"Thank you, mom," he said, turning to face her. "This — this means a lot."

Edyth smiled, her eyes shined with unshed tears. "It's yours now, dear. Make it your future."

As she turned and left the study, Thomas settled into the leather chair. Its surface, polished to a soft sheen by years of use. Time stood still in this room. It was a perfect snapshot of Harold Bauer's life and work. He ran his fingers along the edge of the desk, expecting to feel the warmth from his dad's hand still there.

His eyes scanned the room, taking in details he'd never observed before. A half-finished note laid on the desktop. Its precise handwriting trailing off mid-sentence. Bauer resisted the urge to read it. He felt like an intruder in a sacred space.

The chair creaked as he leaned back. The familiar sound transported him through childhood memories of sitting outside this very room. Straining his ears to hear snippets of his father's world. Now, he was on the other side of that door. The weight of the moment settled heavy on his entire body.

His gaze drifted to a collection of framed photographs on a nearby shelf. Bauer's breath hitched in his throat as he realized he'd never seen these images before. There was his father, much younger, standing proud, in front of Saint Elizabeths Hospital. Another showed his parents celebrating an anniversary. Everyone's face beaming with love. But it was the third picture that caught his attention — a candid shot of himself as a toddler, perched on his father's lap in this very study. Both of them had genuine laughter in their eyes. It was a rare moment of unguarded joy captured forever.

Thomas moved closer to examine the photo. He couldn't remember ever seeing his father so carefree, so present. A lump formed in his throat as he touched the glass, tracing the outline of his dad's face.

The hair on the back of his neck stood up. He whirled around, half expecting to see his father standing in the doorway ready to scold him for being in this forbidden chamber. He was still the only one in the room, but the paranoia continued. Harold Bauer's stern voice echoed through his head: "Thomas, what are you doing in here? This is no place for children."

Thomas' muscles tensed. His reaction was still automatic after years of conditioning. He took a deep breath. Reminded himself that he was a grown man now. Like his father, he was also a respected psychiatrist in his own right. This room was now his to use. His mother had given him permission, and he was no longer here to argue the matter. Still, he felt like an intruder. A child caught somewhere he wasn't supposed to be.

He tried to dismiss the restrictions instilled in him from a young age. The bookshelves lining the walls interested him. Rows of books looked like soldiers standing in formation, their spines bearing titles that sparked professional curiosity. He knew the work of many of the authors well. Freud, Jung, Adler — but some were unfamiliar. Their names lost to time.

One tome stood out. It was older than the others. Its well-worn leather and cracked binding showed years of use. Bauer pulled it from the shelf, noting the absence of a title on its spine. As he opened it, a page slipped out and fluttered to the floor. He bent to retrieve it. His heart quickened as he recognized Harold Bauer's handwriting.

The notes were cryptic at first, filled with shorthand and symbols that he couldn't decipher. But one name stood out: "Dr. Matthias Levi." His brows rose. His father and his colleague once had a close working relationship at Saint Elizabeths Hospital. They collaborated on projects for many years. Thomas always thought it was odd that his father never talked much about his research partner.

He lifted his eyes to look at the bookshelves, then back at the book in his hands. The leather-bound tomes, penned by his father's hand, were his personal journals. What secrets were hidden on these shelves? What research had his father and Levi done that were never shared with anyone else?

Chapter 14

Thomas' fingers trembled as he traced the edge of Dr. Harold Bauer's desk. The polished wood felt cool against his hand, similar to the memories that flooded his mind. He took a deep breath. He kept reminding himself that this was no longer the forbidden sanctuary from his childhood. This study was now his workspace, to explore and make into his own.

Curiosity squelched his initial trepidation as he pulled on the handle of the first drawer. The smell of old ink on discolored paper rose from the confined space. It transported him back to his younger days. When he was a boy, he'd spent countless hours with his ear pressed to the door, straining to catch snippets of his father's private world. Now, he was in the hidden universe of Dr. Harold Bauer, MD, PhD.

Inside was a neat stack of folders. Each one labeled with dates and odd abbreviations. Thomas lifted the top folder from the drawer. He looked over his shoulder, even though he was the only one in the room. His pulse pounded with conviction in his ears as he opened the first file.

He found meticulous notes written in Harold's precise handwriting. Pages filled with observations on patients, theories on different dissociative psychological conditions, and a rough draft of research paper. Thomas' eyes widened. Some of the cases were groundbreaking studies that had shaped and advanced the field of psychiatry.

He moved to the next drawer, pulling it open with growing confidence. This one had a collection of old photographs. He recognized a few faces and places from family albums. Others were new to him.

He looked at the images of a much younger version of his father. Harold looked sharp as he stood tall and confident, with Saint Elizabeths Hospital in the background. Another showed the man deep in conversation with a colleague in a white coat. Bauer didn't recognize the man. Both men's animated gestures were frozen in an image over papers covering a large table.

As he sifted through pictures, an odd mix of emotions came over him. On a personal level, he exhibited a lack of warmth, distance, and emotional unavailability. However, the professional in him had always known his father was a brilliant, well-respected research psychiatrist. Seeing the evidence of his work, the depth of his passion and detail, showed Thomas an unknown side of the man.

Next, he turned his attention to some cabinets that lined a wall in the study. Each nook contained more files, books, and notebooks. He ran his fingers through the pages, reading titles that ranged from classic psychological theories to obscure journal entries. It was like he was inside his father's head, surrounded by the knowledge and ideas that personified his old man.

Thomas continued to explore information he never knew existed. Every drawer, each shelf pulled back the curtain a little more. Harold's professional personality contrasted with the stern, distant father-figure he knew growing up. This man was a complex individual with a rich, secret life.

He returned to the desk to open another compartment. This one resisted his efforts. Bauer gave it a firm tug. When it opened, he found it packed with old letters. Yellowed envelopes, some bearing international postmarks. He lifted out a handful, noting the dates that spanned several decades.

As he read, he realized these were correspondences between Harold and colleagues from around the globe. A few were in German, most were in English. The mail discussed ongoing projects, debated theories, or shared personal news. They were from a man who was warm, and engaged, and had a humorous side Thomas never knew existed.

It was no surprise that Dr. Matthias Levi's name appeared often in his father's papers. The world renowned psychiatrist was a brilliant man and a true pioneer. The man's concepts and methodologies remained a crucial foundation for contemporary research protocols and patient care strategies at Saint Elizabeths Hospital and beyond. They provided him with valuable insight into the working dynamics between Levi and his father.

Hours passed as he lost himself in this once forbidden chamber. The room revealed a few secrets. He felt like a detective in some movies he'd seen. Piecing together elements of stories and uncovering layers of lives he never knew existed.

As the clock struck seven, Bauer's hand came to rest on the last drawer in the desk. This one was locked. He tugged at it, but it refused to budge. Frustration danced with his curiosity as he examined it closer.

His mind raced as he looked around the room for the key. Where would his father have hidden such a thing? It was a rare moment when he wished he knew his father better. His eyes darted about, searching for any hint of where it could be. He opened and closed drawers he'd already explored, hoping to find something he overlooked the first time.

As the minutes ticked by, Thomas grew more determined. He knew the key had to be somewhere in this room. His father wouldn't have locked away information without ensuring he could access it when needed.

Thomas' gaze fell on an old cigar chest tucked away on a top shelf. He remembered seeing it on his father's desk as a child. It was a prized possession his father had brought home from a conference in Cuba. Bauer reached to remove it from its perch.

The wooden box was heavier than expected. As he examined it in his hands, something shifted. His heart quickened. He opened the lid, but only found a handful of old cigars, long since dried out. Disappointed, he set it aside. However, something didn't seem right. It shouldn't have been that heavy, considering what it contained.

He examined the crate closer. He ran his fingers along its interior. There — almost invisible — was a slight gap where the sides met the bottom. He pressed it, and with a soft click, the hidden mechanism popped.

Bauer's hand trembled as he inserted the second of three large brass keys into the lock. The mechanism clicked. He hesitated, then pulled it open. A musty fragrance filled his nostrils. Inside, he found more yellowed documents and bound journals, all stacked neat and seemed untouched for years.

Bauer removed a journal. It was old and worn. His fingers traced over the embossed HB. This was Harold Bauer's diary. It was heavy in his hands. This was more than just paper and ink.

He opened the cover, wincing as the brittle spine cracked in protest. The first page had his father's familiar script. Each line was precise and measured. Bauer's eyes scanned the opening lines, eager to consume the personal thoughts of his dad.

As he read, his brow wrinkled in confusion. Thomas felt like a child once again, trying to decipher cryptic shorthand. It was just like a note he'd found lying around the house when he was younger. This journal contained notes and terms. Some he didn't understand, given the context. Others he had never seen before. Technical jargon peppered the text. Bauer recognized a few from his own studies.

He flipped through more pages, hoping to find something more comprehensible. His eyes darted from one line to another, searching for connections. His eyes froze: Dr. Levi and Case 47. Thomas' heart leaped into his throat as he sat up straighter in his chair.

These words were familiar. Not just because of Harold Bauer's close professional experiences, but from the many whispers and rumors he'd heard circulated through the halls of Saint Elizabeths for decades. Dr. Matthias Levi, the brilliant researcher, vanished in the early 1960s. People knew of Case 47, but none of the current employees had ever seen it. It had become quite the urban legend among hospital staff.

Thomas leaned in closer, his nose almost touching the page as he struggled to make sense of the words surrounding these two men. His father's cramped writing danced before his eyes. It teased him with hints of meaning just beyond his comprehension.

Bauer settled in for an evening of research. He pulled out more journals from the drawer, spreading them across the desktop. He took a yellow notepad from his briefcase and began taking notes, jotting down names, dates, and informational bits that seemed significant even if he didn't know how or why, yet.

His cup of tea had turned cold. Its wet ring threatened to leave its mark on beautiful polished wood. He had forgotten about it long ago. When he first sat down, his hair was neat and in place. Now tufts stood on end after he'd ran his fingers through it in frustration or excitement.

He soon became so engrossed in everything around him. The dimness in the room shifted as the warm glow of the streetlight out front joined the circle of light emanating from the lamp on the desk. He remained lost in his father's world, failing to notice the passage of time.

A place unknown to him. The sudden knock on the door startled him. His heart raced. He failed to hear the soft footsteps approach the study.

"Thomas?" His mother's voice came through the door. "Are you still in there? It's past midnight, dear."

Bauer looked at the clock in surprise. Was it that late already? He glanced down at the mess spread across the desk. All of it seemed unrelated. His father accumulated all this information over decades. He couldn't learn all his secrets in the few hours since his mother unlocked the door.

"I'll be out in a minute, Mom," he called back, his voice sounding exhausted even to his own ears.

He gathered up journals and papers. The order in which he arranged them only made sense to him. He couldn't explain why, but he felt an overwhelming need to keep his discoveries secret, at least for a while. As he shoved the last journal back into the drawer, he knew tomorrow was another day to explore.

Thomas looked around the room. Everything was back in its place. Bauer stood up, stretching his stiff body. He left to find his mother in the living room, waiting, concern etched on her face.

"Sorry, mom," he said, trying to pull off a casual, exhausted tone. "I got caught up in some reading — didn't realize it was that late." It wasn't a lie. He thought to himself as Edyth nodded.

"I just know you have work in the morning. You need your rest, son."

He couldn't argue with her. Especially after how his day had started.

"Do you want me to make sure you're up on time tomorrow?"

He balked at her suggestion, then thought better of refusing her offer. Until his new routine became a habit, he wouldn't deny her maternal love and help.

Bauer closed the door to his father's study. The key turned smooth in its lock. He checked the door three times, ensuring it was secure. Then he slipped it into the pocket of his slacks. His mind was consumed by the discoveries he'd made.

His mother moved ahead of him down the hallway. For a moment, he considered sharing with her what he'd found, but the hour was late, and the secrets were intricate and heavy, and not easy to understand.

"Mom," he began as he walked, then hesitated. Edyth looked at him, her eyes filled with curious concern.

"Yes, dear?"

Bauer's mouth went dry. He wanted to tell her things — about the hidden journals, the cryptic notes, and ask her about the mysterious Case 47, but then stopped himself. There was still an incredible amount of information in his father's office for him to read through.

"I — I just —. Thank you. For letting me use dad's study," he forced his response.

She smiled. Her eyes were tired, her face was peaceful, yet showed years of worry and heartbreak. "Of course, Thomas."

As Bauer got ready for bed, the compulsion to share what he'd found grew stronger. He thought about the documents and journals. So much new knowledge led to a barrage of questions. As he lay staring at the ceiling, his logical mind quieted his racing thoughts. It was foolish for him to think he'd find all the answers in a single day. They would not come easy. He needed a better understanding of what he was reading, first.

The next morning, Thomas rose before his alarm went off. His sleep was restful, considering everything swirling in his head as he drifted off. As he sat at the table, eating his breakfast, he felt drawn to the study down the hall. Bauer knew that giving in to his urge would only make him late for work. The last thing he needed was a repeat of the previous day.

He pulled into his parking spot and cut the engine. Sitting in his car, he savored the solitude before his workday started. Moments like this had become rare in the past several days. He closed his eyes. The doctor inhaled, then exhaled long and slow. The tension in his shoulders eased. For just a few minutes, the weight of recent discoveries and personal intrusions disappeared.

When he opened his eyes, Bauer's eyes fell on the imposing classic façade of Saint Elizabeths Hospital. The building's gothic architecture looked dark against the morning sunrise. There was a complex world that awaited him inside. He took a final breath, gathered his briefcase, and stepped out of the car.

The familiar bustle greeted Dr. Bauer as he entered. Nurses hurried past, clipboards in hand, while orderlies wheeled patients down corridors. The smell of antiseptic and mental illness mingled with the aroma of fresh brewed coffee. He nodded to colleagues as he made his way through the lobby. His mind already shifted to his more professional work persona.

Approaching his office, he slowed his pace. He examined the door frame, his eyes searching for the telltale sign he'd left behind. There it was — a simple blue thread from Sam Harris' cleaning rag, still perched in the doorjamb where he'd placed it. A wave of relief washed over him; no one had been here since he was last here.

The doctor unlocked the door and stepped inside. His eyes scanned the room. The papers on his desk were a mess, just as he'd left them. The drawers of his file cabinet showed no signs of disturbance. Even the pen he'd positioned at an odd angle hadn't moved, confirming what he already knew.

Despite the evidence that surrounded him, a nagging sense of anxiety persisted. He sensed that there was more to this break-in than met the eye. He decided to leave most of his traps in place. Dr. Bauer straightened his tie and pulled on his white coat. He was ready for his first appointment of the day.

A burst of laughter in the distance caught his attention. Two nurses were chatting at a nearby station. Bauer's ears perked up as the subject of their conversation changed.

"Have you seen Sam this morning?" one nurse asked.

"No, not yet. I think he's off today and tomorrow," the other replied.

"Ah, he must be working the weekend, like I am." The woman looked at the light on the wall, and started walking towards her patient's room. "Can you call housekeeping? Shower three needs cleaning."

His shoulders relaxed as their eavesdropped discussion ended. He was relieved that there would be no awkward run-ins with Harris for a few days. Bauer was surprised by the smoothness of his day as it progressed. Patient consultations went well, paperwork seemed less daunting, and staff meetings concluded without major disagreements. It was the most uneventful day he'd experienced in months.

Yet, despite the apparent normalcy of his day, and Sam's absence, he couldn't dismiss his paranoia. As he moved through the hospital corridors between therapy sessions and meetings, a persistent feeling haunted him. He could shake the unmistakable sense that someone was watching, following his every move.

Glances over his shoulder came more often than usual. With a careful gaze, he surveyed the hallways in search of faces. He looked for any sign of lingering eyes or unusual interest. Even though Harris was off work, he couldn't relax. The privacy of his office did little to diminish the anxiety in his gut.

He tried to rationalize these feelings as the day went on. Yet, the sensation persisted. The day's events, or lack thereof, once again left the psychiatrist exhausted at the end of his day. As he prepared to leave, gathering his belongings, he looked around his personal space one last time, locked up, and headed for his car.

Chapter 15

Bauer pulled into the driveway of his mother's home. With the turn of the key, the engine's idle sputtered, then went silent. He sat for a moment, his hands continued to grip the steering wheel. As he took a deep breath, he could feel the day's paranoia melt away. In its wake was a building curiosity about what awaited him inside.

As he stepped out of the car, the aroma of his mom's cooking wafted through the long shadows. The familiar scent of roasted chicken and fresh herbs transported him back to countless family dinners from his childhood. Most of the memories brought a grin to his face.

"Thomas, is that you?" Edyth called as he entered the house.

"Yes, mom," he replied, hanging up his coat. "Something smells delicious."

He made his way to the kitchen, where she stood at the stove, stirring a pot of mashed potatoes. She turned to greet him with a warm smile.

"Perfect timing, dear. Dinner's just about ready. Would you mind setting the table?"

Thomas nodded, then without hesitation, fell into an old familiar routine. His moves were efficient as he placed plates and cutlery down for the place settings. When they sat down to eat, a wave of comfort washed over him as he took his first bite. The tender meat and savory vegetables stirred fond memories of long ago. He was grateful for his rare day of relative normalcy, after the tumultuous events of the past week.

"How was your day?" His mother asked, her eyes filled with genuine interest.

He paused, considering how much to share. "It was uneventful," he said. "Which, to be honest, was a welcomed change of pace."

Edyth nodded, sensing there was more beneath the surface, but decided not to press any further. "Sometimes, a quiet day is just what we need to recharge."

As they ate, Thomas relaxed more and more. The conversation flowed, touching on lighter topics: the weather, a new recipe she wanted to try, an upcoming community event. When they finished, he helped with the cleanup. As they worked next to each other in the kitchen, he realized how much he had missed these kinds of interactions with his mother.

"You know, mom," he said as he dried a plate, "I appreciate you letting me stay here. Thanks again for everything."

She paused her washing, turning to look at him with a soft smile. "Oh, Thomas. You're my son. You're always welcome here, no matter what."

The silence between them wasn't awkward this time. They shared moments filled with unspoken understanding and affection.

As he put away the last dish, Thomas felt a renewed sense of energy. The good meal and his mother's company had pushed away the fatigue that had followed him from work.

"I'm going to read in dad's study, if you don't mind," he said, trying to maintain his casual tone. "There's a lot to look through."

Edyth nodded. A flicker of something flashed in her eyes—curiosity? concern? "Of course, dear. Don't stay up too late, though. You need your rest."

He assured her he wouldn't. Then ran upstairs to change and fetch the key. When he returned, he made his way down the hallway. As he approached the door, his steps slowed, as his well ingrained trepidation kicked in. He heard the soft click of the lock, stepped inside, and closed the door behind him.

The room greeted him with grounding fragrances of old books, leather, and the faint familiar scent of his father that still permeated the room. Bauer settled into the chair. His fingers itched to resume what he'd begun the previous night.

He unlocked and pulled out the drawer containing the journals. He was careful as he lifted the topmost volume. As he flipped through the first few pages, his eyes fell upon a page he hadn't noticed the night before. The date on it was fourteen months before Thomas was born.

"Levi's work is incredible. The implications of his discoveries are staggering, on a global scale," the note began. "What he's discovered challenges everything we thought we understood about the human mind and its relationship to time and space."

Bauer's heart raced as he read. His father's normal, precise, elegant script grew erratic as the entry continued. It betrayed either excitement or perhaps anxiety, maybe both.

"But the risks. The Case 47 protocols, though followed to the letter, go far beyond what is ethically permissible. Still, we must protect the work with our lives.

If we move forward, we must exercise the greatest of caution. God help us if this research ever falls into nefarious hands."

The high-backed chair protested as Bauer leaned back. His mind was reeling. What on earth was his father talking about? Ethics violations? What had Levi discovered? And what was in the protocols that had his father so scared?

He flipped through more pages, searching for additional references to Levi or Case 47. Each mention raised more questions, yet gave few answers. The cryptic notations, and many notes about "temporal displacement" and other odd terms. This information puzzled Thomas but held a great deal of significance for his father and research colleague.

The more he read, the clean, crisp penmanship that definitively belonged to his father became more disorganized. Dates and events scattered all over the place and haphazard in the records. Bauer shook his head, trying to make sense of all of it. He'd never known his father to be this messy.

He ran upstairs to his bedroom and started pulling personal mementos off a large cork board. He brought it down to the study and placed it on a big table against the wall. With a fresh pack of index cards from his briefcase, he began recording his observations. Each card represented a date, an event, or a name from his notes.

Hours passed. Thomas was meticulous in his arrangement notes, trying to connect related pieces of data. He stood up on occasion to survey his board. As the web of information became more complex, a curious observation struck Bauer. Everything on his desk was part of Levi's timeline. Something nagged at him about the glaring omission.

"Where are you, Dad?" Thomas muttered, as he scanned the table for anything he might have missed.

In the hundreds of references to Case 47 and Levi's groundbreaking research, his father's contributions were nowhere to be found. It was as if his father had omitted any explicit mention of himself in his partner's research. But why?

Frustration mounted as Thomas combed through the journals again, searching for any hint of his father's input. These two men had worked together; the rumors at Saint Elizabeths were too persistent to be baseless. So why was their collaboration missing from his father's private notes?

One entry, dated about a year before Levi's disappearance, caught Bauer's attention:

"I am worried about Matthias. He seemed so happy the other day, the happiest I've ever seen him. He was in the lab over the weekend again. The place was a mess when I came in. I don't know why yet, but I fear for his safety. He is pushing himself too hard.

He doesn't seem to see the dangers, or maybe he doesn't care. I've tried to reason with him, but he's stubborn, guarded, and borderline obsessed with something. If this continues, I'm afraid of what might happen to him, to his patients, to all of us."

A chill ran down Bauer's spine. What had Dr. Levi been doing? Why was his father so worried? And was this related to the mysterious Case 47?

He turned his attention to some of the loose papers tucked into the journals. Many had complex equations and diagrams that were well beyond his comprehension. But among them, he found a folded note in his father's handwriting. It appeared to be a draft of a letter, never sent.

Dear Matthias,

I implore you to reconsider your current course of action. The risks you're taking are not just to yourself, but to everyone involved in our projects. This work was started with the noblest of intentions, but I fear that is not the case, now. We've — you've strayed into dangerous territory.

The past incidents with Subject Alpha should have been a wake-up call. We cannot continue to ignore the ethical implications of what we've done. These are people's lives we're dealing with, not just data points in an experiment.

Please, my friend, let's take a step back. We need to reevaluate what we are doing, our methods, and our goals. There's still time to correct the course, but only if we act now.

If you won't listen to reason, I'll have no choice but to...

The letter ended, unfinished. Thomas stared at it, his mind racing. What past incidents with Subject Alpha? And what was his father prepared to do if Levi didn't heed his warnings?

He set the paper aside and reached into the drawer for another journal. This one had notes from an earlier period. As he opened it, a small photograph slipped out and fell to the desk. He picked it up. His breath caught in his throat. He knew the men in the image. It was a group photo, taken in a laboratory.

In the center stood his father, looking much younger than the pictures that hung in the halls of Saint Elizabeths. Harold's arm was around the shoulders of Dr. Matthias Levi from the portrait in the hospital. Both their smiles seemed forced. The excitement of scientific discovery was absent from their eyes.

He recognized a few of the other faces as colleagues of his dad's he'd met over the years. But it was the other face that caught Thomas' attention. Standing to the side, and behind these men, was the face of a man in his early twenties he knew all too well — Sam Harris.

Bauer's mind reeled. Was the old housekeeper somehow involved in Levi and his father's research? But how? And why? He had been nothing but a janitor at Saint Elizabeths for as long as anyone could remember?

He flipped the photograph over. Thomas noted that it was taken around the same time as the unfinished letter. Next to the date, written in his father's script, were the words "The end." The end of what? Another strange puzzle piece that only seemed to complicate things further.

Bauer leaned back in the chair. His head spun with all he'd learned. He glanced at the clock, surprised by the time that had passed since he'd entered the study. He was exhausted, but now his mind was buzzing more than ever with questions and theories.

He knew he should get some rest, but the pull to explore more was too strong. Countless mysteries surrounded him, begging to be revealed. Though he thought better of it, his hand seemed to move on its own as he pulled another leather-bound journal from the drawer and opened it.

Bauer immersed himself in the next log of events. He was soon transported back to the earlier days of Harold's career. He noticed that the penmanship in this one was different, most likely because of the enthusiasm of a young scientist on the brink of groundbreaking discoveries. His father's words painted a graphic picture of late nights at work, heated debates with colleagues, and moments of brilliant discovery. They reignited the fire of discovery in Thomas that was snuffed out at least two years ago.

One entry, in particular, caught his attention:

May 15, 1951

Though I may not be the Godliest of men, today's achievements in the lab can only be described as a miracle. For a brief moment, mere seconds, really, Subject Gamma experienced a vivid hallucination of events that took place well over a century ago. But this differed from the hallucinations we've observed in patients from the East Ward. The historical accuracy and level-of-detail verification surpassed any conventional explanation.

I am prepared to push the boundaries of these discoveries as far as possible. The implications of what we discovered is staggering. The future of the project is truly monumental. It ventures beyond what we've ever understood about the human mind. But, It is hard to say if the benefits outweigh the risks.

Those urging me to proceed are correct about one thing. This is a once in a lifetime opportunity. However, those who push me forward don't seem to care about the ethics, nor the impact this research has on patients or the professionals involved. I no longer feel like I have a choice in the matter.

Bauer read and reread the passage, his brain struggled to comprehend what his father was describing. Was it time travel? Or something even stranger? And who was pushing him beyond his comfort level?

He flipped a few pages, finding another entry that made his blood run cold.

September 3, 1951

Disaster. There's no other word for it. I pushed too hard, too fast, and now, God help us all.

Subject Delta's experience went farther than anything previously seen before. It was more than just a vivid hallucination this time. For several hours, Delta was gone. Physically present, yes, but his mind is absent from this reality.

When he came back, what he described... it's impossible. It goes against everything we thought we knew about time and consciousness.

But the cost; Delta is a broken man. Whatever he experienced, wherever he went, he did not return the same man. He is catatonic now. Completely unresponsive to any stimuli. His eyes remain forever haunted. It's as if he has witnessed things no human should have ever seen.

I am being pushed to continue my work, to further refine my methods. They don't see this as a setback or a warning. I don't want to be part of this. If this is the price paid for this research, I don't want to do this anymore.

I need to figure out a way to shut this all down. Surely the others recognize the risks are far too great. But they won't listen to reason. They kept going because of their excessive investment, obsession with possibility, or fear of punishment if they stop.

Regardless of what happens next, I know that we've unlocked a door that should have never been opened. God, forgive us for what we have done.

Thomas sat back in his father's chair. He ran trembling fingers through his hair as he tried to process what he'd just read. His father and Levi had figured out a way to send consciousness through time. The implications were staggering, but the cost? The fate of Delta haunted Harold. Was this the incident with Alpha that his father had mentioned in the unsent letter? Or had there been other disastrous experiments?

He reached for another journal, this one from a later period. He opened it. A small key fell out, clattering to the floor. Thomas picked it up and examined it. It was old, made of tarnished brass, with an intricate design on the bow. He didn't recognize it as belonging to any lock in the study.

Tucked into the pages, Bauer found a folded piece of paper. It revealed a crude hand-drawn map. It seemed to depict a section of Saint Elizabeths that he didn't recognize. There was a circled room on it.

Bauer's heart raced. Where was this mysterious part of the hospital? What did it mean? He turned his attention back to the journal, scanning for any mention of a key or a map. After several minutes of searching, he found something that made his breath catch:

December 31, 1963

It's all a mess. I tried to correct my mistakes, but that too has been a complete failure. It only made things worse. All that I've learned, everything I've created. It's all too dangerous. However, as much as I want to, I can't bring myself to destroy this body of work. That said, leaving it unsecured endangers all of humanity going forward.

Nobody knows what I'm about to do. They can't know. Their obsessions paired with my own poor judgment have turned my dreams into nightmares. I worry about the future.

All I can do at this point is separate and secure the most dangerous components of this research. It is important that even if someone finds some of the information, there is enough missing to discourage replication on any scale.

No one can know what I'm doing. They can't know. Their obsession has grown too strong, too risky. I fear for all of humanity if they ever gain access to what's been hidden.

If you are reading this, Thomas, be careful. This knowledge is as powerful as it is dangerous. Use it wisely, and always keep in mind: some doors are better left unopened.

He stared at his name on the page, his brain reeling. His father wrote this to him? But why? And why had he never mentioned any of this when he was alive?

He looked at the journal, map and key on the desk with fresh eyes. These items were more than just leather, paper and metal. They were elements that could unlock mysteries that were concealed for decades. Secrets that, according to his father, were incredible, powerful and dangerous.

They had been stowed in Saint Elizabeths. All the time, he'd been working. World-changing knowledge was there somewhere.

He felt a mix of excitement and trepidation. He wanted to rush to the hospital in the middle of the night. To find whatever his father and Dr. Levi had hidden away. But another part of him, the logical voice deep within his mind, urged him to proceed with great caution.

Bauer glanced at the clock, surprised to see it was well past midnight. He'd been so engrossed in his discoveries that he'd lost all track of time. Exhaustion hit him like a wave. The weight of his late nights had caught up with him.

Thomas kept the key, the map, and the most recent journal. He secured everything else in the desk drawer. As much as he wanted to continue, he knew it was already later than he intended to be up. The rest would have to wait. He knew he needed sleep. Tomorrow was another day that would bring new information; the next day he planned to make another visit to the archives.

As Bauer prepared for bed, his mind still had questions without answers. Now there were more secrets to uncover. What dangers might he face? And most pressingly, why did Sam Harris seem to keep popping up everywhere?

Sleep came in fitful stretches that night. Bauer's dreams replayed visions of the figure in the archive watching him and the watchful eyes of an old janitor who seemed to know far more than he let on.

Chapter 16

Bauer's eyes fluttered open. He squinted against the harsh sunlight streaming into the room. He groaned, his achy back protested as he rolled over. The glowing digits from the clock radio on his nightstand read 8:47 AM. He was late.

"Damn it," he muttered, throwing off the bedclothes and stumbling out of bed. His head throbbed, caused by the delayed loading dose of coffee and the residual effects of too many nights poring over his father's journals and papers. The revelations from those pages still swirled fresh in his mind, competing with his urgent need to get ready for work.

He rushed through an abbreviated morning routine. He needed a shower, but there was no time for that, and settled for a quick splash of water on his face. As he threw a tie around his neck, his mother's voice came from downstairs.

"Thomas? Are you alright up there?"

"Fine, Mom," he called back. He winced at the hint of irritation in his tone. "Just running late."

He headed out his bedroom door. Bauer flew down the stairs two steps at a time. He almost collided with his mother, waiting on the landing. Edyth stood there with a full mug of hot coffee and a concerned look on her face.

"I thought you might need this," she said, offering him the cup. "You were up past midnight again last night."

Thomas accepted the steaming drink, feeling a pang of guilt for his earlier shortness. "Thanks, mom. I just got caught up in some reading. I meant to get to bed earlier."

Edyth's expression softened. "I'm glad you're finding use for that old study. Your father would be pleased."

He nodded, not trusting himself to say anymore. If only she knew what he'd already discovered there. He gave her a quick peck on the cheek, grabbed his briefcase, and headed toward the door.

The drive to Saint Elizabeths was a blur of traffic, while his brain swarmed with half-formed theories. Bauer's mind kept returning to the map he'd found, and the cryptic circled room. He did not know where it was or what it meant? Was it somehow connected to Levi's Case 47 he'd heard about only in rumors at the hospital?

He pulled into the hospital parking lot an hour behind schedule. He cursed under his breath as he walked at a brisk pace towards the entrance. As he passed through the lobby, he nodded a distracted greeting to the receptionist, who gave him an odd look.

"Everything alright, Dr. Bauer?" she asked. "You're never this late."

"I'm fine," he muttered, without slowing his steps. "Just overslept this morning."

He made his way through the familiar corridors, his footsteps echoed. As he approached his office, his gait slowed. Something wasn't right.

Thomas paused at his door. Knowing Harris was off for a couple of days, he opted to not set the intrusion trap. However, he knew for a fact that he had locked his door when he left for the night. His door was ajar. His heart pounded. He pushed it and stepped inside.

At first glance, nothing seemed amiss. The desktop continued to be cluttered with notes and patient files, and the bookshelf remained as disorganized as usual. Yet, as he proceeded into the room, he saw irregularities. There was a small shift in the stack of papers on his desk. A drawer that he always kept closed was open a crack. And the pen he balanced on top of the filing cabinet two nights prior laid on the floor.

Someone had been in here, again!

His mind jumped to Sam Harris. Bauer had well-established suspicions before he saw the janitor's face in his father's old photograph the previous night. But if the old man had been off work yesterday and today. Would he come in just to break into his office? If it wasn't him, who else could it have been?

He opened the door and began a more thorough inspection of his space. He searched through drawers and cabinets to ensure nothing else was missing or out of place. As far as he could tell, nothing was taken. The intrusion into his personal space left him shaken.

The doctor stepped back out into the hallway. He flagged down a nurse passing in the vicinity. "Excuse me, have you seen Sam Harris around?"

She shook her head. "No, Dr. Bauer. I heard he was off yesterday and today. Is everything alright?"

He forced a smile. "Yes, everything's fine. Just needed to ask him something about... cleaning supplies."

The nurse gave him an odd look, then nodded and continued on her way. Thomas retreated into his office, slamming the door behind him and locking it.

He would have to deal with this later. He was late for his first appointment before he arrived. Between appointments and meetings, he questioned various colleagues and staff members, but the response was always the same. No one had seen Sam Harris anywhere for the last two days.

Sitting at a nurses' station, Bauer documented on a patient session as lunchtime drew closer. His mind wandered from his task at hand. For a moment, he entertained the idea of confronting the old man and demanding answers. But then reconsidered. If the old man was involved in these break ins, tipping his hand too early could make matters worse. That confrontation would have to wait, at least until Sam returned.

By noon, he found himself back in his office, staring out the window. The constant sense of being watched persisted. He tried to rationalize his increasing paranoia. His work life was anything but remarkable. He hadn't been a part of any new research projects for months.

The rest of the afternoon passed in a haze of appointments and paperwork, but Bauer's mind kept returning to the mysteries swimming in his head. Who had been in his office? What did they want? Was it connected to Levi and his father or the rumors about Case 47?

He thought about the letters, the map, the key from the night before. It would be impossible for anyone at Saint Elizabeths to know what he'd found. Yet, he couldn't shake the feeling that he had stumbled into a situation far more intricate than he expected.

Bauer called the nurses' station to inquire about his next appointment. Despite beginning the day behind schedule, he still got all his work done. He had completed all his scheduled appointments and charting for the day. He looked at his watch. 2:00 PM, he had some time to kill.

With this unexpected extra time on his hands, he secured his office door. Then made his way through the hospital corridors. The doctor stepped into the dim light of the archives. His footsteps echoed through the cavernous foyer. The musty aroma of old books and leather-bound papers filled his senses. It was a soothing familiar scent that grounded his mind and soul. However, today, it had an opposite effect with his heightened paranoia.

His eyes scanned labels as he walked the maze of shelving. He had been in this section many times before. "My father's work should be around here somewhere," he muttered to himself. Filed away among countless other documents and case studies. As he searched, Thomas glanced over his shoulder, half-expecting to see Sam Harris lurking in the shadows. He didn't care if the old man was off for a couple of days. He couldn't shake the feeling of being watched.

His heart raced as he located the section containing Harold Bauer's research. He pulled out one box and sifted through it. As he read through the papers, his excitement shifted to frustration. There was nothing here related to what he'd found in the home study. No mention of Case 47. Nothing that could shed light on the rumored research project that had consumed his father and Dr. Levi during their respective tenure.

Just as he was about to give up, a thick folder caught his eye. "Beyond the Closed Doors: The Hidden Struggles of Psychiatric Professionals." Intrigued, he opened it. What was inside surprised him. He double checked the cover for Harold Bauer's name. His father had written an extensive article about the destruction of psychiatry on those in the field. The detailed observations of Levi and others were enlightening and unsettling. His father described the effects of constant exposure to human suffering and the weight of patients' traumas. Their relentless dedication leads to the gradual undermining of their own mental well-being.

As he read on, a profound realization hit him. His father's chilly response had no relation to disapproval about his chosen profession. It was a misguided attempt to protect him from the very fate Harold Bauer had witnessed in his colleagues.

Bauer's hands shook as he turned the pages. He remembered the day he'd told his father about his career choice, the look of devastation on his dad's face. He'd interpreted it as disappointment. Now, he understood it had been fear.

The deep-seated animosity he had nurtured towards his father for years eased just a little. He could see now that Harold's actions, however hurtful, had come from a place of love, concern and protection. Despite this, the emotional pain he had endured for years would not heal right away.

Thomas shifted his weight and shook his head. *Why didn't he just tell me?* He wasn't quite ready to forgive his father, not yet. That crushing disappointment on that day remained too raw, too painful.

As he stood there surrounded by the ghosts of his father and others, he couldn't help but reflect on his own life. The long hours at the hospital, the strain it had put on his marriage, the distance growing between him and Simon. He thought of Eleanor, of the hurt in her eyes when he'd forgotten a dinner date or to pick up Simon. His life had been in ruins well before his house flooded.

Was this what his dad attempted to protect him from? Had Thomas, in his stubborn determination to prove himself, walked right into the perilous world Harold was so desperate for his son to avoid?

Thomas rubbed his eyes, feeling every one of his forty-five years. He wasn't ready to admit the full extent of the destruction his career had brought to his personal life. But standing there, surrounded by his father's observations and warnings, he could no longer deny that something had to change.

He left the archives, his mind still reeling from the article his father wrote. As he walked through the hospital corridors, the constant sense of being watched persisted. A shadow could conceal a lurking presence. Each prolonged glance from a coworker could hide meaning.

He paused at a water fountain, bending to take a sip. As he straightened, he glimpsed movement in his peripheral vision. He whirled around, heart pounding, but saw nothing in an empty hallway.

"Get a grip, Bauer," he muttered to himself, running his fingers through his hair.

He continued to stroll the familiar hallways of Saint Elizabeths Hospital. As he passed a nurses' station, he nodded to the staff there. He studied their faces for any sign to support his growing suspicion. Everyone just smiled back, oblivious to his inner turmoil.

Bauer reached his office. He fumbled with his keys as he unlocked the door. Once inside, he pressed his back against the door. His eyes closed as he took a deep breath. He couldn't shake off the sense of violation caused by the intrusions into his personal space.

The doctor moved deeper into the room, placing the documents he'd retrieved from the archives on his desk. He leafed through the pages penned by his father. A slip of paper fluttered to the floor. Thomas bent down to retrieve it, his heart racing as he focused his eyes.

He didn't recognize the handwriting, but the content made his blood run cold.

"Temporal displacement—groundbreaking but dangerous. The risks and rewards are tremendous. Investigate with caution. Someone is always watching."

His eyes locked on "Temporal displacement." Two words he'd never seen together before last night. Who was watching? What the hell had he uncovered?

The unsettling note sent Thomas' mind racing. He sat at his desk, pondering what to do next. A knock at the door made him jump and pulled him from his thoughts.

He tucked the paper into the pocket of his slacks., feeling as if he'd just found an important clue. The psychiatrist composed himself before responding, "Come in."

Olivia Kendrick poked her head in. "Dr. Bauer, your 3:30 patient is ready for you."

He nodded, grateful for the distraction. He gathered what he needed for his appointment.

Thomas sat at his dad's desk. The note from the pages of the archives article lay in front of him. His eyes read the words "temporal displacement" followed by "someone is always watching" sent adrenaline coursing through his veins. It was a connection between Levi and his father's work he'd been searching for.

He leaned back in his chair, a smile played at the corners of his mouth. He had been stumbling around in the dark for years. But now he had a match to light his way forward. A few pieces were falling into place.

Bauer reached for his notepad. He jotted down his thoughts with renewed conviction. His anger and bitterness toward his father had blinded him—there was so much more to his father and his work than met the eye. And now, he had a little better understanding of the man his dad was.

A soft knock at the door interrupted his musings. "Thomas?" his mother's voice called. "Dinner's ready."

"I'll be right there, Mom," he replied, covering his notes with a blank piece of paper. As he made his way to the dining room, there was an unmistakable spring in his step that had been missing for several years.

Over dinner, his mom noticed a change in her son's demeanor. "You seem in good spirits tonight, dear," she observed, passing him the roasted carrots.

Thomas nodded as he chewed on a bite of meat loaf, trying to contain his emotions. "Just had a good day at work," he said, not quite meeting her eyes.

Edyth studied him for a moment. "You've been spending long hours in that study," she remarked. "Find anything interesting?"

He paused, fork halfway to his mouth. "Just — getting to know Dad a little better," he said. "There's a lot of history within those walls."

His mother's expression softened. "Your father was a complicated man, Thomas. But he loved you very much."

A twinge of guilt came with keeping secrets from her, but he pushed them aside. He promised to share his discoveries with her at some point, just not now.

After dinner, he returned to the study. He dove back into his father's journals with renewed fervor. Hours slipped by unnoticed as he pored through pages searching for any mention of Case 47 or temporal displacement.

The next morning, Bauer arrived at Saint Elizabeths earlier than usual, eager to continue his investigation. As he walked through the lobby, he noticed a few curious glances from the staff. He straightened his posture, chin held high. *Let them look,* he thought to himself. He was on the verge of discovery. He could feel it.

In his office, Bauer completed his paperwork with remarkable efficiency, determined to clear his schedule for more important matters. When Nurse Kendrick came in with a patient file, she raised an eyebrow at his uncharacteristic behavior.

"You're chipper today, Thomas," she remarked. "New coffee blend?"

Bauer grinned. "Just feeling good, Olivia. Sometimes things just—click, you know?"

She nodded, as a hint of concern flashed in her eyes. "Well, don't work yourself too hard. We need you at your best, doctor."

As she turned to leave, her words of caution failed to register. His sole focus was on a quest that nobody had any knowledge of.

Throughout the day, Bauer found himself more vocal in meetings and challenging ideas he would have ignored before. His colleagues weren't sure what to make of his sudden assertiveness, but he reveled in the rare feeling of control.

During his lunch break, he couldn't resist a quick trip to the archives. As he rifled through more of his father's papers, he detected a presence behind him. Turning, he saw an old man standing there watching at the end of the aisle.

Instead of the usual paranoia, he felt a surge of boldness. His gaze locked onto the elderly janitor's eyes. "Can I help you with something, Sam?"

Harris shook his head. "Just doing my rounds, Dr. Bauer. Don't you mind me." He said as he shuffled away, pushing his cart.

Thomas watched him go, a small smile playing on his lips. Let that old janitor watch; no one there could know what he now knew.

Over the next few days, Bauer's newfound confidence transformed into arrogance. He stayed late at the hospital, arriving home well after dinner most nights. Edyth's concerned looks went unnoticed as he rushed past her to lock himself away in the study.

One evening, as he was locking up his office, Nurse Kendrick caught up with him in the parking lot. "Dr. Bauer," she called, out of breath. "Do you have a minute?"

He glanced at his watch, his impatience evident. "I'm in a bit of a hurry, Olivia. Can it wait until tomorrow?"

She frowned. "No, it can't. I'm worried about you. You've been pushing yourself so hard. Coming in late. Are you sure everything's alright?"

For a moment, Thomas considered confiding in her. But now was not the time or place. "I appreciate your concern," he said through a forced smile. "But I assure you, I'm fine. Better than fine. I'm just focused."

Kendrick didn't look convinced. "Just... be careful, Thomas, okay? Don't lose sight of what's important."

As he drove home, her words replayed in Bauer's mind. What did she mean? Wasn't learning the truth about his father and his work important?

When he arrived, he found his mother sitting in the living room, waiting for him. "Son," she said, "I think we need to talk."

Thomas sighed, running a hand through his hair. "Can it wait? I've got some reports to finish." He lied.

Edyth's expression hardened. "That's what I want to talk to you about. You're spending so much time at the hospital or locked away in that study. I'm worried about you, dear."

"Mom, I'm fine," He insisted, his tone sharp and annoyed. "I've just stumbled on some interesting stuff. It's something big. I can feel it."

His mother's eyes widened a bit in response to the intensity of his reaction. "Thomas," she said with concern in her voice, "you're starting to act like your father."

Thomas flinched at her words. He opened his mouth to argue, then thought better of it. He shook his head, then without another word, he turned on his heels and headed down the hall to the study, and slammed the door behind him.

As he sat in his father's chair, Bauer's mind raced. Was he behaving like his father? He thought about it for a few minutes. No, he decided. This was nothing more than just curious dedication.

Bauer pulled out his notepad and began flipping through the pages of notes and theories he'd compiled thus far. He was making significant strides. Case 47 existed, he now had confirmation. Now he just had to find it. He needed more time and information.

Bauer studied the crude map of Saint Elizabeths he found in his father's desk. He would not return to the archives at the hospital for a while. He knew Sam Harris was watching, but was someone else? For now, he'd focus his energy here, in the study. There was still a lot more for him to dig through.

Chapter 17

Thomas Bauer arrived early to work the next morning. He strode with purpose down the hospital corridor. Each footstep echoed off of sterile walls, as his mind swirled with recent discoveries. He'd had enough of the mysteries, the intrusions, the paranoia. Now he wanted answers.

As he rounded a corner, he spotted Sam pushing his custodial cart. The wheels squeaked against the polished floor. Bauer's jaw clenched as he watched the old man. He quickened his steps, closing the distance between them.

"Harris," Thomas called out, his voice sharp and commanding. "We need to talk."

The old man looked up, his weathered face impassive. He stopped, then turned to face the psychiatrist with an unreadable expression. "Dr. Bauer," he replied, his tone neutral. "What can I do for you?"

The doctor glanced over his shoulder to ensure no one was within earshot. He stepped closer, his tone low. "You can start by explaining why you've been snooping around my office when I'm not here."

Sam's eyebrows rose, but his composure remained the same. "Your office, sir? I'm not sure what you're talking about."

"Don't play dumb with me, Harris," Thomas hissed with frustration. "Someone's been breaking in. They moved my stuff and went through my papers after I left for the day. Some things are missing."

A flicker of something—amusement? concern?—flashed across the janitor's face. "Dr. Bauer, I assure you, I haven't been in there outside of my regular cleaning duties."

The doctor's fists clenched at his sides. "Someone was in there. If it's not you, then who?"

Sam's eyes narrowed, and for a moment, the psychiatrist saw something deeper, more knowing, in the old man's eyes. "Doctor, maybe you should ask yourself why you're so paranoid."

The confident, cryptic response caught Thomas off guard. He took a step back to study Sam's face. "Exactly what are you implying?"

Sam glanced down the hallway, then leaned in closer. His tone dropped to a whisper. "There is so much about this hospital you don't know. Secrets about your father, Dr. Levi, and others. Things no one knows, but I know."

Bauer's blood ran cold. "What are you talking about? What others?" He demanded, his voice hoarse.

Sam's lips curved into a sad smile. "With all due respect, sir, there are some answers you aren't ready for yet."

Before he could press the old man any further, the sound of footsteps approaching interrupted them. The housekeeper straightened, his face once again shifted to a mask of professional indifference.

"Now, if you'll excuse me, doctor," he said, reaching for his cart. "I have work to do."

He watched, stunned, as Harris walked away. The confrontation had gone nothing like he'd expected. What little was said left him reeling. Now he had more questions.

As he stood there, trying to process what had just happened, Nurse Kendrick approached.

"Thomas?" she asked, concern evident in her voice. "Are you alright? You look like you've just seen a ghost."

He shook his head, to clear his mind. "I'm fine, Olivia. Just a strange conversation I wasn't expecting."

She frowned, studying his face. "With Sam? That man knows more about this hospital than anyone. Getting on his bad side… "

"I know, I know," he cut her off, running a hand through his hair. "But I needed information."

She looked at Bauer, confused. She placed a hand on his arm. "Information? From him?"

He looked around. The old man had disappeared. The hallway was empty now. "Yes," he admitted. "But our talk left me with more questions."

As they turned to walk together towards the staff lounge, His mind remained on the confrontation. Sam's strange responses replayed in his head, hinting at something larger than just his father and Dr. Levi. Who were the "others?" How were they involved? Where did the old janitor fit into all of this?

His hands shook as he poured himself a cup of coffee. It was now clear that the old man knew more than he let on. Thomas was just getting to understand his father better. Then Sam Harris comes along to bring him down a notch. Bauer's gut warned him not to disregard or underestimate the man. The only thing he knew for certain was that he had a lot more to learn.

That afternoon, the doctor's mind replayed the unsettling conversation with the old housekeeper. As he returned from a therapy session, once again, he noticed his office door was open. His stomach churned. He knew he'd locked it before heading to his appointments and lunch. He approached, and froze.

The place was in complete disarray. Papers strewn across the floor, cabinet doors hung from their hinges, and books from the shelves peppered the room. It looked like a bomb had gone off in the room.

"What the hell?" Bauer muttered, stepping into the chaos.

He walked through the mess, trying to assess the damage. File folders lay scattered, their contents spilled. The filing drawers were pulled out and ransacked.

Bauer's heart pounded as he reached into his pocket, feeling for the piece of paper he'd found the previous day. He breathed a sigh of relief when his fingers brushed against it. At least the intruder hadn't gotten their hands on that.

He moved toward the phone on his desk. A knock at the door made him jump.

"Dr. Bauer? I have the patient files for your afternoon..." Nurse Kendrick went silent. Her eyes widened as she looked at the state of his office. "Oh my God, Thomas. What happened?"

"I don't know," He replied, his voice tight. "I just got back from lunch and found it like this."

Olivia stepped into the room, careful not to touch any of the mess. "We need to report this right away. I'll call security."

As she called, he tried to make sense of the chaos. He kneeled down, picking up a few scattered papers, trying to determine if anything was missing. But with everything in such disarray, it was impossible to tell.

Within minutes, a security guard arrived, followed by Dr. Jameson, the head of psychiatry.

"What's going on here?" The administrator asked, his brow wrinkled as he surveyed the room.

Thomas explained the situation, mentioning his suspicions and previous break ins. As he spoke, he watched the two men exchange skeptical glances.

"And you're certain you locked your door when you left?" the officer asked, inspecting the frame of the door.

"Of course I did," Bauer insisted. "I always do."

Jameson placed a hand on his shoulder. "Thomas, you've been under a lot of pressure the past few weeks. With everything that's happened with your home, and taking on extra patients..."

He bristled at the implication and condescending tone. "Are you suggesting I did this myself?"

"No, no," Jameson backpedaled. "But a sudden increase in stress can make us forgetful. Perhaps you left the door unlocked, and, well..."

"It happens to the best of us," the security man added.

A surge of frustration came over him. "I didn't do this. Someone broke in here and went through my stuff."

Again the men exchanged another look. " I'll file a report," the officer said, his words placating. "But with no signs of forced entry..."

"Thomas, why don't you take the remainder of the day off? Get some rest. We'll get you some help cleaning this up tomorrow."

Bauer opened his mouth to argue, but the looks on their faces suggested his words would be futile. These two didn't believe him. He just nodded, while continuing to stand surrounded by the mess.

Outside his office door, he overheard Dr. Jameson murmuring to the security officer. "Poor guy. I think he's losing it. He's been working himself to the bone. Probably just needs a good night's sleep."

Anger and frustration seeped deep in Bauer's core. The phone on his desk rang. He just stared at it. On the fifth ring, he moved to answer it. Without a word, he placed the handset to his ear.

"Thomas? Are you there? It's Mrs. Clendin."

There was an unmistakable urgency in her voice. "Yes, Mrs. Clendin, I'm here. Is everything okay?"

"I have a package here for you. I think it's important. Can you please come by after work today? It looks urgent."

"Thank you." Bauer sighed while he ran a hand through his hair. His mail was the least of his concern at the moment. "I will swing by. However, I'm not sure what time that will be. Can I call you when I'm on my way?"

He hung up the phone. He took another look around as numbness overwhelmed him. The prior break-ins were subtle, noticeable only to him. But this was different. He no longer felt safe in his personal space.

Who was in here? What were they looking for? Why would security and administration not believe him? Could Sam have done this? Was this his response from their confrontation earlier?

Bauer started his car. He drove a direct route straight to his home. Whatever had come in his mail had her pretty shaken up. He doubted it was as important as she claimed. He hoped it would provide some answers. He already had too many questions.

He pulled into his driveway, his nerves on edge. The quaint suburban neighborhood looked peaceful in the late afternoon light, unlike the turmoil that occupied Bauer's mind. He took a deep breath, trying to calm himself before exiting his car and making his way across the street.

Mrs. Clendin answered the door just as he was about to knock. She'd been waiting for him by the door. Her typical cheerful face showed creases of concern.

"Oh, Thomas, thank goodness you're here," she said, ushering him inside, and slamming and locking the door behind him. "I'm so worried."

Bauer followed her into the living room, noticing how she kept glancing out the windows. "What's wrong? You said something about mail?"

She nodded as she wrung her hands. "Yes, it came this morning. A strange man delivered it by hand. He insisted I give it to you and only you."

Bauer's eyebrows shot up. "What made him so odd? Did he say who he was?"

She shook her head. "No, but he seemed official. Like he was from the government or something. He was very insistent that only you receive this."

She hurried to a drawer and pulled out a thick manila envelope. As she handed it to Bauer, he inspected it. The well-sealed package had no markings. There was no return address or postage.

"Thank you, Mrs. Clendin," Thomas said, turning it over in his hands. "Did this man say anything else?"

She hesitated. Looked over her shoulder, then lowered her voice. "He said to tell you that 'you'd best watch your step' and, 'you are in great danger.'"

He felt a chill run through his veins. "No," he lied, not wishing to worry her further. "I'm sure it's nothing. I appreciate you letting me know."

"You're welcome." She seemed less stressed now that she handed off the mysterious package.

"I apologize for not stopping by to see you since I moved out." Bauer's words cut through the tension in the room.

Mrs. Clendin motioned for him to take a seat. "That's ok. You are a busy man."

"I have all kinds of excuses, but why waste this visit on that?"

"Would you like some tea? I just brewed a pot."

The familiar scent registered in his brain. "That would be lovely, thank you."

She soon emerged from the kitchen with two cups of Darjeeling and a plate of chocolate chip cookies.

He spoke with his mouth full of cookie, forgetting all manners. "You know, Mrs. Clendin, Simon thinks you make the best ones on the planet."

She blushed a little. "It's my grandma's secret recipe."

An hour passed before Bauer wrapped up his visit. "Thanks for the tea and cookies. They were delicious, as always. If you need anything in the future, please call me right away."

As he made his way back to his car, Bauer's mind raced through recent events. Was he in danger? What the hell did 'watch your step' mean? Who was this mysterious messenger?

Thomas sat in silence. The manila envelope felt heavier in his hands than it did earlier. His memories flashed back through the various warnings penned by his father. The hazards of his profession were more than just the wear and tear on one's own psyche and personal relationships. There were real dangers that lurked in the shadows of the known and unknown. "Trust no one" was now stuck in the forefront of his mind.

He now realized that there were things about his dad and the hospital he didn't understand. There was a lot he didn't know.

With a deep breath, Bauer started the engine and pulled away from his neighborhood. After he drove several blocks, his attention focused on the rearview mirror. The hair on the back of his neck prickled. Something was wrong. A black sedan was keeping pace a few car lengths behind.

His heart rate quickened. He made a sudden right turn, watching as the vehicle did the same. His suspicions were now confirmed. He was being followed.

His grip tightened on the steering wheel. He wove through side streets and alleys. He took random turns attempting to lose his pursuer. It stayed with him, matching his every move. Sweat beaded on Bauer's forehead as he drove faster through unfamiliar roads and neighborhoods. He zoomed through a yellow light.

After what felt like hours, Thomas spotted his chance. He zipped around a large box truck, pulling out ahead of him. For a few seconds it blocked the view behind him. He sped into an alley, threw it in park, and killed the lights.

He held his breath as he watched the rearview. The engine of the sedan roared past then faded into the distance. He waited there fifteen minutes before leaving. He continued to scan the streets for any sign of the black car.

Still on edge, Bauer decided he wasn't ready to head back to his mother's home just yet. He needed a place to think. Ahead, he spotted a hardware store. Thomas pulled into the lot and parked. He sat there, looking at the manila envelope peeking out from under the passenger's seat.

He pushed it out of sight, then stepped out of the vehicle. His best attempts to look casual were awkward as he wandered the aisles. The whole time he kept a vigilant eye on the entrance.

His attention soon shifted to a display next to him. The gleaming metal door knobs and deadbolt locks gave him an idea. After a brief but informative discussion with an employee, he selected a sturdy lock, along with a few essential tools needed for installation. Thomas made his purchase with a sense of urgency he struggled to hide.

Bauer loitered in the parking lot for another twenty minutes. His eyes darted between the rearview and side mirrors, searching for any sign of the sedan. He eased his way out of the parking lot and began a circuitous route to his mother's home. His eyes scanned his surroundings before every turn. Though the black car was nowhere to be seen, Thomas still couldn't shake his growing paranoia.

When he arrived, a thought struck him. Whoever delivered the package to Mrs. Clendin and followed him, didn't know he hadn't been living in his house for the last couple of weeks. They still thought he lived at his house. His knuckles were white as he gripped the wheel.

Dinner with his mother was a quiet, tense affair. They discussed his visit. He was careful to omit the details about the manila envelope and its mysterious messenger and the black sedan. His preoccupied mind replayed the events of his day like some fragmented movie reel.

This wasn't the place to make sense of it all. Edyth noticed the distraction in his absent gaze as he pushed steamed vegetables around on his plate. He created intricate patterns that went uneaten. She didn't press him, sensing her son's need for space. In silence, she worried about what troubled him.

While helping with the dishes, his movements were mechanical and his head was elsewhere. Bauer once again retreated to his father's study. The room felt different now. The energy made him uncomfortable. The air was thick with secrets and things he didn't understand.

The large manilla envelope sat before him. He took a deep breath to steady his nerves. He reached for it and opened it.

Chapter 18

The musty scent of old books and papers wafted from the material inside the manila envelope. Bauer's fingers trembled as he leafed through the package Mrs. Clendin had given him that afternoon. The weight of recent events—his flooded home, the unsettled feelings of being watched, the repeated break-ins into his office—all pressed down on him, but the allure of new information stole his focus.

The light on the answering machine flashed. Another message from Eleanor, no doubt calling about Simon. He reached for the phone, then stopped. Instead, he turned his eyes away, guilt gnawing at his gut. He'd deal with that later. Right now, he needed to find out what was in the package. These papers demanded his full attention.

As he pored over the documents, his eyes locked on the phrase: "Temporal Displacement Experiments." Though he still didn't understand what they meant, they were not foreign to him. The handwriting in the letter was familiar.

Bauer leaned closer, his nose almost touching the yellowed paper. His father wrote this. However, his father's normal precise penmanship became more erratic as he continued to read. It was as if the very act of writing filled him with excitement, or fear.

"Temporal Displacement..." Thomas muttered, his mind racing. "What the hell were you working on, dad?"

He reached for a journal in the locked desk drawer. Thomas flipped through the pages until he found an entry dated around the same time as the note. The words leaped off the page:

"Matthias' work is revolutionary. The potential is staggering, but it is extremely dangerous. The risks—I'm concerned by his complete disregard of ethical protocols. God forgive him. God forgive me. What he is doing is as wrong as it is fascinating."

Bauer's pulse raced. He knew what his father and Levi discovered was groundbreaking, but these notes hinted at research beyond the boundaries of conventional psychiatry. Something outside his comprehension that nagged and annoyed him.

He continued to read. Thomas compared the information with what he found in his father's journal, some clarity emerged. The Temporal Displacement Experiment seemed to involve altering a subject's perception of time. It meant they could experience past events.

His thoughts raced. If this was true, it would revolutionize their profession. It would also advance our understanding of human consciousness as it relates to time. But what were the ethical implications that bothered his father so much, and Levi so little?

He thought of his own patients. Rhyse with his PTSD came to mind. How would he react if he were exposed to these types of immersive mental experiences? Allowing him to witness historical traumas firsthand.

A chill ran through him as he remembered his father's warnings about the destructive effects of their profession. Was this what he'd meant? Was this what led to their dysfunctional relationship?

The phone on the desk rang. He was sure it was Eleanor again. She was the only one with this number. He stared at it, torn between the past and his responsibilities in the present. With a heavy sigh, he reached for it, knowing he couldn't ignore his family any longer.

Bauer moved to answer. His eyes caught on the last phrase in his father's notes: "I am bothered by Subject Alpha's promising progress —"

Bauer's hand froze midair. Dr. Levi's "Subject Alpha?" References to that man came up once or twice at the hospital in discussions about Case 47.

Levi was the one who developed the research protocols for this Temporal Displacement Theory. But if the ethics of the study bothered his father, why would he allow it to continue?

His mind raced. What had they unleashed? And why was it all kept secret?

The phone continued to ring on his desk. Bauer knew he was on the verge of something monumental. These were more than urban legends about Saint Elizabeths Hospital. As more information came in, the puzzle revealed a few answers.

He picked up the handset. Eleanor's tone was full of concern. Something about Simon. He tried to listen, but failed to hear a single word. The call ended.

The papers spread out before him trapped his attention. His gut told him that this information could change everything. Not just for him, but to advance his profession and human consciousness. Somewhere in the back of his mind, a small voice whispered "I must find the missing research".

Thomas sat across from his mother at the kitchen table. His fingers drummed an anxious rhythm on the worn wood. The aroma of tea filled the air. It did little to ease the tension between them.

He'd avoided this conversation for days, wrestling with the decision to involve her. His growing obsession with Case 47 was becoming more challenging. But the burning questions demanded answers. He hoped his mother might know something that would unlock more of the mysteries surrounding his father's work.

"Mom," He began, his voice hesitant. "I need to ask you something about dad."

Her eyes engaged with his. "Of course, dear. What would you like to know?"

"It's about his research at the hospital."

Edyth's hand paused midway to her mouth. The tea cup trembled. She set it down, her eyes narrowed with concern. "I know little, but I will answer what I can, Thomas?"

Bauer took a deep breath. "I've been going through some of Dad's old papers in his study. There are many references to Case 47 and a Subject Alpha. It seems to involve some kind of experimental research he did with Dr. Levi."

The color drained from her face. She pushed her chair back from the table. The legs scraped hard against the floor. "Son, I don't think... "

"Mom," He interrupted, leaning forward. "I need to know what research dad was involved in. It could be important for my work at Saint Elizabeths."

Edyth stood, turning her back to him as she busied herself with something on the counter. "Your father's studies are in the past. It's best left there."

Thomas felt a flicker of frustration. "But these experiments—they are groundbreaking. If I could understand what they were working on... "

"No!" Her voice was sharp as she whirled around to face him. "Thomas, I'm warning you. Drop this. There are dangers there beyond your comprehension."

He stared at his mother, taken aback by the assertiveness in her tone. He'd never seen her like this before. "What do you mean? What is it you aren't telling me?"

Edyth's shoulders sagged, and she leaned all her weight against the counter. "Son, please listen. You must let this go. Your father—he had legitimate reasons for keeping his work secret."

Frustration and determination warred within him. He'd come too far on his own to back down now. "I need answers. What was Case 47? What were Dad and Levi doing? It's clear you know something. Why won't you tell me?"

Her eyes glistened. "You're not ready for the truth. It's a very complicated matter."

"Then help me understand!" He insisted, his voice rising. "I'm not a child anymore, Mom. I can handle whatever it is you're not telling me."

For a long moment, silence hung heavy between them. Her gaze searched Thomas' face as she weighed her decision. She sighed, her shoulders slumped in defeat.

"There's more," she refused to look at him. "More information about their work. In the attic."

"Where? What's up there?"

His mom whispered. "Papers. Journals. Things your father couldn't bring himself to destroy, but couldn't bear to look at any more."

He took a step towards her. "Why? What was so terrible about this research?"

His mother's eyes met his, filled with a mixture of fear and resignation. "The experiments, Thomas. They had catastrophic consequences."

Bauer felt a chill run through him. "Like what?"

Edyth shook her head. "I've already told you too much. It is clear you're determined to pursue this, against both our wishes. You've inherited your father's stubbornness. I can't stop you from doing what you're going to do. But son, I'm begging you, be careful. There are certain things in this world that you should not mess with."As she tried to explain, a strange sensation came over him. Everything around him became blurred. He blinked several times and found himself someplace different. The vision was odd, yet had startling clarity. But this was not his memory. It was nothing he'd ever experienced or witnessed before.

He saw a dim laboratory. There was unfamiliar equipment lining the walls. In the center stood two men. One was a younger version of his father. The other man was tall and intense. Thomas assumed it must be Levi. They were arguing, their voices raised in heated debate.

"This can't continue, Matthias!" his father shouted, his face contorted with anger and fear. "The risks are too great!"

Dr. Levi's eyes blazed with a demonstrative glare. "I can't stop now! There is still a lot you don't understand, Harold."

The vision changed, and Bauer experienced flashes of a different moment - a subject strapped to a chair, writhing in apparent agony. The scene shifted again. Now he saw Levi hunched over a desk in the lab. He was scribbling like a madman in a journal. His expression was fierce, yet unreadable.

As quickly as it had come, the vision was gone. He was now back in his mother's kitchen, gasping for breath. Edyth was staring at him, worried.

"Thomas? Are you alright?" she asked, reaching to touch his arm.

He flinched and pulled away, his mind disoriented. "I—I'm fine," he muttered. "I just need some air."

Without waiting for a response, he stumbled out of the room and down the hall to his father's study. His heart pounded, and his hands shook as he closed the door behind him. He hadn't had one of those episodes since he was a kid. Were those memories?

If they were, they weren't his. But everything was so real, so vivid.

As he tried to collect himself, Bauer noticed the blinking light on the answering machine. Again, there were several missed calls from Eleanor. Without thinking, he pressed play on the voicemail.

Eleanor's voice, tight with worry, filled the room. "Thomas, it's me. Simon's very sick. He's running a high fever, and the doctor wants to run tests. I've been trying to reach you for hours. Please call me back as soon as you get this."

Bauer's first instinct was concern for his son. He weighed the urgency of his son's situation against what had just happened. What had he just experienced? Did it have anything to do with his dad or Levi?

Without conscious effort, he dialed Eleanor's number. When she answered, her voice was a mixture of relief and frustration.

"Thomas, what took so long? Did you get my messages? Simon's... "

"I got your voicemail," He interrupted. "How is he?"

"He's stable, but they want to keep him overnight for observation. Where have you been? I've been trying to reach you all day!"

Bauer hesitated. "I've been working on something important. A breakthrough in my research."

There was a pause on the other end of the line. When Eleanor spoke again, her tone was bitter. "A breakthrough? Thomas, your son is in the hospital, and you're worried about your damn research?"

"It's not just work, Ele," He continued. His voice rose. "This is revolutionary. It could change everything we know about the human mind and consciousness."

"I don't care if it's the cure for cancer!" She shouted. "Your child needs you. He's scared, and he's asking for you. How can you be so callous?"

His overwhelming obsession to find out what had just happened to him extinguished the slight flicker of guilt in him. "Eleanor, you don't understand. What I'm working on... this is bigger than just me or him. It could have implications for everyone."

"I can't believe what I'm hearing," She said, her voice trembling with anger and fear. "You know what? Don't bother coming. Simon doesn't need to see you. Not like this. When you decide you are ready to be a father again, Thomas, let me know!"

The line went dead. Bauer sat in silence. He knew he should feel worse about the argument and the neglect of his son. But all he could think about was the vision he'd just experienced, and the many questions that remained unanswered in his head.

The dim light of the lamp cast long shadows across the room. His fingers trembled as he held a worn envelope with his name on it. He'd discovered it tucked away under the false bottom of the locked desk drawer. The paper was fragile, like it might crumble in his hands. With a deep breath, he opened it:

My Dear Thomas,

If you're reading this, it means I'm not here to protect you from the truth. I've agonized over whether to leave this letter, knowing that my words might only push you further—the same curiosity that nearly destroyed others, myself included.

First, I must apologize for the emotional distance I maintained during your late teens. It was never a lack of love. I now regret my actions. My own misguided attempts to shield you, may have resulted in the opposite of my intentions. My attempts to dissuade you from this profession have failed, and for that, I am sorry.

Thomas, you need to fully understand the gravity of what you're pursuing. The work Levi and I have done — is not just groundbreaking, it's earth-shattering. And like any force powerful enough to reshape our understanding of reality, it comes with terrible risks and great danger.

I've seen brilliant minds consumed by obsession. Their humanity becomes eroded by the relentless pursuit of knowledge. Dr. Levi himself was a victim of his own obsessions — he wasn't the only one. The price of our hubris was always obvious to me.

Others were too drunk on discovery and the potential to recognize what I knew to be wrong. Our contributions to advance the field of psychiatry have been more detrimental than beneficial. It's unclear if the harm we've caused can be reversed or rectified.

I implore you, son: be cautious. The answers you seek come with more questions. They will also introduce you to more danger than you can imagine. Don't let the allure of your quest blind you.

Remember that there are things in this world far more important than scientific achievement or advancement. Your family, your own physical and mental well-being — these are the true measures of a life well-lived.

I love you, Thomas. I always have, even when I struggled to show it. Whatever you choose, going forward, do not proceed in haste. Please know that I am forever proud of you and of the man you've become.

With all my love and deepest regrets,

Dad

Bauer's vision blurred as he finished reading. A flood of emotions welled up in his eyes and flowed down his cheek. The bitterness towards his father shifted. He folded the paper.

Just as he was about to return the letter to the drawer, his phone rang, startling him. Eleanor again, he thought as he reached for the handset.

"Hello?"

A distorted voice crackled through the line. It was familiar, yet still unrecognizable.

"Dr. Bauer, I understand you've been looking for answers about Case 47."

Bauer's heart raced. "Who is this? How did you get this number?"

"Who I am and how I got your number is irrelevant," the man continued, ignoring his questions. "What matters is that I have what you want. The truth about the experiments, about Subject Alpha, and more."

His knuckles turned white as they gripped the phone. "Why should I believe you?"

A low chuckle came through the line. "Because, I was there. I saw things that weren't meant for my eyes. I know what they did. And I can show you too. But this knowledge will cost you."

"Cost me what?" Thomas asked, in a whisper.

"That remains to be seen," the cryptic man replied. "Are you prepared to sacrifice everything for the truth, Dr. Bauer? Your career, your family, perhaps even your sanity?"

Bauer's mind reeled. He thought of his son in the hospital, of Eleanor's anger, of his mother's warnings. Even with all of that, he felt like a moth drawn to a flame.

"I — I need to know," he said, his voice shaking.

"Very well. Sunday night. Midnight. Come alone to the archives of Saint Elizabeths. You'll find your first answers there."

The line went dead, leaving him stunned. Thomas stared at the phone, then at his father's letter. The weight of his decision settled in his neck and shoulders. He had several days to learn as much as he could before meeting with the mysterious caller. There was no turning back now.

Chapter 19

Bauer sat surrounded by stacks of papers, journals, and photographs. The desk lamp cast long shadows late into the night. He'd found bits and pieces about Levi, his father, and hints about Case 47.

With his meeting looming, he felt an urgent need to make better sense of what he had. He spread the documents he had across an expansive tabletop. He added new items to the corkboard in a chronological order. His eyes scanned over dates, names, and cryptic notes. As he worked, more patterns emerged. One left him baffled.

The information on Dr. Matthias Levi was extensive, detailing his work and life until his sudden disappearance in 1964. Thomas could trace Levi's career from his younger years in Vienna, through his controversial research, and right up to his last known days at Saint Elizabeths. But his dad's timeline had a large glaring gap.

Bauer stepped back, rubbing his tired eyes. He'd been over these documents several times. Seeing them laid out in order, the inconsistencies become apparent. Harold Bauer's personal notes were absent before the middle of November 1963. How could that be?

He reached for his coffee mug. He grimaced as he swallowed the cold, bitter brew. The clock on the wall chimed, reminding him of the time. Bauer couldn't shake the feeling that this gap in his Harold's work was significant. It wasn't random; there was something deliberate about it that nagged him.

Leaning forward, he shuffled through papers again, hoping to find something he overlooked. But the result was the same. Plenty of information on

Levi, a wealth of hints about the case itself, but nothing of his father's contributions before that pivotal moment in late 1963.

Had his father only become involved at that point? But that made little sense, given how close the two men were. Had Harold destroyed or hidden his earlier notes? The questions continued to multiply.

He stood there, stretching his stiff body. Thomas walked over to the window. Moonlight bathed the serene landscape outside. It contrasted with the turmoil occupying his head. As he stared out into the night, Bauer knew there had to be more.

He needed to understand Temporal Displacement? What were they doing with unethical research? What caused his father's sudden involvement and Levi's disappearance? It all had to be connected somehow.

He rubbed his tired eyes, glancing at the clock. It was well past midnight. It was time to call it a night. His overwhelmed brain couldn't handle any more. He gave up for the night.

The next morning, Thomas pushed open his office door. His shoulders sagged at the sight that greeted him. The room was still a mess from the previous day. He sighed, running his hand through his hair as he looked around.

There was no point in cleaning it until he could ensure the security of his space. Glancing at his watch, he realized he had twenty minutes before his first session. Just enough time to tackle his most pressing issue.

Bauer reached into his briefcase and pulled out the bag from the hardware store. He pulled the contents and the instructions the clerk had given him. He'd never done handyman stuff like this. He wasn't going to wait for administration and maintenance to get it done.

He read through his notes once again, then got to work. He followed his notes step by step. His fingers fumbled with the tools. He felt accomplished as he tightened the last screw into place.

The doorknob was identical in design as the previous one. Only the locking mechanism inside was different. The turning of the lock was comforting. His office was secure again. Now he wouldn't have to worry about someone getting in when he wasn't around.

A knock sounded at the door. Thomas pocketed the key. He gathered up the screwdrivers and packaging and shoved them into a drawer. He took a deep breath, straightened his tie, and opened the door to see Olivia Kendrick standing there.

"Dr. Bauer, your first patient is ready for you." She said,

"Thank you. I'll be there in a minute."

The hours passed in a blur of sessions and paperwork. He found it difficult to focus. Like his office, his mind was a mess. Each time he returned, he picked up bits and pieces and put them away.

When he returned from his last session of the day, he shut the door behind him. He closed his eyes and pressed his back against the solid surface. His breath escaped long and slow. When Bauer's eyes opened again, the chaos was still there. He had to get this room cleaned up and functional again.

He started with the documents pulled from his filing cabinet. He gathered them in loose piles based on where they needed to go. Most of it was mundane: patient information, administrative memos, and research notes for past or future projects. Bauer sifted through a stack of papers from beneath his overturned wastepaper basket. A yellowed newspaper clipping caught his attention.

"Prominent Psychiatrist Vanishes Without a Trace." The article, dated 1964, detailed the sudden mysterious disappearance of Dr. Matthias Levi from Saint Elizabeths Hospital and the Washington, DC area.

"What the hell is this doing in here?" He murmured under his breath. He'd never seen it before. His intruder must have left it in his trash can?

His heart raced as he did a quick scan of the rest of the text. The official story was that the psychiatric researcher took an unexpected leave of absence for personal reasons. As Bauer read on, inconsistencies jumped out at him. The dates didn't align with what he knew from his father's notes. There were vague references to projects, but not a single word about Case 47.

The most intriguing part was a quote from the hospital administrator. He claimed the man had left his research materials behind. Thomas knew this statement was only half true. He discovered some of Levi's work in the study, which was dated long after the reported disappearance.

This was more than just a story about a man walking away from his career. The discrepancies in the article suggested a deliberate attempt to cover up something. But what and why? And who was doing it?

Glancing around to ensure he was alone, he slipped the newspaper clipping into his briefcase. He couldn't risk leaving it here, even with the new lock on his door. He needed time to study and compare it with what he had at home.

He went back to his cleaning. Bauer's movements became more efficient. He paid more attention to his work. This wasn't just a not just a matter of tidying up his office. Maybe there were more things left behind by his unwelcomed visitor.

He found loads of overlooked information and documents he hadn't seen in months. Thomas emptied drawers and examined their contents. He flipped and shook books in case they concealed some hidden, yet related anecdote.

There, between the filing cabinet and wall, was a manila envelope. It was unmarked and unsealed. It appeared to be stuffed there, intending to be forgotten. He opened it.

He pulled out a photograph, its edges were worn and colors faded with age. Bauer froze as he looked. It defied explanation, challenging everything he thought he knew about his father and Dr. Levi.

The image showed Dr. Levi standing in a bustling 1920s American speakeasy. He was an adult, dressed in period-appropriate clothing. His face was unmistakable. Thomas flipped the photo over, searching for any notation, but the back was blank.

He lifted the manila envelope again and turned it over in his hands a few times. He'd never seen this package or this picture before. He looked again. It seemed authentic.

This was not some elaborate decorations at a costume party. He knew what was true, but the image left him conflicted. He placed it back in the envelope and shook his head. This photo was impossible.

Levi was born in Vienna in 1907. By the time prohibition ended in America, the man would only be twenty-three years old. He didn't even come to the United States until 1945. Yet in this photo, Levi looked like a man in his mid forties. Things he thought he understood now didn't make sense.

A quick look at the clock told him it was later than he thought. It was time to get out of there and process what he'd discovered. He shoved the photos back into its envelope. Then he placed it on top of the newspaper clipping, secured the door, and left.

The drive home was a blur. He checked his mirrors often. No one followed him today. Bauer's thoughts soon became preoccupied.

Edyth greeted him with a warm smile as he entered the house. Thomas failed to acknowledge her. He mumbled something about work, then headed straight for the study. His briefcase was clutched tight in his hand.

Bauer locked the door. He pulled the stuff he found at work. Then he grabbed his notes from the previous night. It was all connected somehow; he was sure of it.

As he was about to dive back into his father's journal, a folded piece of paper from the envelope caught his eye. As he unfolded it, he recognized his dad's neat handwriting. It was a list of names, some crossed out, others circled. Bauer's eyes scanned the page. Thomas didn't recognize most of the people. But one stood out. There, near the bottom, was a name he knew, Sam Harris. Harold Bauer underlined it, as if to emphasize it.

Thomas leaned back in the chair, his mind a whirlwind of conflicted thoughts and emotions. His mother's warnings about what was in the attic mingled with the tantalizing promise of answers from the mysterious caller. He rubbed his temples.

The sudden ring of the phone pulled him from his reverie. It had to be Eleanor again. Guilt flooded over him. He'd been so wrapped up in this stuff that he blew her off the last time they talked.

"Hello?" he answered, his tone betraying his exhaustion.

"Thomas?" Eleanor's voice was tight with worry. "We need to talk. It's about Simon."

Bauer sat up straighter. Something parental stirred in him. "Is he okay?"

"He's home from the hospital. They couldn't find anything wrong with him. He woke up in the middle of the night, he — he had a nightmare."

"What was it about?"

"He woke up crying, talking about being in the trenches in Germany during World War I. He described the smell of gunpowder, the sound of shells exploding. It was so detailed. The look in his eyes. Thomas, it scares me. He told me things that were impossible for him to know."

Bauer's mind raced. The dream sounded like his own recent experience. Could it be a coincidence? A chill ran through him as he considered the implications.

"How long has this been going on?" he asked, trying to keep his tone steady.

"They just started last night," Eleanor replied. "At first, I thought it was just his imagination. But each one is more intense, and more frequent. He's not sleeping well, and I'm worried about it affecting his schoolwork if it continues."

Bauer closed his eyes, shaking his head.

"Thomas?" Eleanor's voice broke through his thoughts. "Do you know anything about this?"

He hesitated, unsure of how much to reveal. "I—I'm not sure, Ele. But I promise you and Simon, I'm going to figure it out."

He reassured her that he would come by to see them the next day after work. The call ended. He sat in silence for a long time.

The possibility of Levi and his father's experiments having some sort of hereditary link was both fascinating and terrifying. If his son was experiencing vivid historical dreams, what did that mean for his son's future? For his mental health?

Bauer's eyes fell on the scattered papers and photographs on the table across the room. The mysterious caller promised answers, but what would it cost him? He had to keep this from his loved ones. He would not risk endangering his family because of this.

Chapter 20

Files and papers lay everywhere. Evidence of his exhaustive search. The room didn't look all that different from his work office after the last break-in. Bauer stood up straight, stretching his stiff back. He walked over to the bookshelf, running his fingers along the spines of old medical texts and journals. His eyes caught on a gap between two books, just wide enough for a thin folder. Heart racing, he reached for it, but found only dust. "Damn it," he muttered, slamming his palm against the shelf. The sound boomed through the quiet room. He'd spent hours in here, combing through every inch of the room. He opened drawers and rifled through papers. Case 47 was not here.

The phone on the desk rang. He hesitated for a moment before answering.

"Hello," his tone betrayed his frustration.

"Thomas," Eleanor's voice was tight with worry. "I need to talk to you—"

"About Simon?"

"No, about you."

Bauer sighed as he pinched the bridge of his nose. "What do you mean?"

"You've been more distracted than I've ever seen you since you moved into your mother's place."

"I've just been busy… "

"This isn't just about work," Eleanor cut him off. "Your son was in the hospital last week, and you didn't even care."

Guilt flooded his head. "I'm sorry."

"The doctor says there's nothing wrong with him. All his tests came back normal."

"That's good."

"No, it's not. His nightmares are getting worse. I do not know how to help him."

Bauer's words caught in his throat. Simon's dreams were becoming more intense. Just like his father described in his journal. "I apologize, I didn't realize they were that bad," he said.

"What do you mean by that? Do you know what this is about?" Eleanor's voice cracked. "I'm worried about our son, and you. You're acting just like—just like your father before…"

She trailed off, but Bauer knew what she meant. His father's obsession with work drove him to the brink of madness.

"It's not like that, Ele," Thomas insisted, as a hint of doubt crept into his mind. "I've been working on something important. Something that may help Simon."

"How?" Eleanor demanded. "By neglecting him? By getting lost in some research that's affecting you and us?"

He opened his mouth to respond, but a knock at the study door interrupted him. "I have to go," he said. "I'll call you back."

He hung up the phone, then turned to face the door. "Come in."

Edyth entered. She looked at the mess in the room, shaking her head. He'd seen that look of concern before. "Thomas, I want to talk."

Bauer tensed, recognizing the tone in her voice. "About what?" he asked.

Edyth's eyes softened. "About this," she gestured to the chaos in the room. "About how you've been spending every free moment in here, just like your father used to do."

"I'm not like him," he said, sharper than he intended. "This is important work."

"Is it worth neglecting what's most meaningful?" Edyth asked. "You haven't spent a minute with your son since you moved in here. You don't eat, and you aren't getting enough sleep."

The words hit Bauer like a gut punch. "You don't understand," he said, his voice low. "There's something here, something Dad and Levi were working on. It's possible that there's a connection between what's been happening to Simon and what they were researching.

Edyth's eyes widened at the mention of Dr. Levi's name. "Thomas," she said, "your father's and Matthias' work — it didn't end well. You know that, right?"

"They were onto something?" He pressed. "Research that could help with his nightmares."

Edyth shook her head with a pained expression. "Listen to yourself. You've become your father. He too believed that he could change the world. But it cost him his relationship with me and you."

He felt a surge of defiance. "This is different," he insisted. "This will not consume me like it did dad. I'm close to figuring it out mom. I can feel it."

"And then what?" She asked. "What happens when and if you 'figure it out'? Do you think that will fix everything? You are running out of time, Thomas."

Her statement surprised him. "Out of time?"

"Yes, you're losing time with your sweet boy, your wife, me. Time you will never get back."

Her words struck a chord. "You don't understand," he repeated. "I can't stop now."

His mother sighed, her shoulders sagged. "I know more than you think I do. Your father did this too. Please don't let this destroy you. Don't repeat his mistakes."

Bauer turned away, unable to meet her gaze. "It won't," his tone was firm. "I know what I'm doing."

He heard Edyth's soft footsteps as she approached him. Her hand touched his shoulder. "Be careful, son. Don't lose sight of what's truly important." With that, she left the study, closing the door behind her.

He stood there in the chaos of his research. Papers covered every surface, journals displayed scribbles in their margins Her words replayed in his head. He rubbed his tired eyes, trying to focus on the task at hand. Organizing his findings seemed like a good idea, but now he was overwhelmed by the sheer volume of information.

His own half-finished notes and diagrams sat near one of many stacks of documents. His father's leather-bound pages laid open on the desktop. The series of random, meaningless doodles had a definite regularity. Unlike himself, his father was always meticulous in recording data pertaining to his work. Thomas had no reason to believe that what those pages contained would be more of the same.

The elusive code he lifted from the journal looked different from this distance and angle. It taunted him. Driven by curiosity, he collected his notes for further examination. His eyes scanned through the letters, numbers, and symbols scrawled in the margins.

The world around him faded away. His focus fixed on the puzzle before him. A word jumped off the page at him. He looked at a few more words. *Unermesslich gefährlich. Zeitverschiebung instabil.* A victorious triumph came over him. His father had written his code upside down and backwards in his native tongue, German!

Bauer now understood what he was looking at:

"Case 47 - Dangerous beyond measure. Temporal displacement is unstable. Subjects experiencing severe psychological trauma far exceeding baseline levels. Levi is pushing boundaries of ethics and sanity. It must stop. Destroy all evidence."

This was penned by a man filled with fear. His father knew the dangers Case 47 presented. Did he try to end the study? If he did, he failed. He knew the research had continued long past the date noted in the article.

As Thomas translated more of the coded note, the full weight of the message sank in. The warning was now clear as day: pursuing this further could have dire consequences. He thought of Simon's nightmares, and his own. They both witnessed incredible, vivid historical details that no living person could know. What was the connection?

For the first time since he'd begun his search for Case 47, Bauer felt overwhelmed by doubt and concern. He glanced at the half-buried photo of Simon on the desk, his son's joyous smile frozen in time. There's no way his father could know the effects of their work on future generations.

By continuing, was he risking more than his own safety? Was he also putting others in danger?

He stood up. The wheels on his chair protested as they moved against the floor. He paced the length of the study. The responsible thing to do now would be to stop, to destroy the evidence as his father had tried to do. If he did, he could focus on being a better father for his son, on repairing his relationship with Eleanor, and on spending more time with his mother.

And yet, he knew he'd only scratched the surface. If there was even a hint of truth to the rumors swirling around Case 47, the research was as incredible as it was dangerous. He knew there was more to it.

The push to continue was intoxicating. He'd already found more than he ever thought possible. He now knew things about his father he never would have known. Could he walk away now?

Bauer caught sight of himself. His dim-lit reflection obscured the picture behind the glass. He didn't recognize the man staring back at him. Dark circles below his eyes aged him. His disheveled hair made him look like a madman. His once starched dress shirt hung loose on his frame, filled with wrinkles after hours of sitting hunched over a desk. If he hadn't been living with his mother, who knows how long he would have gone without a proper meal?

As he studied his face, Bauer saw his father in the intense focus of his eyes. His father had spent countless nights locked away in here, emerging only for an occasional bite to eat or brief interaction with others. However, that was where the similarities ended. His physical appearance and the neglect of personal care embarrassed him.

The parallels were undeniable and terrifying. Was he destined to repeat his father's mistakes? Would he continue to lose himself in pursuit of answers? It had already impacted everyone around him.

He closed his eyes. Something had to change. He needed a different approach. His search for truth could not take priority over his responsibilities to family and patients.

He turned his eyes away from the reflection looking back at him. Bauer's gaze swept over the cluttered room. He would organize his findings and to adopt his dad's methodical methods rather than continuing with his frantic obsession. He would set strict limits on his after-hours work time. Make sure he carved out time for Simon, Eleanor, and his mother.

He began gathering the scattered papers. A new plan was beginning to take shape. He would continue his investigation. Thomas would learn from his father's and Levi's mistakes. He would not repeat them.

Bauer sat at the desk. His revised determination was now strengthened by his recent epiphany. He pulled out a fresh yellow notepad, ready to move forward with renewed focus and discipline. He had a full page of ideas written when his phone rang.

He answered it without hesitation.

"Hello," he said, his tone was strong and steady.

"Listen carefully," a distorted voice crackled through the speaker. "You're in danger. You're not the only one searching for Case 47."

Bauer's grip tightened. "Who is this? What do you know about—"

"There's no time," the man cut him off. "They're getting closer. You need to get to it before they do. The consequences if they get there first—" The caller's words trailed off, leaving the threat unfinished.

"Who are 'they'?" Bauer pressed. "What consequences?"

"I can't say any more now. Watch your back, doctor. I will see you Sunday night."

The line went dead. He stared at the phone. The call confirmed his fear and suspicions. There was more to Case 47 than the legends and rumors suggested. But who else was looking for it?

Thomas felt better about changing the lock on his office door at work. He made a deliberate choice to keep his findings away from the Saint Elizabeths. It was almost 11:00 PM, but he turned back to his notepad. He was determined to finish his new plan.

He drew a column down the center of the page. On one side, he listed his professional and personal obligations: his shifts at the hospital, planned time with Simon, dinner with his mother. On the other, he outlined steps in his investigation.

There would be no more late nights obsessing over every scrap of paper he found. As he worked, Thomas felt a familiar surge of adrenaline. But unlike before, he was in control. He wouldn't let this consume him. He'd find Case 47, uncover the truth his father and Dr. Levi had buried, and he'd do it on his own terms.

The next morning, Bauer arrived at the hospital earlier than usual. He nodded a greeting to the night staff as they finished their shift. He concentrated on his day ahead. He had forty-five minutes until his first appointment, he intended not to waste it.

In his office, he locked the door and pulled the blinds. He couldn't shake his paranoia. The caller's warning echoed through his mind. From his pocket, he retrieved the notes he'd compiled the previous night.

The first thing he needed to do was learn more about Sam Harris. There had to be a reason the man was everywhere he turned. He began with human resources, searching for anything that connected the mysterious man with his father, or Dr. Levi.

Bauer knew the man had been at Saint Elizabeths for decades. He was the longest tenured employee at the hospital. However, his personnel file was thin. It lacked the usual performance reviews and disciplinary documentation one would expect from such a long career.

The doctor reached for the hospital's current staff directory. He looked for Harris' contact information. Thomas shook his head. The old man's name was not there. He returned the files to their rightful places and walked back to his office.

There was so much he still needed to learn. His father's journals told him nothing about the old man. Yet, there he was, puttering around the hospital, pushing his cart day in and day out. He had even confronted him just a few days ago about the break-ins. Something wasn't right.

A knock at the door startled him from his thoughts. Bauer shoved his notes from home into his pocket, "Come in."

The door opened to reveal Nurse Kendrick. Her usual warm smile was gone. She looked concerned.

"Thomas, is everything alright?" she asked, looking at the mess as she stepped into his office. "You've been so distracted."

He forced a grin. "I'm fine, Olivia. Overwhelmed by some personal matters. Nothing work related."

She didn't look convinced. "You know you can talk to me if you need to, right? As a friend, not just a colleague."

"Thank you, I appreciate that," he said, touched by her concern. "I'm okay. Just working through some things."

She nodded. Her eyes continued to display a hint of worry. "Alright. But don't forget to take care of yourself, Thomas. We can't help our patients if we're not at our best."

As she turned to leave, a thought struck him. "Olivia, wait. Actually I could use your assistance with something."

She paused, turning back to face him. "What do you need?"

He hesitated for a moment, weighing his words. "You know Sam Harris?"

"Yes, of course." Olivia's brow furrowed as she nodded. "Why do you ask?"

"Just trying to track down some old records," he said, keeping his tone casual. "I thought it might be nice to do something in recognition of all the years he's worked here, but he doesn't seem to be in my current staff directory."

"That's odd," she mused. "He's been here so long, he should be in there. Have you checked with Human Resources?"

"Not yet." Bauer lied. "I want this to be a surprise."

"Do you want me to check around?" Olivia offered. "I'll be discreet, of course."

"That would be great, thanks," he said, relieved to have another pair of eyes in his search efforts. "Let me know if you find anything."

The doctor glanced at his watch. His next appointment was in a few minutes. Thomas took a deep breath to center himself. He had made a promise to maintain balance, and he intended to keep it.

Chapter 21

Bauer made his way past a nurses' station. A calendar hung on the wall. It was Friday. He just needed to keep his cool for a few more hours, then he could get out of there.

The anxiety of being watched had become a constant over the last several days. Conversations in hushed tones were no longer dismissible as simple paranoia. This was a byproduct of his recent discoveries, the mysterious phone calls, and his upcoming secret meeting.

As he passed, he caught a fragment of whispers.

"Olivia told me Dr. Bauer was asking her about Sam Harris."

"That's odd. Why?"

Thomas paused near the patients' charts, pretending to look through them. He strained to hear more of their conversation without being noticed.

"I don't know. He sure has been acting strange the last few weeks."

"Well, he had that emergency at home right about then."

"Yeah, what was that all about?"

"Who knows? He's never talked about it with anyone here."

"Whatever it is, I think the pressure is getting to him."

A burst of loud, maniacal laughter from a nearby patient room drowned out the rest of the exchange. Bauer's jaw clenched as he left. He didn't tell her their earlier discussion was to stay between them. However, he never once considered it would go any further.

It seemed odd that no one knew a lot about the old man. He almost never called in sick. Four or five days a week, Harris was here wheeling his cart around the hospital. The doctor shook his head and turned toward the cafeteria for some much-needed coffee. He noticed a small group of staff members huddled near a vending machine. Their conversation stopped as he approached. Awkward smiles and nods greeted him.

"Dr. Bauer," one nurse acknowledged, her tone too cheerful to be genuine. "How are you doing today?"

"Fine, thank you," he replied through a forced smile. He felt their eyes on him as he filled his cup. Their silence spoke volumes.

As he turned to leave, he overheard someone mutter, "The man's been through a lot. It's no wonder he's acting so strange. I feel for him. That kind of pressure isn't healthy."

Bauer's grip tightened around his mug. It took everything within him to not respond. He wanted to explain the reasons for his behavior, that he wasn't losing his mind. But who would believe him? Hospital security and administrators thought he'd ransacked his own personal space the week before. Would the truth dispel whatever rumors were circulating?

Throughout the day, similar scenes seemed to play out on repeat. Hushed conversations ended when he entered a room. Concerned glances from colleagues. Even a few of his interactions with patients were odd. Their eyes searched for some sign of instability.

The doctor retreated to the privacy of his office for a moment to regroup and prepare for his next appointment. The phone on his desk rang. His hand reached to answer.

"Dr. Bauer speaking."

"Tom? It's Andrew."

"Oh hey, it's good to hear your voice,"

"It's been a while since we last talked. How have you been?" His cheerful tone came through the line.

He leaned back in his chair, his eyes darting around the room. "I've been — managing," he replied, being careful with his words.

"Right, of course. How are things now? Did you find a place to stay?"

Recalling conversations from a few weeks ago his knuckles turned white. Andrew's questions seemed innocent, but he wasn't about to have a repeat of his conversation with Frank. "I found something." He deflected. "It's temporary, but it'll work for now."

"That's great to hear," Andrew said. "Listen, if you need anything, just let me know. The guys and gals from the group would be more than happy to pitch in."

Bauer's instinct was to refuse the help outright, but he forced himself to pause and sound grateful. "I appreciate that, but I think I've got stuff under control for now."

"Alright. But the offer always stands, okay?"

"Thank you," Thomas said, then changed the subject. "Hey, I'm sorry again about missing the last meeting. I know everyone was looking forward to my presentation."

A chuckle came through the phone. "Don't worry about it, Tom. Things happen."

There was a brief silence. He could almost hear Andrew shifting gears. "Oh, while I've got you on the line, I was hoping you could help me with something."

Bauer tensed. "Oh?"

"Yeah, we're putting together that reenactment project at Saint Elizabeths in a few weeks. I was wondering if you could please get me some reference materials."

Bauer's heart rate quickened. The archives? He was trying to avoid going there until his meeting. It was where someone had watched him. The place where things didn't add up. How could he refuse without arousing suspicion?

Andrew explained what he needed.

"That's quite a request."

"I know it's a lot to ask," His friend said. "But you are the only one who has access, and the information would be awesome to have. I hope you don't mind."

"No, no," he interrupted, his mind racing. "It's no trouble at all. I'd be happy to get them for you before I leave. Things have been—busy so I'm not sure what time that will be."

"Of course. No rush. Whenever it's convenient, will be fine."

He nodded, even though he was on the phone. "Alright. I'll see what I can find for you."

"Thanks, Tom. I appreciate your help. And remember, if you need anything, just let me know."

"I will," Bauer lied. "Take care, Andrew."

As he ended the call, his head rested against the back of his chair, closing his eyes. He didn't want to go to the archives. He opened his eyes and looked at his schedule for the rest of the day. His trip would have to wait until he was done with his next two appointments. With a deep sigh, Thomas headed out of his office door.

The doctor settled into a seat, notebook in hand. His patient entered the therapy room. Rhyse Scott flopped into the seat across from him. The man's eyes darted around, never quite settling on anything for too long.

"Good afternoon," the psychiatrist said, in a welcoming tone. He remembered how fast a past session escalated. "How have you been?"

The man shrugged, his fingers tapping an erratic rhythm on the armrest. "Same ol' stuff, Doc. Nightmares, flashbacks, the usual. They never stop."

The psychiatrist nodded, jotting down a few notes. "I see. Has the new medication been helpful?"

"Yeah, I guess," the patient muttered. "It helps sometimes, but other times —" His voice trailed off, his gaze fixated on something behind the doctor.

Following a quick glance over his shoulder, Bauer issued a gentle prompt. "You were saying?"

Rhyse's attention snapped back to Bauer's face. A strange intensity had settled in his eyes. "They're different from my regular nightmares. In these ones, I'm not even here or back in Kuwait. I'm somewhere else. In another war zone, but I don't know where."

Thomas leaned forward, his interest piqued. "Can you elaborate on what you experienced, Rhyse?"

The young man shifted in his seat. "Hard to explain, Doc. Have you ever felt like you were living someone else's life? Like you were there, even though that'd be impossible?"

Thomas sat up in his chair. The man's words were reminiscent of visions he and Simon had and some notes he'd found in his father's study about temporal displacement. He forced himself to maintain a neutral expression. "That must have been an intense experience. How many times has this happened?"

The man shook his head. "Not often, but when it does, it's — I'm there, you know? In some other time, some other place, in some other body."

Thomas' hand hovered over his notepad. Was this related to Case 47? Or was it just a coincidence? He cleared his throat. "These experiences you're describing—"

"It's funny," Rhyse interrupted, a wry smile twisted on his lips. "I always thought this kind of time travel stuff was only in sci-fi books and movies. But sometimes, I wonder —"

His heart skipped a beat. "Time travel?"

The patient leaned forward, his voice dropping to a whisper. "Yeah, like what they were working on here, back in the day. You know, the secrets and all that."

The doctor's grip on his pen tightened. "I'm not sure I follow. What are you talking about?"

The young man's eyes narrowed. "Come on, Doc. You work here. You must have heard the stories. About the guys who tried to send people's minds back in time. I think it was Case 47, or somethin' like that?"

For a moment, Thomas forgot how to breathe. His mind raced to process what Rhyse had just said. How did he know about Case 47? Was this some kind of demented test, or a trap?

Forcing himself to remain calm, he cleared his throat. "Where did you hear about these studies?"

Rhyse shrugged. He looked uncomfortable. "Rumors. You know? People talk. Especially in places like this." He gestured at the walls. "Anyway, it's probably all nonsense. Just my messed-up brain messin' with me."

The doctor nodded, trying to understand. "Um, right. Of course." He glanced down at his notes. His professional composure faltered. "Let's — Can we go back to your nightmares? You mentioned they've been persistent —"

As the hour progressed, Bauer struggled to remain focused on Rhyse. His mind was obsessed with Case 47. How much did he know? And who else might be privy to what he knew?

When the appointment ended, he watched the man leave with a mixture of feelings he could not identify. The psychiatrist slumped back in his chair, running a hand through his hair. The world felt heavier than ever. He glanced at the clock. One more patient, he muttered to himself.

The doctor returned to his office following his last session of the week. He tossed his notepad on the desk next to a handwritten reminder. Andrew's research materials still needed fetching. Even though his friend said "no rush," he knew better than to believe it. He was tired and ready to go home. The archives now seemed like a million miles away.

Bauer froze in place as a soft rustle caught his attention. Mice? Rats? He frowned, leaning forward to investigate the source of the noise. He looked down to see something being slipped under the door. His hand shook as he reached for the doorknob. With sudden force, it flew open, and he stepped out into the empty hall.

He threw his hands up in the air. Annoyed frustration replaced his fears. This insane cat-and-mouse game was getting old. Thomas returned to his office and locked the door. He then picked up the paper.

He unfolded the crisp white sheet. The message inside was brief, written in a script that very much resembled his dad's:

"Beware, Dr. Bauer. What you think is secret, is not. You aren't the only one searching for it. Proceed with caution."

Bauer's blood ran cold. He read it again. It was similar to the warning from the mysterious caller. How could anyone know what he was doing at his mother's home in his free time? He'd been discreet, hadn't he?

He thought back to his talks with Olivia. His late-night searches at home. His inquiries about Sam Harris. Had he been careless? Too obvious?

The cryptic note in his hands raised more questions. Was it a threat or some genuine attempt to protect him? And who could have slipped it under his door and disappeared so fast?

Bauer slumped back in his chair, the page clutched tight in his hand. The whispered conversations that stopped when he entered a room. His session with Rhyse and now this — it was clear to him that whatever was going on was bigger, and far more dangerous than he'd ever expected.

For a brief second, he considered stopping his investigation, forgetting about Case 47 and focusing on his work, his patients. But then he saw Simon's eyes peeking at him over the pile on his desk. This mystery had sunk its hooks into him. He wouldn't let it go, not until he figured out what was happening to him, Simon, and now Rhyse.

Thomas refolded the paper. He needed to be more careful, more discreet. But he couldn't stop, not yet.

Bauer's footsteps echoed through the long empty corridor as he made his way towards the archives. The cryptic note was still in his pocket. He tried to piece together the fragments of information he'd gathered over the past few days.

As he rounded a corner, a hushed voice caught his attention. His pace slowed. He pressed his body against the wall, then peered out. His heart leaped into his throat as he recognized the hunched posture of Sam Harris.

The janitor stood in a secluded alcove with his back to the doctor. Sam was engaged in an intense, animated, whispered conversation with someone Thomas couldn't see. The unknown person hidden in the shadows, their features were indistinguishable in the dim light.

He strained to hear their words, but their words were too quiet, their voices too low. He watched as the old man nodded, then jabbed his finger into the chest of the man. The unseen figure then handed something to Harris. After a quick glance around, the object disappeared into the janitor's pocket.

The discussion continued a few moments, then Sam straightened up, and scanned his surroundings with furtive glances. Bauer ducked behind the corner, afraid to breathe. When he dared to look again, both of them were gone. The alcove was now empty and silent.

Who was he talking to? What did he give him? He couldn't understand why his co-workers thought he was losing his mind when he asked about the old housekeeper. It was impossible to ignore what he had just seen.

He shook his head to clear his thoughts, then continued on with his task. He needed to focus and find the materials Andrew had requested. As he approached his destination, the familiar, comforting musty smell of old paper greeted him as it always did.

The archives were once a place of solace and discovery. Now they felt oppressive and dangerous. He struggled a little to open the heavy door. The room was silent, save for the soft buzz of the fluorescent lights overhead. He glanced over his shoulder, half-expecting to see the shadowy figure or Sam lurking. But he was alone — at least, as far as he could tell.

Bauer headed towards the section labeled Civil War-era. As he scanned the shelves, something caught his eye. A folder he remembered was taken from his office after his house flooded. It was now back where it belonged.

He was relieved that whoever took it had returned it. His heart pounded as he pulled it from the shelf. The documents were disheveled and out of order. The culprit had gone through it. This was not the time nor the place to look through it. Bauer gathered the materials Andrew had requested, along with the mysterious file. He then hurried towards the exit.

Chapter 22

Thomas Bauer rushed back to his office and locked the door behind him. He placed the retrieved files in his briefcase nearby. Out of habit, his eyes darted around the room, expecting to find something else out of place. He settled into his chair and exhaled. He was grateful he'd changed the lock on his door.

As he reached for the phone, it started ringing.

"Dr. Bauer speaking."

"Thomas, it's Andrew."

"Oh, hey, I was just going to call you. I've got what you need from the archives."

There was a brief pause. "Excellent, I appreciate your promptness."

His friend was silent on the other end of the line. "Hello, Andrew? Are you there?"

"Yeah, sorry about that. We must have a poor connection. Can you hear me?"

"Yes. How would you like me to get these to you?" Bauer prompted, his free hand drumming on his desk.

"Meet me at the old boathouse in Anacostia Park at 6 pm. We can discuss the materials there."

"That's a bit out of the way, isn't it?"

"Listen, I gotta run," His tone left no room for argument. "See you at six."

Before he could respond, the line went dead. He returned the handset back to its cradle. He'd known this man for years. That was a conversation unlike any other he had with his friend. "The boathouse?" He whispered to himself, shaking his head.

Glancing at his watch, he realized he had just over an hour to get to the park. As he got up to leave, his phone rang again. Thinking it was Andrew again, Bauer picked it up.

"Hello"

"Thomas, are you busy?" Eleanor asked, with an unmistakable hint of concern in her tone.

"I was just getting ready to head home. What's up?"

"You said you were going to come by tonight. Simon's been asking about you. We were wondering if you'd like to join us for dinner at our place?"

Guilt and disappointment gripped Bauer's core. Despite his silent vow to be a better husband, father and son, he hadn't gotten off to a great start. Once again, he had been so focused on work that he'd forgotten his promise. His attention returned to their conversation.

"Yes, I will be there. I have one stop to make on the way. I should be there no later than 7:30."

A quick call to his mother let her know of his change in plans for the evening. There was delight in her tone. She was glad he was spending some time with his family and away from the hospital and his father's study. "Tell Simon I need to schedule a marble rematch!"

Bauer smiled as he hung up the phone. He threw a few things in his briefcase, then closed the clasps. He then grabbed his coat and secured the door behind him. As he stepped away from his office, he almost collided with a man pushing a cleaning cart.

"Sorry, excuse me doctor," the man mumbled. He proceeded on his way without lifting his head.

Out of respect, he moved aside. The man continued with no further interaction. By the time Thomas turned for a second look, the man was already disappearing around a corner.

He shook his head. Bauer needed to hurry if he was going to make it to Eleanor's in time for dinner.

"I can't be late, not tonight," he muttered to himself. Remembering his promise, Thomas spun on his heels and headed toward the main exit.

When he exited the hospital, he drew in a deep breath. The hint of wood smoke in the cool, damp evening invigorated him as it replaced the stuffy, recycled indoor air in his lungs. He pulled his coat tighter around his chest against the chill of the early fall night as he made his way to his vehicle. The setting sun cast long shadows across the pavement.

He fumbled for keys as he approached his car. When he opened the door, something fell. Near his feet was a small piece of paper. Bauer glanced about, now aware of his surroundings. The parking lot was quiet and had very few cars. The hair on the back of his neck bristled, telling him otherwise.

He reached down to pluck the note from the ground. It was crisp and white, and folded like the one he received earlier under his office door. Thomas threw his briefcase onto the passenger's side, slid into the driver's seat, and locked the door. For a moment, he sat there, staring at his hands. They had a slight tremble to them as he unfolded it. His eyes widened as he read the scribbled words:

"Careful, they're watching you."

Bauer looked around the parking lot. He saw nothing but the lengthening shadows of dusk. His attention once again returned to the note. He noticed that there was no signature, no information that would suggest who might have sent it. Just four ominous words with a simple message, written in the same script.

With a quick check of his watch, Bauer slammed his fist against the steering wheel. There wasn't time for this, not tonight. He was already running late for his meeting with Andrew, and soon later for his dinner plans. Jamming the key into the ignition, he gave it a turn.

The engine roared to life, breaking the silence that surrounded him. He took one last glance at Saint Elizabeths Hospital as he pulled away.

His eyes glanced often at the rearview mirror as he drove to Anacostia Park. The emptiness of the streets on a Friday night surprised him. As he got closer, "make this quick" became the mantra in his head.

The cool air nipped at his exposed skin as he stepped from the car. He clutched the file tighter under his arm as his eyes scanned the growing darkness. The parking lot had only two cars in it. His and a sleek, black sedan parked near the footpath entrance that led into the park. Its tinted windows reflected the dimming light. It was not Andrew's beat-up old Volvo.

According to his watch, it was now 5:55 PM. Where was Andrew? His friend always ran early for everything. He should be here by now. A quick glance at the unfamiliar car got his stomach churning. He second-guessed every shadow he saw.

Bauer looked around, then started on the path. When he reached the trail, the gravel beneath his feet crunched loud against the ambient sounds. The river's gentle lapping at the water's edge failed to soothe him.

As he rounded a bend, movement up ahead caught his attention. There, in the distance, he could see a figure moving towards the boathouse, coming from a different route. Relieved, he picked up his pace as he continued to watch the silhouette. Andrew's casual, slight bow-legged walk was unmistakable. The gait of the man was all wrong. He did not know who this man was, but he knew it couldn't be Andrew.

Something wasn't right. Just then the man stopped and turned his direction, Thomas ducked behind a thick oak tree. His chest pressed into the rough bark. He peered around the trunk. His eyes strained for a better look.

He watched as the person moved with purpose. Their steps were quick and efficient. As the man drew closer to the boathouse, the light over the door illuminated the stranger's profile. This guy was shorter, and had broader shoulders. The man paused at the door. Following a few furtive glances, he slipped inside. That was not his friend, but he had seen this man before somewhere.

Who was this man? Why was he here? And where the hell was Andrew? He hesitated, weighing his options. What seemed like a simple favor for a friend had turned far more complicated. He thought about heading back to his car and leaving. But he'd promised Andrew he would get him with the stuff he needed.

Hidden behind a tree, Bauer watched the boathouse when a second man approached from a different path. The newcomer walked with confident, purposeful steps. Unlike the first man, this one didn't bother to check his surroundings before entering. The door creaked shut. Thomas stood alone in the growing darkness.

He crept forward. He kept low and off the gravel, using the shadows and bushes for concealment. A twig snapped underfoot. He winced as the noise disturbed the quiet evening. He froze, holding his breath, expecting to be discovered at any moment.

Satisfied no one had heard him, he once again moved toward the boathouse. As he neared his destination, voices drifted through a cracked side window. Thomas pressed himself against the rough wooden wall, straining to listen.

"...I tell you it's not there," a husky voice said, frustration evident in his tone.

"It has to be somewhere in Saint Elizabeths." the second man replied. His tone was smoother but no less tense. "We've searched everywhere."

"I'm telling you, Case 47 is not there. I've been searching every inch of that place for months."

Bauer's breath caught in his throat. Case 47? These two men were looking for it, too. He leaned closer, desperate to hear more.

"Maybe your sources were wrong," the gruff man suggested. "Or someone got to it first."

"Impossible," the smooth-voiced man snapped. "No one else knows about it."

"But the rumors."

"Ignore them. If anyone found the damn thing, they wouldn't be talkin' about it."

"What about Bauer?" the gruff voice asked. "He's been snooping around the archives a lot."

Bauer's heart hammered in his chest.

"He's harmless," the other man dismissed. "He can't even keep up with his patients' and his own problems."

"He has been acting weird the last few weeks."

"Trust me, that doctor is not our problem. All you need to concentrate on is finding that research."

The conversation continued, but Thomas' mind drifted. Who were these men? What did they know about Case 47? It was clear they knew who he was and where he worked.

He was so lost in his own thoughts, he almost missed them approaching the door. Panic surged through him. Thomas looked around, desperate for a place to hide.

Several old canoes leaned against the boathouse. The door flew open. Without thinking, he dove behind one. He contorted his tall, lanky body to fit into the narrow space. The smell of damp wood and mildew filled his nostrils. He froze praying no one had seen him.

The door creaked, followed by heavy feet crunching on the gravel. Bauer's muscles screamed, but he didn't move a muscle.

"Anything?" the smooth man called from inside.

"All clear," the gruff voice replied. "No sign of anyone."

The footsteps retreated, and the door closed once more. His breath shook as he exhaled. His heart pounded. As he crouched behind the canoes, his mind warred with burning curiosity and his instinct for self-preservation.

Bauer now knew that he wasn't the only one looking for it. The voices in the boathouse grew louder. Their frustration was palpable through the walls. He strained to hear more, his body tense and ready to flee at a moment's notice.

"We're running out of time," the smooth guy said, with an edge of desperation in his voice. "If we don't find Case 47 soon, everything we've done the past few years will all be for nothing." Bauer's muscles protested from being in the cramped position behind the canoes. He tried to catch every word from inside the boathouse. In the distance, he heard a car pull into the parking lot, followed by the slamming of a door. He looked around a canoe to see Andrew nearing the path.

Without making a sound, Bauer bolted from his hiding spot. He made his way towards his friend, walking among the bushes, just off the trail. The crunch of footsteps on gravel approaching filled his ears. He held his breath, fearing discovery.

"Thomas?" Andrew's voice carried well on the evening breeze.

Bauer's heart leaped. He peered around the old oak he hid behind earlier, as his friend's familiar silhouette grew closer.

"Over here," he hissed, waving him over.

Andrew crouched down beside him, confusion etched into his face. "What the hell is going on? Why are you hiding?"

"Shhh, there are two men in there—" Thomas recounted as he pointed, without mentioning the details of the conversation he just overheard. He watched as Andrew's expression shifted to concern.

"Jesus, Thomas," he muttered, running a hand over his stubbled chin. "What have you gotten yourself into?"

"Me?" He whispered back, indignant. "You're the one who told me to meet you here with this file."

Andrew shook his head. "I never called you today. I've been stuck in traffic for the last hour trying to get here after I got a message saying you needed help."

Bauer's blood ran cold. If he didn't call him, who did? And why?

The sound of a chair scraping inside the boathouse made them both freeze.

"We need to get out of here!" Andrew whispered.

Bauer nodded, his earlier curiosity was overshadowed by the growing threat. They inched away from their hiding spot.

As they reached the edge of the path, the door swung open. Light spilled out onto the gravel, and two silhouettes emerged.

"I'm telling you, I heard something," the gruff man insisted.

The two friends exchanged panicked looks. Without a word, they bolted toward the parking area.

"Hey!" a man shouted. "Stop right there!"

Bauer's vehicle was on the far side of the lot. He figured these two knew his car. His lungs burned as he sprinted as fast as he could. Andrew kept pace beside him.

The men's footsteps behind them made them run faster.

"My car's just ahead." He panted.

They burst out of the tree line towards the old Volvo. Andrew fumbled with his keys. His hands shook as he tried to unlock the door.

Bauer glanced back. The two men were closing in fast. "Hurry!"

The car door flew open. Andrew jumped into the driver's seat while Thomas threw himself into the passenger side. The engine roared to life just as their pursuers reached the edge of the gravel.

He slammed the transmission into reverse. Tires screamed as they tore out of the parking space. He shifted gears and floored the accelerator. The old Volvo lurched forward with a protesting groan.

Bauer's heart thundered as Andrew's sedan sped away. He glanced in the mirror, half-expecting to see the men hot on their tail. Instead, his eyes widened as he caught another figure walking through the lot.

"Sam?" he muttered under his breath, craning his neck for a better look.

There was no mistaking the janitor's hunched posture and shuffling gait. What was he doing here, of all places? The question gnawed at Bauer as the old man's silhouette disappeared into the darkness.

Andrew's hands gripped the steering wheel as he sped through the winding roads leading away from Anacostia Park. The silence in the car was thick, broken only by the occasional squeal of tires around a sharp turn.

Thomas' mind tried to make sense of what had just happened. The mysterious phone call, the men in the boathouse, their pursuit, and now Sam's unexpected appearance—it was all too much for his brain to process. He opened his mouth several times to speak, but his words remained silent.

What could he say? How could he explain something he didn't understand himself? He knew he couldn't tell anyone about Case 47 without putting them in danger. He needed to know more.

Andrew cleared his throat, breaking the silence. "Thomas, what the hell was that all about?"

Bauer turned to his friend. He could see the worry and fear in Andrew's expression. He wanted to share everything that had occurred since his house flooded. But something told him not yet. The memory of the conversation he'd overheard in the boathouse echoed in his mind: "No one else knows about it."

If what the men said was true, then sharing anything with anyone could put them in danger. He hadn't several notes warning him about being watched? No, he had to keep everyone in the dark, at least for now.

"I'm not sure," he half-lied, hating himself for the deception. "It must have been some kind of weird misunderstanding."

Andrew shot him a skeptical glance. "Thomas, we were just chased by two dudes ready to beat our asses! That's — that's not a mix up!"

Thomas sighed, running a hand through his hair. "I know, I know. It's just — it's complicated. I can't explain it right now."

"Can't or won't?" His friend pressed. His tone was sharp.

The question hung in the air. Bauer looked out the window, watching the streetlights blur past. Unspoken questions and growing mistrust were heavy.

"Both," said Thomas after a long silence.

As they neared Eleanor's neighborhood, Bauer's stomach twisted into knots. He glanced at his watch and winced. They were over an hour late for dinner. Eleanor was going to be furious.

"Look, Andrew," he began, trying to salvage something from this disastrous evening. "I'm sorry about all this. There are a few things I know, but I can't say yet. I swear I never meant to drag you into whatever this is. All I can say is that you phoned me earlier asking for stuff from the archives. When I got them, you told me to meet you at the park. "

"But Thomas, I didn't call you today. Not once." Andrew's expression remained unreadable as he focused on the road.

"You didn't?" Bauer replayed his afternoon in his head. "It sure sounded like you."

"No, you called me. You said you needed help."

"Now that I think about it, I didn't call you either."

"Something weird is going on here." His friend's voice softened a little. "I just wish you trusted me enough to tell me what's going on. We've been friends for years. You can trust me."

Bauer nodded, guilt gnawing at him. "Believe me, Andrew, trust has nothing to do with this. It's just ... something in my gut tells me that until I find out more, you're safer not knowing. Once I know it's safe to do so, I promise I'll explain everything."

As they pulled up in front of Eleanor's house, he could see his estranged wife's silhouette in the window. Anger and disappointment were evident in her posture, even when viewed from a distance.

"You want me to come in with you?" His friend offered. "Help smooth things over with Eleanor?"

Thomas shook his head. "No, I'll handle it. Thanks for the ride, and for getting us out of there."

As he climbed out of the car, Andrew called after him. "Thomas? Be careful, alright? Whatever's going on, just watch your back."

With a nod, he shut the door and watched as the Volvo drove away. He took a deep breath, preparing himself for the fury that awaited him inside.

Chapter 23

Thomas Bauer stood on the sidewalk and watched Andrew's tail lights disappear around the corner. The events at Anacostia Park still overwhelmed his head. However, now a different dread settled in his stomach. He turned to face the house, his old home, noting the warm glow of the lights within. It should have been inviting, but to him, it was the calm before a storm.

He trudged up the walkway, his shoes scuffed against the concrete. As he neared the door, it swung open with significant force. Eleanor's face failed to contain her fury. Her eyes blazed with a mixture of anger and disappointment.

"It's nice that you finally showed up," she said, her voice dripping with sarcasm.

He winced at her tone. "Ele, I'm so sorry. I can explain—"

"Save it," she cut him off, stepping aside to let him in. "Simon's already in bed. He waited up for you as long as he could, but—"

The unfinished sentence hung in the space between them, filled with accusation. Guilt made it hard to breathe as he stepped into the house. The aromas of a now-cold dinner lingered in the air, further reminding him of his failure.

Eleanor shut the door behind him with more force than necessary. "Do you have any idea what time it is? You're over an hour late, Thomas!"

Bauer ran a hand through his disheveled hair. He caught his reflection in a distant mirror. His clothes were dirty and rumpled, his face was pale. But she never noticed his appearance. Her focus was on his tardiness.

"I know, and I am sorry," he began, trying to find the right words. "Something came up and I—"

"Work?" She interrupted, her voice rising. "It's always the same with you, isn't it? Even when your son needs you, you can't tear yourself away from that damn hospital. This isn't the first time, Thomas."

Frustration soon accompanied Bauer's guilt. He wanted to tell her the truth, to explain the strange phone calls, the men at the boathouse, the chase through the park. But how could he? He didn't even understand any of it himself. Hell, he couldn't even tell Andrew, and he was involved in some of it.

"It's not that simple, Ele," he said, his voice strained. "There are things happening that I can't talk about right now."

She let out a bitter half-laugh. "Oh, I'm sure there are. So what else is new? There's always some big 'something' that's 'important.' It takes precedence over everything and everyone."

Her words penetrated deep into his heart. The truth hit with blunt force. She wasn't wrong. Over the years, he was always dedicated to his profession, trying so hard to prove himself to his father. But his recent situation was different. This was not about him or the hospital.

"Will you please just listen?" he protested weakly. "I'm not even late because of work. Not this time. I even called to tell you I had to make one stop, then I'd be right over, remember? Andrew needed a file."

"That's more important than your son?" She shot back. "More important than promises you made to him, to me?"

Bauer felt his own anger rising now. "Of course not! How can you even suggest that? Simon means everything to me."

"Are you sure? Because your actions tell me otherwise. Do you have any idea how disappointed he's been when you don't show? How many times I've had to tell him, 'Just a little longer, sweetie. I'm sure Daddy will be here soon.'"

Each word was like a knife twisting in Bauer's core. He could picture his son waiting, his excitement slowly fading into disappointment. He couldn't deny that it was a scene that had played out far too often.

"Look Ele, I didn't mean for this to happen," Thomas said, his voice softer now. "There were unforeseen circumstances. Things outside of my control."

She shook her head. Her anger seemed to deflate a little, replaced by weariness. "Always some excuse, some reason you can't be here when he needs you."

Bauer wanted to argue, to defend himself, but no words would come. Deep down, he knew she was right, even if it wasn't the case tonight. His work had already cost him his home, his family. And now it was on the verge of consuming his sanity.

"I'm trying," he said, his tone softened. "I really am."

Eleanor looked at him, it was the first time since he'd arrived.

The sound of footsteps on the stairs interrupted the tense silence between them. They both turned to see their boy rubbing the sleep from his eyes as he descended.

"Dad?" His voice was a mix of drowsy surprise and excitement. "You're here!"

Bauer's heart clenched as his eyes came to rest on his child. Despite the late hour, Simon's face lit up with a smile that seemed to push away the remnants of disappointment.

"Hey, son," Bauer said. His words were soft and warm. "I thought you'd be asleep by now."

Simon bounded down the last few steps and threw his arms around his father. "I was, but you and mom talking woke me up."

As the boy pulled away from the hug, the boy's brow furrowed, as his head cocked to the side. He looked his father up and down, taking in his dad's appearance.

"Dad? What happened to you?" He asked, his tone tinged with concern. "You look like you've been rolling in the dirt."

Bauer glanced down at his clothes, now acutely aware of how he looked. He noticed smudges on his once-crisp shirt and saw that his slacks had wrinkles and stains. He didn't get a chance to clean up.

"Oh, this?" He tried to sound nonchalant. "It's nothing, I ah—I just tripped over some logs at that old park where you and I used to go fishing. You know how clumsy your old man can be sometimes."

Eleanor, hearing Simon's comment, looked at her husband. Her eyes widened, as some of her anger drained from her face.

"Thomas, are you alright?" she asked, her voice much softer, with a sense of concern.

He nodded, forcing a smile. "I'm fine. Just a long day."

She hesitated for a moment, then sighed. "Well, you must be hungry. I can reheat some dinner leftovers if you'd like."

"I appreciate that, thank you," Thomas said, grateful for the olive branch offered.

As his wife moved toward the kitchen, Simon tugged on his father's dirty sleeve. "Can I stay up a little later, Dad? Please? I want to sit with you while you eat."

They both looked at Eleanor, who nodded. "Since it's Friday night, sure." She conceded.

Soon, they were all seated around the dining table. The aroma of reheated spaghetti filled the air surrounding them. Bauer took a bite, savoring the taste of his meal. Though he had no objections to his mother's food, he missed Eleanor's cooking, and all of them sitting down to dinner together.

"So, Simon," his dad said between bites, "how's school been?"

His son shrugged, his gaze lost in the tablecloth's pattern. "It's okay, I guess. Today I was really tired. I had this weird nightmare last night."

There was a sudden change in Simon's demeanor. His eyes became distant, as if he were looking at something far beyond the walls of the dining room.

"Do you want to tell me about it?" Thomas asked. His fork paused halfway to his mouth.

"I was a soldier. In a war. But not like the stuff I've seen on TV or in movies. This was different."

A chill came over Bauer. "In what way?"

"There were long trenches," the boy continued, his voice taking on an eerie, detached edge. "Deep ditches in the ground. We were all crammed in there, covered in mud. The noise was — it was so loud, dad. Constant explosions, and a weird whistling sound. I've never heard it before."

Bauer's mouth went dry. He glanced at Eleanor, who was also watching their child with a mix of concern and confusion.

"And the smell," Simon's nose wrinkled. "It was awful. Like rotten eggs and something worse. All of us had these gas masks, but they didn't help much."

"Masks?" Thomas asked. His voice was now just above a whisper.

The boy nodded. "Yeah, because of the poison in the air. They told us that it would melt our lungs if we breathed it in."

Bauer's blood ran cold. The details being described were too specific, too accurate for a mere child's imagination. He noticed the detailed similarities of what Simon was saying and what Rhyse had described during some of their sessions. The only difference was his son was recounting experiences from the World War I trenches, while his patient talked about similar ordeals from the Korean War.

Eleanor watched with growing concern as the boy recounted more of his vivid dream. Her eyes darted between her son and husband, noting the intense focus on her husband's face. It was a look she recognized all too well; his expression was cold with a measured detachment, like he was analyzing every word.

"Son," Thomas said, his tone took on a clinical tone, "can you tell me more about the masks? What did they look like?"

Eleanor tensed. Her knuckles were white as they gripped the edge of the table. She watched as Simon's brow wrinkled, his eyes filled with fear.

"They were big and clunky," the kid replied, his voice eery and detached. "Made of some thick rough material and rubber, I think. They had these round glass eyepieces and a long snout-like can thing at the front."

Bauer nodded, leaning forward. "And the trenches? How deep were they?"

His wife had heard enough. She stood, her chair scraped loud against the floor. "Thomas, can I speak with you for a moment? In the kitchen?"

Her husband looked up, almost startled by the interruption. He snapped out of his professional, analytical trance as he noticed the tension in Eleanor's words. With a nod, he followed her, leaving Simon confused and sitting alone at the table.

Once in the kitchen, she whirled on him. Her eyes flashed with more anger than concern. "What the hell do you think you're doing?" she hissed, keeping her voice low to keep their conversation from reaching Simon's ears.

Bauer blinked, taken aback by her sudden intensity. "I'm just trying to understand —"

"Understand?" She cut him off. "He's your son, Thomas, not one of your patients. He's had a nightmare, and you're interrogating him like he's on your psychiatrist's couch at work."

Bauer's face fell as he realized her point. "I — I wanted to know more. I didn't mean to —"

"No, you never mean to," Eleanor sighed, her anger deflating some. "But this is exactly why I worry about him spending time with you. You can't seem to turn off your doctor mode, and just be his father."

Bauer ran his fingers through his hair, frustration evident in his gesture. "Ele, you don't get it. These dreams Simon's having, they're not normal. The level of detail —"

She held up her hand and shook her head. "Just stop. I think it's best if you leave now."

Bauer's eyes widened. "Leave? But I just got here. I didn't get to spend any time with Simon."

"And whose fault is that?" she retorted. Her earlier anger had returned. "You were late, Thomas. And now, instead of just being present for your son, you're treating him like a case study at work."

He opened his mouth to protest, but the words died on his lips. He didn't have a valid argument. Not one she would believe. How could he explain to her the significance behind Simon's dreams? How could he convey the growing knot in his gut, or the similarities between his son's nightmares and his own?

"But, I can't," Bauer said. His voice was low and defeated.

Eleanor's eyebrows shot up. "Excuse me?"

"My car," Thomas explained, feeling the weight of the entire evening press down on him. "It's still in Anacostia Park. We took off in Andrew's car when we were being chased. That's why I was so late, and my clothes are such a mess."

Eleanor stared at him for a moment, her expression a mix of disbelief and exasperation. After a few minutes, she let out a long sigh. "Fine. I'll drive you to get it. Regardless, you're going home, Thomas. Your son needs his father and some rest, not an interrogation."

He nodded, knowing there was no point in arguing any further. They returned to the dining room, where Simon continued to sit and stare at the tablecloth.

"Hey, bud," Bauer said, trying to keep his tone light. "I've got to head out now. But I'll see you in a couple of days, okay?"

The boy looked up, disappointment evident in his eyes. "Already? But you just got here."

Pain gripped Bauer's heart. "I know, and I'm sorry. We'll spend more time together soon, I promise. Maybe we can go fishing, you know, like we used to."

"Yeah, that sounds good." Simon's voice trailed off and his gaze became distant as he moved from the table and wrapped his arms around his father.

Bauer couldn't help but notice an unmistakable tightness in his son's embrace. It was now clear that his son didn't want him to leave, and he didn't want to go. His mind wandered as he held his son a little tighter. He could admit his past screw-ups, but he would not own all of tonight's failures, regardless of what Eleanor thought she knew or understood.

He knew he still had a lot to prove to them and himself. There was no question about that. However, this time, the boy's pain and disappointment were not all on him. It was on her, too. He would do as she requested without making a scene, but only after Simon released his hug.

The two of them finished exchanging their goodbyes. She then stepped between them and gestured towards the stairs. "I'll be up in a minute to tuck you in, again." she said. His disappointed eyes remained on his father as he lowered his head a little and turned away.

Together they rode back to Anacostia Park, surrounded by an awkward silence. The only sound was the hum of the car's engine and the occasional rustle of clothing. Thomas sat rigid in the passenger seat, his eyes looking out the window. From the stolen glances over at his wife, he couldn't help but notice Eleanor's anger gripping the steering wheel.

The tension between them was a palpable, invisible barrier that neither of them seemed willing to breach. He opened his mouth several times. Each time, he swallowed his words, unsure of what to say or how to begin.

Eleanor, for her part, kept her gaze fixed on the road. Her jaw set firm, without expression. The streetlights cast intermittent shadows across her face, highlighting lines that were deeper than he ever remembered.

As they neared Anacostia Park, he cleared his throat. "Ele, I—"

"Don't," she cut him off, her voice low but steady. "Just — don't, I don't want to hear it, Thomas. Not now."

He sunk further into his seat. The remainder of their shared journey passed in complete silence.

When they pulled into the parking lot, Eleanor brought the car to a stop next to Bauer's vehicle. The engine idled for a moment, then she turned it off, plunging them into darkness broken only by the golden glow of lights off in the distance.

"Thank you for the ride," he said, his hand on the door handle.

She nodded, still refusing to look at him. "Just — Thomas. Whatever you're mixed up in, whatever's going on, be careful."

For a second, he detected a hint of concern in her voice, but before he could respond, she was already reaching to start the car again. He stepped out, closed the door behind him, and watched as she drove away, her taillights disappearing into the night.

Alone, Bauer leaned against his vehicle, as a mix of emotions crashed over him like a tidal wave. He fumbled in his pocket for his keys, his hands shook as he unlocked the door and slid into the driver's seat.

The interior felt like a comfortable hug, with its solitude. A small secluded sanctuary of familiarity in a world that continued to spiral around him, most of it beyond his control. He sat there, resting his head on the steering wheel, making no effort to start the engine.

His mind replayed the events of his day like some insane, disjointed slideshow. The cryptic notes, the chase through the park with Andrew, his arguments with Eleanor, and the bizarre nightmare. Each memory brought with it a fresh wave of emotions and confusion.

He took in a shaky breath. His work, his family, and the growing mysteries involving his father and Dr. Levi threatened to crush whatever he had left.

But it was his son's dream that kept pushing its way to the forefront of his mind. The vivid details, the historical accuracy that someone his age shouldn't know. Something in his gut told him that this was not just a nightmare. The similarities between Simon's and Rhyse's experiences were astonishing. Was there a connection? There was a piece of an insane puzzle he was missing.

Bauer reached for the key and gave it a turn. The engine's rumble and roar broke through the stillness, grounding him back in the present. He drove out of the parking lot, his mind still churning with unanswered questions.

It was late, and the streets were nearly empty. Thomas navigated on autopilot as thoughts swirled in his head. He pulled into the driveway of his mother's home. The house was dark and silent.

He was glad his mother hadn't waited up for him. Thomas was careful not to make any noise that might wake her. He paused in the hallway. His gaze was drawn to the closed door at the end of the hall.

Bauer slumped into his father's leather chair. Exhaustion settled over him like a heavy blanket. His eyes burned from lack of sleep, and his muscles ached from stress and physical exertion earlier that evening. He needed rest. The mysterious caller's words echoed in his mind; 24 hours until their meeting in the archives. The thought wasn't enough to overcome the fatigue that had seeped into his bones..

He glanced at his watch; the hands blurred as he tried to focus. It was well past midnight. With a groan, Bauer pushed himself up from the chair and made his way out of the study. In silence, he trudged up the stairs. His body collapsed onto the bed, fully clothed.

Sleep claimed him quick, but it was far from restful. His dreams were a chaotic mess of images from his day. He tossed and turned. His subconscious mind replayed all that had consumed his waking hours the previous day.

Chapter 24

The shrill ring of the house phone jolted Bauer from his deep, fitful slumber. His eyes were still heavy with sleep. The clock on his nightstand read 7:30 AM. He closed his eyes again, not quite ready to move.

A gentle knock on his door was followed by Edyth's soft, sweet voice. "Thomas, are you up?"

"Come in," he mumbled, his words thick with fatigue.

The door opened a crack. "The phone's for you. It's Eleanor. She sounds anxious and upset, but she won't tell me what was wrong."

He was now only more awake. "Thanks mom, I'll take the call in your room."

Bauer rolled over. HIs hands rubbed some life into his stubbled face trying to get some blood to his brain. The clothes he had on were still filthy, yet more wrinkled than they were the night before. He shook the fatigue from his head, then headed down the hall.

He picked up the phone as he laid down across his mother's bed. "Hello, Eleanor?"

"Thomas?" Her voice came through, thick with worry. "It's Simon. There's something wrong—"

Bauer sat up, more awake. "What's happened?"

"There are these marks on his skin," she said, her words coming out jumbled and rushed. "They weren't there last night. They look like — like burns or something. And he told me they're because of his nightmares."

"What do they look like? Where are they?"

"All over his arms and chest," his wife replied. "They're red and raised, almost like welts. It's not random. There's a pattern to them."

He tried to process everything she was saying. "Have you called a doctor yet?"

"No," she said. "I wanted to call you first. He's scared, Thomas. And he's asking for you. He says the marks are from the gas in his dreams."

He closed his eyes, fighting back a wave of nausea. "I'll be right there. Don't take him anywhere. I need to see this for myself first."

He hung up and went to change out of his dirty clothes, his head raced with possibilities. As he rushed down the stairs to grab his coat and keys, a thought entered his mind.

He ran to the phone in the kitchen. His fingers were fast over the numbers.

After three rings, a groggy voice on the other end picked up. "Hello?"

"Andrew, get dressed! I'm on my way to pick you up. Bring your WWI medical manuals with you!"

"What? Thomas? What the hell for?!"

"I'll explain everything when I get there! Just get ready, hurry!"

Bauer ended the call and stood there for a second. His world was crashing down around him. It was no longer affecting just his life, but also the lives of those he loved. But now wasn't the time for that.

He dialed Eleanor's number again. "I'm on my way," he said as soon as she picked up. "But Eleanor, I need you to do something for me. Can you take some pictures of Simon's marks with the Polaroid? I — I have to make two stops, then I'll be there."

There was a pause on the other end of the line. When his wife spoke again, her voice was bitter. "It's about work, isn't it? Even now, when your son needs you?"

Thomas winced at her tone. "It's not like that. It's complicated, and now is not the time for me to explain. Please, just get the snapshots for me. I'll be there as soon as I can."

He hung up before she could respond, knowing that every second he delayed would only make Simon's condition worse.

Bauer's car screeched to a halt in front of Andrew's house. His friend stumbled from the door, arms laden with leather-bound books, their golden edges glinting in the early morning light. With disheveled hair, a half-tucked shirt, and a bewildered expression, his friend approached the vehicle.

"Thomas, what in God's name is going on?" Andrew asked, fumbling to reach the door handle.

He leaned across the passenger's seat and opened it. "Get in. I'll explain on the way."

As the man piled into the car, depositing the stack of manuals between them, Bauer gunned the engine. The tires squealed as they peeled away from the curb.

"It's Simon," Thomas said, his knuckles white on the steering wheel. "He's got these marks on his skin. Eleanor said they look like burns, and he says they're just like the ones he saw in his nightmares about the war."

His passenger's eyes widened. "What war?"

"World War I," Thomas confirmed. "The same kind we were researching for the reenactment a while back."

They sped through the quiet Saturday morning streets. The city was still waking up around them. He pushed his sedan faster, as he tried to piece together fragments of information from his father's journals and Simon's sudden, inexplicable injuries.

"We're not going straight to Eleanor's," he announced as they approached a familiar intersection.

"Where are we going now?"

"Saint Elizabeths. I need to grab something."

The hospital loomed before them, its imposing façade was unmistakable in the soft glow. He parked crooked near the main entrance. He shifted the car into park and exited, leaving the door open and the engine running.

"Stay here," he instructed. "I'll be right back."

He sprinted through the doors. His eyes darted around for any sign of the staff. The lobby was empty. Then he saw what he came for.

Without hesitation, Thomas grabbed a green tank from a nearby wheelchair and a bag of oxygen masks. His heart pounded in his ears. As he turned, a movement caught his eye. Sam Harris stood at the far end of the room, watching him with an unreadable expression.

Their eyes locked for a second. Then the old man gave the doctor a slight nod. Bauer rushed out of the door and back to his car with the pilfered equipment.

Andrew's eyes bulged as his friend tossed the stuff into the backseat. "Thomas? You're stealing stuff from the hospital? What the hell—"

"No, just borrowing it," He cut him off, half explaining as he threw the sedan into gear. "We need to get to Eleanor's."

They drove in tense silence for the rest of the way, only interrupted by the occasional squeal of tires as they took corners too fast. They pulled up in front of the house.

Bauer jumped from the vehicle before the engine died. He grabbed the oxygen tank, masks and his stethoscope from the backseat. He hurdled up the walkway steps toward the entrance, leaving Andrew to gather his things.

Eleanor flung the door open as they approached, her face a mix of relief and confusion. Her eyes widened as she saw the equipment in her husband's hands. Exiting the car, she could see a strange man with an armload of books.

"What is all this?" she demanded, her voice rising. "Who's he? What's going on?"

Bauer pushed past her into the house, his eyes searching. "Where is he?" he asked.

"Upstairs in his room." She replied, following close behind. "Thomas, I demand an explanation. Right now."

He bounded up the stairs two at a time. His heart pounded. He burst into his son's room. The oxygen tank clanked against the metal doorknob. Simon lay in bed, his face pale and drawn, his eyes wide with fear from the sudden intrusion.

He was careful as he took the boy's arm. He'd seen these kinds of angry lesions before, but only in pictures. The inflamed welts covered his arms and chest, forming patterns that seemed to pulse with each labored breath. Some patches blistered, while the surrounding area developed a sickly, yellowish hue that contrasted with the redness of what looked like burns.

Tears flowed down Simon's face in a continuous stream. The whites of his eyes were bloodshot and red. Thomas watched in horror as his son's breathing became more ragged and shallow, punctuated by fits of a harsh, wracking cough that produced small amounts of blood tinged mucus.

The boy's skin felt cool and clammy to the touch. Droplets of sweat had formed on his ghostly white forehead. Noticing the bluish tint to his lips, Thomas looked at Eleanor, who was standing behind him wringing her hands. "Hand me that tank and that bag! Hurry!"

He ripped open the plastic packaging and attached it with mastered efficiency. When he turned the valve, they could hear air flowing. He lifted his son's head and placed the mask on his face. For the moment, all they could do was wait and see how Simon responded to the oxygen.

"Dad?" The kid's eyes fluttered as he seemed to return to the present. He was weak, and spoke in whispers.

"I'm here, bud," he said. His voice was steady despite the panic wracking his brain. He ran a hand through his boy's hair, feeling the clammy sweat on his forehead.

Simon's eyes darted about, filled with fear, as if scanning for threats. Thomas grabbed his hand and held it. "How did you find me in the trench with all the mud? The place smells like garlic and rot and death."

Bauer turned and shot a glance at Andrew, who still stood in the doorway with his mouth agape. "What do you think?"

"Mustard gas?"

Thomas issued a nod. "Yeah, that was my thought, too."

"Dad, there were explosions all around us," Simon continued, his voice growing stronger with less coughing. His face began to regain its color. "The ground shook. The guys were screaming. Then, I saw it. This greenish-yellow cloud coming our way."

Bauer's eyes went wide. He glanced over his shoulder to see his friend standing there, flipping fast through WWI medical manuals.

"The air," the kid explained, his breath hitching as he spoke. "It hurts. Real bad. It burned my eyes and throat. I couldn't breathe. I tried to put my mask on, but I wasn't quick enough."

He squeezed his son's hand. His heart broke listening to the terror in his the boy's words. "It's okay, Simon. You're safe now. Your mom and I are here now."

Andrew stood in disbelief as he witnessed the physical manifestations described in the book he was holding. "Thomas," he called, his voice urgent. "I think I've found something."

As Bauer looked at his wife, he noticed worry and confusion displayed on her face. He motioned to her to come take his place as he released his grip on his son's hand. He then joined his friend in the doorway.

Andrew pointed to a page in the manual. "Look here. This describes a mustard gas attack during the Battle of Ypres in 1917. The symptoms match Simon's description exactly! The burning, the difficulty breathing, and the distinctive marks on his skin."

Thomas connected the dots between his own dreams, things he read in his father's notes, and the kid's inexplicable condition. The gravity of the situation hit him like a physical blow.

"Oh my God," he muttered under his breath as he ran a hand through his hair. "It's real. It's all real."

"What is?" She demanded, her patience gone. "Tell me what the hell is going on!"

He ignored her, turning his attention back to Simon. He adjusted the mask on his son's face.

"Is the air helping?"

The boy nodded. His breathing was less labored. The redness in his eyes started to fade a little. His dad increased the flow, watching as some of the tension eased from the kid's face.

"Thomas," Eleanor said, her voice low and dangerous. "I want answers. Now."

He looked at his wife. Her eyes were full of fear and anger. How could he explain the truth floating through his head without sounding insane?

When his attention returned to his son, the boy was breathing easier with the oxygen flowing into his lungs and through his body. Everyone in the room exhaled as they watched the boy's symptoms continue to improve. Following a few more minutes of observation, Bauer felt comfortable enough to step out of the room, leaving Simon to rest.

He gestured, then led Eleanor and Andrew down the stairs. The living room seemed small, like the walls were closing in on him as he struggled to find his words. He motioned for them to have a seat while he paced the floor.

Eleanor's eyes followed him, filled with concern and frustration. "Thomas, please. Just tell us what is happening to our son."

He stopped pacing and ran his hand through his hair, then exhaled. "It's extremely complicated." He started, methodical in his explanation. "I've been investigating some unusual cases at the hospital that occurred in the 1950s and 1960s. Simon's condition seems to be very similar to some that I've been reading about."

Andrew leaned forward, his brow furrowed as his elbows came to rest on his knees. "Tom, that doesn't even make sense. Why are we talking about incidents from the 50s and 60s? What would they have to do with a mustard gas attack from 1917?"

Thomas hesitated. Now he was aware of the gaps in his knowledge and what was safe for him to share with them. "There's been a pattern of patients experiencing vivid, historically accurate dream-like events. Some even showed physical symptoms corresponding to their nightmarish experiences, just like Simon has."

Eleanor's eyes widened. "Like chemical burns?"

Bauer nodded, relieved that she was following along. "I'm not sure if there is some sort of environmental factor at play. Something that's affected his brain chemistry and caused these intense, realistic visions."

It wasn't all lies. He omitted the temporal displacement theory and Dr. Levi's and his father's involvement didn't sit well in his gut. He watched as Eleanor and Andrew exchanged glances, telling of their skepticism.

"Environmental?" His friend repeated, his tone doubtful. "That seems pretty far-fetched. If that were the case, there would be more cases like this popping up around the city. You know, like at the school, or other places he's been."

Bauer shrugged, trying to appear a little more confident than he felt. "I know it all sounds really strange. But I will not lie and pretend I have any actual answers when I don't. That said, it's the best explanation I have right now."

Eleanor sat up a little straighter. Andrew leaned back and pressed his backs against the sofa. Thomas stared off into space. He started pacing again. When he stopped, he looked them both dead in the eyes. "Until I can figure out what the hell this is, I'm going to need your help."

After what they had just witnessed upstairs, neither one felt like they could deny him. "Alright, what do you want us to do?"

He outlined his plan, watching their faces for signs of disbelief or suspicion. "Eleanor, keep a detailed log of Simon's symptoms and his nightmares. Make sure you note the date and location of his dreams. Also, note any physical changes, no matter how insignificant they might seem."

"Of course." She nodded, her lips pressed into a thin line. "But, shouldn't we take him to a hospital?"

Her husband shook his head. "No, not yet. His condition is improving with the oxygen, and I don't want to risk exposing him to anything else until we know more about what's really causing his symptoms." He turned to his friend. "Can you continue researching historical connections? Focus on World War I for now, but keep an eye out for any similar incidents throughout history."

Andrew agreed, though his expression remained skeptical. "I'll do what I can, but this all seems—"

"I know," Bauer cut him off, not wanting to hear his doubts spoken aloud. "For now, it's our best chance at staying one step ahead of whatever this is. If that makes sense."

As they discussed more details of his strategy, Thomas could feel the weight of his secrets suffocating him. Now that others were at risk, he needed answers more than ever. The upcoming midnight meeting in the hospital archives loomed in his head.

Eleanor's voice pulled him from his head. "Thomas? Are you listening?"

He blinked, realizing he had zoned out. "Sorry, what were you saying?"

She sighed with frustration. "We should have a plan, in case Simon's condition deteriorates."

Her husband nodded, grateful for her suggestion and the distraction from his thoughts. "Yes, we need to be prepared for anything. I'll order some medications from the pharmacy just to err on the side of caution —a bronchodilator inhaler, corticosteroids, antibiotics and an oxygen tank. They will help if his breathing and other symptoms return. They will also keep his lesions from getting infected."

He looked at Eleanor and Andrew, their concerns and confusion on full display in their eyes. They were trusting him, following his lead despite their unspoken doubts. There would be time for disclosure later, he told himself. For now, he had to focus on finding more information and keeping them all safe.

Chapter 25

The adults returned to Simon's bedroom. They all were relieved the kid's condition continued to improve, and his breathing grew stronger. They watched the oxygen mask fog with each exhale. The angry red welts on his skin had faded, replaced by a more healthful pallor.

A wave of relief washed over everyone in the room. Bauer remained cautious, but still optimistic. He knew they weren't out of the woods yet. He also knew things could change fast if the boy slipped back into his "nightmare-state."

Eleanor hovered nearby, her eyes darting between Simon and her husband. The tension in her shoulders had eased somewhat. However, creases of concern showed on her forehead. "He looks a lot better," she admitted.

Andrew nodded in agreement from his position closer to the bedroom door. "It's remarkable, really. I've never seen anything like this."

Bauer flashed a hint of a smile. "I'm not ready to celebrate just yet, but this is a good sign." He turned to his wife, his expression serious. "Ele, do you want to do a quick run to the pharmacy? I've called in some prescriptions that will be crucial, should his symptoms return."

She hesitated, her gaze shifted toward her son. "Are you sure? What if—"

"We're not going anywhere until you get back." Her husband assured her, gesturing to himself and Andrew. "We're not his mother, but I'd say he's still in pretty capable hands." Thomas said with a slight smile and a wink.

After a moment's consideration, Eleanor nodded. She leaned in to kiss her son's forehead. "I'll be as quick as I can," she promised before disappearing from the room to grab her purse and car keys.

As Eleanor's footsteps faded down the stairs, Bauer pulled his chair closer to Simon's bed. He took his son's hand in his, careful not to disturb the non-rebreather oxygen mask.

Andrew took a seat on the other side of the room, his eyes scanning through the old medical textbook in his hands.

The boy's eyes fluttered open. His face was a mix of comfort and relief as he noticed his dad's presence.

"How are you feeling, bud?"

His eyes blinked, trying to focus on his dad. "Better," he mumbled through the mask. "Tired."

"That's okay," his father said, with a gentle squeeze of his hand. "You rest. We'll be right here. I promise."

As Simon drifted off again, Bauer studied his son's face. The fear and pain that had contorted his features earlier were gone. A peaceful expression shown in their place. He couldn't believe that just an hour prior, the boy had been through some real-life horrors in a World War I trench.

Andrew's voice, just above a whisper, broke the silence. "Thomas, I've been thinking about what you said downstairs. About the cases from the '50s and '60s."

Thomas tensed, suddenly aware of how much he'd revealed in the heat and confusion of the moment. "What about them?"

"Well, it's just—" Andrew paused, being careful with his words. "It seems like an incredible coincidence that he would experience something so similar to what's in these books. The historical accuracy of this is — it's uncanny."

There was so much he still didn't understand himself. "I know it all pretty far-fetched," he began. "But over the years, I've come to realize that we know very little about the human mind. More often than not, in situations like these, we have to make the most educated guesses possible, and hope for the best."

His friend leaned forward, his voice low. "Do you think it could be some kind of past life regression? Or maybe some sort of genetic memory?"

Bauer couldn't help but issue a slight chuckle at Andrew's suggestion. However, part of him wondered if there might be more plausibility in those explanations than the man realized. "I'm not sure I'd go that far with a hypothesis," he said. "But I know that there's a hell of a lot more going on here than we understand right now."

They lapsed into silence, broken only by the soft hiss of the oxygen tank and Simon's steady breathing. Bauer's mind drifted to his upcoming meeting at the hospital that night. Deep down, he hoped for crucial answers to what was happening, especially with his son.

The sound of Eleanor's vehicle pulling into the driveway returned Bauer to the present. A few moments later, Eleanor appeared in the doorway, her arms laden with stuff from the pharmacy.

"I got everything you ordered, but the oxygen is still in the car." She said, a little out of breath.

"I'll go get it," Andrew volunteered without hesitation.

"Thank you," she nodded, then turned her attention back to her husband. "How is he?"

Thomas stretched his stiff muscles. "Sleeping like a baby and still improving," he reported. "He's been asleep most of the time you were gone."

His wife looked relieved as she set the bags down on a nearby dresser. She moved to her son's bedside, brushing a strand of hair from his forehead. "My brave boy," she murmured.

Her husband stood in the bedroom, his gaze shifting between his son's peaceful form and Eleanor's less-worried face. He'd done all that he could for Simon. He was thankful his son was responding so well to his interventions.

The clock next to the bed read 10:30 AM. Bauer couldn't believe only three hours had passed since Eleanor first called him. Exhaustion seeped into his bones, replacing the stress of the earlier situation.

"Ele," he said, placing a hand on her shoulder. "I have to take Andrew home. But I want you to let me know right away if Simon's condition changes for better or worse, no matter how small it might seem."

She nodded, her eyes never leaving Simon. "Of course. Are you sure? What if—"

"I'm just a phone call away," Her husband reassured her, though the promise sounded hollow even in his own ears. "I need to return that tank before someone finds out it's missing."

He set up the oxygen she brought back from the pharmacy. After some brief instruction, he gave a final glance at his son, satisfied by the boy's remarkable improvement.

Thomas motioned for his friend to follow him. They made their way downstairs in silence. Both men were exhausted.

The drive back to Andrew's place was quiet. Each man lost themselves in their own thoughts about the events of the day and the prior evening. His friend stared out the window. Once in a while, he jotted down a note in a small notebook he kept in his pocket.

"I really appreciate your help today," Bauer said as he pulled up to the house. "I know this isn't what you signed up for when we became friends."

Andrew managed a weak smile. "No, I can't say that it was. But I'm glad those old books were helpful. Hey Thomas?" He paused as he gathered the old books. "Whatever's going on here, I hope you find some real answers soon."

Thomas nodded, watching him exit and make his way to his front door. Once he was sure his friend was safe inside, he set off for Saint Elizabeths Hospital.

The parking lot was emptier than usual when he arrived, however it was late morning on a Saturday, so most of the weekday staff was off. He grabbed the oxygen tank from the back seat, intent on just sneaking in for a quick drop-off before he could head home and finally take a shower.

As he approached the main entrance, a familiar figure burst through the double doors to greet him, almost colliding with him.

"Dr. Bauer!" Dr. Rachael Chang, one of his colleagues, exclaimed. Her usual neat appearance was disheveled. Her white coat appeared wrinkled and askew. Strands of hair had escaped her usual pristine bun. "Thank God you're here. I was just about to call you."

He looked at her, confused. "What's up?"

"It's my patient, he was admitted early this morning with some unusual symptoms, but in the last hour, things have escalated fast," she said, her words tumbling out in a rush. "I don't know what's wrong with him, and everything I try seems to make him worse. I've never seen anything like it. I thought, given your experience with these odd cases…"

Bauer's grip tightened on the oxygen tank in his hands. "Show me," he said, following her back into the hospital.

Bauer felt odd and out of place in his blue jeans, t-shirt and sneakers as he followed her to the third floor. Dr. Chang filled him in on the details as they walked. The patient is a 32-year-old male with no significant medical history. He arrived with complaints of vivid nightmares and the sudden onset of unexplained physical symptoms.

As they entered the patient's room, Bauer's breath caught in his throat. The scene before him was similar to what he'd seen earlier in his own son.

The man was thrashing weakly, his skin covered in painful crimson welts that seemed to shift and change as Bauer watched. His eyes burned with a blood-red color, and he struggled to breathe, gasping in short, ragged breaths.

"He keeps mumbling about trenches and gas," Dr. Chang said, her voice low. "At first, we thought it might be some kind of PTSD episode, but the physical symptoms don't make any sense."

The doctor approached the bed, thinking. The similarities to Simon's condition were undeniable, but there was something else. Something that nagged at the edges of his memory, tugging at fragments of information he'd gleaned from his father's notes.

He leaned in to study the pattern on the man's skin. They weren't all that different from Simons.

"Chemical burns," he murmured, more to himself than to Dr. Chang.

"What?" she asked, moving closer to her colleague.

He straightened up. His mind worked fast to piece together remote connections between this man and his son. "These welts," he said, gesturing to the patient. "They're consistent with chemical exposure. The kind you might see from exposure to mustard gas."

Her eyes widened. "But that's impossible. There hasn't been a confirmed use of that stuff in decades, and not anywhere near here."

Thomas nodded, his gaze never leaving the patient. "I know. But I've seen something very similar to this before. In fact, not that long ago."

He turned to the nurse standing nearby. "Put him on high-flow oxygen and a non-rebreather."

"Yes, doctor!"

He then faced Dr. Chang, his expression grave. "Can I see the man's chart?"

"Of course, Dr. Bauer."

He flipped through pages. He searched for anything that would reveal more about what might be happening to this man and his son. Then his eyes locked onto something. Thomas slammed it closed and ran from the room.

When he reached the nurses' station, he grabbed the nearest phone and dialed as fast as he could.

The other end of the line rang three times before a voice came over the line. "Hello?"

"Ele, it's me. How is Simon doing?"

"He's continuing to improve. He woke up a bit ago and said he was hungry."

"Mmm, that is some good news." Her husband commented, relieved by his son's continued improvement. "Listen, do you know the name of Simon's teachers at school?"

She began going through the list of names. Bauers stopped her. "Did you say Sanchez?"

"Yeah."

"Would that, by any chance, be Raul Sanchez?"

"Yes," this time with more frustrated confusion in her voice. "Why are you asking me all this?"

He ignored her question. "What subject does he teach?"

Eleanor was quiet for a second, "World History, I think."

"Do you know what they've been studying the last week or so?"

Again, the line went silent for a moment. "I think they've been studying—" Her words came slower and softened to a whisper, "World War I. Thomas? Do you think that's what's triggered Simon's nightmares and—"

He cut her off before she could finish. "I can't say for sure yet, but I think we might be onto something. I will call you back as soon as I know more." Thomas hung up the phone. His mind raced with the new information. He turned to his colleague, who had been hovering nearby with concern on her face.

"Rachael, I need you to trust me on this," Bauer said, his voice low and urgent. "You're going to keep Mr. Sanchez on high-flow oxygen."

She waited for more instruction, but none came. "And?"

"That's it, just high-flow O2."

"But doctor, what about the lesions all over his arms and chest? I thought you said he had mustard gas poisoning?"

"I know it makes little sense, but I've seen this before."

She hesitated for a moment, her eyes searching Bauer's face for something more.

A nurse emerged from the man's room and approached the nurses' station. "Sorry to bother you two, but I thought you'd want to know. The patient is awake and asking to speak with you."

Chang looked at Thomas then responded to the woman. "Thank you. We'll be right there."

As they made their way into the room, they could see that the welts on the man's skin had already become less inflamed, and his breathing easier. Dr. Chang listened to his lungs, amazed by how her patient's condition had improved so fast. "I don't understand," she murmured, shaking her head. "How did you know?"

Bauer allowed himself a small smile. "Let's just say I've been doing some research. Sometimes, old school approaches can yield the most effective treatments.

Word spread quickly through the hospital about Mr. Sanchez's remarkable improvement. He was approached by colleagues who had dismissed his unconventional ideas weeks earlier.

He nodded, accepting the praise of his peers with muted pride. Considering Simon and this man's cases, he realized his environmental cause was correct, but in a way that no one could understand. There had to be a connection between his son and Sanchez that went beyond their student-teacher status.

The similarities in their symptoms were too striking to be coincidental. But what was the link that caused this?

Satisfied with the stabilization of the patient's condition, Thomas checked in with Eleanor one more time before heading home for a shower and some rest.

"The marks on Simon's skin have almost disappeared," she reported. "Thomas, I don't know what you did, but thank you."

Bauer felt a warmth spread through his chest at her words. It had been a long time since he'd heard that tone in Eleanor's voice; a mixture of gratitude and something that might have been admiration. For a moment, he hoped that maybe, just maybe, this could be a turning point for their relationship.

Bauer's feet were heavy when he stumbled through the front door of the house, his exhaustion betrayed in every movement. The events of the past forty-eight hours had left him drained. He leaned against the door and closed his eyes, gathering the strength to haul himself up the stairs.

"Thomas? Is that you?" His mother's voice called from the kitchen.

"Yeah, Ma. It's me," he replied, his words hoarse from fatigue.

Edyth appeared in the hallway, concern showed on her face. "You look terrible, dear. Are you alright?"

Bauer forced a weak smile. "Just tired. It's been a long couple of days."

"Well, go get some rest. I'll wake you for dinner."

He nodded without protest, grateful as he turned to make his way upstairs. The hot shower washed away the grime and some of the tension he carried for the past forty-eight hours. As the water cascaded over him, Bauer's mind drifted to his upcoming midnight meeting. A flutter of anticipation stirred deep inside, despite his exhaustion.

Clean and somewhat refreshed, Thomas collapsed onto his bed. Sleep claimed him within minutes, pulling him into a dreamless slumber.

Later, he awoke to the soft knock of his mother at the door. "Thomas? Dinner's ready if you're hungry."

He groaned, rolling over to check the time. 7:30 PM. He'd slept for five hours, he still felt exhausted. "Be right down, Mom," he called back, while struggling to sit up.

Over a simple dinner of pot roast and vegetables, Edyth watched her son with worried eyes. "You're working too hard. It's not good for you."

He paused, fork halfway to his mouth. "I know. But this — this is important. I can't explain the details yet, but I'm making great headway. I can feel it in my bones. This is something that could change the world."

She reached across the table and put her hand on his. Her eyes never faltered. "Just be careful, dear. Your father used to say things like — "

Her words stopped, but her son knew she had more to say. "I will. I promise."

Following dinner and dishes, Bauer retreated to his father's study. He had only a few hours before he needed to leave for the hospital, and he intended to use that time well. Settling into the high-backed leather chair behind the desk, he pulled out a yellow legal pad and began organizing his thoughts.

At the top of the page, he put "QUESTIONS" in bold letters. Below, he started listing everything he wanted to know:

What was Case 47?

How were the temporal displacement experiments connected to Levi's and his father's work?

Who was Subject Alpha?

What happened to Dr. Levi?

How is Sam Harris involved?

How are Simon and Mr. Sanchez's conditions related to all of this?

Who has been watching me, and why?

As he wrote, more questions came to mind. Each new question led to more. By the time he finished writing, he had filled the page with a complicated web of interconnected inquiries. He sat back as he rubbed his eyes. The scope of what lay before him was tremendous, but there was a sense of clarity emerging from the chaos.

He glanced at his watch: 10:00 PM. He wanted to get to the archives early. It was time for him to go. Thomas grabbed his jacket and keys. He patted the back pocket of his jeans for his list of questions and wallet, then paused at the door of the study.

The drive to Saint Elizabeths was quiet. The late-night streets were deserted. Bauer's mind ran through plausible scenarios for his evening ahead. When he pulled into the hospital parking area, anticipation and apprehension settled in his gut.

He parked his car in a secluded corner of the lot. He sat for a moment. Then, with a deep breath, he got out and made his way towards a side door of the building.

The night air was cool and still against his skin. Only the distant wind blowing through the trees broke the silence. Bauer's footsteps echoed off the pavement as he approached the remote entrance he often used when he worked late. His fingers punched in the four-digit code without a thought. The lock clicked. Bauer glanced over his shoulder, then stepped inside.

Chapter 26

Bauer's footsteps were silent. He walked the dim corridors of Saint Elizabeths Hospital. There was no one in this wing of the building because of the late hour. The only person he might cross paths with was the occasional security guard.

He checked his watch. It was only 10:30 PM. His gut churned from nervousness. He had to wait ninety minutes for his mysterious caller to arrive.

Thomas made his way towards the weighty wooden double doors of the archives. He froze, listening for any signs of movement in the long hallway. He was alone. Putting some weight into his effort, he pushed a door open.

The creak of the hinges announced his arrival, making him wince. He slipped inside, letting the door close behind him. Before him was an endless maze of towering bookcases and filing cabinets. Among the shelving, he found the occasional cart with materials that needed to be returned to their proper place.

The air was thick with the musty scent of old leather, canvas, paper, and faint hints of dust and ink. The green hue of dim emergency exit lights cast long unearthly shadows across the floor, creating an eerie atmosphere that further set Bauer's nerves on edge.

Over the years, he'd probably spent more time lost in this sea of collected information than he had in his own office. Few people at Saint Elizabeths had as much knowledge about what was there as he did. His moves were swift and silent through aisles. He scanned his surroundings, looking for a suitable hiding spot. Some place where he could watch and wait.

He selected a secluded corner at the end of the aisle. It was where two large shelving units came together. Book carts overflowing with thick, leather-bound volumes helped obscure his hiding spot. He positioned himself behind a cart.

He sat with his back against the shelf. The tall, lanky man tucked his long legs to minimize his visibility. From his vantage point, he could not see the double doors. However, he had a clear view of the entire length of the main walkway down the center.

He could also see the entrance of every row that flanked the central aisle, including the one where he was to meet the mysterious caller. Obscured by the shadows, he peered between the tomes loaded on the cart once more. Thomas glanced at his watch. He still had plenty of time before his man would arrive. He settled in to wait, his senses on high alert for any sound or sign of movement.

Each second felt like an eternity as he sat in the oppressive silence. The heating system kicked on. The sudden noise from the antiquated ducting made him jump. "Get a grip, Bauer", he thought to himself.

Thomas checked the time again. His man was now almost fifteen minutes late. Just as he thought he'd been stood up, the unmistakable, yet distinct, sense of air shifting within the confines of the archives caught his attention. The sound of the archive door opening indicated that someone had arrived, although he couldn't see them.

He held his breath and pressed his body further into the bookshelf against his back. He peered through gaps in the library cart contents. A dark figure appeared as he entered the main aisle in the distance. He turned his head, surveying the vast space between him and where he hid, waiting in the shadows.

The newcomer began creeping amongst the shelves toward his hidden location. His movements were graceful, fluid, deliberate, cautious, and familiar. There was something about the way this man tilted his head.

It was unsettling for him to not remember where he had seen this man before. The man's face was impossible to make out in the low light. The doctor watched as the man stopped at the entrance of each row to make sure no one was in them. The man looked over his shoulder often. A gesture suggesting paranoia that didn't escape the psychiatrist's notice.

This man lingered a little near where he was supposed to meet his caller. Thomas' pulse quickened as the man moved deeper into the archives. The visitor was now walking toward the spot where he hid.

The doctor pressed himself further against the shelf at his back, wishing he was invisible. The familiar stranger stood within arm's reach, close enough for him to catch a whiff of cologne, a scent that stirred memories but refused to reveal the man's identity.

Satisfied that he was alone, or so he thought, the mysterious figure turned on his heels and made his way back down the aisle. He now moved with purpose. He stopped at the end of the row where Bauer was to meet his caller.

Thomas watched as the man disappeared among the shelves. The familiarity of the stranger gnawed at him. He'd seen this person before, he was certain of it. But where? A patient? A colleague? Someone from his past? He remained frozen in place.

He considered revealing himself, but something held him back. His instinct to remain hidden conflicted with the fact that he could not see the other man. Something in his gut told him that whoever this man was, he was not the man he had come in here to meet this evening.

Suddenly, a cacophony of disturbing sounds erupted from the row in which the man had vanished. The unmistakable sound of scuffling feet echoed through the cavernous space. Next came the muffled voices engaged in a barely audible, heated argument. Bauer's breath caught in his throat.

Someone was in there with them. But how? Thomas strained his ears as he heard books and papers falling from shelves and crashing to the floor.

The altercation continued. What was happening? Who else was here? His instincts urged him to stay hidden, but his curiosity compelled him to move to where he could get a better look.

With great caution, he emerged from his hiding spot. He crouched low as he moved in the shadows toward the source of the commotion. As he crept closer, the muffled words grew louder and clearer. Bauer could now distinguish between the two distinct voices. One belonging to the man he'd watched enter the archives. His tone was deep, and he spoke with an eastern European accent.

He'd heard the other voice before. It was softer, and filled with fear. Their conversation was hushed and intense, punctuated by the occasional sound of more books hitting the floor.

"I don't have it," the familiar man strained.

"Where is it?" The larger man hissed.

Thomas ducked into an adjacent row. He pressed his back against the shelf. He was now close enough to better hear the confrontation that was taking place a few rows away. What he could see made his blood run cold.

The European man had the other man pinned forcefully to the stack of books. The smaller man struggled to keep his feet under him.

"I don't know," came a forced whisper as more books fell and scattered.

"Don't lie to me," the big man growled, leaning his forearm into the other man's throat.

Whatever he had come in here for was far more dangerous than he could have ever anticipated. What did this violent confrontation the next row over have to do with Levi's and his father's research?

The caller was right. Thomas wasn't the only one searching for the illusive Case 47. Adrenaline surged through his veins. His pulse thundered in his ears as he crouched down, unsure of what to do.

Should he intervene? Run for help? A loud crashing noise of metal on the floor came from the entrance area, cutting his indecision short. He and the two men froze in place and held their breath, plunging the repository into absolute silence.

From his vantage point, he could finally see the big fellow's eyes. The eastern European's eyes darted around, as if searching for an escape route as footsteps grew louder in the main aisle. In that moment, the man's gaze locked with his. The dim light cast long shadows across his face, making it difficult to see his features.

"We're not alone," the man snarled, loosening his grip on the familiar stranger a little. He moved in Bauer's direction. Thomas' heart pounded in his chest as the large man turned toward the entrance of the row.

A concealed frenzy of violent movements erupted around the man. Horrific screams of pain echoed through the archives. Then everything went silent, followed by the dull thud of a body hitting the floor.

Thomas pressed his back tighter against the shelf, his arm clamped tight over his own mouth to muffle his ragged breathing. The silence that descended upon the room was oppressive, broken only by the sound of the blood rushing through his ears.

His mind raced. Who had fallen? The familiar stranger or the man with the accent? Was someone dead? Injured? The weight of the situation threatened to crush.

Bauer's muscles tensed, ready for action, but fear kept him rooted in his spot. His instinct to help warred with his need for self-preservation. The ethical part of him screamed at him to intervene, but his body remained frozen.

Sweat beaded on his forehead as he strained his ears, listening for any sign of movement or life. The silence stretched on, punctuated only by the occasional creak of the old building settling around him. Each second felt like an eternity.

His fingernails dug into the bookcase behind him, the rough wood grounding him in reality. He could feel splinters embed themselves into his skin, but he failed to notice any discomfort. He focused all his senses on the situation two rows away. The area where the altercation had taken place now remained eerily quiet.

Bauer closed his eyes, trying to steady his breathing and calm his racing heart. The darkness offered no respite from the turmoil that racked his mind. When he opened his eyes again, the dimness was even more ominous. Dark shadows stretched into sinister fingers across the floor.

Bauer's legs trembled, muscles taut by the strain of remaining still for so long. He wanted to move, to act, to do something other than hide like a coward. But the potential consequences of even the slightest movement kept him paralyzed where he was.

The silence seemed to grow, if that were possible. It pressed firm against his eardrums, making him wonder if he'd gone deaf. He swallowed hard. The sound boomed loud in the suffocating stillness.

Time stretched and wrapped around him as he remained frozen in place. Each breath threatened to expose his position. The air was thick and oppressive, heavy with tension and the faint metallic scent of what Bauer feared must be blood.

His eyes darted and searched for any sign of movement, any clue what was happening just a couple of rows away. But the bookshelves stood between them as silent sentinels, revealing nothing of the drama that had occurred beyond them.

He shifted, his muscles protesting the prolonged lack of movement. The smallest of movements caused a floorboard to creak beneath his feet. It sounded loud in the stillness. Thomas froze once more. He held his breath as he waited to see if the noise had given away his position.

Thomas saw the man turn on his heels without a sound. He retraced his steps through the foreboding silence. The man stopped at the end of his row where the altercation had taken place. However, there was no mistaking the way the man moved; cautious yet purposeful.

The man paused in the distance. His head swept up and down the main aisle of the archives. Thomas watched him. He knew what would happen if the man ventured closer toward him. He pressed himself deeper into the shadows, once again wishing he could somehow become invisible.

For a moment, the man stood motionless, cocking his head, listening. The only sound was the faint hum of the building's ancient heating system.

Bauer's pulse thundered so loud in his ears, he wondered if the man could not hear it. He could not take his eye off the man.

The man turned, then walked. His heels clicked against the hardwood floor. He was now heading in the direction where Thomas hid in the shadows. Each step grew louder as the visitor drew closer. Bauer backed himself into the book shelves, desperate for a way out of his predicament.

The shelves that had seemed like the perfect hiding place had become a trap. He had nowhere to go if the man came his way. The deeper he went, the darker it became. As he retreated to the deepest part of his row, then came to a sudden stop.

Against his back, near his left kidney, something poked him in the ribs. The man's footsteps grew near. He averted his eyes to see the red glow of a light on the wall. His hand came to rest on a fire alarm.

The familiar man was now just a few feet away from Bauer's row. His pace slowed, and Thomas could now hear the soft rustle of fabric as the man walked toward his row. Every nerve in his body burned as his fingers wrapped around the white grip of the alarm. In a matter of seconds, he would have to make a decision; try to remain hidden, or pull the handle?

As the man grew closer to one of the functioning overhead lights, the doctor's blood ran cold as he caught a clear glimpse of the man's face. He was one of the men who had chased him and Andrew from Anacostia Park.

He struggled to process this new information. What was he doing here? How had he known about this midnight archive meeting? The man was now mere steps away from where he hid.

His fingers gripped tighter around the fire alarm handle. His muscles, ready to pull it at any second. He could hear the visitor's steady, somewhat labored breathing. The faint scent of cigarette smoke and cologne clung to the man's clothes. The doctor held his breath, afraid that even the slightest sound would give him away.

The man reached Thomas' row and stepped to enter it. A sudden loud commotion came from the archives entrance, shattering the weighty silence, causing them to jump.

"Lacheu, are you still in here?"

"Over here." Responded the man with the accent.

"Someone's coming. We gotta get out of here!"

Bauer recognized the other voice. It belonged to the other man that had chased him and Andrew through the park the night before. The one he saw Harris running toward, as he and Andrew sped away in a panic. Both men were here now, in the archives. Why? Did the old man arrange this weird secret meeting?

The Eastern European man paused and looked into Bauer's direction. He swallowed hard, certain the man saw him. The man took one more step closer to him.

"Lacheu, come on, what are you waiting for?!" Came the other man's concerned, shouted whispers. "They're going to find us if we stay here any longer!"

The man hesitated for a split second, staring into the darkness of the row. Then, without warning, the man turned. His retreating footsteps echoed through the archives. The two men's whispered conversation reached Thomas' ears as he quickly made his way towards his companion.

"Was he there?"

"Yeah."

"And?"

"We don't have to worry about him anymore."

"Good work Lacheu, I'm sure Shimba will be pleased."

Thomas remained frozen in place, still afraid to move. He listened as their voices faded away in the distance.

It was only when he heard the distant sound of the archive door slam closed did Bauer exhale. He hadn't even realized he'd been holding his breath all this time. His legs were weak. He leaned against the bookshelf, his breathing now ragged as he felt like passing out.

Chapter 27

Bauer remained frozen in place. His back pressed against the wall and bookshelf at his back. The adrenaline that coursed through his veins made his body shake with every thunderous beat of his heart within his chest. He waited another minute before he finally felt safe enough to move.

His legs were weak from the prolonged tension of trying to stay still for so long. He stumbled with each trembling step he took toward the main aisle of the archives. The silence that had seemed so oppressive just moments ago was now eerie and unnatural. Bauer gasped for breath as he tried to calm himself.

His mind raced with all that he had just witnessed. Who were Lacheu and Shimba? What were they after? And who was the unfortunate soul who had become their victim?

As he reached the row where the altercation took place, his steps faltered. Gripped with fear, he hesitated as he peered into the darkened space. His eyes widened in horror as they fell upon the crumpled form lying motionless on the floor.

Books and papers were strewn about, evidence of the violent struggle that had occurred just moments earlier. The figure lay sprawled face-down, surrounded by the chaos and a growing pool of dark liquid. The doctor's stomach sank as the distinct metallic scent of blood filled his nostrils.

Bauer stood frozen at the entrance to the row. He thought about chasing after the attacker and his accomplice. They couldn't have gotten far, and perhaps he could catch up to them, maybe even overhear more of their plans.

The names Lacheu and Shimba echoed through his head. Tantalizing clues of some larger mystery, he now found himself involved in.

His eyes remained fixed on the motionless form before him. Another part of him knew it was in his own best interest not to follow the perpetrators of this crime. They never knew he was there, and he planned to keep it that way for as long as possible. Besides, he couldn't leave. Someone lay hurt, maybe dying, and Bauer had a moral obligation to help. His ethical duty and innate compassion warred with his ill considered burning curiosity and desire for answers.

His hesitation dissolved as he noticed the alarming amount of bright red blood pooling around the fallen man. His medical training kicked in, overriding his remaining fear and indecision. With quick, methodical steps, he approached the victim. His brain shifted to doctor mode. Each calculated move was to save the life of the man laying on the floor.

As he drew closer, Thomas' breath slowed, then caught in his throat. The prone victim didn't appear to not be breathing. As he stepped next to the unconscious figure, his gaze became fixed on the unmistakable body of Sam Harris. The old janitor's familiar weathered face was ashen, his eyes closed and mouth agape.

"Oh my God, Sam," Thomas whispered, dropping to his knees beside the injured man. His hands moved fast over the old man as he performed a rudimentary initial assessment of injuries.

Soaked with blood, the housekeeper's shirt stuck to his skin. There were several tears in the fabric.

The physician's fingers probed, searching for the source of the blood. He found a deep gash in the janitor's abdomen. The bright red streams pulsed with each beat of the old man's heart.

The doctor recalled his emergency medical protocols. He quickly shrugged off his jacket, wadding it up and pressing it against the wound. "Hold on, Sam," he muttered, his voice tight.

As he applied pressure, his eyes darted around, looking for anything he could use to help slow the bleeding. But as he took in the full extent of the injuries, a cold realization settled over him. The victim's breathing was shallow and irregular, his pulse weak and thready under his fingers.

The cut in the abdomen was deep. The lacerations could have penetrated vital organs. There were other wounds too, defensive cuts on arms. The red-tinged, matted gray hair that surrounded the nasty gash on the side of his head oozed of thick red liquid. Thomas' stomach lurched as he realized the severity of the wounds brought on by the brutal attack.

This was no accident, nor some random act of violence. Lacheu, whoever he was, had come here to eliminate the old man or him for good. The thought chilled Bauer to his core, even as he continued to work, trying to stem the flow of blood.

"Sam, can you hear me?" He called out, leaning close to the old man's face. There was no response, not even a flicker of movement behind the man's closed eyelids. "Just hold on. I'm going to get you out of here."

Bauer's hands trembled as he tried to apply pressure to bleeding wounds. His mind raced as he executed long established protocols intended to stop the incessant hemorrhaging.

As he continued his futile efforts, he reflected on the precarious situation he now found himself in. He was alone in the archives with an injured old man, who was dying, and the attackers could still be nearby, ready to finish the old man and him off. The old man was slipping away right before his eyes.

Through a surge of desperation, Thomas realized that only surgery would save this man. He needed to get him out of here fast. Thomas shifted position to get better leverage. He noticed something shoved in the interior pocket of the blood-soaked coat. A crumpled piece of paper, its edges stained red, peeked out from beneath the lapel of the overcoat. Bauer lifted it from his clothes.

His eyes widened. Through the smears of red, he could make out familiar phrases and notations. Harris was the mysterious caller he was supposed to meet in the archives that night. This man promised him crucial information he'd been looking for.

The connection between Case 47 and Dr. Levi to his father was on the verge of being lost forever. There was no time to examine it any further. With shaking hands, he stuffed the bloodstained note into his pants pocket.

"Damn it, Sam," Bauer muttered, refocusing his life-saving efforts. "You've got to hold on. I need to get you out of here."

The urgency of the situation hit him. The old man was fading fast, his breaths became more shallow. It was now or never. He had to act now.

With a deep breath, Thomas steadied his legs under him. He couldn't afford to be gentle, not with the man's life hanging in the balance. In one fluid motion, he scooped the unconscious man into his arms, ignoring the protest of his own muscles. The surge of adrenaline coursing through his own veins made the physical effort easier.

The body was limp, his head drooped and bobbed against Bauer's chest. The doctor struggled to maintain his balance. The smell of blood overwhelmed Thomas' senses. The warm stickiness seeped through his own clothes. He pushed aside any personal discomfort, focusing only on getting Harris to a more advanced level of care as fast as possible.

With determined steps, the physician ran out of the exit of the archives. The hallways of Saint Elizabeths seemed darker and longer than usual. His pace quickened. Beads of sweat flowed from his brow. His breath came in quick gasps from the exertion. Every second was an eternity, each step a battle against time itself.

The startled faces of night shift staff turned towards him as he burst through the doors, Harris' bloodied form cradled in his arms.

"Help!" Bauer called out as he approached the nearest nurses' station. "I need some help over here, stat!"

For a moment, everyone stood frozen in place. Then the room erupted into organized chaos.

"What happened?" a nurse asked as she rushed forward, already reaching for the bloody victim. As an orderly wheeled a gurney over

"Somebody attacked him!" Thomas explained panting for breath. He laid the old man down. "Multiple stab wounds, possible head injury. He's lost a lot of blood."

The room became a flurry of activity as the medical staff sprang into action. Bauer worked alongside the night shift people he almost never saw.

"I need someone to get some lactated ringers and high flow O2 started on him, stat!"

"I've got the IV!" yelled one nurse as she ran to grab the supplies she needed.

On the other side of Harris, another RN ripped open the packaging on a non-rebreather mask, hooked it up to oxygen, and placed it over the old man's face. Bauer's own hands moved with efficiency as they all worked together to stabilize their coworker. They cut away his bloodied clothes, revealing the full extent of his injuries.

"My God, so much blood," Thomas' voice was tight with concern. "I need some hemostats, sutures, anything. I gotta get this bleeding under control, or he's not going to make it!"

He stopped the flow from the last severed artery.

"Come on, Sam," the doctor muttered, his fingers moving like a master's to make sure all the bleeding had stopped. "You can't die on me now."

"Not when so many questions were so close to being answered." Thomas thought to himself. The minutes ticked by so slow, each one felt like an hour.

Outside Saint Elizabeths Hospital, the distant wail of an approaching siren grew louder by the second.

The ambulance arrived, paramedics crashed through double doors. They brought in their gurney and equipment as they followed an orderly. The doctor stepped back, allowing them to take over. His eyes remained fixed on Sam's pale face as he delivered his verbal report. As they prepared to transport the old man, he was flooded by a mix of hope and dread. He was still alive, for the moment. Whether he would survive the journey to the trauma center was now out of his hands.

As they wheeled Harris away, Bauer stood in the middle of the now quiet hall. His clothes were covered with blood. With a sigh, Thomas sank into a nearby chair. The adrenaline that had fueled him for the past hour was wearing off, leaving him exhausted. He reached for his handkerchief. The edges of the crumpled bloodstained pages brushed against his fingers.

The contents of Bauer's pocket felt heavy. He would have to wait until he returned to his father's study to look at it closer. Who were Lacheu and Shimba? What did Harris know that was worth killing him? Now even more questions burned in his mind as sirens once again blared through the night, announcing Sam's departure from Saint Elizabeths Hospital.

Thomas could feel the weight of medical and ethical responsibility and all that had occurred the past several weeks settled on his upper back and shoulders. He'd done everything he could. He prayed that it would be enough.

The sound of heavy footsteps approaching interrupted his reflection. Two large men entered the area, their faces set with grim expressions.

"Dr. Bauer?" the taller of the two asked, his tone gruff. "We need to ask you a few questions about what happened here tonight."

Bauer's stomach tightened. He wasn't ready for this. Not now, not when he was still trying to process all that had occurred.

"I'm sorry, but I've got to follow that ambulance," Thomas said, his voice strained. He started to get up from the chair where he sat, but the man stepped in front of him.

"Sir, we have to know what transpired here. It's protocol," the security guard insisted.

He couldn't tell them what he had seen, couldn't risk exposing himself or putting Harris in even more danger. "Look, I found Sam injured in the archives. I brought him here. That's all I know. Now, if you'll excuse me, I have an ambulance to catch."

The guards exchanged glances. They were not satisfied with his response. "Dr. Bauer, we'll get a more detailed statement — "

But he had already pushed past them, his feet carrying him fast down the hallway. He could hear their calls behind him, but he refused to slow down. His breath came in short gasps. He burst through the hospital doors and into the cool night air.

The parking lot was a blur as Thomas rushed to his car. He fumbled with keys, his hands shook as he moved to unlock the door. He slid into the driver's seat. His heart pounded in his chest. He wanted to just sit there for a moment, but this was not the time for that.

The night replayed in his mind several times like an odd, distorted record. There were bits of conversations he had overheard and the struggle he had seen. The sight of Harris lying on the floor. Then his frantic efforts to save the old man's life.

There was something about this Lacheu character. Something familiar beyond the events at Anacostia Park. It nagged at the back of his brain. Everything came together in a surreal nightmare he could never wake up from.

Bauer's stomach churned as he looked down at his clothes. After years in the medical field, the gore didn't bother him. However, this was different. This was Sam Harris' blood on him. The doctor moved his hand to his chest. The bloodstained document he had removed from the housekeeper's coat was still in his pocket. A physical reminder of the dangers he experienced that evening.

The security guards that approached him earlier zipped through the parking lot in their golf cart. Bauer wouldn't wait for another interaction with him. He watched as the men disappeared around the side of the hospital. Without hesitation, Thomas started his car and left.

The sedan sped through the intersections, trying to catch up with the ambulance. Keeping a safe distance, he knew couldn't tell anyone what had happened that night. Doing so would not only put him in danger and further jeopardize Harris' safety as well.

The dark early morning streets of Washington D.C. passed by in a blur of streetlights and shadowy building facades. Thomas' hands gripped the steering wheel tight. He navigated the winding route on autopilot through the city to the trauma center.

His throat was dry. He swallowed hard. All his life, he had always prided himself on a very personal form of integrity. He always did what he knew was right by his patients and his research. He never backed down, despite pressure or professional reprimand from administrative higher-ups.

His head was a mess as his car sped through the night, ever closer to the ambulance. This old man whose life hung in the balance had risked his life to meet with him in the archives tonight. Bauer shook his head. Other than his own mother, the old man was his only living connection to his father and Dr. Levi.

Going forward, he had no choice but to be deliberate with what he knew and the answers he sought should he continue this quest. Thomas had some tough decisions to make. His eyes became fixated on the flashing red lights as Sam Harris clung to life inside the ambulance.

His selfish actions had jeopardized the safety of his family, Andrew, himself, and now the old housekeeper. How could anything be worth risking life, limb, and sanity?

Chapter 28

Dr. Thomas Bauer burst through the emergency room doors of the trauma center. His heart pounded hard in his chest. The smell of antiseptic and fear hung heavy in the air as he stumbled forward in his blood-stained clothes. He'd followed the ambulance's wailing sirens through the dark streets of Washington DC, His mind consumed by confusion and fear.

The fluorescent lights overhead cast harsh shadows across the doctor's face, accentuating the lines etched deep into his features. His eyes darted around the bustling emergency room, searching for any sign of Harris or the EMTs who had wheeled him away from Saint Elizabeths Hospital.

The cacophony of beeping monitors, urgent voices, and patients in pain assaulted Bauer's senses. He pushed his way through the crowd of patients and staff, ignoring their curious, concerned glances. His disheveled appearance and wild-eyed desperation made him stand out in the chaos of the ER.

A young nurse with kind eyes approached. Her brow wrinkled with concern. "Sir, are you injured? You're covered in blood."

"No, no, it's not mine." Bauer shook his head. "Sam Harris," Bauer continued. His voice was hoarse and strained. "Where did they take him? I'm looking for a patient who just came in by ambulance, Sam Harris. He was stabbed. Where is he?"

The nurse's expression softened with understanding. "Are you family?"

"I'm his—" Bauer hesitated, realizing he did not know how to define his relationship with Harris. Colleague? Adversary? Victim? "I'm his doctor," he finished in a lame attempt to gain him access.

"I'm sorry, sir, but only immediate family is allowed back there right now," the nurse explained in a firm yet gentle tone. "If you'd like to wait, I can update you on his condition as soon as we know more."

Bauer was numb as he nodded. He watched the nurse disappear behind a set of heavy double doors. He stood there for a moment, feeling lost and helpless, before shuffling over to a row of uncomfortable plastic chairs in the waiting area.

As he sank into a seat, he felt drained and shaky. Bauer ran a trembling hand through his hair, grimacing as he felt the tackiness of residual dried blood still on his hand.

Nothing about this evening turned out the way he'd expected. Bauer had been so certain that Sam Harris was the one who'd been following him. The one breaking into his office, leaving cryptic warnings. He'd even confronted the old janitor.

He felt disappointed with himself. He hid like a coward as Lacheu assaulted the man. Bauer's only defense was that he didn't know it was Harris two rows away with his assailant. The sounds of struggle, the cries of pain, and the sickening thud of his body hitting the floor all replayed in his head.

Thomas' stomach churned as he again watched the expanding pool of blood. He shuddered, opening his eyes and stared at the scuffed white floor of the waiting room. He thought he was so close to unraveling mysteries that haunted him. Now he felt more lost than ever.

Who was this Lacheu figure seen at the park and in the archives? The altercation made it clear the two knew each other. Harris had knowledge worth killing for.

A gentle touch on Bauer's shoulder startled him from his thoughts. Bauer looked up to see the same kind-eyed nurse from earlier standing next to him.

"Dr. Bauer?" she asked. Her voice was comforting, but professional. "I need some information about Mr. Harris, if you don't mind."

Bauer nodded, looking up at her from his seated position. "Of course. What do you need to know?"

"Please come with me, where we can talk in private."

In the triage room, the nurse pulled out a clipboard and pen. "We're having trouble locating any next of kin for Mr. Harris. As his doctor, do you have any information about his family or emergency contacts?"

Bauer's eyes drifted as he realized just how little he actually knew about the man he'd suspected of stalking him all this time. He'd been so focused on the potential threat that Harris represented, that he'd never for a moment stopped to consider the janitor as a person with a life outside the hospital.

He racked his memory for anything that might be helpful from the old man's personnel file. "I — I'm afraid I know very little about his personal life," Bauer admitted, feeling a twinge of guilt. "He's worked at Saint Elizabeths for decades, but beyond that—" He trailed off, shaking his head.

The nurse's pen hovered over the clipboard. "What about his age? Medical history? Any allergies or medications we should be aware of?"

"He's in his late sixties." Bauer's mind raced, trying to recall any scrap of information about Harris that might be useful. "I'm sorry. I can't remember off the top of my head." He lied.

The nurse nodded, making a few notes. "That's alright, Dr. Bauer. We'll do our best with the information we have. Is there anything else you can tell us that might be helpful?"

Bauer hesitated, wondering how much he should reveal about the circumstances that brought Harris and himself to the emergency room. "I found him lying on the floor bleeding."

The nurse's eyes widened, then relaxed some. "Thank you for your help, Dr. Bauer. We'll update you on Mr. Harris' condition as soon as we can."

Bauer exited the triage room and returned to the ER waiting room. He slumped back into a chair, overwhelmed by frustration and guilt. He'd suspected Harris, to accuse him of spying and breaking into his office, but now he realized he knew nothing about the janitor beyond his work at Saint Elizabeths.

Bauer's gaze drifted to the television mounted on the wall in the upper corner of the waiting room. The volume was off, but closed captions scrolled across the bottom of the screen as a local news station replayed the 11:00 pm news broadcast. His absent eyes watched as his mind wandered.

A familiar face flashed across the screen. Bauer's gaze became fixated on the man's image on the television. His heart raced as he recognized him as Lacheu, the man who had assaulted Sam Harris in the archives that night. The caption beneath his face said he was a "person of interest" in connection with a recent break-in at a government research facility.

Bauer leaned forward to get a better look at the words scrolling across the screen. The words moved too fast for his tired brain to process. He only caught fragments about a "top-secret research facility" and "stolen classified documents," but before he could piece together more information, the report moved on to another news story.

Before Bauer could consider the new information, a doctor in blue scrubs approached him. He looked tired and stressed, but maintained his professionalism.

"Dr. Bauer?" the physician asked, extending his hand. "I'm Dr. Reeves. Could you please come with me to the trauma bay? Mr. Harris is stable but remains in critical condition, but there's something we need your help with."

Bauer stood up. His heart pounded in his throat. "Of course. What is it?"

Dr. Reeves hesitated, glancing around the crowded waiting room. "It's — unusual. We've found some markings on Mr. Harris' body that we can't explain. Given your connection to him and Saint Elizabeths, we thought you might be able to shed some light on the situation."

Bauer nodded, then followed with a mix of curiosity and apprehension. The two doctors walked through the double doors and into the restricted area of the emergency department. Bauer's mind raced with possibilities. What could be so unusual that the trauma team needed the input of a psychiatrist?

Dr. Reeves led Bauer through a maze of curtained-off areas. The beeping of monitors and murmurs of people in pain contributed to the urgency of the moment. They stopped in front of a closed door, and Dr. Reeves turned to face Bauer.

"Before we go in, I need to prepare you," the doctor said, his voice low. "Mr. Harris' condition is serious. He lost a lot of blood, and we're still working to stabilize him so we can get him into surgery. The markings we need you to look at — they're unlike anything I've seen in my career."

Bauer took a deep breath, then nodded to Dr. Reeves. The trauma doctor pushed open the door. Bauer followed him into the room. The steady beeping of monitors filled the air as Bauer's eyes adjusted to the bright lights. His gaze fell upon the unconscious form of Sam Harris lying in the hospital bed.

The old janitor looked small and frail, his skin pale against the bleached white sheets. IV tubes and wires snaked around his body, connecting him to various machines that monitored his vital signs.

Bauer approached the bedside. His heart was heavy with concern. He had spent so much time suspecting him, viewing him as a potential threat, that he never saw the vulnerable human being before him.

Dr. Reeves cleared his throat, drawing Bauer's attention. "The markings we mentioned are all over his body," he said, lifting the sheet to reveal Harris' limbs and torso. "The wounds are recent, but healed over. At some recent point, they were significant injuries.

Bauer leaned in, his eyes curious as he examined the old man's skin. At first, he saw nothing unusual — just the wrinkled, age-spotted arm of an elderly man. But as his eyes traveled up towards the man's shoulder, he froze.

There, inked into Harris' skin, was a tattoo unlike anything Bauer had ever seen. The number 47 entwined with the sinuous form of a snake. Its body twisted into the shape of a lowercase Greek letter alpha. The design was as beautiful as it was unsettling. The black ink looked darker than usual against Harris' pale skin.

Bauer's mind raced. The number 47; it couldn't be a coincidence. Case 47, the mysterious file he had been searching for, the key to understanding his father's research and Dr. Levi's experiments. And the alpha symbol, it had to be a reference to Subject Alpha, mentioned in the documents he had found?

"Dr. Bauer?" Dr. Reeves's voice cut through his thoughts. "Look here. Do these marks mean anything to you?"

The marks in question appeared as though Harris had been a victim of some sort of torture. Bauer opened his mouth to respond, but before he could form a single word, the slightest of movements caught his eye. Harris' eyelids fluttered, and his fingers twitched.

"He's regaining consciousness," Bauer said, moving closer to the bed. "Mr. Harris? Sam? Can you hear me? It's me, Dr. Bauer."

Harris' eyes opened, unfocused and glassy. His lips moved, forming words that had no sound. In that brief instant of lucidity, Harris grabbed Bauer's wrist with surprising strength and pulled him closer. Without thinking, Bauer leaned in, placing his ear right up to the old man's mouth.

Harris' breath was weak, just more than a whisper, but Bauer could only make out a few words: "Passage...archives...Case 47...dangerous." Harris' voice was weak and raspy. "You have to find it. Before they do."

Bauer's heart raced as he processed Harris' whispered words. The old janitor's grip on his wrist loosened, and Bauer straightened up. He glanced at Dr. Reeves, who looked at him, curious.

"What did he say?" Reeves asked, staring at him with concern.

Bauer hesitated, weighing his options. He couldn't risk revealing what this man had just told him. They had no bearing on potential treatment protocols. Bauer still didn't understand the information himself. "Nothing coherent," Bauer lied, his voice steadier than he felt. "Just the ramblings of a man coming out of unconsciousness."

Dr. Reeves nodded, satisfied with the explanation. Before he could press further, a commotion erupted in the hallway outside. Raised voices and hurried footsteps sounded through the closed door.

Reeves moved toward the door to investigate. He cracked the door open slightly. Bauer strained to hear tense fragments of the conversation that filtered through.

"—government agent—"

"—demand information—"

"—speak with the old man—"

Bauer was confused. A government agent? Here? Now? Wanting to talk to Sam? Just when a few of the pieces were falling into place, he realized the situation was far more complex and dangerous than he could have ever imagined.

He looked back over his shoulder at Harris, who once again laid there unconscious. The old janitor's secrets ran deep. And now, those secrets had attracted the attention of powerful entities far beyond anything at Saint Elizabeths Hospital.

The presence of a government agent added yet another layer of danger to the mystery of Sam Harris. Being seen in here right now would only make matters worse for both of them. Panic set in as Bauer realized he needed to get out of there. His eyes landed on an exit on the other side of the room.

When he turned to make his way towards the door, a shrill alarm pierced through the relative calm. The steady beep of Harris' heart monitor had changed to a continuous, high-pitched tone. The line on the EKG machine flatlined. Bauer whirled around, his eyes wide with shock as he watched Harris' body go limp on the bed.

"He's coded!" Dr. Reeves shouted, rushing to Harris' side as he smashed the blue button mounted on the wall.

In an instant, the room erupted into organized chaos. Medical staff poured in, their voices overlapping as they called out orders and readings. Bauer was shoved out of the way. Nurses and doctors swarmed in around the old man. "Clear the room!" Someone shouted.

Bauer felt hands on his shoulders, guiding him out the nearest door. He stumbled into the hallway, his head spinning from the sudden turn of events. Bauer caught sight of a man in a dark suit pushing his way through the throng of hospital staff. The man stared at the trauma bay door. His expression looked like a mix of determination and frustration.

Bauer's heart hammered in his chest. This had to be the government agent he'd overheard mentioned just moments ago. The man was trying to force his way closer to Harris' room, even as the medical staff attempted to hold him back.

"Sir, you can't go in there!" a nurse insisted, her voice strained as she blocked the agent's path. She created enough of a distraction while Bauer distanced himself a little from Harris' room.

The agent's face contorted with anger. "I need to speak with that man immediately. This is a matter of national security!"

"That man has been unconscious since he arrived," explained the nurse.

Bauer pressed himself against the wall, trying to make himself as inconspicuous as possible. He watched as more medical personnel rushed into the room to help try to revive Harris. The government agent hovered not far outside the door like a vulture ready to pick apart his dead prey.

The gravity of the situation crashed down around Bauer all at once. Everything he wanted to know, everything he thought was so damn important, now seemed so trivial. He had lost sight of the human cost of all this.

Guilt washed over him as he remembered how he used to suspect the vulnerable old man was a threat. The man had secrets and fears of his own. Now, because of his own stupid pursuit of answers, Harris lay dead in the other room while others fought to bring him back.

Anger bubbled up along with his guilt. He was mad at his selfish actions. He never once suspected that they would subject Harris to torture in order to get at the secrets he continued to hide. His dad tried to warn him. Hell, Harris even tried to warn him, protect him.

As the medical team continued their desperate efforts to revive Harris. Bauer could feel his future and his past slipping away, along with the old man in the other room. It was all too much.

The shouts of the medical staff, the insistent beeping of machines, and the frustrated demands of the government agent all blended into a cacophony of chaos around Bauer. He stood there, pressed against the wall, overwhelmed by the swirling emotions of guilt, fear, and anger.

In that moment, as he watched the frantic scene around him, Bauer did not know if Harris would survive. What did Harris know about Case 47 that was so vital to national security? He couldn't fathom what consequences might await him if his involvement with Harris was ever discovered.

Chapter 29

Dr. Thomas Bauer stood frozen with his back against a wall across from the trauma room, where Sam Harris lay dead. His heart broke deep within his chest as he watched the frantic efforts of the medical team through a small gap in the door. The brilliant white walls and buzz from the harsh fluorescent light overhead made him uncomfortable. He adjusted his posture, hoping to shake himself from the chaotic nightmare that surrounded him.

Inside the room, doctors and nurses swarmed around the old man's motionless form. Their voices carried an urgent tone as they called out medications and instructions. A continuous, haunting sound had replaced the rhythmic beeps of the heart monitor.

"Clear!" One doctor shouted, pressing the defibrillator paddles to Sam's bare chest. Thomas flinched as Harris' body jumped from the bed, then fell still once more.

He watched the medical team continue their desperate efforts. A new fear gripped Thomas' chest. If they failed to bring the old man back, all the answers he sought would be lost forever. The crucial information about Dr. Levi and his father, the truth behind Case 47 - it would all slip away, leaving him with so many unanswered questions and a lifetime full of regret.

The scene before him blurred as his mind drifted back to the contents of one of Harold Bauer's journals. He saw himself sitting at the old desk in the home study, poring over the yellowed pages filled with his father's neat handwriting. Scattered among the entries were photographs; pale snapshots of a Sam Harris standing alongside his father outside Saint Elizabeths.

In his mind's eye, he could see the images now. The old man, looking much younger but still recognizable, his eyes bright with life and curiosity. His father, next to him tall and proud in his white coat, a small smile played at the corners of his mouth. The hospital loomed behind them, its imposing façade that contained many secrets.

As the memory faded, Thomas' gaze refocused on the present scene. The contrast between the vibrant young man from those photographs and the pale, lifeless form on the bed was jarring. How did it come to this? Despite the repeated warnings, he pressed on with his relentless search. It was his selfish quest that led to this tragic turn of events.

Something he'd forgotten popped into the doctor's head. He became dizzy, on the verge of passing out. An overlooked detail he missed until now. Bauer finally remembered where he recognized Lacheu from. He was the odd man pushing the housekeeper's cart outside his office the night he left to meet Andrew at the Anacostia Park!

His head flooded with memories of all the other places in the hospital where he'd seen Lacheu. The man, like Sam, was a constant, yet more inconspicuous presence around Saint Elizabeths. Bauer's blood ran cold as he realized that it wasn't Harris, but his merciless attacker that was responsible for the break-ins.

This realization hit Bauer like a physical blow. That dangerous man had been there all along, a silent but dangerous person concealed in the shadows. How could he have missed such a crucial detail? How could he have been so stupid?

Before he could think about it too much, a commotion from within the trauma room pulled his attention back into the moment. The medical team's movements became more frantic, their voices thick with urgency.

"We're losing him, again!" One nurse called out, her voice tinged with desperation.

Thomas pressed his hands against his racing heart and closed his eyes. Harris had risked his life to share his secrets with him. The information he was so desperate to get made him blind.

"Come on Sam, please fight back!" He whispered under his breath. The continuous tone of the flatlined monitor filled his ears. The psychiatrist glimpsed the old housekeeper's pale, lifeless face.

Bauer's body slumped in his chair. His eyes drifted to a bloodstain on his pants. The urgent voices from the other room faded into a dull hum as his mind spiraled into an all-consuming vortex of self-recrimination.

How could he have been so blind? So consumed by his obsession with Case 47 that he failed to see the dangers lurking in the shadows? His stomach churned as he recalled his suspicions of the man now fighting for his life just feet away. He was so certain, so smug. He knew it was the old janitor. Now he faced the brutal reality of Sam's broken body, and his own horrible misjudgements.

Each breath mechanically forced into the man's lungs, every frantic chest compression by medical staff to keep life-giving blood flowing, felt ineffective.

"I'm such a fool," he muttered, running a trembling hand through his hair. The weight of responsibility pressed down on him like a physical force, threatening to crush him beneath its mass. This was all his fault. His reckless pursuit of answers had led them both to this dirty, semi-sterile hallway awash with fluorescent light and the acrid smell of antiseptic.

Memories of his interactions with Harris flooded Bauer's mind, each one accompanied by a fresh stab of remorse that pierced his own heart. He saw the old man's gentle smile as he mopped the hospital floors. He heard his quiet "Good morning, Dr. Bauer" echo through the corridors. How many times had the housekeeper tried to help him, to warn him perhaps, only to be met with suspicion and disdain?

"I'm such a fool, Sam," He whispered, his voice thick with emotion. "Sorry for being so stupid. I didn't listen. I should have seen—"

A movement at the end of the hallway caught his attention, snapping him back into the moment. The federal agent who had arrived earlier was prowling near the nurses' station, his eyes scanning the area with a predatory intensity. Bauer's heart rate spiked as he realized the true extent of the danger nearby.

These were not just shadowy figures in the periphery of his mundane world. Lacheu, this governmental menace - they were very real, dangerous threats. And he, in his arrogance and obsession, had stumbled right into their crosshairs. His mind tried to piece together what he actually knew. How deep did this conspiracy go?

The man's gaze locked onto him. He walked toward him with purposeful strides. Panic clawed at his brain as he realized he would have to lie and deceive if he were going to protect not only himself but also Sam, if the old man somehow survived.

"Dr. Bauer?" The agent's voice was crisp, authoritative. "I'd like to ask you a few questions about the incident involving Mr. Harris."

Thomas straightened, forcing his features into a mask of professional concern. "Of course, Mr.—?"

"Agent Sullivan, FBI." The man flashed his credentials. "Can you tell me what you were doing at the hospital at such a late hour this evening?"

Bauer's mind raced, searching for a plausible explanation that wouldn't further raise suspicion. "I was catching up on some paperwork. Time got away from me. I heard a commotion as I was leaving. I investigated to make sure everything was alright."

Sullivan's eyes narrowed. "And your relationship with Mr. Harris?"

"The janitor?" The doctor feigned mild surprise. "I know him only in passing. We exchange pleasantries now and then, nothing more."

"Yet you stayed to ensure his well-being," the agent pressed.

Bauer nodded, hoping the tremor in his voice could be mistaken for simple concern. "Of course. He's been a fixture at Saint Elizabeths for decades. Everyone knows Sam. I couldn't just go home without knowing how he was."

The agent studied Bauer's face, searching for the slightest hint of deception. Thomas held his breath, aware of how much hinged on his statement. One wrong word, one slip, and his house-of-cards façade would come crashing down.

"I see," Sullivan said following an extended pause. "Well, Dr. Bauer, I may have more questions for you later. Please don't leave the hospital until we've spoken with you again."

As the agent turned away, he felt a mixture of relief and dread wash over him. He had deflected suspicion for now, but for how long?

Bauer's stomach churned. He swallowed hard. The taste of bile lingered in the back of his throat. His hands trembled as he ran them through his hair, as he noticed for the first time the dried blood caked under his fingernails. He scrubbed at them several times. His breath came in short, sharp gasps.

A nurse hurried past, while casting a concerned glance his way. Bauer attempted to smile, to fake a normal appearance, but his facial muscles failed him. Instead, he issued something of a grimace, then turned away. He could feel the nurse's gaze linger on him a moment before she continued on to whatever she was doing.

Despite being surrounded by fellow professional personnel in a medical environment, the palpable weight of isolation left him breathless. Here he was among the familiar, yet felt alone. These weren't his friends, his colleagues, or his patients. They were complete strangers, moving through their own orbits, oblivious to the turmoil raging within him.

Bauer's eyes darted around as he took in the constant bustle of activity from his immediate surroundings. Doctors consulted charts. ER techs wheeled people to radiology and back. In the waiting room, he could see family members huddled together, seeking comfort in each other's presence as they waited for any bit of news on the condition of their loved one. And there Bauer remained, an island unto himself.

The urge to leave, to run as far away as possible from everything he had sought to understand, grew stronger with every passing minute. What was the point of it all? This relentless pursuit of truth had led him here, to this odd organized insanity. Harris' blood was all over his hands and clothes while men and women fought to bring him back from death just a few yards away.

A sudden wave of dizziness swept over him. Bauer leaned forward in his chair. He gripped the armrest to catch himself before he fell. The floor seemed to tilt beneath him. The walls drew in closer around him. He closed his eyes, trying to find his balance, but the spinning only intensified. Each beat of his heart sounded like a thunderclap in his ears.

Thomas reached for something solid as he struggled to regain his equilibrium. His mind drifted back to conversations with his father many years ago. When he was young, eager and filled with ambition as he announced his intention to pursue a career in psychiatry. The look on his old man's face forever etched into his memory.

"This field will consume you, Thomas," his father warned. "It will take everything you have and leave you hollow."

Back then, the foolish, naïve, and cocky version of himself had dismissed his dad's concerns as the ramblings of an old man full of regrets and past his prime. Now, as he sat in the trauma center, feeling more alone and lost than he ever had before. His father's words now haunted him with incredible clarity.

Despite all his years of work, research and all the warnings from his dad, mom, Eleanor and Sam, he still failed to see the implications of blind ambitions, and his desperate need to prove himself. His pursuits of truth seemed to be noble. However, that was not the case anymore. His marriage was in ruins, his relationship with his son was ok, but not great. He paid no attention to his mother while living in her house. And now, the life of a man he knew little about hung in the balance, all because of his stupid selfishness.

As despair threatened to overwhelm him, a fragment of memory flickered in Bauer's mind. This time, he saw himself sitting at his father's desk in his home study, poring over old journals and photographs. The thrill of discovery, the excitement of piecing together a long-hidden mystery, was at that point intoxicating. For a moment, he remembered the growing ambition that had driven him. He believed that he was on the verge of discovering something significant.

That spark of intellectual passion and curiosity remained a faint ember deep within him. It was a tiny, fragile glow, but it still had yet to be snuffed out. Even now, a part of him needed to understand, to make sense of this tangled mess of secrets and lies that had surrounded him his entire life.

The guilt was so overwhelming that it extinguished any glimmer of redemption. Bauer wanted to run, to abandon his dangerous pursuit and retreat to the safety of his ignorance. Here he stood there, at the crossroad of hope and despair. Uncertainty and danger lay ahead on one path. But the road back to the life he had known was gone forever. He had seen and learned too much, to ever return to the naive man he used to be.

Every decision he'd made in the past weeks seemed to mock him. The late nights spent poring over his father's cryptic documents, the visit with Mrs. Clendin, his growing paranoia - all of it had led him to this chaotic hallway that reeked of bodily fluids and desperation.

Bauer's mind drifted to Eleanor and Simon. How often had he brushed aside their concerns, their attempts to connect with him? He saw Eleanor's face, etched with worry and disappointment so many times, as he canceled yet another family dinner. He heard Simon's voice, small and uncertain, asking if he'd make it to his school play or baseball game this time.

"I'm sorry," he whispered, though there was no one there to hear him.

The image of Sam Harris, pale and lifeless on the hospital bed, flashed before Thomas' eyes. He felt a fresh wave of nausea as he recalled his treatment of the old man. How quick he'd been to cast the housekeeper as his enemy in his personal twisted drama, when in reality, the man had been trying to help, even protect him the whole time.

"I wouldn't listen," Bauer said, his voice thick with regret. "I should have seen the signs."

The sound of hurried footsteps drew Bauer's attention. He looked up to see a nurse rushing past; her face etched unreadable. He wondered about the man's condition, but the words died in his throat. What right did he have to inquire about this old man he knew very little about? The man who risked his life for him?

His gaze drifted to the trauma room exit. Beyond it lay the world he'd known before all this madness began: his patients, his routines, the comfortable predictability of his life at Saint Elizabeths. A life that was now so far behind him.

He thought of his office, of the stacks of neglected patient files waiting for his attention. How he longed for the once trivial daily concerns that never seemed to hold a candle to the tantalizing mystery surrounding Case 47. Now, he would give anything to return to those simpler days. To lose himself in the familiar rhythm of the mundane.

"What have I done?" He whispered, as he buried his face in his hands.

He thought of the first time he'd ventured into the hospital archives. Getting lost for hours in the heart pounding thrill of rediscovering long forgotten notes and studies. He remembered the rush of adrenaline as he'd pieced together fragments of his father's research, convinced he was on the verge of something new and groundbreaking.

Now, those moments of excitement were hollow, and tainted by dire consequences. He sat, shaking his head. This knowledge, no matter how profound, was not worth all this.

"We're losing him again!" A voice cut through Bauer's reverie. His head snapped up, eyes wide with fear as he realized it was coming from Harris' room. He had never been so helpless, yet so responsible, as additional medical staff rushed past him.

"No, no, no," Thomas muttered, rising to his feet. He took a staggered step toward the room, then stopped, frozen in place. What could he do to help?

As the frantic activity continued behind the closed doors, The research psychiatrist felt the final ember of his personal and professional self being extinguished. The enormity of what he'd set in motion crashed over him like a tidal wave, leaving him gasping for air.

"I can't do this anymore," he whispered over the chaos that surrounded him. He looked down at his blood-stained hands. He knew it was his only choice. "I'm done," he said, with a finality that surprised even himself. "No more chasing ghosts. No more risking the lives of others for the sake of my stupid, selfish pursuits."

As he exhaled long and slow, he could feel a great weight lift from his exhausted frame. Going forward, he would focus on mending bridges and the painstaking process of rebuilding trust. For the first time in weeks, he felt his true heart once again beating strong within his chest.

As Thomas rose to leave, he made one last glance into the trauma room. A nurse came into view, her face flushed from physical exertion, but her eyes were bright.

"We got him back!" she announced to no one in particular.

"After we get his vitals stable, we need to move him to surgery without further delay." Said another voice from inside the room.

Bauer's knees became weak. Tears blurred his vision, as the medical team continued to work, encouraged by Harris' strengthening pulse and rising blood pressure. The old janitor's face was still pale, but there was a steady rise and fall to his chest that spoke of a life reclaimed from death.

Chapter 30

"**D**r. Bauer," came the voice of the surgeon as he entered the doctors' lounge close to the operating room.

The unexpected intrusion jolted him from his slumber. Lost in a haze of momentary disorientation, he conducted a quick scan of his unfamiliar surroundings. He looked down at the GWU imprinted on the pocket of the scrub top he had on. It had been a long time since he wore hospital scrubs.

It took a minute for him to remember. It was kind of the George Washington University Trauma Center physicians to take pity on him. They escorted him into the doctors' lounge for a shower and something to wear so he could change out of his blood-stained clothes.

The few hours of sleep he got while Sam was in surgery did little to counter the level of fatigue that had settled deep within his bones.

"Dr. Bauer," the surgeon repeated. "I just wanted to let you know Mr. Harris' operation was a success, and he is now resting in recovery."

A mix of relief and latent anxiety washed over him as the man's words registered in his exhausted brain.

With cautious optimism, the surgeon continued. "He's stable now and his vitals continue to improve."

Thomas nodded, unable to find his voice. The albatross of guilt that had consumed him for hours lifted a little, only to be replaced by a new sense of dread. He was grateful his coworker was alive, but how could he face the man who almost died because of him? What would he have to say about the attack in the archives?

The doctor escorted Thomas towards the old man's room. The squeak from his shoes against the polished floor sounded unnatural and loud in the quiet hallway. Banks of fluorescent lights buzzed overhead. They cast a harsh glow that made everything seem like a surreal dream.

As the two men approached the door, Bauer's steps slowed. His palms grew damp, and he wiped them on his wrinkled scrub pants. The events of the past few weeks again flashed through his mind. It all seemed so foolish now, so dangerous.

The surgeon stepped aside and made an openhanded gesture. Thomas' hand hovered over the door handle. He was ready to walk away from all of this. Forget about Case 47, about the mysteries of his father's and Dr. Levi's research. He wanted to go back to his patients, to the predictable routine of his life at Saint Elizabeths.

However, before he did, he had something extremely important to do. Thomas had to face the old man. He owed this man a most sincere apology, at the very least.

Bauer drew in a deep breath, then leaned into the door and pushed it open.

The hospital room was dim. The only sound was the steady beep of machines that monitored his cardiac rhythm and blood pressure. The old man laid there, looking small and fragile against the white sheets. IV tubes and EKG wires snaked around the man who was reclaimed from the clutches of death.

Bauer's throat tightened as he approached the side of the bed. Each step grew heavier the closer he got closer. Guilt had continued to gnaw at his core since the near-fatal altercation in the archives became overwhelming.

Sam's eyes opened. "Dr. Bauer," his voice was weak but clear. Thomas' head snapped up, surprised to find the old man awake.

"Sam," Thomas stammered, "I uh — how are you feeling?"

A glint of a smile tugged at the corners of the old man's mouth. "Like a Mack Truck hit me. But I'm alive, thanks to you."

He blinked as he became confused for a moment. "Me?"

Harris nodded. "You got me out of there after they left me to die on the floor of the archives. You got me the care I needed. The doctors say if you hadn't been there—" His weak words trailed off.

He felt his face flush. He hadn't expected gratitude. He'd been prepared for anger, for accusations. This only made matters worse.

"Sam, I — I don't deserve your gratitude," He said, his voice just above a whisper. "If it wasn't for me, for my obsession with Case 47, you wouldn't have been in danger last night."

The old man's eyes, clouded with pain, fixed on him with surprising intensity. "Dr. Bauer, it's clear that you don't understand. I've been the one trying to protect you from the men who did this to me. To keep you from repeating the mistakes of your father and Levi."

It was as if the floor had dropped out from under the doctor. He stared at Sam. The thoughts that took over his mind left him dizzy. Nothing made sense anymore.

"What do you mean?" he asked, his tone hoarse. "What mistakes?"

The housekeeper's eyes fixed on his coworker with surprising intensity. "You know, you remind me a lot of your father," his voice was weak, yet clear.

A slight reflexive flinch came over him in response to the comparison. A mix of emotions flooded his head. Despite all he'd just learned about his father, the old man's words hit hard.

His jaw firmed, as a familiar tightness once again formed in his chest. Harris' had transported him back to a memory he'd tried for years to suppress.

A young, scrawny version of himself stood in his dad's study, with clenched fists, filled with determination. His father's icy decimation of long established hopes and dreams blindsided him.

Harold Bauer looked up at his son from his paperwork. His eyes were frigid and focused. "No, Thomas. I won't allow it. This field will consume you, destroy you."

His old man's reaction had left a deep psychological wound that had never healed. He worked hard for many years to prove his father wrong. However, with age and experience, came wisdom. Though his father failed to communicate his reasons, Thomas now understood better than ever that his father was only trying to protect him. Bauer's experiences over the last few weeks had opened his eyes. The rejection still stung, but not like it had in the past.

Thomas shook off the memory, refocusing his attention on Harris. The old man continued on, unaware of the turmoil his words had stirred. "I knew your father, well, you know. And Dr. Levi too. We were friends for many years."

He tried to keep his face neutral. He did not want to reveal the extent of what he knew. A faint twitch of Bauer's eyebrow was the only outward sign that the housekeeper's revelations were not novel. This was all information he'd already gleaned from his father's journals and the photographs he'd discovered.

"Is that so?" Thomas said, with a controlled tone.

The old man nodded, with a distinct distance in his eyes. "Oh yes. We were all quite close back then. I was the only one in housekeeping your father and Levi trusted to clean their offices and lab. You know, your father was a brilliant man, just like you. He was always searching for answers, always questioning."

He made an uncomfortable shift in his chair. The constant comparisons kept him on edge. He'd spent his entire life trying to prove his worth, then distancing himself from his old man's shadow. Yet here he was entangled in the same dangerous mysteries. The ones his dad tried so hard to protect him from.

"Harold was obsessed with finding the missing Case 47 file too," Harris continued. "He searched for years, well until —" His voice trailed off, leaving the words hanging in the air.

Bauer waited for the man to finish in vain. The parallels between Harold and him were undeniable. He was following in his dad's footsteps, just like he said he would. In the end, he was still driven by the same desire to help others and the driving quest for answers.

Thomas had become the very thing his father tried to protect him from. A man consumed by the mysteries of the past, while neglecting the present. Now it was as if he was being pulled down this path against his will. He was like a ship caught in a whirlpool, spiraling ever closer to some predetermined destiny he wanted no part of.

"I — I need some air," Thomas said, his voice strained. He turned and left the room. A concerned look from the old man followed him out of the room.

In the hallway, He pressed his back against the wall. His breath came in short gasps. The weight of choices, of failures, was suffocating. He'd spent so long running from Harold's shadow, only to find himself in this unconscious emulation was overwhelming.

The doctor reentered Harris' room. His shoulders slumped as he settled back into the chair beside the old man's hospital bed. His hand ran through his disheveled hair. It took conscious effort to avoid making eye contact with Sam.

"Sam, I —" Bauer began, with a strained whisper. He cleared his throat and tried again. "I — I can't do this anymore. I'm — I'm done trying to find Case 47."

The leaden words hung in the air with a certain finality to them. His chest tightened as he forced himself to continue.

"I never meant for anyone to get hurt. My family, friends, or you." His voice cracked. "All of it, whatever this is — it's too dangerous. I was a fool to think I could unravel it all without consequences."

His gaze rose to meet Harris' eyes. The old man's face remained stoic, but there was a glimmer of something. It resembled disappointment, but this was different. It looked nothing like what was seared into his memory by his father.

"I'm so sorry, Sam." Thomas grabbed his chest. "I can't — I won't put anyone else in danger. It's over."

The battered man winced as he shifted his body on the bed. His eyes bore through Thomas as he spoke. His voice was suddenly low and urgent.

"You can't, Dr. Bauer. Not now. Not when we're so close."

The doctor shook his head. His mouth opened to further protest, only to be cut off by the old man.

"Lacheu is a dangerous man, as is his boss, Shimba. It is them who have drawn the attention of the feds to me once again."

"Again?"

Sam continued without a hitch. "That federal agent? He's not who he claims to be."

The sudden change in Sam's tone made Bauer sit up straighter. The old man's eyes darted toward the door, then settled back on him.

"What do you mean?" Thomas leaned in closer, forgetting his earlier declaration to walk away from all that endangered family, friends and himself.

Harris' voice dropped to the quietest of whispers. "It is not safe here. Too many eyes and ears. But you need to know, there's a lot more at stake here than you realize."

Bauer's brow furrowed. "What are you —"

"Not here," he hissed, his eyes once again looking at the door. "Dr. Bauer, I'm afraid you don't have a choice in the matter. You are the only one who can redeem the wrongs of your father and Levi. You are the key to everything."

"What the hell are you talking about?" Bauer asked with a voice full of confusion and frustration.

Harris shook his head, his lips pressed into a thin line against his raised, frail finger. "I've already said too much. But remember, Thomas, your father knew. And so do they."

The cryptic warning sent a chill through Bauer's veins. Despite his earlier declaration, he found his determination waning as he was drawn back to the mystery like a drunk to his drink.

"Sam, please. You've got to give me more than that. Who are 'they'? What did my father know?"

Harris closed his eyes and shook his head. The old man's face looked older and more tired. When he opened them again, there was a fierce intensity in his gaze. He motioned for Thomas to take a seat next to him on the bed. With what strength that remained in him, the old man tugged at Bauer's clothing to pull him closer.

"Be careful, Thomas. Trust no one. And whatever you do, you can't let them find—"

The door to his hospital room swung open, cutting the old man's words short. A nurse entered with a clipboard in hand.

"I'm sorry, Dr. Bauer, but Mr. Harris needs to rest now," she said. Her tone was clear and pragmatic. She would hear no arguments about the matter.

The doctor stood, his head reeling from his coworker's warnings, interrupted by the nurse's sudden intrusion. He looked back at the old man, who gave him a meaningful wink.

He moved to exit the room, but he wasn't quite ready to leave the old man's side.

"Remember what I told you," he murmured with a reassuring nod, just loud enough for his ears.

Filled with conflicting emotions, he rose from his seat. The weight of his earlier decisions had lifted, only to be replaced by something he still did not understand.

Once again, Thomas stood alone in the hospital corridor. The harsh fluorescent lights overhead assaulted his eyes after being in the darkened room for so long. He turned to make his way towards the exit, each step carrying him further away from his decision to leave it all behind.

His father's efforts to warn him had failed. This man had almost gotten himself killed in order to protect him. Sam, like his father, was right. He couldn't walk away, not now.

Harris' words, though brief, had renewed within him a desire to continue what his father had begun decades ago. He would proceed, only this time with the most extreme caution and whatever guidance the old man could offer him.

As he passed through the hospital's automatic doors, the coolness of the new day hit his face, bringing with it a moment of clarity. Bauer paused, drawing fresh air into his lungs. In that instant, the full implications of his previous actions crashed over him like a tidal wave. As it receded, he could see every decision that had led him to this point in his life.

Throughout his career, his relentless pursuit for answers had become a blinding searchlight, illuminating only what lay in front of him, while casting deep, impenetrable shadows all around him. Family, friends, even his own personal well-being became lost in that darkness, and sacrificed on the altar of professional ambition.

Bauer was so intent on chasing rabbits he'd failed to see the collateral damage left in its wake. He'd even tossed aside things that were fun and enjoyable. His historical reenactment group meetings and projects with Andrew, these were all casualties of his hyper-focused pursuit.

As he stood surrounded by the cool night air, whispers of accusations came with the breeze. Random gusts full of guilt from those he'd neglected or those he'd put in harm's way. The spotlight of his ambition, once so alluring, now was on him and his faults. This exposure was harsh and unforgiving.

As this new realization threatened to overwhelm him, something else stirred. Harris' words echoed through his mind, hinting at deeper mysteries, at dangers still to be revealed. With only the best of intentions going forward, he felt a familiar spark of professional curiosity reignite deep within him.

His hunched and defeated posture began to straighten. The set of his jaw tightened. His eyes gained clarity as they scanned the hospital parking lot. As Bauer made his way to his vehicle, his steps became more purposeful. The weight of guilt still pressed down on him, but it was now countered by a defined sense of responsibility. Harris' warnings, the hints of greater dangers at play, all tugged at his conscience.

Thomas' hand hesitated on the door handle. As he reached into his pocket for his keys, his fingers brushed against something. He pulled out a wrinkled and folded piece of paper.

He turned it in his hand, then froze in place and looked over both shoulders. "Don't open it until you're alone."

He looked around, then unlocked his car, threw in the bag with his bloody clothes, and slid into the driver's seat. The morning sun rising in the east cast an odd glow into the vehicle's interior. With trembling fingers, he unfolded the note from his pocket.

As his eyes scanned the simple message contained inside. Bauer's eyes widened, and he, without a thought, gripped the steering wheel tight.

"I know where Case 47 is hidden."

After all this time, all the searching, all the danger, Harris had known all along. He gasped for air in the confines of his car. The answers that both he and his father had sought most of their lives were now within reach. Thomas could not resist what lay before him, even if he wanted to. He sat there, the simple note clutched in his trembling hand. All that lay before him was the uncertainty of his future, filled with promise, answers, and peril.

Chapter 31

The hospital garden outside the George Washington University Trauma Center was nothing like the bright-lit organized chaos inside. Vibrant flowers in hues of red, yellow, and purple dotted their surroundings, their sweet fragrance mingling with the earthy scents of the early fall day.

A gentle breeze rustled through the leaves of a nearby oak tree. Its limbs were heavy, full of acorns almost ready to drop. The canopy overhead created patterns of dappled shade over a weathered wooden bench. The soft burble of a fountain added to the soothing backdrop of chirping birds that flitted among the branches.

Thomas wheeled Harris out into the peaceful sanctuary. He couldn't believe the miraculous improvement in the old man's health. Just hours ago, The old man was pale, weak, and for a brief while, dead. Now, the old man sat upright in the wheelchair with the occasional wince of pain.

Sam's eyes were clear and alert. He scanned his surroundings with keen interest. His recovery was dramatic. The doctor almost second guessed the severity of the man's condition earlier that morning.

"You're looking quite well, Sam," he said, unable to contain the overwhelming relief in his voice as he positioned him next to a secluded hedge.

Sam chuckled. It was stronger than expected, coming from his frail frame. "Amazing what a good team of doctors, a bit of rest and some good drugs can do, eh, Doc?"

He settled onto the bench. His facial features changed often as he looked over at his friend across from him. The color had returned to the old man's cheeks. There was a certain glint in his eye that Thomas had never seen before. The restorative health benefits of just sitting out in nature had always fascinated the seasoned physician.

For a moment, they sat in silence, basking in the warmth of the diminishing fall sun. The doctor felt some of the tension release from his shoulders as he listened to the gentle sounds that surrounded them. It was an appreciated respite from the constant beeping of monitors and hushed urgency inside the hospital.

The tranquility was short-lived. Harris winced as he leaned closer. His voice dropped to a near-whisper. "Did you find my note, Dr. Bauer?"

Thomas' pulse quickened. The garden shifted to something far more ominous. He nodded as he glanced around to ensure they were still alone. "I did, Sam. But I'm not sure what you want—"

"Good, good," he interrupted, his gnarled hands gripped the doctor's arm with surprising strength. "Then you know you are at a point of no return. Also, with what happened in the archives this morning, we are running out of time."

A chill went through Thomas despite the warmth of the late-day sun on his back. He straightened his body. Holding it taught as if preparing for a physical confrontation. "I don't understand. What do you mean?"

The housekeeper's eyes once again looked around his surroundings. It was reminiscent of his own recent paranoia. When the man spoke again, there was an urgency in his tone. "They're watching, you know. They've always been there for as long as I can remember. Your father knew too. But I don't think they know too much about you yet."

"About me?"

"Yes. They don't know that you're about to pick this up where your father left off."

Thomas leaned back to put some distance between himself and Harris. He ran a hand through his hair, then shook his head. "Sam, your words sound like the ramblings of a madman. Maybe we should head back inside so you can get some rest."

The doctor stood up. As he reached for the brakes of the wheelchair, a weathered hand gripped him with incredible strength.

"No!" The old man hissed. His eyes went wide with a mixture of fear and purpose. "You don't understand. Case 47 isn't just some old files most have heard about in rumors. It's the key to everything. And they'll do anything to get their hands on it."

Thomas pried Sam's fingers from his wrist. His medical training kicked in as he did a quick check of the old man's physical and mental status. The man's pulse was racing, his skin cool and clammy to the touch. Signs of stress, but was it from some genuine concern or some sort of latent delusional episode caused by medication?

"Sam, you've been through a lot in the last nineteen hours." He said, his tone gentle but firm. "I need to get you back to your room. We can talk more about this once you've had more time to rest."

As he moved to push the wheelchair back towards the hospital entrance, the doctor knew deep down that the old man's warnings weren't from delirium.

Thomas stopped. His grip on handles loosened as Sam's words sank in his conscious mind. The old man's eyes were no longer clouded by pain. They now burned with an intensity that made him freeze in his tracks.

"Your father, Harold," he began, his voice, once again just above a whisper, "he was more than just a colleague of Levi's. They were more than that. Partners. Confidants. Guardians of secrets that can and have caused epic change."

Bauer's brow wrinkled. He leaned in closer, despite himself. "What are you talking about, Sam?"

"The Bauer family tree. It's not what you think it is, Thomas," his aged hands tightened on the armrest. "Your father. Levi. There are connections you know nothing about."

Thomas sank back onto the bench. His legs grew weak under him. The garden setting that surrounded them seemed to fade away, leaving only Sam's intense gaze locked on him.

"What do you mean?" He asked. His whispers were hoarse.

The old man shook his head. "I can't tell you everything. Not here. Not now. But in Case 47 and Levi's research files — there are answers. Your father knew it. That's why he drove himself insane looking for them. And now, it is your turn to carry the torch. You are the one who must find it."

Bauer's mind whirled. The persistent, burning questions about his family's history, which his father always brushed aside, now loomed larger than ever. His shoulders tensed. He leaned forward with calculated purpose.

"Why me? Why now?"

The man's eyes scanned the garden once more then settled back on his visitor. "Because you're the only one who can. The only one who should. Dr. Levi's work, your father's legacy — it's more than just research, you know. It's you, Thomas."

Sam's words were ambiguous, yet hit Bauer like a physical blow. He sat with his back pressed against the bench. His eyes blinked and darted. It was difficult for him to process what was just said. A barrage of thoughts overwhelmed his curiosity.

Questions that gnawed at him stirred a newfound drive for answers. Images of Eleanor and Simon flashed through his mind. The guilt of neglected responsibility tugged at him. The conflict that raged within him was a battle between his need to know and the desire to repair his failing relationships with his wife and son.

Harris sensed the internal struggle. He leaned forward, his voice urgent. "Thomas, listen to me. Case 47 is a hell of a lot more than just a collection of dusty old files. It's the key to everything. It's tied to you in ways that you can't even begin to comprehend."

Bauer's head snapped up, his eyes wide. "What?"

"Without Case 47 and Dr. Levi's research on Psycho-Temporal Displacement, you wouldn't even be here."

The words hung heavy in the air. Bauer recoiled. He almost fell off the bench. He could not grasp what this man was trying to say.

"What do you mean? What you suggest — is not possible. How could some dusty old files tie me to being here, now?" He stammered.

The old housekeeper's grip on Bauer's arm once again tightened. "It is possible. And it's why you must find it and the notes that go with it before the others do. In the wrong hands, that information would be catastrophic."

Bauer's mind exploded. "How am I connected? What exactly did my father and Dr. Levi, do? Who else knows about this?"

The floodgates had opened. He leaned in. His earlier decisions to walk away were now forgotten. He now hung on Sam's every word. The old man's revelations had stirred a fire deep within his soul. It was a desperate need to uncover the truth about his family, its history and his very existence.

As he was just about to answer, a shadow fell across the two of them. Thomas looked up to see a nurse approaching. Her face displayed a mask of professional concern.

"I'm sorry, Dr. Bauer, but Mr. Harris needs to return to his room now. Doctor's orders."

The doctor nodded, his mind still spinning. As he stood to push the wheelchair, the old man grabbed his wrist once more.

"Remember, Thomas," he whispered, "You must find Case 47. Before it's too late."

Bauer's car rolled to a stop on the gravel driveway in front of his mother's home. The quiet purr of the engine faded from his awareness. He sat there for a moment in the ambient silence. His hands still gripped the steering wheel. He stared at the familiar façade. The afternoon sun cast long shadows across the manicured lawn. Bauer didn't notice the play of light and dark.

His mind struggled with conflicting thoughts and emotions. Harris' words echoed. "Without Dr. Levi's research on Psycho-Temporal Displacement, you wouldn't be here, Thomas."

The constant attempts to process this cryptic bit of information made Bauer's head throb. He closed his eyes and pressed his head against the headrest. The weight of it all had taken on a physical form that settled on his chest.

Should he continue or stick to his previous decision? Could he walk away? The question loomed before him, the largest fork in the road he'd ever faced in his life. Walking away meant a return to what was comfortable and routine. It was an unfulfilling future. However, it would give him the chance to mend his relationships with Eleanor and Simon. The alternative was far from practical, yet tantalizing with its mysteries, promises of answers to long burning questions and hidden dangers to himself and others.

Bauer's thoughts drifted to a favorite childhood memory. His father had taken him fishing once, a rare moment of genuine connection and bonding between them. They had sat near a swift-flowing stream. His father warned him not to get too close to the water. His father spoke of the treacherous currents and unassuming dangers that lay hidden beneath the calm surface.

"Life's very much like this river, Thomas," his father explained. His voice was gentle. "You need to decide whether to stay on the shore or take a leap of faith and jump in. If you choose to leap into those waters, you must know there's no easy way back."

Now, decades later, Bauer stood at the proverbial edge. Dr. Levi's research, Case 47, glimmered with promises of answers, but some dangers that lurked in the undercurrents below had already started to bubble up from below.

With a heavy sigh, he exited his car. His movements were automatic. Thomas' mind was busy as he trudged his way up the path to the front door. He didn't notice the chirping of birds or the rustle of leaves in the gentle breeze.

Inside, the house was quiet. Bauer moved through the rooms like a ghost. His footsteps were muffled by carpeted floors. He soon found himself in the kitchen, staring into the refrigerator without seeing what was in it.

The decision before him consumed all cognitive functions. He weighed his professional reputation, his family, his safety against the tantalizing prospect of learning the long-buried truths and how it all connected to him.

Up to this point, he had been trying to solve a jigsaw puzzle with more than half of its pieces missing and no picture to guide him. The new information that came with Harris' revelation clarified nothing. The old man's words only added to the complexity of the mystery. He felt like he knew nothing of substance.

Thomas closed the refrigerator door. His reflection in its polished surface caught his eye. He didn't recognize the man staring back at him; disheveled, eyes haunted by a lack of sleep and an overabundance of questions.

Preoccupied by thoughts, he made his way to the laundry room. He remembered the bag of bloodstained clothes was still in his car. The events at the hospital the previous night seemed like a lifetime ago. But the physical evidence remained where he'd left it, waiting to be dealt with.

As he turned to head back outside, he almost collided with his mother. Edyth stood in the doorway, her eyes wide with concern.

"Thomas! Are you okay?" Her gaze dropped as she looked him over, then snapped back to his face. "What happened?"

He opened his mouth to respond, but the words caught in his throat. How could he explain the events of the past twenty hours without it sounding unhinged?

"I — I need to get something from my car," he managed, trying to sidestep his mother.

Edyth's hand on his arm stopped him. "Please. Talk to me. I'm worried about you, son."

The genuine concern in her voice made him stop in his tracks. He looked at his mother, really looked at her, for the first time in ages. The lines around her eyes seemed deeper, her silver hair a little more disheveled than usual. She'd been concerned about him for a while. His realization came with a fresh wave of guilt.

"I'm sorry, ma. It's been a long twenty-four hours. There was an incident at the Saint Elizabeths, and I had to stay with a patient."

Edyth's brow furrowed. "Are you sure you're alright?"

He nodded, feeling the exhaustion settling over him again. "I'm fine. Just tired. I need to get something from my car."

Making his way out of the laundry room, he was aware his mother's eyes were still on him. The dirty clothes felt heavier than it should have as he retrieved it from the backseat. When he returned, his mother was still there, waiting for him.

Bauer set the bag down on top of the washing machine. Then, without thinking, he removed the items. Edyth gasped as the dark stains on his clothes became visible.

"Thomas! Is that blood?" Her voice trembled as she raised a hand to her mouth.

Her son winced. He'd hoped to avoid this conversation, at least until he'd had time to process everything himself. But now it was too late for that.

"Yes, but it's not mine," he said quickly, seeing the panic in his mother's eyes. "It's — it's Sam Harris'. He was attacked at the hospital last night. He's okay now, but it was touch and go there for a while."

"Sam Harris?!" She repeated, her face losing all color. "Oh, Thomas —"

Something in her tone made him turn toward her. "You know him?"

Edyth hesitated, her hands twisting upon themselves. It was a nervous gesture Bauer hadn't seen since childhood. "I — I knew of him. He worked with your father, didn't he?"

Bauer's pulse quickened. "Yes, he did, ma. What else do you know about his relationship with dad?"

Her eyes darted away, then back to her son's face. She seemed to wrestle with what to say next. She took a deep breath.

"I know more than I've let on, Thomas. About your father's work. About Dr. Levi and Case 47."

The words hung in the air between them, filled with implication. It was as if the ground had shifted beneath his feet.

"What do you know?" he asked, his voice just above a whisper.

Edyth's shoulders rose, as if she had cast off a heavy burden. "Mmm, not everything. Your father, he tried to keep it from me, to protect all of us, by keeping much of it secret. But I knew what they were doing. I knew it was dangerous. It had something to do with Dr. Levi's research."

Bauer just stared at her. All this time, his mother knew about the mysteries that consumed him. "What do you mean?"

Edyth reached out her hand and cupped her son's cheeks. The gesture was so tender, so maternal, that a lump formed in Bauer's throat.

"Oh, my boy. I've wanted to tell you what I knew for so long, but I was afraid. Your father made me promise to keep his secrets, for your safety." Her eyes glistened with moisture. "But now I see that keeping this from you hasn't protected you at all, has it?"

Bauer shook his head, unable to form a single word. His mother knew about Case 47. She had been carrying his father's secret all these years. It was all too much.

Edyth's hand dropped from his face, and she squared her shoulders. "I don't know any of the details, Thomas. I know that Levi's work connects to our very existence in ways I don't understand. Your father went insane searching for answers. He tried to protect us. He wanted to make sure we were safe."

The echo of Harris' words made the hair on the back of Bauer's neck stand on end. "Ma, I have to know more. Please, tell me all you know."

"I will." Edyth nodded, then paused. "But before I do, you need to know this stuff is dangerous. I know little. Your father always said that if the wrong people found what he was looking for, it would change everything. Are you positive you want to pursue this?"

At that moment, Bauer stood in the laundry room with the blood from the previous night's violence in his hands. His mother's worried eyes locked on him. He felt the last of his indecision melt away. The river of mystery was in front of him. He was ready to jump into its dark swirling, fast moving currents.

"I'm sure, ma. I think it's time that we all learn the truth."

Edyth's expression was a mix of pride and fear. "Then I'll tell you what I know. But first, let's take care of these stains. We don't want any more questions than necessary, now do we?"

As they sorted through the bloodstained clothes, Bauer felt a strange sense of conviction in the decision he had just made. The rush of cold water filled the washing machine. Its rhythmic churning continued as he and his mother left the laundry room. Edyth didn't even ask if her son was hungry. She just pulled some leftovers from the refrigerator and heated them up for him.

Chapter 32

The next morning, Bauer's alarm blared, jolting him from a deep, disorienting sleep. He reached for the phone. Squinting to focus his half-opened eyes. He dialed the number to Saint Elizabeths Hospital. After a brief conversation, he hung up. His head was far too preoccupied with Sam Harris and the small, yet significant, revelations revealed the previous night to keep his mind on his routine professional duties.

As he dressed, several calls came in from colleagues and coworkers inquiring about their co-worker's condition. He responded with vague reassurances, careful not to divulge any actual information. He couldn't risk compromising the housekeeper's safety any further or his own involvement in what happened in the archives the other night.

The return trip to the GWU Trauma Center felt longer than usual. Every red traffic light seemed to last an eternity. Bauer's fingers drummed on the steering wheel, while his mind formed new questions he hoped his new friend could answer.

Upon arrival, the doctor made his way to the man's room. He met each nurse he'd seen during his prior visits with a curt nod. He paused as he looked in. Thomas couldn't believe what he saw. The man who almost didn't survive the previous night, now sat upright in his hospital bed. The color had returned to his cheeks.

"Dr. Bauer," the old man greeted. His voice was stronger than Thomas had ever heard it before. "I was hoping you'd come by this morning."

The doctor approached. His medical training kicked in as he did a quick head to toe assessment of the old man. "You're looking rather well, Mr. Harris. How are you feeling?"

"Less like I took a hit from a Mack Truck. Mmm, more like a VW bug, maybe." He chuckled. "I'll live, thanks to you."

He waved off the gratitude. A pink flush to his cheeks came with the discomfort caused by the words of gratitude. "The trauma team did all the important stuff. I just got you here in time."

The man's eyes twinkled with subtle amusement. "Don't sell yourself so short, Doctor. They are already talking about discharging me."

As Harris continued to talk of his pending release, a knot formed in Bauer's stomach. The image of his body lying in a pool of blood in the archives flashed through his mind. He was sure that Lacheu knew where he lived. If he didn't, it wouldn't be too difficult for him to figure it out.

He was also certain that his attacker and his accomplices knew Sam had survived the attempted murder. There was no way to assure his safety once he left the hospital?

Thomas' protective instincts surged. He couldn't let this man be released after nearly losing his life. He racked his brain for another, safer alternative. As the old man continued talking. Thomas didn't hear a word.

"Mr. Harris," Bauer interrupted the old man's monologue. His voice was firm. "I don't think it's safe for you to return home just yet."

One eyebrow shot up. "What do you mean? I can't stay here forever, Doctor."

"I agree," his coworker leaned in closer and dropped all formalities in their whispered conversation. "Sam, I have an idea. What if you came to live with me and my mother for a while? Just until you've recovered."

The look on Sam's face was clouded with skepticism. "That's very kind of you Thomas, but I couldn't impose."

"It's not an imposition," he insisted, his voice taking on an edge of urgency. "Please consider it. It's for your own safety. Whoever did this to you last night might track you down to finish the job."

A tense silence fell between them. His eyes narrowed, studying Bauer's face. "You're not going to let this go, are you?"

Thomas replied. His words were firm. "No, I'm not."

The man's shoulders sagged a little as he exhaled long and slow. "Very well, Thomas. If you insist."

Relieved, Bauer nodded. "I need to make a quick phone call. You'll be safer with us, Sam. Besides, a few days of my mother's cooking will put all the pink back in your cheeks."

He left the hospital room. His mind was ready to move on to the logistics of his plan. He stepped to a payphone in the hall and dialed the number.

"Ma?" he said when Edyth answered. "I need to ask an important favor."

He explained the situation to his mother, his words tumbling out in a rush. To his surprised relief, her response was immediate and enthusiastic.

"Of course he can stay with us, Thomas!" she exclaimed. "I've heard so much about him over the years. It will be wonderful to finally meet him."

He felt a wave of gratitude wash over him. "Thanks! We'll arrive sometime around five."

As he hung up, Bauer couldn't help but smile. Despite the danger and uncertainty that awaited them, his mother's warmth and support provided a huge boost to his exhausted brain.

Sam Harris winced several times as he placed what few belongings he had in a drawer. Thomas got him set up the ground floor bedroom of Edyth Bauer's home. His host exhaled once he got the guest settled.

The doctor never felt confident of the old man's safety while he was at GWU. How could he? Lacheu had attempted to kill the man in the archives the other night. Then there was the federal agent, demanding to speak to him as he lay dying in a trauma room. None of it sat well with him.

His coworker's presence in the house brought a sense of security. It also provided a safe, private place to discuss what had remained secret for many decades. Thomas thought as he helped his mother with the dinner dishes.

After the evening chores were complete, he approached the downstairs room. His footsteps were hesitant on the creaky floorboards.

Bauer knocked. "Sam? Can I come in?"

"Come in, Thomas," the voice called from within.

He entered, finding Harris sitting on the edge of the bed, his eyes distant and thoughtful. The room was dim. A single bedside lamp cast long shadows across the walls.

"Did you get all settled in?" He asked, stepping into the room.

He smiled weakly. "You and your mother's hospitality are unmatched. And that dinner was delicious. I'm forever grateful for the kindness of you both."

"You're welcome here anytime." His co-host nodded, then took a deep breath. "Would you like to join us for a cup of Darjeeling? My mother just brewed up a pot."

"I'd love a 'spot of tea,'" replied Sam with a horrible rendition of a British accent.

The two sat in silence across from each other for a moment, surrounded by the scent of Darjeeling.

"Sam, could you tell me all you know about the hospital? About Dr. Levi and my father? About their work?"

The old man's eyes sharpened, then locked on Thomas. "More than anyone else there. More than I ever wanted to know."

"Like what?"

Harris leaned forward. His voice had dropped to a near-whisper. "Saint Elizabeths has never been just a government run institution for the insane, you know. It's always been one of many secret facilities where questionable research studies were conducted."

Bauer's expression shifted from curious to deadpan. "You — you mean on humans."

"Mmm, many were on humans. A few were on animals." His gaze was distant, his tone matter-of-fact. "It's always been a place where the boundaries of reality and ethics blurred."

A wave of nausea came over Bauer. "Dr. Levi's and my dad's studies were part of those experiments, weren't they?"

"Yes, but you should know, they were the most ethical of all the researchers. The cruelty of some of the others didn't sit well with your father."

"And what about Case 47?"

His gaze dropped to his hands on his lap. "Those were the darkest days of Levi's work."

"And my father's?"

He rubbed the back of his neck. His eyes avoided Bauer's "Um no, your father wasn't involved with that project."

"I don't understand. I thought the two were collaborators throughout their careers."

"That's what the rumors would have everyone thinking. But it's not true."

"What do you mean?"

"Trust me, Thomas, it's something you have to see to believe."

"Then show me, Sam. All of it, no matter how profound or horrific. I want to know the truth."

"Very well, but you must promise me that what I give you stays just between the two of us. There are others who have been desperate to find it for decades now. In the wrong hands…" The old man's words trailed off as he sat shaking his head.

His voice took on a note of urgency. "We have to get to Case 47 first. Before anything else happens to me. It's the only way for you to understand the complexities and scope of what we're dealing with."

The doctor looked up, meeting the man's intense gaze. "And how do we do that?"

"We'll need a plan," he began, a glimmer formed in his eyes Thomas had never noticed. "One that will keep us one step ahead of Lacheu and whoever might be prowling around that hospital."

He issued a slow nod. His mind already thought of a few possibilities. "Alright, Sam. Let's get this figured out."

As the night wore on, Bauer and his co-conspirator pieced together a strategy. Their whispered conversation came with moments of tense, silent contemplation. Their thoughts and ideas were complex. The occasional wince of pain from Sam served as a constant reminder of the genuine danger involved.

The next morning, the two men sat at the kitchen table, papers spread out before them. Edyth bustled around, preparing breakfast. Her curiosity piqued by their intense discussion.

"We need to get back into the archives," Sam said. "From there, I can show you where the files are located."

"The archives?" He paused for a moment. This man almost didn't survive their last visit there. "What about security?"

"It's usually minimal there, especially that section," he said. "I can get us through any electronic locks."

She approached, setting down a plate of bacon and scrambled eggs. "Electronic locks? What are you two up to?"

Her son hesitated, then exchanged a glance with the old man. "It's complicated, ma, and quite dangerous."

"And it requires breaking into locked areas?" His mother asked, her words tinged with concern.

Sam leaned forward. "Mrs. Bauer, I assure you, this is of utmost importance. The safety of your family and mine depend on it."

Edyth's eyes widened. "Thomas, is this true?"

Her son nodded with a grim expression on his face. "I'm afraid so."

She sat down, her face drained of color. "But why? What's this all about?"

Her son took a deep breath. "It's about Levi's and Dad's work. There are documents I must find."

"Mrs. Bauer, Dr. Levi and your husband were both brilliant men," the man added. "But their discoveries seem to have put all of you in danger."

Her hand trembled as she reached for her cup of tea. "I always knew Harold was involved in something — unusual. It drove him mad. But I never imagined — "

"We are going to fix this, ma. So no one else gets hurt." He said, reaching out to squeeze her hand.

"But we're going to need your help," He interjected.

Thomas shot an alarming gaze of disapproval at Sam. "No! My mother will have no part in this."

She looked between the two of them, her expression a mix of fear and determination. "What do you need, Mr. Harris?"

Sam smiled. "You've already done a great deal by letting me stay here, Mrs. Bauer. And perhaps..." His voice trailed off.

The two men continued to work on the details of their plan. Edyth listened intently, offering a few suggestions and insights that surprised both of them. Her knowledge of the hospital, its long-established social events and traditions proved invaluable, even after all these years.

"It sure would be helpful if there was some sort of distraction." Their guest thought out loud.

"If you time it just right," she said, "you could use the annual staff picnic on Saturday as cover. Security is always lighter that day."

Sam grinned. "Mrs. Bauer, you're an absolute genius!"

As the plan took shape, the gravity of their mission became clear. Bauer's pen raced across the notepad, mapping out every detail.

"We'll need to move fast," he warned. "In and out in under an hour."

"What about Lacheu? I'm certain he will be there at the hospital."

"A valid concern," the housekeeper agreed. "But I've been watching him for years. He is sneaky, yet predictable. A decoy would be helpful."

"I could assist with that," she offered.

Bauer shook his head. "No, ma. It's too dangerous."

"Thomas," Edyth said, "I may not understand everything that's happening, but I know when my family needs me. Let me help."

"Your mother's right. We could use all the support we can get."

The two of them sat at the kitchen table, hunched over papers. Their voices were low and urgent as they compiled their list of resources.

"What about access keys," the doctor said, tapping his fingers.

"I've had all those for years. Whatever I don't have, I can get from my old friends over in maintenance."

Thomas nodded, scribbling in his notebook. "And security?"

"Most of them should be focused on those attending the picnic."

"But how can we get into the archives without drawing attention to ourselves?"

"There's a blind spot near the east wing door," the housekeeper replied. "We can use that to our advantage."

He remembered using that entrance the other night.

He pulled an old pocket watch. "Dad's timepiece. We need to synchronize our watches. Our movements must be precise."

As night fell, they stood in the dim light of the kitchen, surveying their coordinated effort.

"I think we're about as ready as we'll ever be," Bauer said, a mix of determination and apprehension in his words.

Harris nodded. "Now, for the final pieces of the plan."

Thomas picked up the phone. His fingers hesitated before calling Andrew's number. It rang twice then his familiar voice came on the line.

"Andrew? It's Thomas. I need a favor."

"Of course. What's up?"

He took a deep breath. "It's about the historical reenactment at the picnic this weekend. I was wondering if you could make some slight adjustments to the performance."

There was a pause on the other end. "What are we talking about here?"

"Nothing major," his friend said quickly. "Just a few tweaks to create a bit more excitement."

"Why?" There was a touch of suspicion in Andrew's voice. "What's really going on here?"

He closed his eyes. He wanted to be careful with what he said next. "Look, I can't get into details. I need some help. It's important."

"Does this have anything to do with what happened the other night at the boathouse, and with what happened to Simon?"

"Yes," he admitted. "But believe me, the less you know, the safer you'll be."

"I don't like the sound of this." His friend sighed. "What do you need me to do?"

"Just make your reenactment a little more attention-grabbing. Maybe add some mock battles and a dry-fire cannon. Something to keep everyone focused on you."

There was a long silence on the other end of the line. Andrew spoke. "Alright, we'll do it. But you owe me one hell of an explanation when this is all over."

"Of course, when and if it is safe to do so. Thank you. You do not know how much this will help."

As he hung up the phone, a wave of guilt washed over him. He hated the idea of involving anyone else in their dangerous plans. His mind was filled with worst-case scenarios, meshed with recent events.

Bauer closed his eyes, and he was back at Saint Elizabeths, watching Harris bleed out on the archive floor. The image changed, and now it was his friend lying there. His friend's eyes were wide with fear and betrayal.

Then the scene shifted to Eleanor and Simon, their faces twisted in anguish. The government agent he saw at the trauma center was dragging them away. Thomas could hear Simon's screams, as Eleanor's eyes were scared and filled with condemnation, locked with his.

Bauer's eyes snapped open, his heart pounded in his chest. He gripped the edge of the table, trying to steady himself as he took a seat.

"You okay?" Sam asked, with deep concern on his face.

He nodded slowly. "It's just that we had a close call with you. I don't want anyone else getting hurt as we execute this plan."

Harris placed a hand on his shoulder. "It's not too late to abort our plans, Thomas."

He sat silent for a moment, then shook his head. "You're right. We've come too far already. That's what you told me in the hospital yesterday. We need to get this done."

With trembling fingers, Bauer picked it up again. He dialed his wife's number. Each unanswered ring was excruciating.

"Hello?" Eleanor's tone was warm on the line.

"Ele, it's me. I — I was wondering if you and Simon had anything going on this weekend?"

There was a silent pause. "Thomas, what's going on? You sound so strange."

He swallowed hard. "I can't explain everything over the phone. But I could use some help from both of you."

"From us?" Her voice filled with concern. "For what?"

"Please. Look, I know I have no right to ask you two, but it's important, and it's bigger than our personal problems."

Another long minute. "I'm not agreeing with anything until I get a full explanation."

Thomas stood in his mother's living room. His eyes scanned the faces of everyone assembled. He paced near the window, as Andrew watched his every move with a furrowed crease in his brow.

His wife was seated on the edge of the sofa. The frequent darting of her eyes betrayed any external perception of the calm she was trying to project. Simon was on the couch, flanked by the two women. His son inched a little closer to his grandmother, prompting her to wrap an arm around him.

Andrew's, Eleanor's and Simon's eyes lingered on the strange old man covered with cuts and bruises who sat in an armchair. The atmosphere was heavy with unasked questions and poorly concealed anxiety.

Bauer cleared his throat. His voice was steadier than the turmoil that churned in his head. "I appreciate you all for coming with such short notice," he began, his eyes scanning the room. "As much as I'd like to explain the full details," with an open hand, he gestured to the battered old man seated among them. "Mr. Harris' here is a poignant example of why it's not safe for me to do so."

With all eyes still on Sam, Andrew cleared his throat. "You must be able to tell us something about what you need and why."

Bauer took a deep breath. "This involves research my father and another psychiatrist were conducting at Saint Elizabeths Hospital in the 1950s and 60s."

"Like what?" Asked his friend.

"I can't get into that at the moment. The less you know, the safer it will be for all of us."

Eleanor's eyes widened, then shifted to a look of disdain. "Thomas, what on earth are you talking about?"

"I'm asking you to trust me when I say that I can't get into those details right now," he said. "Sam and I could use your help so we can retrieve some crucial documents hidden deep within the hospital archives."

"And why do you need us for that?" Andrew asked, with obvious skepticism dripping from his words.

Harris leaned forward in his chair. "Because it's not as simple as just walking in and taking them. There are people who have been searching for this information for decades."

Simon, who had been quiet until now, spoke up. "Daddy, does this have anything to do with my nightmares? About the soldiers?"

Bauer stopped pacing and stood in front of his son. Their eyes met. "Yes, I believe it does. I just don't know how or why yet. But I have a feeling that with these documents, we'll be able to better understand what's been happening to you."

"This is insane, Thomas." Eleanor shook her head. "You're going to break into a secure part of a government facility. We could all go to jail."

He looked out at the cars parked out front, trying to find his words. "I know it sounds crazy…"

Harris cut him off. "It's not 'breaking in,' I have keys. Besides, that section of the hospital wasn't locked. It's just very well hidden."

"I wouldn't be asking if it wasn't important or necessary." explained Thomas as he turned away from the window.

Andrew scratched at the stubble on his chin. "And what do you need us to do?"

He outlined the plan, explaining each person's role. As he spoke, he could see the doubt in their faces and the fear in their eyes.

"I know it's a lot to ask," Bauer said, with a hint of optimism in his voice.

Eleanor's eyes locked on Bauer's. "And you're sure this is the only way?"

"It's not the only way," Harris interjected. "But it is the safest way."

He stood in the middle of the room. His gaze jumped often between his wife and friend.

"I think we should do it," Simon spoke, shattering the oppressive silence that lingered in the room. "If it can get rid of my nightmares, maybe it will help other people, too. We have to try."

Eleanor looked at her son, surprised, then back at her husband. She sighed. "Alright. We're in."

His friend nodded. "Count me in too. But Thomas, if this goes south—"

"It won't," responded Harris with a little more strength in his voice.

Andrew and his wife looked over at the battered and bruised old man. The prominent cuts and bruises covering the old man's body did little to bolster their confidence in him.

"We're going to do this right." Sam continued. "We're going to do this together in such a way that the men who did this to me will not know your connection to any of this. And that includes you, Thomas."

"I don't see how that is possible, Mr. Harris." She commented.

"I know the fellas who did this to me. I've been watching them for years. They still know very little of my involvement in this, and they know nothing about your husband, Mrs. Bauer. And I have every intention of keeping it that way."

Following a brief silence, Sam grimaced as he stood from his chair. A small smile came over his face. "Well, ladies and gentlemen, shall we get started?"

Everyone in the room nodded.

"I'll put on a pot of tea," Edyth announced. "Simon, come help me with the cookies."

Her grandson jumped up from the couch. "Coming grandma."

The group discussed the details of Sam and Thomas' plan. He felt an unfamiliar feeling of relief wash over him. He watched Andrew and the old man pore over a crude map he'd drawn of the hospital grounds, Eleanor and her son listened as they sipped their drinks and brushed away cookie crumbs.

For the first time in months, the psychiatrist didn't feel alone. A shared sense of purpose had replaced the initial doubt and tension that had consumed the room earlier.

As night fell, the group gathered in the dining room, surrounded by maps, diagrams, and lists. Thomas looked at each of them, with a feeling of gratitude.

"Alright, is everyone clear on what all needs to happen and when?" Bauer inquired.

Simon's eyes were wide with a mix of excitement and nervousness, chimed in, "What if something goes wrong?"

He stepped next to his son, placing a protective arm around his shoulder. "Then we shift and stop the plan. We all know the emergency exit routes. Safety remains a top priority throughout all of this.

As the clock in the living room struck midnight, "We should all get some rest," he said. "Saturday is going to be a long day."

Andrew was the first to leave. "I'll see you all in a few days. "Tom, call me if you need help with anything else, before then."

"Will do, and thank you."

As Eleanor was about to head home with Simon, she paused, then turned back to her husband. "Hey Thomas," she said, "whatever happens, I'm proud of you for doing this. For trying to find answers to Simon's nightmares."

Bauer felt a lump form in his throat. "Thank you."

After his mother retired for the night, He pulled Harris aside. "Are you sure about this?" he asked in a low voice. "Are you strong enough to do this? It's not too late to back out."

Sam gave him a wry smile. "After all these years, Thomas, I'm more ready than ever. We need to get this done."

The doctor nodded, feeling a renewed sense of determination. He said goodnight to the old man and turned towards the stairs. Alone in his room, he checked his father's watch from his pocket. He rubbed his fingers over the worn surface. "I hope we're doing the right thing, dad," he whispered.

With all the preparations done, Bauer laid his head down on the pillow. He closed his eyes, trying to calm the racing mind.

Come Saturday, they would collectively embark on a mission that could change everything. As sleep claimed him, Bauer's last conscious thoughts were of the group he had assembled – unlikely allies united by a common purpose. They would accomplish this together.

Chapter 33

Dr. Thomas Bauer stepped through the main entrance of Saint Elizabeths Hospital. His footsteps echoed through the bustling morning corridor. The familiar smells of cleaning products and floor polish filled his nostrils. Today, everything felt different, almost oppressive. He straightened his tie, took a deep breath, and steeled himself for what he knew would be a challenging day.

As he made his way to his office, he noticed the furtive glances and hushed whispers of the staff. The rumors had three days to fester and spread to every corner of the facility. He kept his face and words professional and neutral, offering polite nods to those he passed.

"Dr. Bauer!" a voice called out. It was Olivia Kendrick, her eyes wide with concerned curiosity. "Is it true about Sam? Everyone's saying you found him in the archives, bleeding!"

He paused, choosing to be careful with his words. "Yes, I did. I understand he's doing better now."

"But what happened? Was he attacked?"

"He doesn't remember anything from that night." He replied with a measured tone. "The important thing is that he's receiving proper care and continues his recovery now."

As he continued through his day, more staff members approached him, each with questions and their own version of what they'd heard about the early Sunday morning incident. Thomas returned vague responses that revealed little while assuring everyone that Harris was on the mend.

Alone in his office, he closed the door and pressed his back against it and exhaled. He knew that returning to work would complicate things. The constant barrage of inquiries was more draining than he'd expected. He moved to his desk, sinking into his chair, and rubbed his temples.

Bauer turned to look out his window. He knew he'd have to navigate these conversations with great care over the coming days. He needed to balance discretion with the natural curiosity of his colleagues.

Throughout the morning, a steady stream of staff members had their reasons to pass by his office or stop him in the hallway. Each time, he repeated his well crafted narrative: yes, he had found Harris in the archives; no, he didn't know what had happened; as far as he knew Sam was recovering with family.

By lunchtime, he was exhausted. He sat in the cafeteria, picking at the salad he had no appetite for. He overheard bits and pieces of conversations from nearby tables.

"Someone told me it was some sort of break-in gone wrong," one orderly whispered.

"No, no, I heard he was looking for something," another replied.

The psychiatrist kept his eyes on his plate, resisting the urge to correct or engage. He knew that the less he said, the better chance there was of him contradicting his well-crafted version of the story or revealing his connection to Sam's activities that night.

As the days passed, Thomas grew more adept at deflecting questions and redirecting conversations. When pressed for details, he maintained his false ignorance. He then made a point of expressing concern for Harris' well-being, which seemed to satisfy most of his colleagues' curiosity.

By the time his shift ended on Friday, he felt he had navigated his way through the minefield of rumors and speculation. As he packed up his briefcase, preparing to leave, there was another knock at his door.

"Dr. Bauer?" It was Marcus Sinclair, the hospital administrator. "Do you have a moment?"

He nodded, gesturing for him to enter. "Of course, Dr. Sinclair. What can I do for you?"

The man closed the door behind him, his expression serious. "I wanted to discuss the incident with Mr. Harris. Given your involvement, I think it's important that the administration has a clear understanding of what transpired."

A flicker of anxiety came over Thomas, as he kept his face impassive. "I understand, sir. What would you like to know?"

"Why don't you start from the beginning?" Marcus said, settling into the chair across from Bauer's desk.

Thomas took a deep breath, then recounting the events as he had been doing all day, careful to stick to what he knew was safe to share. He described finding the housekeeper in the archives, carrying him to the nurses' station, and began to assess and treat the old man's wounds. He emphasized he knew nothing of what had caused the old man's injuries.

Sinclair listened with the occasional nod. When the physician finished, he leaned forward. "And you do not know why Mr. Harris was in there at that hour?"

"No, sir," Thomas replied, meeting his visitor's gaze. "I'm sorry, I don't."

The man seemed to consider the psychiatrist's response for a moment before speaking again. "Well, Dr. Bauer, I appreciate your handling of this situation. It's a delicate matter, and your discretion is commendable. Please keep me informed if you learn anything new about Mr. Harris' condition or the circumstances surrounding his accident."

"Will I see you tomorrow, Dr. Bauer?"

"Tomorrow?" A sudden lump formed in Thomas' throat.

"At the Staff Picnic?"

"Oh yes, of course. I'm bringing my family with me."

"Wonderful! It will be nice to meet them."

As the administrator stood to leave, the doctor felt a mix of relief and lingering tension. He had navigated the week's rumors and conversations without compromising Sam, himself, or their plan.

The late morning sun climbed higher in the sky. A festive celebration took over the sprawling campus of Saint Elizabeths Hospital. Coworkers and their families bustled about and mingled. The annual picnic was in full swing.

Colorful tents looked beautiful against the lush green lawns and the aroma of grilled food wafting through the air. Dr. Thomas Bauer stood alone near a cluster of tables, his eyes scanning the crowd.

He watched as Andrew gathered and directed their historical reenactment group with animated gestures. The men and women, dressed in period-accurate Civil War garb, listened as their leader went over the final preparations for their upcoming mock battle. Their polished brass buttons glinted in the sunlight, and the wool uniforms looked stifling in the heat of early fall.

Bauer's attention shifted toward the parking lot. There in the distance he spotted his mother, as she made her way towards the picnic area. Seeing her sent a subtle jolt of heightened awareness through him. It was the predetermined signal that Sam Harris was now in place, hidden away somewhere in the hospital. Edyth's face was a mask of casual cheerfulness as she joined her son. Her son was the only one aware of the underlying nervousness in her eyes.

"Thomas, dear!" Edyth called out, waving. "What a lovely day for a gathering."

He smiled and reached out to hug and kiss her. "It is, ma. I'm so glad you could make it."

As she and Bauer engaged in conversation with colleagues and their families, Eleanor and Simon approached. The boy's face lit up at the sight of his grandmother, and he rushed forward to wrap his arms around her.

"Grandma!" he exclaimed. "Did you bring the cookies you promised?"

She laughed, ruffling Simon's hair. "Of course I did, sweetheart. They're in my bag."

The extended Bauer family settled in at a nearby table, where Thomas had a clear view of Andrew. The white linen tablecloth fluttered in the gentle breeze. Following a brief welcoming address by Dr. Marcus Sinclair, they all left to get their food, drinks, and cutlery. The chatter between hospital staff and their families created a constant hum of background noise as they all returned to their tables.

Bauer's eyes darted from his assembled party, to Andrew's group and the building. He took a deep breath and held it. He could feel a tremendous weight on his shoulders, but he knew there was no turning back now. Everything was ready, everyone was in place.

As they ate, Thomas engaged in small talk, all the while keeping a watchful eye on Andrew in the distance. When their gazes met across the lawn, Bauer issued an almost imperceptible nod. It was time.

Under the table, Bauer's foot found Simon's leg. He gave his kid a gentle kick, their prearranged signal. Simon, mid-sip of his drink, executed the kickoff of the plan. He faked a sneeze and his full cup of lemonade flew forward, spilling its contents all over the front of his clothes. "Oops!"

The cold liquid soaked through the fabric, as his father jumped to his feet with a convincing yelp of surprise. "Simon!" he scolded, his voice sharp, but his eyes twinkled at the boy with a hint of mischief. "What have I told you about being careful?!"

The kid hung his head, playing his part like a master. "I'm sorry, dad. It — it was an accident."

His father sighed as he grabbed a napkin and began dabbing at the wet mess.

"Thomas, calm down. It was an accident." His wife intervened. "He said he was sorry."

He looked at his wife and took a deep breath. "You're right Ele. I apologize, Simon, I overreacted. It's alright, son. But I need to go change." He turned to her and Edyth as he excused himself. "I'll be back in a bit. I have a spare shirt and pants in my office."

As he made his way through the crowd, he heard Andrew's voice rise above the general chatter as he took the microphone to address everyone. "Good afternoon, everyone! It's time for our reenactment to begin. Come with us as we transport you back to 1863!"

The excitement in the air was palpable as people moved around to get a better view of Andrew and his assembled group. The doctor slipped away unnoticed and headed towards the building as planned.

Just as he reached the edge of the picnic, a loud boom echoed across the grounds. Thomas turned to see a plume of smoke rising from one of the replica cannons. The sound of muskets firing followed, accompanied by the shouts and yells from the re-enactors.

The chaos of the mock battle provided the perfect cover. As children squealed with delight and adults gasped at the realistic display before them. The psychiatrist slipped through the east entrance of Saint Elizabeths, and the door closed behind him.

Inside, the hospital corridors were eery and quiet when compared to the commotion outside. He paused for a moment, listening for any sign of movement. He heard nothing. His moves were swift down the hallway, his lemonade soaked shoes squeaked against the polished floor.

When neared the archives door. His heart stopped. There, at the far end of the corridor, pushing a housekeeping cart, was Lacheu.

"Shit!" He whispered under his breath. He wouldn't be able to slip in there now unnoticed.

Thomas didn't break stride, The doctor continued to walk without even looking at the double doors. With a napkin in hand, he dabbed at the stain down the front of his shirt. He forced his face into a mask of mild annoyance, as if his only concern was his soiled clothing.

His pulse thundered in his ears. Bauer's mind raced as he executed the contingency plan they had put in place. He needed to maintain Lacheu's attention long enough to dismiss the man's suspicions. He hoped that would be all that was needed to throw him off his trail.

As he passed closer, Bauer issued a curt nod while avoiding eye contact. He continued down the hallway, his shoes left faint damp footprints on the polished floor. Only when he turned the corner out of the man's line of sight did he allow himself a shaky exhale.

The doctor made his way to his office door. He was aware of every sound in the creepy, quiet hospital. The muffled boom of cannon fire from outside seemed surreal in contrast to the tense silence inside.

Once inside, Thomas changed into the spare clothes he kept there. As he buttoned up his fresh shirt, a flicker of movement from underneath his door caught his eye. He knew Lacheu was lurking in the hallway, watching his door.

Bauer's jaw clenched. This complicated things, but he wasn't about to give up. Not yet.

Emerging from his personal space, he pretended not to notice Lacheu's presence. He started back towards the corridor to the east exit that passed by the archives. His pace was deliberate and unhurried. As he drew nearer to the entrance, he slowed. He glanced over his shoulder as if sensing he was being watched or followed.

He stopped. Then, in a calculated move, he turned around and scanned the hallway with narrowed eyes.

In the distance, he watched Harris' attacker duck out of sight. A grim smile tugged at the corner of his lips.

The moment he disappeared from view, Bauer acted. With swift, silent movements, he slipped into the double doors. His heart pounded as the door clicked shut behind him.

Inside the archives, the familiar musty smell of old paper calmed his restless soul. Thomas paused, letting his eyes adjust to the dim light that surrounded him. Sam's cryptic instructions echoed in his mind: "Go to the oldest part. It is there where time stands still, but history continues to move forward."

His gaze swept across the towering shelves, as horrific memories of his last visit flooded in; the struggle, the blood, the housekeeper lying motionless on the floor. A shudder ran through him. He was sure Lacheu would follow him in there. What if he ended up like Harris, bleeding out among old files and dusty tomes?

The doctor's footsteps were soft as he navigated the familiar maze of bookcases to the oldest section of the archives. The air was heavy with the scent of aging paper that held long forgotten knowledge. His eyes darted around for any sign of Sam.

"Sam?" he whispered. No response.

The silence pressed in, broken only by the faint creak of old wood beneath his feet. His heart skipped a beat as he stood in the spot where the old man had said to meet him. Empty.

A bead of sweat trickled down his back. Where was the old man? Had something gone wrong?

Bauer felt the air in the room shifted. The hairs on the back of Thomas' neck stood up. He was no longer alone in the archives.

The soft squeak of rubber soles on linoleum reached his ears. Lacheu had entered to look for him.

A lump caught in his throat. His back was against a shelf. He wished he was anywhere but there. He struggled to control his breathing.

He could hear Lacheu's footsteps draw closer. His pulse pounded. He held his breath, every muscle in his body tense.

Just as panic threatened to overwhelm him, a hand seized his shoulder. Bauer almost cried out, but another hand clamped over his mouth.

The doctor's eyes widened in surprise, then relief as Sam placed a finger to his lips. The housekeeper then tugged on his shirt, pulling him further into the back of the archives. The doctor followed. His trust in this man overrode his fear of Lacheu for a second.

They moved in silence, weaving through the shelves. Harris led them to what appeared to be a dead end. With practiced ease, he pressed a hidden mechanism. A section of the wall swung inward, revealing a dark passage.

The old man gestured, ushering him inside.

As they slipped into a tunnel, Thomas heard Lacheu's getting closer as Sam closed and secured the secret door behind them without a sound.

The two men stood motionless, afraid to breathe. They listened as the footsteps stopped. When they started again, they faded into the distance.

"That was close," Harris whispered, his relief palpable.

His accomplice nodded, still too shaken to speak. It took a few minutes for the adrenaline to subside. He had saved this man's life a week ago, and today, this man had returned the favor.

"Where does this go?" Bauer asked, keeping his voice low.

"You'll see, but first, we need to move. Follow me. Watch your step," he said, his words just above a whisper. He led Thomas deeper into the hidden passage. "These old tunnels can be treacherous."

The space grew darker, as if someone had thrown a thick blanket over them. The air was heavy with the scent of dust, mold and something indistinguishable, yet unpleasant. The doctor continued on with his coworker with a mix of excitement and trepidation.

Thomas nodded. Then he realized his guide couldn't see him. "Alright," he murmured back.

Their footsteps echoed off the narrow walls. As they made their way through the winding passage, Thomas had so many questions, but he held his tongue, focusing instead on following the old man's lead.

After what felt like an eternity, Harris stopped dead in his tracks. Bauer could hear the sound of metal scraping against metal, followed by a soft click. A sliver of light pierced through the darkness.

"Welcome," Sam said, with a distinct hint of pride in his voice, "to the underbelly of Saint Elizabeths."

As the door swung open, Bauer's eyes squinted, then widened in amazement. They walked into an old wing that appeared to be abandoned, as if time had stood still. Dust motes danced in the shafts of light filtered through the grimy windows. Rows of rusted old wheelchairs and bed frames lined the hall, their fabrics rotted away some time ago.

"What is this place?" Bauer breathed as his gaze swept through his surroundings. "How long has this been here?"

Harris chuckled. "Longer than you'd think. This ward's been sealed off for decades. Forgotten by everyone — well, except for me."

They moved through the ward, their footsteps echoed through the cavernous space. Thomas' fingers traced along the edges of peeling paint, touching the history beneath his hands.

"There's more," he said, gesturing towards a door at the far end of the room. "Much more."

As they ventured deeper into the hidden spaces of Saint Elizabeths, Thomas felt himself stepping back in time. They navigated through old stairwells, their steps creaked on the worn metal. Patient transfer tunnels stretched before them, their walls adorned with faded murals depicting serene landscapes. There were a few portraits of the patients who had once wandered these halls.

In one corridor, the doctor paused, his brow furrowing. "Wait a minute," he said, pulling out a folded piece of paper from his pocket. It was a crude copy of an old blueprint he'd found in his father's study. "According to this, there should be a room here."

The housekeeper raised an eyebrow. "I've been through this part more times than I can count, Thomas. There's never been a room there."

Thomas approached the wall, ignoring the old man. He ran his hands along its surface. His fingers caught on a slight indentation. With a grunt of effort, he gave it a push, and a section of the plaster swung inward, revealing a hidden chamber.

"Well, I'll be damned," Sam muttered, impressed. "How did you know that was there?"

"My dad's notes," he explained, with a hint of pride in his voice. "I bet he knew every nook and cranny of this place, like you do."

As they explored the newfound room, Thomas felt an increasing sense of connection to his father. The knowledge he'd gleaned from his father's study seemed to complement what the janitor knew in unexpected ways to unlock more of the hospital's secrets. They discovered old treatment rooms that contained antiquated equipment waiting for another patient to arrive, and storage areas filled with old records on the verge of turning to dust.

"You know," his guide said as they paused to catch their breath, "your father would be very proud of you. I can see you've got his eye for detail."

Bauer felt a sense of warmth spread through his chest as his friend stood in silence a few feet away. "I think I understand why he was so fascinated by this hospital."

As they pressed on, the dynamic between them shifted. The old man now looked to Bauer for insights. The younger man relied on Harris to navigate their way through most of the hidden spaces.

They worked together to clear a blocked passage, Sam's knowledge of the building's structure guided their efforts, while Thomas' strength and practical skills made the task possible.

"We make a good team," the housekeeper observed as they broke through. The doctor nodded, a smile tugging at his lips. "That we do."

Chapter 34

Harris led Bauer deeper into the abandoned recesses of Saint Elizabeths Hospital. He struggled to draw the thick air into his lungs. The corridor they walked became narrower. Continuing on, the walls closed in around them.

The cracked bare plaster and peeling paint combined with curled and dangling strips of wallpaper. Together, they created time's bizarre art piece in the media of neglect.

Bauer's footsteps echoed, soft and hollow, off of the broken flooring. Each step stirred up dust that had laid undisturbed for ages, causing particles to dance in the weak light filtering through the dirty glass.

"Watch your head," Harris warned as he ducked under a low-hanging pipe. On it were the words "Hot Water" and a red arrow, showing the direction of flow.

Bauer heeded the old man's instruction. He squinted and blinked a few times as his eyes adjusted to the more oppressive gloom. The musty scent of decay filled his nostrils, mingling with the acrid tang of old chemicals and the hint of old rusted metallic equipment. As they rounded a corner, the space opened wide. Bauer's breath caught in his throat. Before them stretched a vast, cavernous room, its high ceiling disappeared into the shadows.

"Welcome to the heart of the old ward," Harris said, his voice just above a whisper.

Rows of ancient hospital beds lined the walkway. Their once-white sheets had become yellowed and tattered. Abandoned wood and metal wheelchairs were scattered about the room, their wheels frozen in time. On a nearby stainless steel table, a collection of tortuous medical instruments lay strewn about, their sinister purposes long since forgotten.

Bauer's gaze swept across the room, taking in the faded murals on the walls — pastoral scenes meant to soothe troubled minds, now eerie in their decay. The hair on his arms stood up as he imagined the countless men and women who had once inhabited this space. It wouldn't surprise him if more than a few of their disturbed, restless souls still wandered these old parts of the hospital.

As they walked through the ward, Thomas' foot caught on something. He looked down to see a weathered patient file. Its pages had spilled out across the floor. With trembling hands, he picked it up. The brittle paper crumbled in his fingers.

"Careful," Harris cautioned. "Some things in here are better left undisturbed."

They pressed on, their footsteps muffled by the thick layer of dust. The air grew colder as they ventured deeper into the abandoned wing. Thomas couldn't shake the feeling of being watched by unseen eyes.

Sam stopped short. Bauer plowed into him, almost knocking the old man to the ground. "Here we are," he said, gesturing to a nondescript door.

Thomas' face looked puzzled. "Is this where Case 47 is hidden?" he asked.

The housekeeper shook his head and chuckled a bit. "No, this is Levi's old office."

His eyes locked onto the door. As his eyes focused in he could just make out the name Dr. Matthias Levi on the dirty, faded nameplate on the door. Thomas' mind drifted back to the home study, poring over old photographs and documents. One image stood out; a younger, proud Harold Bauer standing in front of this very room. One arm wrapped around the shoulders of his colleague and the other leaning on Sam. All three men displayed smiles that reached their eyes.

With no warning, the memory shifted, as Thomas recalled a passage from his father's journal:

"Levi's work is groundbreaking, but I fear the consequences of such research. The line between genius and madness is thin, and I fear Levi has already crossed it, without even realizing it."

Thomas blinked. The vision faded as fast as it had formed. He stared at the closed door, his hand hovered over the tarnished doorknob.

"Should we go in?" he asked, his voice just above a whisper.

The old man shook his head. "No, not yet. There's something else I need to show you first."

Harris continued the macabre tour toward another corridor. Their soft footsteps and the occasional creak of the settling building broke the oppressive silence. When they turned another corner, Bauer's eyes widened. Before them was a massive pile of debris–broken furniture, and twisted metal lay mangled under fallen chunks of plaster and ceiling tiles. Their path forward was blocked.

"Damn," he muttered. "This wasn't here last time. Must've been another collapse."

Thomas surveyed the obstacle, his mind racing. "We can't go back," he said, more to himself than to the old man. "Not with Lacheu snooping around the hospital. Besides, we've come too far."

Sam nodded in agreement as he looked at the rubble before them.

Bauer approached the pile, testing the stability of some sections. "Our only options are over or through."

"Maybe if we can create a small opening," he mused, "We can crawl through."

Together, they began removing pieces of plaster, only to cause a cascade of off-balanced larger chunks. "I think over is a safer option." Suggested Thomas.

As they helped each other climb over the mess, Thomas reflected on how his feelings towards his father and the old housekeeper had changed. Just a few weeks ago, he would have balked at the idea of crawling over dangerous mountains of debris in this abandoned old hospital wing. Now, here he was, working by the side of a man he once thought was his enemy, driven by an insatiable need to find hidden truths.

As they emerged, covered in dust and sweat, the doctor turned to help him through the last steps. The older man's face was red with exertion, but his eyes shone with a mixture of pride and excitement.

"Well done, Thomas," he said as he dusted himself off. "Your father would be proud."

He felt a warmth spread through his core. He realized that he was not following in his father's footsteps. He had started to forge his own way.

"What now?" Bauer asked with a breathy voice.

Harris smiled, a mysterious glint in his eye. "Now," he said, "we find what we came for."

The old man led him a little way down the new corridor. The space looked familiar, but the younger man didn't know why. They came to a stop in front of a weathered wooden door. Its once-polished nameplate was now tarnished and illegible. Dr. Harold Bauer, it read. Thomas' hand trembled as he reached for the doorknob amid a torrent of memories.

His father's stern face, disappointment etched in every line, flashed before him. "This field will consume you, Thomas. Just as it has so many others."

Bauer's fingers wrapped around the cool metal, hesitating. He could almost hear his younger self arguing back, full of naïve determination. "I can handle it, Dad. I'm not like you."

With a deep breath, he turned the knob and pushed. The door opened a few inches. With a little more force, the hinges creaked in protest, disturbing the room's silence. Bauer went inside, waiting for his eyes to adjust to the dimness.

The office was a virtual time capsule, frozen in the moment his father had last been in there. Dust-covered books lined the shelves, their spines faded but still legible. A large oak desk occupied the center of the space, its surface cluttered with long forgotten papers and files, as if his father had just stepped out. Thomas expected him to return at any second.

Bauer's throat tightened as he approached it, his fingers traced the edge, leaving a trail in the thick layer of dirt. How many nights had his father spent here, poring over research, while he waited at home for a bedtime story that never came?

"Your father was a mysterious and complicated man," Harris said, breaking the silence. "Brilliant, but haunted by Levi's work and his connection to it."

Thomas nodded, unable to speak. His eyes fell on a framed photograph, half-buried by papers. With trembling hands, he picked it up. He wiped away years of grime with the back of his hand.

The image showed a much younger Harold Bauer. His arm was around a boy's shoulders. Both were smiling, their eyes bright with genuine shared joy. He recognized himself, only six or seven years old, holding up a small trophy.

"My first science fair," Thomas whispered, as a lump formed in his throat. He had forgotten about this moment, it was lost beneath years of disagreement and disappointment. His father had been so proud of him that day, beaming with unmistakable happiness.

As his attention moved from the photo, something in the dark recesses of the books caught his eye. A leather-bound book, almost lost among dusty tomes. Bauer's heart skipped a beat as he pulled it from the shelf, recognizing his father's handwriting under the cover.

Bauer opened the journal. Its pages were brittle and yellowed with age. As his eyes widened with surprise.

"November 6, 1963," Thomas read aloud, his voice just above a whisper. "Something has changed in Levi, but he won't tell me what it is. He seems to be in a euphoric daze, yet when he looks at me, it's like he's seen a ghost. His temporal displacement experiments seem to have progressed further than they were ever intended. Levi is ecstatic, but something isn't right, but I can't figure out what. I fear he's tampering with forces we don't fully understand."

Bauer's hands shook as he turned the pages, devouring his father's private thoughts. The journal revealed a man torn between scientific curiosity, moral responsibility, and his wife and son. It was a far cry from the cold, distant man Bauer remembered.

"March 3, 1964," he continued. "I held Thomas today, watching him sleep. The innocence in his face. I'm not sure how long I can continue this work. Nothing is as it once was. My only hope is it's not too late to save my family, my son, from the dangers we've unleashed."

Tears welled in Bauer's eyes as the realization crashed into him like a wrecking ball. His father's distance, his temper were all attempts to dissuade him from following in his footsteps; it was all done to protect him and his mother.

"He was trying to save me," he choked out, looking up at the old man. "All those years. I thought he didn't care. His looks of cold disappointment. He was just scared."

Sam nodded. "Your father carried a heavy burden. He wanted to spare you from the same fate as those around him."

Bauer clutched the journal to his chest, overwhelmed by a mix of grief and newfound understanding. The complexity of his relationship with his father was unraveling in his mind.

"We should move on," Harris whispered, placing a hand on Bauer's shoulder. "There's still more to show you, but we are running out of time."

Thomas wasn't ready to leave, but knew the old man was right. He tucked the leather book and framed photograph into his pocket. As they left the office, he cast one last glance at the desk where his father used to sit. Bauer took a deep breath, then closed the door behind him.

They continued down the short corridor until they reached a set of heavy double doors. A faded sign above read: "Research Laboratory—Authorized Personnel Only."

"This is it," Harris said, his voice tinged with a mix of excitement and apprehension. "Dr. Levi and your father's old lab."

Bauer's heart raced as Sam produced an ancient looking key and unlocked them. They swung open with a groan, revealing an open room filled with antiquated equipment and a dust-covered workstation. The space was complete chaos. Most of it packed up like it was all waiting for movers to come and haul it all away.

As they entered, Thomas' eyes darted from one spot to another, recognition dawning on his face. "The temporal displacement chair," he breathed, approaching a large, dentist-like seat with restraints in the center of the room.

Harris raised an eyebrow. "You know about this?"

The doctor nodded, running his hand along the cool metal surface. "From my dad's information. It's designed to create a localized field of temporal instability. In theory, it would allow for the displacement of consciousness across different points in time."

He moved to a nearby workstation, examining the complex array of dials and switches. "This must be the chronometric stabilizer. It's meant to anchor the subject's consciousness to their original timeframe, preventing complete dissociation."

As he explored the lab, his excitement grew. The scientific details he had pored over in his father's notes had come to life before his eyes. He explained the function of each piece of equipment to his friend, who listened with curious attention.

"And this," he said, gesturing to a helmet-like device connected to a tangle of wires, "is the neural interface. It's designed to synchronize the subject's brainwaves with the temporal field, facilitating the displacement process."

He paused, a frown creasing his brow. "But according to my dad, they never solved the problem of temporal feedback. The risk of psychological trauma to the subject was extreme."

Harris' face was grim as he nodded. "I think that may have been what led your father to abandon the research."

Bauer's mind raced, connecting dots he'd never seen before. "The nightmares," he muttered. "Could some sort of residual temporal displacement somehow be connected to his and Simon's vivid dreams of historical events?"

As Sam opened his mouth to respond, something from outside the door froze them both.

"We're not alone," he whispered, his eyes wide with alarm.

Thomas' heart pounded in his chest as they searched for a place to hide. The sound drew nearer, echoing through the hall.

Thomas and Sam crouched behind one of the large pieces of equipment, their breath held in tense silence. The sound in the corridor grew louder. Each echo sent a fresh jolt of adrenaline coursing through their veins. His eyes looked for potential escape routes and improvised weapons.

As the noise got closer, Bauer felt a growing sense that went beyond their immediate danger. Something about this situation was off, a nagging sensation at the back of his mind that he couldn't quite put his finger on. He glanced at Harris, searching the old man's face for any sign of recognition or concern, but Sam remained focused on the lab's entrance.

Whatever it was stopped just outside the door. Bauer's muscles tensed, ready to spring into action. His own heartbeat thundered in his ears, drowning out the faint sounds of his shallow breathing. Time seemed to drag and stretch, turning each second into an eternity.

Then, as quick as it had appeared, the noise faded. Bauer let out the breath he hadn't realized he was holding. His body sagged some, but the tension never dissipated. The nagging feeling remained with him. He was now sure something wasn't right.

The old man motioned for them to stay put a few more minutes. His eyes stayed focused on the door. When he spoke, his voice was just above a whisper. "We need to hurry. The Case 47 files aren't in here."

Thomas' brow furrowed in confusion. "What do you mean? I thought this was where..."

Sam cut him off with a sharp gesture. "There's another chamber. Hidden. That's where I found them."

They made their way out of the lab and back into the corridor. The unsettling feeling continued to grow in the doctor's gut.

Sam led them through another abandoned hallway, revealing more decay and neglect. Thomas' senses were on high alert. Every creaky window or distant echo set his nerves on edge. He looked over his shoulder several times, half-expecting to see some shadowy figure trailing them.

They exited the hallway into an old musty stairwell. The metal stairs groaned under their weight as the sound of their footsteps echoed through the vertical shaft. The further down they went, the air grew colder and more damp. Thomas' breath became short as his heart pounded in his ribcage from a mix of exertion and anticipation.

When they reached the bottom, it was a dead end. A look of confusion came over the doctor's face as he looked over the blank wall in front of him, then over at Harris. The old man ran a gnarled hand along the edge, searching for something.

"Here," he muttered, pressing against a specific spot. A grinding noise came from a section. Then it swung inward to reveal a hidden room.

His eyes widened in amazement. "How on earth did you—"

"Your father showed me," he replied, a hint of sadness in his voice. "When he was losing his mind, but just before he went completely mad."

"Did Levi know about this?"

"No. He didn't know that I knew either. It's been my secret all these years. I don't think Levi ever intended for this information to be seen again."

"If that were the case, why didn't he just destroy it?"

"That I can't say. In his final days at this hospital, he seemed to be haunted by something. I know your father tried his best to help him, but by that point, his colleague had already decided to hide this stuff and leave."

The two men stepped into the hidden chamber. Colder air mixed with Bauer's conflicting emotions. The rush of learning secrets his father never knew awaited. With it came a deep, aching sadness for a man he never knew.

It was small, no larger than a walk-in closet. Shelves lined the walls, filled with dusty files and a few pieces of antiquated equipment. Sam gestured toward a file cabinet in the corner that seemed out of place.

"Bottom drawer," Harris said in a matter-of-fact tone, as he kept his eyes focused on the entrance to the room.

Thomas approached. His hand trembled as he reached for the handle and pulled. Metal slid against metal as it moved an inch or two, then stopped. He braced his foot on the base. He shifted his hand to get a better grip. He put his other hand into the gap he'd just created. With some body weight behind his effort, it opened.

There, in the back of that cabinet, was a thick leather attaché. Thomas grabbed it and placed it on the small table in the middle of the room. He flipped it open to see a series of large files all labeled "Case 47."

As his fingers brushed the folder, a sudden realization hit him. The nagging feeling that had been plaguing him since they entered the lab crystallized into a clear thought. He turned to Harris, his voice tight with suspicion.

"How did you know about this place? You said my father showed you, but I've read all his journals. He never once mentioned this room. You didn't learn that Case 47 was here from my father, did you, Sam?"

Harris's expression changed. A flicker of something, regret? fear? guilt? flashed over his face. "Thomas, it's—"

Before he could finish, a loud crash echoed from the stairwell above them. The entire staircase structure shuddered. Dust rained down on them from higher points in the stairwell. Bauer pulled Sam into the room with significant force. He then grabbed the attaché containing Case 47 as his eyes scanned his surroundings.

"We need to get out of here!" Harris shouted over the noise of crashing metal and crumbling debris.

But as they turned toward the exit, a section of the ceiling collapsed, blocking the entrance to the hidden chamber. The impact knocked Thomas to the ground, forcing the air out of his lungs. Through the haze of dust and debris, he saw Sam pinned beneath a fallen chunk of concrete.

"Sam!" He cried out, scrambling to his feet. He rushed over to the old man, assessing the damage as a stream of dirt continued to fall from above. The housekeeper was trapped, but did not crush him. If they worked together, they might lift it enough for him to slip free.

Thomas braced himself to move the material. The old man grabbed him by the arm. "No!" he screamed. "There's no time. Get out of here."

"I'm not leaving here without you," He insisted.

Sam shook his head, his eyes filled with a mixture of pain and stubbornness. "You have to. That file, Case 47, it's more important than I am. You need to get it out of here, keep it safe. Keep it far away from Lacheu and the others."

Thomas hesitated, torn between duty and a strained sense of loyalty to this man.

"I'll come back for you. I promise."

The old guy managed a weak smile. "I know you will. Now get the hell out of here!"

With a heaviness in his heart, he turned away and faced the blocked entrance. There near the top of the fallen debris was a space just large enough for him to squeeze through. It was his only option.

As he climbed, he struggled to find firm footing. Case 47 had become an albatross. Its contents were cumbersome and heavy with responsibility as he navigated his escape.

When he emerged from the hidden chamber, the scene around him was more chaotic than the last. He could see the door to the stairwell above him. He didn't trust the stability of the structure, but it was his only way out. Thomas removed his belt to create a makeshift shoulder strap, then secured the attaché across his torso.

In his moment of crisis, Bauer found clarity. He thought of his father, of the man he had misunderstood for so long. He thought of all he had learned on this journey. Lessons about family, loyalty, and responsibility that came with the burden of knowledge.

With a deep breath, he climbed up the rickety, twisted metal staircase. Case 47 remained strapped to his body. As he reached the landing to the door, they used to access the stairwell. He looked down at the rubble below, blocking the hidden chamber. He would come back for Harris once he had the files secure. Despite Sam's instruction, there wasn't a choice between one or the other — he had a duty to protect both.

When Thomas exited the door. He peered through one of the grimy windows. It surprised him to see his vehicle parked outside. Now he understood why Sam had instructed him to park it there when they were laying out their plans for today. With brute force, he forced open an old emergency exit. He placed a stick in the door to prevent it from slamming closed behind him.

He fumbled for his keys as he moved toward his car. Bauer wrenched the lock on his trunk. He threw in the attaché and the journal from his pocket, then slammed it shut. He closed his eyes and drew in a deep breath.

"Mission accomplished," he whispered. Now he needed to go find Andrew. Together, they had to figure out a way to rescue Sam without being noticed, if that was even possible.

Chapter 35

It was a brisk walk from the far side of the building, near where Bauer parked his car. His heart panicked as he scanned the crowd scattered about the hospital grounds for his friend's familiar face. The cheerful chatter from co-workers and their families sounded out of place. Every outburst of laughter mocked him as their banter grated on each of his raw nerves.

With laser focus, he set out to find his friend. The doctor weaved through clusters of people, muttering apologies as he bumped into shoulders and avoided colliding with a group of children squealing with delight as they chased others around the picnic area. His eyes darted from one face to the next, growing more desperate with every passing second. Where the hell was Andrew?

The heat of the day was oppressive for early fall. Away from protecting shade, the sun beat down without mercy. Thomas could feel beads of sweat trickling down his back. He wiped at his brow with the back of his trembling hand, unaware of the dark smear of dirt left across his forehead. He failed to notice the curious and concerned glances cast his way. Hunching his back and shoulders, he tried to make himself smaller, less conspicuous.

As he approached another group of tents with tables set up under them, a sense of relief washed over him. There, in the distance, seated in the shade of a large oak tree, sat his friend leaning against it with his eyes closed. The man had shed the top part of his wool Civil War uniform and was lounging in his soaked t-shirt. His suspenders laid at his sides. A big half-empty glass of lemonade clutched loose in his fingers.

Thomas' approached, his shoes crunched on the grass. Andrew looked up as he heard footsteps. His eyes widening as he recognized his friend approaching. His friend was unaware of his dirty, disheveled appearance; his clothes caked with dust and grime, hair matted with dirt and sweat. Every step closer made with urgency and sorry attempts to draw attention away from himself.

"What the hell happened to you?" He exclaimed, sitting up straighter.

Bauer glanced over his shoulder, ensuring no one was within earshot. "I'll have to fill you in on the details later," he said in a low, urgent tone. "Right now, I need your help to rescue Harris. He's trapped at the bottom of a collapsed stairwell under some rubble."

Andrew's expression shifted from shock to concern. "Where?"

"On the other side of the building. Over near where I parked my car. We got to move fast, follow me. Bring a flashlight, some rope, and bring two entrenching tools. I'll meet you back here in a few minutes."

Andrew nodded, getting to his feet. "Alright, let me grab the gear. See you in a bit."

As his friend hurried off, the doctor took a deep breath, steeling himself before heading back to the where his mother, wife and his boy waited for his return.

Thomas approached the picnic table where Eleanor, Simon, and Edyth sat, their cheerful conversation dying as soon as they saw him. His son looked at his father, open-mouthed and stunned. His mother's eyes were wide with shock, while his wife's brow furrowed deeper than usual.

"What the hell happened to you?" they exclaimed in near-perfect unison.

His head raced as his words poured out of him. "I don't have time to explain," He said, keeping his voice low and urgent. "Son, I need your help. It's important."

Eleanor's eyes narrowed. "What's going on? You can't just come here looking like that and whisk our son away without an explanation."

"Elr, please." His frustration grew to a fever pitch. "Every second counts. I promise I'll tell you everything later, but right now—"

"No," she cut him off. "You always say that, Thomas. But 'later' never comes. Your work, your obsession with whatever this is, they always come before your responsibilities to your family."

His jaw clenched. He could feel the weight of his mother's and son's eyes upon him as he and his wife engaged in their tense, whispered argument.

"This has nothing to do with my work, Ele. A man's life is at stake. He could die if we don't act fast."

Eleanor's face softened a little, but the disappointment in her eyes remained. "And you need our son for this rescue mission?"

She closed her eyes and took a deep breath. From her expression, he wasn't sure if she believed him. He was just getting to know the old man after all the years he'd been at Saint Elizabeths. On top of all that, Harris owed him answers that were interrupted by the cave in.

Losing patience with his wife's delayed response, He leaned in closer, his voice just above a whisper. "It's Sam, he's trapped. Andrew and Simon have to help me get him out."

Her eyes shot open. "Trapped?!" Eleanor hissed. "Where? How? Why on earth would you need our son for this?"

Thomas looked her square in the eyes. "He's smaller than both of us. It's easier for him to fit through the tight spaces. It could make all the difference."

"Fine. But I want a full explanation when this is over, Thomas. No more secrets."

"Agreed," he said, relief washing over him. He turned toward Simon, who had watched the entire exchange with wild-eyed curiosity. "Come on, kid. We have to hurry."

As they walked away from the table, he could feel Eleanor's eyes boring through him. She was correct. He owed her more than that; he owed her a change. But right now, Harris' life hung in the balance.

Bauer led them around the building. They move towards his parked car near the hospital maintenance yard. He moved fast toward the concealed old emergency exit. He felt bad about withholding crucial details, but it was necessary for their own safety.

"Alright, guys," he said as they neared his vehicle. "He's trapped in an old stairwell that's collapsed. We need to be quick, but careful, so we can get him out."

Andrew frowned. "I don't remember any of that on the maps used for our reenactments."

Thomas hesitated. "It's not a part of the hospital shown on modern maps. Few people know about it."

"Like a secret passage?" Simon's eyes lit up with excitement. "Cool!"

"Something like that," he mumbled, avoiding Andrew's apprehensive gaze.

He wrapped the coil of rope across his body, then they each grabbed one of the replica entrenching tools. He then handed Simon the flashlight.

"Dad, how did you find this stairwell? And how did Mr. Harris get trapped down there?"

Thomas' stomach churned. He should have known his son's curiosity would lead to challenging questions. "Mr. Harris was showing me some of the oldest parts of the hospital," he said. "Sam knows a lot about this old building and its history."

His friend stopped in his tracks, fixing Thomas with a hard stare. "Thomas, why aren't you telling us everything? This sounds bad, and you're involving your son. We deserve to know the entire story."

Bauer's mind raced, trying to find a balance between dangerous truths and discretion. He knew he could never tell them anything about Case 47 and the experiments, but for now, he wanted them to trust him and he needed their help.

"Look," he began, his voice low and serious. "Harris and I have only been working together for a week. He knows things about this hospital, my father, and my family that I never knew. I wish I could give you more information, but to be honest, that's all I know right now. All I can tell you is that it's important."

Andrew's frown deepened. "You're willing to risk our lives for this?"

A twinge of guilt shot through Bauer as Andrew mentioned his son's name. "Trust me, I wouldn't have even asked if Harris' life wasn't in danger." Bauer's mind drifted for a second to his conversation with Sam just before the cave in.

A heavy silence fell over the group as they thought about what he just said. He held his breath, hoping he had convinced them to continue.

His friend spoke. "Alright, we'll help. But I want a full explanation when this is over, Thomas. And if at any point I feel it's too dangerous for any of us, it will all stop there. Understood?"

Thomas nodded. Relief flooded through him. "Agreed. Thank you, both of you. Now, let's go get Harris out of there."

As they got closer to his car, he walked off the paved path. He moved deeper into the tangled thicket of dense bushes that had grown up against the building walls. His help watched as he appeared to be frantic as he looked for something.

"What the hell are you looking for, Thomas?" Questioned Andrew. "There's nothing here."

Bauer's heart and mind raced as he continued to search in silence for a few more minutes. "Here it is." He announced, with a hint of relief in his tone.

As his friend got closer, he could see pieces of wood that were almost unnoticeable in the wild foliage. His friend seemed oblivious and unbothered by the thorny branches scratching at his arms as he got further into the bushes.

When Thomas placed his hand on the wall. He could feel cool air seeping out from an invisible space. His hands were wet with sweat, as he pressed his fingertips into a gap in the door, while pulling on the stick.

A low, eerie creak of resistant protests from the hinges echoed in the tense silence surrounding them. Bauer winced at the sound, praying no one would hear it. The coolness of the space on the other side of the door sent a shiver through him as he took a deep breath and wrenched the door open wider.

As they stepped inside, the door slammed behind them. The musty smell of abandonment assaulted each of their senses as their eyes adjusted to the dim light. Andrew's eyes widened, his attention hijacked by the archaic remnants of the old hospital wing. He felt a twinge of irritation as his friend became distracted. A growing sense of urgency soon overshadowed his annoyance.

Simon's small voice broke the silence. "Dad, what is this place?" he whispered, his tone a mix of fear and excited curiosity. His eyes darted from the peeling wallpaper to the rusted equipment covered in dust scattered about, soaking in every detail of this forgotten world.

Thomas second guessed himself. What was he thinking, bringing his friend and son into this dangerous situation? He should have just called the fire department and let them figure out how to get Harris out.

He then shook his head and swallowed hard. In a moment of clarity, he knew that option would also bring with it the attention of the curious, the nosy, and certain men like Lacheu and others. Unwelcomed visitors intruding into this long forgotten space before he explored it in its undisturbed state.

He promised that the firefighters would only be a last resort. Now was not the time for second guessing himself.

Simon tugged at his arm, drawing him back to his question. "Ahh — it's the oldest part of the hospital, son," he replied, keeping his voice steady. "No one has used it in decades. Stay close to me or Andrew, and be very careful where you step, okay?"

The kid nodded. His eyes were wide with wonder and apprehension as he took another look at his surroundings.

They came to the door leading to the stairwell. He opened the door, trying not to knock loose any more debris. his friend found something secure to attach the rope to. They clung onto it as they climbed down the mangled steps.

A small stream of dirt cascaded down into the space below. Thomas held his breath with every step they took, terrified that one wrong move could send them crashing down.

His mind raced once again. Maybe Eleanor was right. He was being selfish. If something happened to either of them, he'd never be able to live with those traumas.

When the three of them reached the bottom, Bauer exhaled. His son, driven by a mix of curiosity and concern, secured the flashlight and started to wiggle his way through the small opening into the hidden chamber to check on Harris. His heart leaped into his throat.

"Simon, wait!" he called out, but his son had already disappeared into the room.

He and Andrew exchanged a worried glance. Then they both unfolded their entrenching tools. Gripping them tight, they needed to work fast. As they dug through the rubble, the sound of shifting stones filled the air, punctuated by labored breathing.

Thomas' muscles strained with each scoop of debris he cleared away. Sweat trickled down his back, and dust clogged his nostrils. But he wouldn't stop.

They could hear the boy rummaging around in the next room echoed from the other side.

"Simon? How's Mr. Harris doing in there?"

The seconds stretched into an eternity as he waited for his son's voice to return a response. Confirming Sam's condition. Instead, an eerie silence hung in the air, broken only by the sound of shifting rubble and their own labored breathing.

Simon's head poked back through the opening, his face pale and streaked with dirt. "Dad," he called out, his words trembling, "Mr. Harris isn't in here. He's gone!"

Simon's words hit Bauer like a physical blow. "Gone? What do you mean he's gone?" he demanded, his confusion echoing through the confines of the stairwell. His knees buckled, causing him to stumble. His gaze darted from Andrew's confused face to Simon's worried eyes.

"Thomas, what the hell?" Andrew's tone cut through the silence, a mixture of justified anger with a hint of genuine concern evident in his tone. "You drag us down here, putting us both in danger, and Harris isn't even down here?"

His mind raced, trying to figure out a way to explain the situation. He opened his mouth to speak, but he choked on his words and the dust in the air. How could he justify any of this without compromising everything?

Simon crawled back out of the opening, his slight frame covered in dust and debris. "Dad, there's something else," he said, his voice just above a whisper. "I found this in there." He held out a crumpled piece of paper. The edges of it were torn and stained.

With trembling hands, Bauer took the paper from his son. As he unfolded it, his eyes widened with instant recognition. It was a page from Case 47. It had handwriting all over it that wasn't Levi's. At the bottom, scrawled in what looked like fresh ink, were the words: "The truth will set you free, but first it will make you miserable."

Bauer's legs gave out, and he fell to the ground. How could he have been so stupid? He had dragged his son and his best friend, even his mother and estranged wife, into this mess. He had pulled them all into potential danger of one form or another. All for what looked like a wild goose chase.

Harris had delivered what Bauer had demanded. However, this game of cat and mouse was far from over. Harris was a man shrouded in his own mysteries. He also seemed to always be one step ahead. His only slip up was when he almost got himself killed by Lacheu in the archives a week ago.

As he grappled with the shock of Harris's disappearance and the look of betrayal on Andrew and Simon's faces, Andrew's voice cut through his thoughts. "Thomas, we deserve an explanation. Now."

For a moment, his words failed to register. Bauer looked at his friend, then at his son with a blank expression. He owed them an explanation, but he wouldn't tell them the whole truth. That would only put them in even more danger. What he had secured in the trunk of his car was far too dangerous.

"Andrew, Simon, I do owe you an explanation. But first we need to get out of here. Then we need to get my mom and Eleanor away from here. We can all meet back at my mother's place. Once we're all there, I promise I will explain everything."

Bauer crawled into the chamber for one final look at the room where he last saw Sam Harris. He then rejoined the others. With a deep breath, Andrew, Simon and he began the arduous climb up the rickety metal staircase to the door above.

By the time they reached the landing above, their legs were weak from exertion. It felt good to have solid ground under them once again. They moved fast toward the old emergency exit in which they entered.

Thomas froze in place as a shadow fell across the dingy window near the place where they entered. His blood ran cold as he recognized the silhouette. It was Lacheu. In that moment, all other concerns faded as he shifted into protective mode. He put a finger to his lips as he motioned for them to move.

"Get behind me," he hissed, pushing his kid and Andrew towards the far corner of the room. His eyes darted around, searching for another escape route.

The sound of footsteps outside grew louder with each passing second. Bauer's heart pounded as he realized their only option was to go back through the archives. The only way out was through the narrow passage Harris had brought him.

"Dad, what's happening?" Simon whispered. His voice trembled with fear.

He turned to his son. He looked his son dead in the eyes, trying to maintain what little calm and reassurance he could muster. "It's all going to be okay. I promise." But his words sounded hollow to him as they escaped his mouth. After what had happened to Sam a week earlier, deep down, he knew he couldn't guarantee either one's safety.

The footsteps stopped just outside the old emergency exit door. Thomas held his breath, his body tense and ready to move. He then issued a silent gesture. He then turned on his heels and led his friend and son back through the old wing of the hospital to the passage at the back of the archives.

Chapter 36

Bauer's mind was a mess. It made it difficult for him to remember. Retracing his and Sam's steps through this maze of the abandoned and forgotten was not as easy as he expected. The faded wallpaper and peeling paint served as landmarks and constant reminders of the dangers that lurked all around them.

With each turn, his eyes darted about, scanning for any potential unknown threat concealed in the shadows and dark corners. The musty air and dust burned in his lungs, making every breath a struggle. He strained his ears, listening for any noise other than their soft footsteps and ragged breathing.

"This way," he whispered, gesturing towards a narrow passageway. His muscles screamed in protest as he struggled to push aside an old rusted gurney blocking their path. The metal groaned and screeched against the floor. He cringed as the sound reverberated through the empty halls.

Simon stumbled as his foot caught in a crack in the flooring. His smaller frame shook. His father reached out to steady his son. Guilt threatened to overwhelm him when he saw the unmistakable look of fear in the boy's eyes.

"Dad, where are we going?" Simon's voice trembled. "Who was that man?"

He tried to respond, but Andrew cut him off. "Yeah, Bauer, who was that? And why the hell are we running from him?"

The anger and confusion in his tone was palpable and justified. However, the tone of betrayal hurt.

Bauer's mind raced, searching for an explanation that wouldn't lead to more danger. "Listen, I can and I will explain everything, just not now," he said, his words strained. "First we need to get out of here!"

His best friend scoffed, his face contorted in disbelief. "You can start explaining right now. You and Harris dragged us into this risky situation, and where the hell is he?"

The accusation hit Bauer like a physical blow. He stumbled, his hand bracing against the wall for support. The peeling paint and plaster crumbled beneath his touch, reminiscent of the crumbling mess that was his existence beyond the walls that surrounded them.

"I know, I know. This is all my fault. I'm not even going to deny or deflect responsibility for any of this. No one else is to blame but me." Thomas said, his words just above a whisper. "I'm sorry. I never meant for any of this to happen."

As they came around another corner, his son spoke again. "Dad, you promised to tell us. You lied about Mr. Harris, about everything."

Simon's words cut and twisted through Bauer's core. In his head, his father's voice echoed, disappointment dripping from every syllable. "You've ended up just like me, Thomas. You always put your work, your wants and needs first, no matter who gets hurt."

Bauer shook his head, trying to clear the memory. "I didn't lie, Simon. I just — I didn't know how dangerous this all was going to be."

"Dangerous?" Andrew spat. "You knew how bad this was, didn't you? I saw the cuts and bruises on Harris the other day. You knew. You just didn't care."

The new wave of accusation hung heavy, suffocating the air between them. Every muscle in Bauer's body burned from exertion. Exhaustion threatened to overwhelm him. His legs felt like lead as he struggled to push him forward.

He was relieved when they reached the dark narrow hidden passage that led back to the archives. His hands shook as he fumbled for the mechanism to open it. Before he opened it, he turned to face them in the dim light.

"Listen, I admit it, I messed up. I know I've put you all in danger. But right now, we need to focus on getting out of here and away from this hospital safely. Can you please stick with me just a little longer?"

Andrew's eyes narrowed. He then gave a reluctant nod.

HIs son, however, remained silent. His eyes avoided his father's. "Like I have a choice." The boy refused to look him in the eyes.

Bauer turned away. The door creaked as it opened. As they emerged into the archives, and made their way to the exit, he pushed down the crushing pain that tore at his core as his mind raced through their next steps. He faced his son.

"Simon, can you do something very important, not for me, but for your mom and grandma?"

The kid nodded, his eyes still distant and filled with a potent mix of hurt and confusion.

"I need you to go back to the picnic area. Find your mother and grandmother. Tell them they have to leave right away. We will all meet up at grandma's house. Can you do that?"

Simon issued a defeated nod. Without further hesitation, he turned towards the archives door. Bauer's heart clenched as he watched his son walk out the door. "He has to get out of the hospital safely" he thought to himself. Guilt swirled deep within his gut as his son disappeared out the East Wing exit.

He turned his gaze back to his best friend. The look of betrayal on his friend's face was almost unbearable.

"Alright Thomas," Andrew said, his voice low and threatening. "You better start explaining yourself."

Bauer sighed, his shoulders sagged, his legs shook under him. This wasn't the time nor the place for this discussion. Besides, there was nothing he could say in that moment that would restore this man's faith in him. As he opened his mouth to speak, a noise from down the corridor made him freeze.

They weren't out of danger yet.

"I hate to ask. But I need your help. One more time. Please, I beg of you! Once we are all safe and away from here, I swear I will explain everything to everyone." Thomas whispered with urgency in his voice.

Andrew's jaw clenched, his eyes narrowed, burning with a mix of anger and frustration. He hesitated for what seemed like an eternity. The man nodded. "Fine. But this doesn't mean I'm not still pissed at you."

"Thank you. I know that guy who chased us the other night is still around here somewhere."

"Wait, the guy from the boathouse? He's here?"

"Not now, Andrew." Bauer cut him off as he grabbed him. "He might still be out by where I parked. I can't just walk over there alone. I need you to give me a ride to my car."

They moved fast through the hospital toward the main exit. Bauer's eyes darted to each shadow, every corner. As they approached, he held his breath, half-expecting the menacing man to materialize at any second.

The sea of vehicles stretched out before them. It was full for a Saturday afternoon. They could hear sounds coming from the picnic area. Clueless families clapped and cheered as the music paused between songs.

A quick scan of the parking lot. There was a deceptive calm over the vehicles, plenty of places for someone to lurk. Bauer could see in the distance, Simon followed by his mother and grandmother, heading to their cars. Then his gaze drifted toward the maintenance yard.

Lacheu was nowhere to be seen, but that only made Thomas more nervous. "Let's go," he muttered, his voice tight with anxiety.

As they raced across the lot, his friend's presence was both a comfort and a reminder of his selfish stupidity. How much he'd been willing to risk, and lose in his pursuit of the Case 47 files. As they neared where Andrew parked, every sound seemed amplified. Their hurried footsteps on the asphalt, the distant sounds coming from the picnic, even the wind in the trees, grated against his frayed nerves.

Bauer's whole body shook as he climbed in. He fumbled for his keys with shaky hands as the car navigated around the building. The old Volvo pulled to a stop. "Thanks," he said to Andrew, guilt and gratitude wearing deep within his core. "I'll explain everything, I promise."

"You better." Andrew's expression remained hard and unforgiving, but he nodded. "Now go."

With a quick glance of the area, Bauer slid into his sedan and started the engine. His tires squealed as he accelerated towards the nearest exit.

He merged onto the main road. His eyes flicked between what was ahead and his rearview mirror. He took notice of every vehicle behind. His knuckles turned white as he gripped the steering wheel. His breath came in short, shallow gasps.

A red sedan two cars back caught his attention. It seemed to match his moves. Was it following him, or just heading in the same direction? His mind considered possibilities, each more paranoid than the last. He took a sudden right turn, then another. His erratic driving caused horns to blare at him.

He'd lost the sedan, but now a black SUV appeared behind him. Beads of sweat formed on his brow. His hands were slick as his grip slipped on the steering wheel. He swerved around a slower car, almost colliding with another. Their angry shouts and honks that followed in his wake failed to register.

His vision began to blur. Shadow on the road morphed into a lurking figure, every glint of sunlight came from a potential weapon. Bauer blinked hard, trying to clear his head, but fatigue and paranoia clung to him like a second skin.

When he turned onto his mother's street, a wave of nausea came over him. He was safe, for now. But as he pulled into the driveway, the sight of Eleanor's car and Andrew's truck made his stomach churn. The taste of bile in the back of his throat accompanied the dread of the confrontation that awaited him.

Bauer stumbled from his sedan. His legs were weak and unsteady. When he walked through the front door, his family and Andrew greeted him with infuriated faces.

"Where the hell is Harris?!" Eleanor demanded, her tone sharp with fury and frustration.

"I don't know." He whispered. His eyes refused to meet hers.

His friend stood at the back of the room, next to the fireplace. His arms crossed, his expression was more of anger than concern. "Start talking. Now!"

Edyth stepped forward, her face pale with worry. "Thomas, dear, you look horrible. Go upstairs. Catch your breath. Get out of those dirty clothes and get in the shower."

"Mrs. Bauer," Andrew protested, but she cut him off.

"You two, also. Come with me, let me get you some fresh towels. Simon, I think I have something around here that still fits you."

Everything in the room was still.

The portrait of Harold Bauer on the wall caught Thomas' eye. Andrew's stern expression was superimposed on his father's face.

"Dad, are you okay?" Simon's voice trembled. Concern warred with the hurt and betrayal in his eyes.

Bauer's shoulders sagged as he shook his head. Then, without a word, he turned up the stairs.

He could hear his mother and Andrew coming from downstairs. "I have a change of clothes out in my car, Mrs. Bauer."

The door clicked behind him. He collapsed, clothed, onto the bed. His body sunk into the familiar comfort.

The muffled voices soon returned, this time in the hallway outside his room. His mother's voice came through the walls as she escorted her guest to the bathroom in the master bedroom. Within a few minutes, he heard the distant sounds of the shower turning on.

In the silence that surrounded him, the adrenaline that had propelled him through his day had faded, causing fatigue to settle deep into his bones. Bauer's eyes closed, allowing his body to relax, followed by a slow release of air from his lungs.

A sound outside his window jolted Bauer awake. Disorientated, he wasn't sure how long he'd been lying there. He stretched and rubbed his face with filthy hands before pulling his exhausted frame from the bed. He reached into his back pocket and produced the photograph he'd taken from his father's old office. His fingers trembled as he held it. He studied the youthful faces, frozen in time.

There he was, a boy with eager eyes and a proud smile, standing next to his father. His dad didn't have his characteristic stern and imposing look on him. His hand rested, relaxed on the shoulder of young Thomas. There was something in his old man's eyes that Bauer had never seen before. It was unmistakable pride, and even a hint of affection.

As he undressed, he winced at the various cuts and scrapes he'd accumulated during his venture through the old abandoned wing of the hospital. His head pounded as his reality settled in. Harris, wherever he was, had delivered on his promise, which was more than he could say for his family and friends.

Bauer's hands shook as he unbuttoned his shirt. His stomach felt uneasy about the collateral damage of his actions. He had put his life and the lives of family and his closest friend in danger, risked everything he held dear. For what?

He now realized that his obsessive pursuit of the elusive Case 47 files, his obsession to uncover his father's secret truths all stemmed from a place he'd failed to acknowledge. His unresolved issues with his father, the constant need to prove himself, to earn the approval and pride he'd always craved but never received.

In his mind's eye, he was a young boy, poring over textbooks late into the night, hoping to impress his father with his knowledge and dedication. He remembered the disappointment that would wash over him when his efforts netted him a cursory nod or some hollow, distracted acknowledgment.

Case 47 tugged at his conscience from the trunk of his car out front. He wanted to go back downstairs and tell them all the truth, explain the dangers, and why they were all necessary. But he knew all of them well enough to know how that would go. Without the old housekeeper around to back him, he had no chance at convincing them. He was certain it would only make matters worse.

Then he remembered Lacheu's face, twisted with determination and malice, as he pursued him and Andrew in Anacostia Park the other night. Then he recalled the sight of Sam Harris, bleeding and left for dead on the archives floor.

No, he couldn't reveal the truth to them. Not yet, and probably never. The information in those files was far too dangerous. Lacheu almost murdered a man to get his hands on Case 47, the less everyone else knew, the better. A sinking feeling settled deep in Bauer's gut. He was now forced to keep these secrets from his friend and family, just as his father had done.

The irony of the situation was obvious. How many times had he resented his father for his secrecy, for the walls he'd built around him and his work? And now, here he was, doing the exact same thing.

Bauer slowly lowered himself onto the edge of his bed, his shirt half-unbuttoned. He could feel barriers in his mind beginning to crumble. Forgotten memories of his father flooded in. But these were not the stern, disapproving flashes that had dominated his mind for years. The rare instances when his father had expressed his pride and affection shook loose and bubbled up from somewhere deep within his own psyche.

His father's face filled with worry and exhaustion, bent over his study desk late at night. One night before some big presentation, lying in this very bed, pretending to be asleep as his dad came in to check on him. He heard his old man's quiet words, whispered in the darkness, when he thought his son was sleeping.

"You can do this, Thomas. I know you can. You're so much stronger than you know, and that's what scares the hell out of me."

The full complexity of their relationship hit Bauer with startling clarity. His father had been far from perfect. But he had been human, struggling with his own secrets, trying his best to protect his family the only way he knew how.

Thomas grabbed his robe and towel and headed across the hall to the bathroom. The water from the shower stung as it seeped into every wound. It washed away the dirt and grime of the day and tears that had been waiting for years to fall. He now knew he'd misunderstood his father. He'd wasted so much time resenting a man who was really not too different from himself? They had similar blind spots from their obsessive work ethic. Despite those flaws, they both love their families and friends in their own imperfect ways.

The water removed years of regret and left in its wake a strange sense of calm. He now understood the secrets his father had carried. The secrets, the constant vigilance, the fear of what might happen if the information fell into the wrong hands. It was a lonely journey, one that had cost Harold Bauer in terms of his family, sanity, and his peace of mind.

And now, Thomas Bauer was alone on that same path, carrying his dad's burdens. But unlike his father, he would not continue until he mended his relationships with Eleanor, Simon, Andrew, and his mother. And though his relationship with his mother was the least strained at the moment. He still had a lot of work to do.

He would learn from his father's mistakes. He had the chance to make changes. To do things right for him and his father. He would find balance between being present for those he loved and having a more fulfilling career.

As he finished dressing and prepared for his return downstairs, Bauer made a silent promise to himself and to the memory of his father. He would uncover the truth without sacrificing everything. He would protect his family and friends, not just from external threats, but from the isolation and distance that had plagued his own childhood.

He had a long road ahead of him, filled with difficult conversations and hard truths. But for the first time in a while, he felt ready to face it. He had stepped out of his father's shadow and into his own understanding of the man Harold Bauer had been.

Thomas took one last look at the photograph before tucking it into the mirror of his dresser. He would face his family and friends with honesty; as much as he could without endangering them further. It was time to start healing the rifts he'd created, to be the husband, father, and friend they deserved.

With a deep breath, he opened the door and made his way downstairs.

Chapter 37

Bauer descended the stairs. His footsteps were heavy with the weight of the impending confrontations. When he entered the living room, he met a wall of angry silence. Andrew stood by the fireplace, arms crossed. The look on his face failed to contain his fury. The woman he loved sat on the couch, her posture rigid, eyes blazed with fury. Simon seated on the arm of a loveseat, his boyish face etched with painful disappointment.

"Sit down, Thomas," Eleanor commanded. He complied, sinking into the chair his father used to occupy, feeling the exhaustion of the last few weeks.

His friend was the first to break the tense silence. "What the hell were you thinking? You put us all in danger. You lied to us, manipulated us, and for what? Your obsession with finding some documents?"

Thomas opened his mouth to respond, but was cut off by Eleanor. "Do you have any idea what you've done to this family?" Her voice trembled with outrage. "You've missed every single one of Simon's baseball games so far. Do you even know he made the all-star team this season?"

The boy's eyes widened at his mother's words, a flicker of something unrecognizable crossing his face as he looked at his father. Bauer felt a deep stab of guilt as he realized he did not know about his son's recent accomplishment.

"And what about us, Thomas?" Eleanor continued, her words cracked with painful emotion. "Did you remember our anniversary was last month? Of course you didn't, because you were too busy with your precious work. Your research was too important for you to even acknowledge it."

Each accusation hit Bauer like a physical blow. His body slumped further into his chair. Memories of his own father saying similar things years ago came flooding back. The parallels were clear. His face got hot as a wave of shame crashed over him.

Andrew stepped forward, his face red with anger. "And let's not forget about the other night at Anacostia Park," he said, his voice low and dangerous. "You dragged me into that, and we ended up being chased out of there by some maniac. And what about today, at the picnic? Where the hell is Harris?"

"I don't know." Bauer just shook his head. He wished Sam was there to help him explain this mess. "I swear. The last time I saw that old man, he was buried in rubble up to his chest, trapped in that room."

"After you put Simon and me in danger like that?" Andrew paced the room, shaking his head. "Give us one good reason any of us should believe you, Tom?"

Bauer's shoulders sagged further under the weight of their words. He ran a hand through his hair, noticing for the first time how much he was shaking. "I — I'm sorry," he said. "I never meant for any of this to happen to any of us."

"But it happened, Thomas," Eleanor said, her voice still tight with anger. "And it's been happening for years. Your work, your research, they're destroying everything, including you. We can see it. Why can't you?"

Bauer lifted his head. His eyes met those of his family and friend. The pain and disappointment looking back at him cut deeper than any physical wound ever could. He took a deep breath, noticing for the first time the great wall that stood between them.

"You're right," he said, choking through emotions. "All of you. I've — I've been foolish and stupid. I've been so caught up in my work, so busy trying to prove myself, that I've completely lost sight of what's important."

He turned to his son, feeling a lump form in his throat. "I'm so sorry, Simon. Congratulations on making the all-star team." His dad couldn't look him in the eye. "I had no idea. I should have been at all those games for you."

The boy nodded, his eyes glistened with tears forming. "It's okay, Dad," he said, but Thomas could hear the hurt in his words.

He forced himself to look his wife in the eyes. The crushing weight of his failures as a husband was unbearable. "And our anniversary — My God, Eleanor, what can I say? You are a wonderful wife and an even better mother. You deserve so much better than that, than me."

He turned to Andrew last, shame and regret coloring his face. "I pulled you into this. I betrayed your trust." Bauer touched a closed fist to his chest a few times. "I have no excuse for that, but I am sorry."

The room fell silent as Bauer's words hung in the air. He could feel their pain and anger dissipate as a heavy sadness settled in to take their place.

"I — I need to explain," Thomas said, his voice inaudible. He leaned forward, elbows on his knees, hands clasped together. "I've been trying so hard to prove myself, to live up to some impossible standard. And I've now come to realize that it's because of my relationship with my father."

He closed his eyes, a vivid memory surfaced. "When I was sixteen, I stayed up all night working on a science project. I was so sure that if I could just make it perfect, my dad would finally be proud of me. But when I showed it to him the next morning, all he said was, 'Good job, Thomas,' and went back to reading his newspaper."

He opened his eyes, looking at all their faces. "I've been chasing his pride and approval ever since, even though he's been gone for many years now. I thought if I just worked hard enough, somehow I'd be worthy of the Bauer name."

As the words left his mouth, Thomas felt a sudden clarity. His need for his dad's encouragement ran so deep. It had shaped every decision, both good and bad, he'd made for years. He could feel a sinking feeling in his core. He also knew that change would not be easy.

"Look, this is not an excuse," he said, his voice a little stronger now. "I just want you all to understand. This can't continue like it has. I will work hard to change. There is no other option. I can't keep living like this and hurting the people I love most."

He looked at each of them, seeing the mix of emotions on their faces. There was still anger there, still hurt, but also a hint of understanding.

"I don't expect forgiveness now," Bauer said. "But I hope you'll give me the chance to make things right. I want nothing more than to be a good husband, father, friend, and son." Bauer's gaze drifted over to his mother. "You all deserve better."

Edyth cleared her throat, drawing the room's attention to her. Her eyes, usually sharp and clear, now held a distinct misty quality. She leaned forward in her chair, her hands clasped in her lap.

"Thomas," she began, her voice soft but steady, "there's something you need to know about Harold Bauer."

He felt the reflex of his chest muscles tighten as he spoke his father's name. He braced himself, expecting another tale of his disappointment or frustration.

"The night before your big science project was due," Edyth continued, "your father didn't sleep a wink."

Bauer's brow furrowed deep with confusion. What she was saying was nothing like he'd remembered it.

"He paced the floor all night," she said, her eyes distant in the memory. "I found him in his study at dawn, with his nose buried in books. He was scared, Thomas. Terrified he wouldn't be able to understand what you were working on, that he couldn't show you how he felt."

The room fell silent as Bauer sat with this new information. It contradicted everything he thought he ever understood about his father, that day and beyond.

"But — he didn't even look at it," He protested.

She shook her head, a sad smile on her face. "Oh, son. That gruff, stubborn old man, it was all a mask to hide his own insecurities. He was so damn proud of you, yet so concerned about your future. He wanted to protect you from the dangers he'd seen in his work, but he did not know how to express himself well."

As his mother spoke, memories flooded into Bauer's head. Brief moments he had dismissed or misinterpreted over the years took on new meaning. His father's terse "good job" now seemed less of a dismissal and more of an attempt to conceal his own overwhelming emotions.

"He — he was proud of me?" Thomas choked.

Edyth nodded, reaching for her son's hand. "More than you could ever know. He just had a horrible way of showing it."

Her words made him dizzy. His world had just tilted on its axis as years of what he thought was rejection transformed into misinterpreted love, pride, and concern.

Eleanor, who had been listening to the entire exchange, slowly stood up. She approached Bauer. Her movements were cautious, but deliberate. She placed a hand on her husband's shoulder. Her touch spoke volumes about her willingness to give him another chance.

"Thomas," she said, her tone softer than earlier. "I think — I think we all need to work on communicating with each other better."

Simon, watching from his perch on the arm of the sofa, nodding in agreement. He slid off the armrest and moved close to his father. His face displayed more forgiveness than his mother's. His eyes had hope, with the smallest hint of wariness.

"Dad," he said, his voice small but steady, "do you think, maybe you could come to my next game?"

He looked at his son, seeing him for the young man he was becoming for what felt like the first time in ages. He was unable to speak past the lump forming in his throat.

Andrew, who had been silent through all this, stepped forward. He extended a hand to his best friend, a gesture of understanding between them.

"We've got a lot to talk about, Tom." He said, his voice rough with emotion, but no longer angry. "But I think I understand you a bit better now."

He looked his pal in the eyes and took his hand. The handshake was firm, a symbol of cautious moves forward.

As his world resettled around him, Bauer felt something inside him break into a million pieces. Years of pent-up emotions, of misunderstood gestures and unspoken words, rushed to the surface.

Tears flowed down Bauer's face as years of suppressed grief, anger, and longing poured out of him. His body shook with incredible force. Each new wave of emotion seemed to release another layer of pain and misunderstanding.

Eleanor's hand tightened on her husband's shoulder, and he could feel Simon's small arms wrap around him. Thomas became more aware of their presence, their love, and their attempts to understand despite the hurt and confusion he'd caused them.

As the sobs subsided, he stared at the cuts and abrasions on his hands. For years, he had been trying to build a tower of his own achievements. Each brick he'd laid was a desperate attempt at receiving approval from his father. Something that had been there all along, hidden behind a façade of stubbornness on both their parts.

He knew from clinical and now personal experience that changing the patterns of thought and behavior that had defined him for so long would not be easy. It would require constant effort and vigilance. A daily struggle as he chipped away at well ingrained habits and beliefs.

Bauer's breath shuddered as he drew it in. He looked each of them in the eyes. They may not be ready to forgive him, but at least their anger was gone. He knew what he had to do.

"I — I think I need to step back from my research for a while," he said, his voice hoarse from crying. "Focus on my clinical work, and on rebuilding what I've neglected for far too long."

When he stood up, his legs were shakier than ever. Thomas walked over to his briefcase sitting next to the dining room table. He pulled one thing out of it, then snapped it shut.

Then he picked it up. With deliberate movements, disappeared into his father's study. When he stepped back into the hall, he closed the door behind him. He heard the soft click of the lock engage and turned away from everything he'd been obsessing over for the last many months.

"This will not be easy," Bauer said, returning to the living room to face his family and friend. "This has been my way of doing things for so long. But I want to change."

Eleanor nodded, a sliver of a smile displayed on her face. "One day at a time, Thomas," she said. "That's all any of us can do."

Simon's arms tightened around his father as he looked up at him with hopeful eyes. "Does this mean you'll come to my games?"

His dad returned the hug as his eyes met his son's gaze. "I'll be there," he said. "I promise. Every game. And I want to hear all about the ones I've missed."

As he spoke the words, Bauer felt something stir in him. Anxiety and fear crept into his determination. He knew that the only thing worse than missing his kid's activities was breaking his promises. Lasting changes to years of ingrained behavior could never happen overnight. He looked at the faces of those he cared about most. They were willing to give him a chance. He'd already failed them more times than he could count. He could not let them down again.

Thomas walked over to the kitchen table and grabbed his appointment book. He picked up a pen and returned to the living room. He took his seat and opened his calendar to the week ahead. His hand hovering over the pages as he contemplated the empty squares. With a deep breath, he filled them in.

"Simon's game, Tuesday at 4," he muttered, writing it down. He flipped to the following weeks, adding games, practices, and even a team dinner. He then added upcoming historical reenactment group meetings. As he entered one date after another, a feeling of excitement and trepidation consumed him. It had been so long since he'd been this involved in anyone else's life but his own.

Everyone in the room seemed satisfied with Bauer's conscious first steps. The exhaustion on display before them was something far beyond physical. Andrew stood up to leave.

"I'll call you in a few days, Tom."

Bauer nodded and stretched out his hand. "Thanks for sticking with me. Your friendship means a lot to me, despite my own moments of stupidity."

"It's alright, I'm here for ya, man." He grabbed his hand and pulled him in for a hug.

"I appreciate that."

As he walked out the front door, his wife and son weren't far behind him.

"Simon, I have some leftover cookies to send with you," Edyth said, reaching out a hand toward him. They disappeared into the kitchen wearing smiles filled with love and joy.

Bauer reached for his wife's shoulder and looked into her eyes. It had been a while since they last shared even a moment alone together. "Ele, I —"

He dropped his hand and moved toward the window.

She grabbed his arm and turned him back towards her. "You what?" she asked, looking into his eyes.

"I — I was wondering if you'd like to have dinner with me next Friday? Just the two of us?"

There was a long silence. Just as he was certain she was going to turn him down, Eleanor replied, her voice cautious but warm. "That — that would be nice, Thomas,"

As they talked, making plans for their evening, Bauer felt a flutter in his stomach. Despite all the distractions that had pulled him away from her, they still loved each other. However, it had been so long since they'd done anything like this together. He was both looking forward to it and worrying about how it might go.

As he watched his wife and son pull out of his mother's drive, he ran a hand through his hair. He was committed to making these changes. But his full calendar in the other room ramped up his anxiety. Could he really maintain this?

He pushed the thought aside, focusing instead on the warmth he felt when Eleanor agreed to go out with him. His family, his friends, his relationships with them. They were far more important than anything related to work; he reminded himself.

Chapter 38

Monday morning arrived way too soon. Bauer stood in his father's study. He'd removed the Case 47 files from the trunk of his car. He put the attaché and other documents and journals in waterproof bags, then placed them in a lockbox. Everything went into a hidden compartment underneath a loose floorboard he remembered from his childhood.

As he pushed a heavy bookcase over the hiding place, he felt a pang of guilt. The mysteries within pulled at him, begging to be investigated. But he had made a promise to himself and to his family. With a sigh, he turned and left the study, and locked the door behind him.

At the hospital, he was bombarded with questions about Harris.

"Dr. Bauer, how's Sam doing?" one nurse asked as he passed.

"I heard he's making a miraculous recovery," another staff member chimed in.

He mumbled noncommittal responses, trying to navigate his way through this sea of inquiries without revealing his own confusion about the housekeeper's whereabouts. As he made his way to his office, he caught sight of Lacheu down the hall. The man's eyes locked on him, his expression unreadable. Thomas continued on, pretending not to notice him, as his heart raced in his chest.

As the day went on, the psychiatrist overheard snippets of conversations as he moved through the hospital. The whispers and rumors grew more and more outlandish.

"I swear I saw him at the staff picnic the other day," one orderly insisted. "He looked fine to me. Not like someone who'd been attacked a week ago."

"That's impossible," another argued. "I heard he's still in the ICU across town, just hanging on."

The conflicting stories swirled around, making it hard for him to focus on his patients. He fought the constant urge to investigate. To find out the truth about what had happened to the old man.

As he left his office that evening, Bauer's mind was a battlefield of competing priorities. The mystery of Harris warred with the contents of the Case 47 attaché. They pulled at him, threatening to drag him back into long-established habits. But the memory of his family's faces, their cautious faith in him as he'd promised to do better, grounded him.

As he walked to the parking lot, keys in hand, he continued to feel torn between the two worlds. His eyes fell on his trunk. It was as if those files were still in there. He ran his fingers through his hair. He was glad they weren't.

"One day at a time," his wife's words echoed through his head.

With a deep breath, he got into his car and drove to Eleanor's house. As he pulled up, he saw Simon in the front yard, tossing a baseball with a friend. The sight of his boy, carefree and happy, strengthened his commitment.

Bauer got out, his eyes once again lingered on the trunk for a second. Then, with deliberate steps, he turned away and moved towards the house. Eleanor appeared in the doorway, a tentative smile on her face.

As he walked up, she gestured for him to take a seat on the porch. They sat together, discussing their day as they watched their son play. Thomas closed his eyes as a sense of peace came over him. For now, in this moment, he was right where he needed to be and where he wanted to be.

Later that night, he tucked his son into bed. He pulled the covers over the boy's chest, smoothing out all the wrinkles. As he leaned down to kiss him on the forehead, he felt a weight lift off his shoulders. The simple act of being present, this opportunity to participate in this evening ritual, filled his heart with a warmth he'd almost forgotten about.

"Thanks for tucking me in," Simon mumbled, already half-asleep.

"You're welcome."

"Goodnight, dad." The boy yawned and drifted off.

"'Night, son," Thomas whispered back, his voice tinged with emotion.

He lingered for a moment, watching Simon's chest rise and fall with each breath. He placed an open hand on his heart and felt it beat, then turned to leave.

As Thomas drove back to his mother's house, the streets were quiet. The world seemed at peace. He was content. A feeling that had been missing for months.

Pulling into the driveway, he cut the engine and sat savoring the stillness of the evening. The porch lights cast a warm glow over the familiar façade of the house. He could see a shadow moving about in the kitchen, likely preparing herself a late-night cup of tea.

He stepped from the car and made his way inside. When he entered the house, the comforting scent of chamomile and honey greeted him.

"Thomas?" his mother called. "Is that you?"

"Yes, mom," he replied, hanging his coat on a hook. "I'm home."

As he walked through the living room, Bauer's eyes drifted to the end of the hall. It came to a stop at the door to his father's study. There behind that door, hidden beneath the floorboards, lay Case 47 - its mystery still unsolved, so many questions still left unanswered.

Chapter 39

Bauer stirred in his childhood bed. Consciousness seeped into his brain. The familiar scents of this old room surrounded him. A mix of aged wood, with a hint of mustiness from the old books on the shelves. His eyes opened to the soft morning glow filtering through the curtains. He lay there for a few moments more, a little disoriented, caught between what once was and what is now.

The warmth of contentment lingered in his core from the previous night. He enjoyed tucking Simon in and spending time with Eleanor. For that evening, the weight of his professional world hadn't intruded into the personal. A slight tug played at the corners of his lips as he remembered Simon's sleepy "Goodnight, dad."

Following a quick glance toward the nightstand, he realized his alarm had yet to go off. The digital display of his clock radio read 5:47 AM in the room's muted tones. He lay there, savoring the quiet, allowing himself to savor this rare moment of peace.

The house creaked, settling in the early morning stillness. He could hear his mother moving about downstairs in the kitchen, the soft clink of dishes signaling the start of her day. He stretched, back popping as vertebrae shifted to more comfortable positions.

He swung his legs over the side of the bed. Bauer's feet touched the cool hardwood floor. He paused, taking in everything around him. Posters from his high school years still adorned the walls, faded reminders of his past interests and aspirations. A bookshelf sat in the corner, filled with his old medical texts and psychology journals from his college days.

As he stood, he caught sight of himself in the dresser mirror. His disheveled hair had a few salt-and-pepper strands sticking out at odd angles. Dark circles still lingered under his eyes, substantiating the many weeks of stress and sleepless nights that came with his relentless selfishness. But now, in its place, was something different; a clarity, a calmness that hadn't been there for a long time.

He made his way downstairs, following the aromas of bacon and fresh brewed coffee. He found his mother in the kitchen, humming to herself as she stood over a frying pan on the stove. The sight of her was familiar and comforting.

"Good morning, mom," he said, his voice still rough with sleep.

Edyth turned. A warm smile lit up her face. "Thomas! You're up early. I hope I didn't wake you."

"Nope, I just woke up on my own. Slept well, for once." He shook his head, moving to pour himself some coffee. "Can I get you some more?"

"Thank you," she said, passing him her mug as she looked at him. "That's wonderful to hear, dear. You look more rested than you have in weeks. Have a seat. Breakfast is almost ready."

He handed her mug back to her and sat down at the table facing her. He cradled his cup between his hands. The warmth seeped into his palms, grounding him in the moment. Sunlight streamed through the window, casting a golden glow over the worn but well-loved kitchen.

Edyth bustled about, placing some over-easy eggs, bacon, and toast in front of him, then took her place with her own plate. "So, how was your evening with Simon and Eleanor?"

He took a sip of coffee, savoring the rich flavor before answering. "It was great. He and I chatted about his upcoming games, then I got to tuck him in for the night. After that, Ele and I, we just enjoyed each other's company on the porch for a while, and talked."

"That sounds lovely, Thomas." Edyth reached over the table, patting his hand. "I'm so glad you're making time for them."

He nodded, a mix of emotions playing across his face. "I've missed so much, mom. But being there last night, it felt right. Like I was where I needed to be."

"That's because you were, dear." she said, her voice soft and understanding. "Family is what matters most. Your father understood that, even if he didn't always show it."

At the mention of his father, Bauer's gaze drifted towards the living room and the hallway. He noticed the familiar pull of what remained locked behind that door. But it was not the all-consuming force it had once been.

"I know, mom," he said, turning back to his plate. "I get that now."

They enjoyed their breakfast in warm silence for a while. The only sounds were the clinking of cutlery and the gentle ticking of the old clock on the wall. He found himself relaxed, enjoying the simple pleasure of sharing a morning meal with his mother.

As he finished his eggs, he glanced at his watch. "I should get ready for work," he said, standing to clear his and his mother's plates.

Edyth nodded, taking another sip of her coffee. "Of course, dear. Will you be home for dinner tonight?"

He paused, considering. "I'm not sure. I'll call you later to let you know, okay?"

"That's fine, Thomas."

"Thanks for everything, mom," he said as he kissed her on the cheek before heading upstairs to shower and dress. As his fingers worked at the knot in his tie, he caught sight of himself once again in the dresser mirror. The man staring back at him now looked more put-together, more at peace than he had been in months.

Descending the stairs, his steps slowed as he moved closer to his father's study. He took a deep breath, and stepped inside. The warm hues of morning filled the room. Dust motes danced in the one shaft of bright sunlight streaming in.

Books lined the walls, their spines old and faded. They displayed Harold Bauer's varied interests and many years of research. The heavy old desk sat in the center of the room. Its surface was neat and orderly.

The hefty bookcase, then the floorboards, drew his gaze. He turned to the window, allowing his fingers to run over the smooth leather of the chair. For a moment, he could almost see his father sitting there, poring over notes and muttering to himself. The memory snuck up on him, bringing with it a slight, sad smile to his face.

"I'm trying to understand, dad," he whispered to the empty room. "I'm trying to do better."

His eyes came to rest on his briefcase. It was where he had left it the night before when he returned from Eleanor's house. Thomas grabbed it from behind the desk. Then, with one last glance around the study, he exited, and closed the door. The mysteries contained within would stay right where they were. He had a life to rebuild and relationships to mend.

Chapter 40

Thomas noticed details he'd overlooked in recent weeks during his commute to work. The crisp fall air. The changing colors of the trees lining the streets played with the light. Cheerful morning waves from neighbors out on their walks invigorated his spirit as he passed.

Walking through the hospital doors, everything was so different. The same halls he'd walked countless times before seemed brighter somehow, more alive. He nodded to the receptionist, and exchanged pleasantries with a passing nurse.

In his office, he settled behind his desk, looking at his schedule for the day. Patient names jumped out at him; people he'd been treating for weeks, months, even years. He felt guilty as he realized how his personal pursuits had interfered with his patients' care.

"It's time to do better," he murmured to himself, picking up the first file.

As he further got into his daily routine, a gentle knock on his door interrupted his concentration. "Come in."

He looked up to see Nurse Kendrick standing in his doorway with a tentative smile on her face. "Good morning, Dr. Bauer," she said, her voice warm. "I hope I'm not interrupting anything important."

He leaned back in his chair, offering a welcoming gesture. "Not at all, Olivia. Please, come in. Have a seat. What can I do for you?"

She stepped into the room, closing the door behind her. She lowered herself into a chair across from him. Her eyes studied him with a mix of curiosity and something else. "I just wanted to check in on you this morning. Thomas. You seem, dare I say, out of sorts these past few days. In a good way, I mean."

A small smile tugged at the corners of his mouth. "I suppose I am feeling different. I've had some time to reflect on my life's trajectory and I've made some changes."

"That's wonderful to hear." Olivia nodded, her expression softening. "I must admit there are several of us around here who've been worried about you. Especially after what happened with Sam in the archives."

At the mention of the housekeeper, Bauer felt a pain grip his chest. He struggled to keep his face neutral. He did not want to betray any sort of emotion.

"I was wondering if you had heard anything about how he's doing?"

He shook his head. "No, nothing."

A frown creased her brow. "It's all quite strange. I noticed that another guy from housekeeping has taken over his shifts. I don't recognize him, his name is Lacheu. He seems to know his way around well for someone who's only been here a short time."

It took everything within him to push down the urge to probe further. "That is interesting. Well, I'm sure the administration needed to get Sam's position covered until he returns." After an awkward moment, he issued a thoughtful nod. "So, how are things going with Rhyse and the other patients?"

As Nurse Kendrick began updating him on various cases, he found himself engaged in the conversation. He asked questions, offered insights, and felt a renewed sense of purpose in his work. By the time Olivia left his office, he realized that an hour had passed.

Throughout the morning, he noticed curious glances and warm smiles from his colleagues. Dr. Amelia Hawthorne, a fellow psychiatrist and long-time friend, stopped him in the hallway.

"Thomas, you're looking well," she said, clapping him on the shoulder. "Whatever you're doing, keep it up. It's good to see you back to your old self."

A warmth spread through his body from her words. "Thanks, Amelia. I am feeling more like myself these days."

As lunchtime approached, he found himself in the hospital cafeteria, a tray of food before him. He sat alone at a table near the window, his mind wandered as he consumed his meal. The changes he had committed to were challenging. He knew that rebuilding his relationships with Eleanor and Simon wouldn't be easy, but he was determined to see them through.

"Dr. Bauer, call on line three, Dr. Bauer, call on line three." Came the operator's announcement on the public address system.

He made his way to the nearest phone and pushed the blinking button and picked up the phone. "This is Dr. Bauer."

"Thomas," Eleanor's voice came through, a mix of surprise and warmth. "I wasn't sure you'd answer. I figured you were busy when you didn't pick up in your office."

"Nah, I was just grabbing some lunch."

"Oh, then I won't keep you long. I just wanted to thank you for stopping by last night. Simon didn't stop talking about it all morning."

He felt a lump form in his throat. "No thanks necessary. It meant a lot to me, too."

"Thomas, I was wondering if you'd be okay with coming over after work? Maybe you could help him with his homework or something?"

Without a hint of hesitation, he responded. His tone was full of happiness. "Of course. I'll be there a little after five."

After ending his call with his wife, he dialed his mother's number. "Mom? It's me. I just wanted to let you know I won't be home for dinner tonight. I'm going to spend some time with Simon and Eleanor."

Edyth's voice was warm, delighted, and filled with understanding. "That's wonderful, dear. Don't worry about me. I'm so proud of you, Thomas."

As the call ended, he noticed a janitor pushing a cart down the hall outside the cafeteria. His heart skipped a beat. For a moment, he could have sworn it was Sam Harris. But as the man turned to speak to another staff member, he realized it was just another housekeeper

The sight mingled with his earlier conversation with Olivia. It stirred within him a flicker of curiosity. "How the hell could he have just disappeared?" He thought to himself. He took a deep breath, shaking his head before returning to his lunch. That mystery would have to wait, His family could not.

Late that afternoon, he left work right at 5 PM, something he couldn't remember doing in months. As he drove to Eleanor's house, his heart beat a little faster. He pulled into the driveway. His son was waiting for him, homework spread out on the small table.

"You're here!" Simon called out, waving. "Mom, he's here!"

He felt a surge of emotion as his boy greeted him with a hug as he stepped away from his car. "Hey, Simon, how was school today?"

"It was alright, but I'm having trouble with math and English."

"Well, let's see if I can help you with that."

For the next hour, Thomas sat on the front porch, helping with long division problems and grammar exercises. He found himself engaged, patient, and attentive in a way he hadn't been for months. Eleanor watched from the window, a small smile played on her lips.

As the sun continued to set, shadows formed across the yard. He helped his kid pack up his books, and together they went in and washed up for dinner.

Later, he went to tuck the boy in for the night before he left. "Great job today, Simon. I'm proud of you."

Simon's face beamed up at him. "Thanks, dad. Will you come help again tomorrow?"

He glanced over at his wife, who gave a slight nod from the doorway. "You bet, son. I'll be here!"

Thomas Bauer lingered in the hall, watching as Simon drifted off to sleep. The cool evening air from an open window carried the scent of oak and a hint of wood smoke from a neighbor's chimney. He turned to see Eleanor leaning against a doorframe, her arms crossed over her chest.

"Would you like a cup of coffee?" she asked, her voice soft and tentative.

He nodded, following her down the stairs. The familiar surroundings stirred a mix of emotions within him. Nostalgia, regret, and cautious hope. She busied herself in the kitchen while he settled on the worn leather couch in the living room.

"Here you go," she said, handing him a steaming mug before taking a seat in the adjacent armchair. "It's decaf. I remember how you used to toss and turn if you had caffeine too late in the day."

Thomas smiled, touched by her consideration. "Thank you. I'm glad some things around here haven't changed."

They sat in the comfortable silence of each other's company, sipping their coffee. His gaze wandered about the room, noting the subtle changes since he'd last lived there. New throw pillows on the couch, a unique arrangement of family photos on the mantle.

"Eleanor," he began, his voice low and earnest. "I want you to know how sorry I am. For everything. For letting my work consume me, for neglecting you and Simon. I was so caught up in trying to prove myself, to live up to my father's legacy, that I lost sight of what mattered."

Eleanor's eyes softened, but there was a hint of wariness in her expression. "I appreciate you saying that, Thomas. But I've heard similar promises before."

He nodded, acknowledging the truth in her words. "I know, and you have every right to be skeptical. I want to be here, to be present. Something's changed in me, Ele. I now know that no amount of professional success is worth sacrificing my relationships with my family. I want to be the husband and father the two of you deserve."

She set her mug down on the coffee table, leaned forward a little. "What brought about these changes? They seem so sudden."

He took a deep breath, choosing his words with extreme care. "It's been building for a while, I think. But, I've had some experiences that opened my eyes, made me reevaluate my priorities. I saw the consequences of my professional life. I didn't like the person I had become."

He paused, running a hand through his hair. "I've also gained some new perspective on my relationship with my father. Things I believed most of my life were never true."

Eleanor's expression softened further. "Your father loved you, Thomas. He was proud of you. Even though he struggled to show it, I remember seeing hints of it once in a while."

He nodded, a lump forming in his throat. "I know that now. And I don't want to repeat his mistakes with you and Simon."

There was a silence that hung in the air between them.

Eleanor spoke, her voice was soft. "I've missed you. The real you. The man I fell in love with years ago. Not the workaholic Dr. Bauer guy, who was always chasing after something just beyond his reach."

He felt a surge of emotion. "I've missed you too. Both of you. More than I ever realized."

She met his gaze, her eyes shimmering as a tear formed. "I want to believe that things can be different with us. But I'm scared, Thomas. I can't go through that pain again, and I won't put Simon through it again, either."

He leaned forward, his voice earnest. "I understand. I know I have a lot to do to prove myself. I'm not asking for everything to go back to the way they were overnight. But I'm hoping you'll let me show you I've changed. To rebuild what we had, over time and on your terms."

Eleanor was quiet for a long moment, considering his words. She gave a small nod. "Okay. We can try. But Thomas, this is your last chance. I mean it."

He felt the weight of responsibilities and promises settle onto his shoulders. "I understand. Thank you, Ele. I promise you and Simon, I won't let you two down this time."

They spent the next hour talking. Their conversations were cautious at first, then with growing ease. They talked about happier times, shared updates about their lives, and tentative discussions about their hopes for the future. As the clock struck eleven, he hesitated as he stood to leave.

"I should get going. It's late, and I don't want to overstay my welcome."

She walked him to the door. "This was nice. Thank you for coming over."

On impulse, he leaned in and placed a gentle kiss on her cheek. "I appreciate you and Simon giving me another chance. I'll see you tomorrow."

She nodded, a small smile played on her lips. "Goodnight, Thomas."

Pulling into the driveway of his mother's house, he felt at peace with his choices. He noticed a light still on in the living room. He was quiet when he entered. He didn't want to wake his mother if she had fallen asleep. From the foyer, he could see his mother seated in her favorite armchair, with a book open in her lap.

Her eyes opened and a warm expression spread across her face. "Welcome home, dear. How was your evening?"

He hung his coat and joined her. Placing his briefcase next to the couch before sinking into it with a contented sigh. "It was great, Mom. Simon and I worked on his homework, and then Eleanor and I had a nice talk after he went to bed."

Edyth's eyes sparkled with interest. "Oh? And how did that go?"

"Better than I could have hoped," He admitted. "We're going to try to work things out. We're taking it slow, on her terms. It's a start."

"I'm so glad to hear that, Thomas," Edyth said. "You do seem happier than I've seen you in a long time."

He nodded, feeling a rush of affection for his mother. "I am. I feel like I'm on the right path."

They sat in comfortable silence for a moment. Thomas's gaze drifted towards the hall that led to his father's study. Tonight, the pull was weaker. He took a breath and turned his attention back to his mother.

"How about you? How was your evening?"

Edyth's face lit up. "Oh, it was lovely. I had dinner with the neighbor next door. We had the most interesting conversation about her travels in Europe."

As his mother chatted about her night, he felt content. When Edyth yawned and announced she was heading to bed, he stood and gave her a warm hug.

"Goodnight, mom. I love you. Thank you again for everything."

"Goodnight, dear. Sleep well."

He watched as his mother ascended the stairs. A yawn escaped him. A few minutes later, he too made his way upstairs. His eyes were heavy as he brushed his teeth and slipped into his nightclothes. He drifted off. His head was free of the anxieties and obsessions that had plagued him for so many years.

As he slept, his mind took him on a walk through a familiar landscape. The grounds of Saint Elizabeths Hospital stretched out before him, but they looked different, more vibrant, almost ethereal. The grass was a lush green beneath his feet, and the trees swayed in a breeze he could not feel.

As he approached the main building, he saw someone in the distance. A man stood on the steps, silhouetted in the bright sunlight. His heart skipped a beat as he recognized the broad shoulders and commanding posture of his father.

"Dad?" He called out, his voice sounded strange in the dreamscape.

The man turned toward him. There was a warmth in his father's eyes. Something he couldn't remember ever seeing before.

"Thomas," Harold said, his tone was deep and rich. "I've been waiting for you."

As they stepped toward the entrance, he felt a mix of emotions swirling in him – love, longing, and a lingering trace of the old need for approval. But there was something else too, a sense of understanding and acceptance.

"I'm sorry it took me so long," he said as he reached his father.

His dad shook his head, placing a firm hand on Thomas's shoulder. "No apologies necessary. You're here now. That's what matters."

Together, they turned and went into the hospital. But instead of the familiar corridors, they found themselves in the old wing he'd explored with Sam Harris. The floors shined with fresh polish and everything was shiny and new as far as the eye could see. Without a word, they walked to his father's office and entered.

"Your life's work," he murmured, taking in the sight.

His dad nodded. "And yours too. But Thomas, there's something I need you to understand."

They stopped in front of a particular shelf. His father gestured to the books and files there. He recognized some of the titles; case studies he had read, and papers his father had published.

"You've done some good research, son," Harold said, his voice filled with pride. "And you still have some work to do. But it's not the most important thing."

He felt a lump form in his throat. "I know that now. I just wish I had realized it sooner."

Harold's expression softened. "It's never too late to change course, Thomas. I had to, but that's a complicated matter."

As he spoke, the surrounding scenery shifted. The endless shelves of the library faded away. The scene shifted to the coldness of the lab he once shared with Dr. Levi. He recognized it right away.

He turned to his father. "Dad, there's so much I don't understand. About your work, about Case 47, about—"

But Harold just stood there, shaking his head. "Fix yourself and your family first, son. Focus on what matters most. The rest will fall into place."

With those words echoing through his mind, Bauer drifted back to consciousness. His eyes opened to the early morning sunlight streaming through his bedroom window. For a moment, he lay still. The remnants of the dream clung to him like a warm, comfortable blanket.

The vision felt so real, so vivid. He could almost still feel his father with him. He could hear the pride in his voice. He took a deep breath, letting the emotions stay with him a few more minutes.

As he went through his routine, he caught himself humming. A sense of optimism lifted his spirits. He joined his mother for breakfast, sharing a loving smile over coffee and French toast.

"You're in a good mood this morning," Edyth observed, her eyes twinkling.

He nodded. "I had a fantastic dream last night. About dad."

Edyth's expression softened. "Oh? Do you want to talk about it?"

For a moment, Thomas thought about telling her about it, but something held him back. It felt private, personal. Like a gift meant just for him.

"Maybe later," he said. "But it was a good one, mom."

He finished his breakfast and ran upstairs to brush his teeth. When he returned to the living room, he paused in front of his dad's portrait, remembering his dream. He then made his way down the hall to the study. He walked in, grabbed his briefcase, then turned on his heels and left for work.

Epilogue

He pulled into the parking lot of Saint Elizabeths Hospital like he always did. Thomas smiled, remembering fond moments from his dream. The building contained over a century's worth of history within its walls.

The doctor greeted the receptionist with a warm smile as he entered. He exchanged pleasantries with a passing nurse. As he made his way to his office, he couldn't shake the feeling that something was off.

It wasn't anything tangible at first. The corridors looked the same. The usual bustle of his work life was all around him. But there was a thick tension in the air, something that prickled at the back of his neck.

Reaching his door, he paused with his hand hovering over the doorknob. He gave a gentle push, and it opened, setting off alarms in his mind.

Thomas was certain he had locked it when he left the previous evening. He always did, without fail. He was the only one with the key to that door. His pulse quickened as he entered.

At first glance, nothing seemed out of place. His desk was as he left it, papers stacked neat. A family photo in its usual spot. But as he stepped further into the room, he noticed subtle signs of changes.

A drawer that didn't quite closed all the way. A book on the shelf that was a little out of alignment with the others. And there, next to his pencil holder, a small scrap of paper that he was certain wasn't there the night before.

With trembling fingers, Bauer picked it up. On it were only two words, scrawled in a familiar handwriting:

"Alpha awaits."

A chill ran through his veins. Everything he had been trying to put behind him leaped to the forefront of his brain. Sam Harris's disappearance, the murderous Lacheu, Case 47; all of it came rushing back, threatening to undo the peace he was so desperate to continue.

The doctor sank into his chair, the scrap of paper clutched in his fist. He had thought he was making significant progress, focusing on what was important. But it seemed the past wasn't quite done with him yet.

As he sat there, struggling to make sense of this recent development, he couldn't help but recall his father's words from the dream: "Fix yourself and your family first, Thomas. Focus on what matters most. The rest will fall into place."

"What the hell am I supposed to do now, dad? This shit won't leave me alone." Bauer whispered to himself, with a heavy sigh.

Also by

Jane M. Bell

Yesterday's Ruin — Prequel to the Case 47 Series (Free Download)
www.books.janembell.com

Children's Books – Under the Pen-Name J. Margaret Bell
Timeless Tides: Monterey Through the Ages
Mystery at Sea Edge — www.books.janembell.com

About the author

Jane M. Bell

My Journey...so far...

I suppose it was inevitable that I finally became a writer. Growing up, I was surrounded by the constant tap tap tap ding of my grandmother's manual typewriter as she constantly worked on a myriad of writing projects.

I grew up just south of Modesto, California, and graduated from Ceres High School. During my days of study at Modesto Junior College I developed an interest in psychology when I began working in a locked mental facility. In 1988 I began my 20 year career with the Army Reserves where I served as an Armorer, Drill Sergeant, and Combat Medic Instructor.

After earning my AA from Modesto Junior College, I went on to study at Sonoma State University where I earned my BA in Psychology with distinction, and did Post-Graduate studies in Neurobiology. During my post graduate days I worked at the San Francisco VA Medical Center at Ft Miley where I worked in a schizophrenia research lab.

Following my graduate work, I went on to work in the medical field as an Obstetrics Technician at a local hospital.

Today I make my home just outside of Modesto, California with my two sons, daughter two dogs and cat. I still try to find time to serve as a docent at Columbia State Historic Park in the Sierra foothills east of Modesto.

My Work

I find inspiration everywhere, especially in the lesser known chapters of historical events. I feel compelled to bring these interesting, hidden historical gems back to life. Our greatest lessons in life and as a society come from the successes and failures of those who came before us.

Milton Keynes UK
Ingram Content Group UK Ltd.
UKHW020113181024
449757UK00012B/800